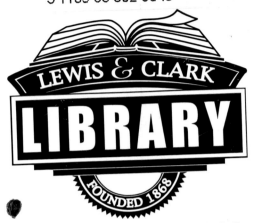

The Last Man

**Center Point
Large Print**

Also by P. T. Deutermann and available from Center Point Large Print:

Pacific Glory

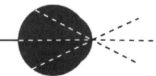

This Large Print Book carries the Seal of Approval of N.A.V.H.

The Last Man

P. T. DEUTERMANN

CENTER POINT LARGE PRINT
THORNDIKE, MAINE

This Center Point Large Print edition
is published in the year 2012 by arrangement with
St. Martin's Press.

The text of this Large Print edition is unabridged.
In other aspects, this book may vary
from the original edition.
Printed in the United States of America
on permanent paper.
Set in 16-point Times New Roman type.

ISBN: 978-1-61173-517-8

Library of Congress Cataloging-in-Publication Data

Deutermann, Peter T., 1941–
The Last man / P. T. Deutermann.
pages ; cm.
ISBN 978-1-61173-517-8 (library binding : alk. paper)
1. Americans—Israel—Fiction. 2. Missing persons—Fiction.
  3. Temple of Jerusalem (Jerusalem)—Fiction. 4. Large type books.
  I. Title.
PS3554.E887L37 2012b
813'.54—dc23
                                           2012009856

Given the tectonic power shifts taking place in the Near East these days, this book is dedicated to the fond hope that Israel will survive, both as an island of modernity in a sea of resurgent medievalism and as an outpost of democracy in an increasingly barbaric world.

ACKNOWLEDGMENTS

I want to thank my editor, George Witte, for letting me do this one after so many years, and also my copy editor, India Cooper, for doing her usual excellent job with the manuscript. Rick Cavey gave me invaluable advice on the diving technicalities; any errors there, whether intentional or not, are of my own making. The Ministry of Tourism in Israel was very helpful. Finally, I want to acknowledge the power of the Masada site, itself. There's nothing quite like it in the world.

THE VISION OF THE DRY BONES

The hand of the Lord came upon me. He took me out by the spirit of the Lord and set me down in the valley. It was full of bones. He led me all around them; there were very many of them spread over the valley, and they were very dry . . . (Ezekiel 37: 1–2)

From a scroll fragment found on the fortress of Masada during the Yigael Yadin archaeological expedition

The Last
Man

Part I

*The Mountain Fortress of Masada
in Judaea, A.D. 73*

Judah scrambled across the earthen floor of the watch-room as the ceiling fell in, barely staying ahead of the tumble of dust, timbers, and royal plaster as he rolled into a corner, covering his face against the flying debris. A battered round rock about a foot in diameter, fired from a Roman ballista, smashed a final massive dent into the end-wall masonry before rolling to a stop three feet away. Through the wreckage of the ceiling, Judah could now see the sheets of fire consuming the tops of the western ramparts. He barely had time to collect himself before another stone came hissing across the night sky, passing invisibly over the ruined timbers of the watch-room to batter down a building somewhere beyond him in the darkness.

Damn them and their machines, he thought. Their machines and their implacable Roman power. A distant crash marked the impact of yet another ballista stone, hurled across the night sky by the catapult in the burned-out siege tower. Ever since the treacherous desert wind had turned on them, firing the wooden ramparts overlooking the siege ramp, the Zealots' fate had been sealed. By dawn the casemate walls would have burned through and the howling hordes of the Legio X Fretensis would spill in like a swarm of armored beetles. Even now, at the third hour, the ominous rumble of kettledrums and the cheering roars from the Roman formations gathering below echoed in waves across the desert darkness. It was the same sound the mob made in the hippodrome at Caesarea during the procurator's games.

I am Judah, Sicarius. I shall be the Last Man, he thought, as he tried to make himself small in his corner of the watch-room. He had drawn the final tile, the tenth lot, and with it the horrific responsibility to finish it. The room shook as another ballista round careened across the open ground outside and ricocheted off a nearby storeroom wall. A woman shrieked, a pathetically human sound amid the dull thudding of collapsing masonry. Had she cried out from fear of the stones, or from seeing her husband coming for the family with a knife?

Not long now, he thought, rolling over on his side and shifting his own glinting dagger from his left hand to his right. Not long at all. The smell of burning timbers was suddenly strong as the streaming, treacherous wind veered across the top of Herod's fortress, pushing acrid smoke through the holes in the building, stinging his eyes to sudden tears. The tears ambushed his memory. He had lived a very long time. It had been almost forty years since those heady days in Galilee, when the teenagers who would become Sicarii formed their first cell in the mountains. Now he was the last of them, the last man in more ways than one. The Daggermen were a bloody memory now, their bones scattered over Galilee and beyond, along with the bones of the thousands slaughtered in the broken streets of Jerusalem. Death to Rome, indeed. He shivered again, imagining he could hear his own bones rattle. The Romans were about to show them the final cost of their supremely naive rebellion.

Another stone rocked the walls of the watch-room. He inspected the dagger again, his badge of honor as a Sicarius, the Roman word for Daggerman. Judah, son of Joseph, later outcast son of Kerioth. One of the very first Galileans to take up the long knife against Romans and other undesirables. *Old* Judah Sicarius. The oldest Kanna'i, or Zealot, as the people called them. Sixty-one seasons he had lived. Gray now in beard, long in tooth, but still tough as an Egyptian chariot harness. Without a doubt, he had been the oldest warrior on this mountain. The last of the Kanna'im, too, after the judgment of the ostraca, the fateful tiles, cast earlier in the royal precincts. *I shall be the Last Man!*

A smaller projectile crashed down somewhere up along the casemate walls, and this time the prolonged screaming of a mortally injured child rent the night air. Judah winced but did not move. On this night of nights, one way was as good as another to die. In a little while he would have to go out there, dodging across the deadly open spaces, within sight of Roman archers in the fighting tops of the charred siege tower. He would be a scurrying bundle of old rags under the deadly gaze of their catapult, one more rebel to nail with their iron quarrels if they could manage the shot. Nevertheless, this old Jew had a final mission. If he could just make it across the open ground, glinting dagger in hand, he was honor-bound to carry out Eleazar's final, terrible orders. By so doing, would he finally make amends for what he had done forty years ago? Was this final, bloody mission the cost of his redemption? *Could it be?*

He drew his tattered cloak closer as he thought about their glorious leader, Eleazar ben Jair. Kanna'i extraordinary, a stunningly effective demagogue right to the very end. It had been ben Jair's idea to fire the casemate timbers in order to destroy the siege tower, and it had worked, too. For a while. He recalled with relish the screams of the Romans as the lower hide shields caught fire, and then the lashings and the very timbers of the eighty-foot-high tower, crouched atop the blood-soaked siege ramp. He had watched with the other Zealots, secreted like rats in their burrows along the western wall, firing arrows into the blaze each time a roasting Roman poked his head out of the smoke, screaming desperately for help from the legionaries behind the tower.

Then, just after nightfall, with the tower's

massive timbers only half consumed, the fateful desert wind, the very breath of their own vengeful God, had turned on the defending Jews. It had veered into the north and then swept back onto the western wall, *away* from the tower. The Zealots, who had cushioned the outer face of the wall with sand and timbers to defeat the tower's battering ram, could only watch in horror as the capricious flames began to burn the wall timbers, sealing Masada's fate. The Romans had been able to withdraw the siege tower to just beyond the flame front and put out the fires in its fighting tops, but the great battering ram and even the tower were superfluous now because, with the makeshift wooden walls ablaze on the mountain's rim, the fortress would be totally exposed by dawn.

Ben Jair's coal black eyes in the guttering lamplight had revealed the extent of their calamity. "The core of the walls is aflame," he croaked, his voice hoarse from the smoke. "They have finished the ramp, and by first light the maniples of the Tenth Legion, soldiers in their *thousands,* will break through. By the Lord God, we tried, we surely tried, but the accursed wind . . ."

Ben Jair had paused to catch his heaving breath and to drink some water. "So now," he continued, "now that the fateful hour is at hand we must choose. We are the final warriors of the Jewish race. God's Temple is demolished; Jerusalem is a defiled, corpse-ridden ruin. Our lands, our villages, our hearths and homes, gone, all gone. Our kinsmen's bones bake in the desert. The Romans have hunted down every last patriot and slaughtered them all like leprous dogs. They even buried the old hermits alive in their caves at Qumran and then posted guards until the smell told them it was finished. They leveled Machaerus and killed everyone who surrendered, and now they have laid siege to this final fortress, here at the bottom of the world, for nearly three years. At dawn, it will be finished here as well. At third cockcrow, the Roman juggernaut will march up the ramp to kill and rape and torture, and any survivors here will envy the dead."

Ben Jair had stared at the hollow-eyed warriors standing around the main audience room in Herod's palace, his gaze hot, eyes blazing like a demon's as he seduced them one last time with all the hypnotic urgency of a prophet. Always the posturer, he had gathered himself in front of them, coiling his dirty robes like a Levite, chanting his final exhortation.

"We long ago, my generous friends, resolved never to be servants to the Romans, nor to any other than to God himself. The time is now come that obliges us to make that resolution true in practice. We were the very first that revolted from them, and we are the last that fight against them. I cannot but esteem it as a favor that God hath granted us that it is still in our power to die bravely and in a state of freedom. It is very plain that this place shall be taken in a day's time. We are openly deprived by God himself of all hope of deliverance. That fire which was driven upon our enemies did not, of its own accord, turn back upon the wall which we had built. This was the effect of God's anger against us, for our manifold sins which we have been guilty of in a most insolent and extravagant manner with regard to our own countrymen, the punishments of which let us not receive from the Romans, but from God himself, executed by our own hands.

"Let our wives die before they are abused, and our children before they have tasted of slavery, and after we have slain them, let us bestow that glorious benefit upon one another mutually and preserve ourselves in freedom as an excellent funeral monument for us. But first let us destroy the fortress and our money by fire, and spare nothing but our provisions, that they may be a testimonial when we are dead that we were not subdued for want of necessaries, but that we have preferred death before slavery."

Judah's face twisted in a grimace as a ballista stone cracked the steps by the doorway. He wiped some dust off his face and realized that it was getting cold. The final hours before dawn were always the coldest. He waited and listened. The artillery bombardment seemed to be slacking off.

It had been an amazing exhortation, and, equally

21

amazing, the surviving warriors had done exactly what ben Jair proposed. Men went among their families, gathered most of them into Herod's palace, shawled their faces and heads, and then killed them all. Then they reassembled and drew lots to choose ten among them "to bestow that glorious benefit" on themselves. The second slaughter completed, the bloodied ten had assembled one last time to again draw lots. Judah Sicarius had drawn the fateful tile. He had withdrawn to the southern end of the fortress to wait until the last hour before dawn, so that the remaining nine could fulfill their compact with honor. If they failed to do that, well . . . He ran his fingers along the well-oiled blade of his own dagger.

It had been an amazing exhortation. Also a glorious, masterful lie, of course. Yes, they would die, and willingly. They were Kanna'im. Zealots. Fanatics. Yet they chose death not just to deprive the Roman beast of its final triumph. This self-inflicted immolation was for something far more important than that. Over and above a final, glorious defiance, their mass suicide would also protect the holy relics hidden in the heart of the mountain. The holy *things* spirited out of the Temple on that last horrific night, when the combined legions of Titus and Vespasian had run amok through ankle-deep gore in the streets of Jerusalem, their sandals splashing blood onto the very walls in a manner reminiscent of the times of Moses and the plagues in Egypt.

He peered through a hole in the building's walls again. The flames inside the western palace and along the walls were unremitting. It was time to move, time to begin the hunt through the battered ruins atop the mountain. The final ten had included ben Jair. Judah, as the Last Man, must now ensure that all had died before he took his own life. Especially ben Jair himself. He could make a fine speech, ben Jair, and he had been a stalwart commander and lethal warrior, but Judah knew the man of old. He did not think Eleazar had the courage to turn his dagger upon himself.

It was strangely quiet now across the open ground outside. He shook his head in wonder at all that had happened in these past six years, and the dreadful duty he faced. Once he had confirmed that all the defenders were dead, he would be the last Jew alive of all the uncounted thousands of warriors flattened beneath the Roman yoke during the civil war. They would never find him, though. He would be with the treasure, a treasure to which he, the last Daggerman, the despised Judaean, the last of the Kanna'im, would add one final, supremely ironic object before honoring the fate decreed by the tiles.

I shall be the Last Man.

The wind shifted yet again, and the smoke suddenly surged thick in the ruined room. He could not breathe. It was definitely time. He hefted the long dagger with a deep sigh. In a way, he would have it easy. He had had no wife or children to slaughter this dark night. All that was left was for him to go through the surviving buildings in search of any stragglers and, especially the body of ben Jair. Coughing in the smoke, he lunged for the door, pausing only to get a breath before launching himself into what was now indisputably the Roman night. From the plains stretching below the sheer red walls of the mountain he could hear the soldiers' massed cheers swelling over the crackle of flames and the keening of the bitter desert wind. You bastards won't be cheering on the morrow, he thought grimly as he bolted from the smoke-filled building. We have rebuffed your best efforts for almost three years, and now, in death, we shall defy you.

I shall be the Last Man!

Judah barely avoided the slashing bolt from a catapult as he rolled into the rubbled floor of the mikveh, the ceremonial purification baths near the western palace. Roman *bastards!* He peered back through a crack in the wall. Above the billowing flames, the charred tops of the siege tower, hulking just below the rim of the mountain, harbored a dozen or so snipers who were probably calling targets for the ballista artillery catapult farther down the ramp. The hard rock plain that was the top of the mountain was totally illuminated now by the burning western walls, and his mad dash across the open space between the palace watch-room and the mikveh had apparently been spotted. He winced as another bolt came ricocheting through the doorway and skittered around the cluttered anteroom. The demons knew he was in here, he thought. There were weapons stacked in one corner. He longed to return the fire, although the tower was probably out of range now. Besides, he had things to do.

He looked around. The mikveh consisted of two buildings, with the purifying baths, now empty and dry, between them. The first room was for undressing and ritual cleansing. It had remained relatively intact since the bombardment, except that one glancing hit on the roof had covered the mosaics of the floor with bits of mortar and broken roof tiles. Three families had taken refuge in the small building directly across from the purification pools after their quarters had been overtaken by the fire along the western walls. Most of the Zealots' families had lived inside the casemate walls themselves during the siege, existing in tiny rooms that allowed them to defend against climbers and stay out of range of the Roman snipers on the other side of the deep ravine called Wadi Masada. If they had not sought shelter in the palace, and the killing had been done, he should find bodies in the building on the other side of the empty pools.

He peered out the doorway, scanning the terraces, then drew back as another ballista stone came hissing directly overhead. It missed the pool building roof by a few feet and shattered in the darkness against the hardpan rock of the mountain. He bolted across the pool terrace and dived into the anteroom of the other bathhouse building as a bolt from a catapult whined behind his back. He stood up, brushed off his robe, and drew the long iron dagger. He had no need to test its edge; a Sicarius with a dull weapon was a contradiction in terms.

There was a ragged cloth curtain hanging between the anteroom and the chamber inside. He paused, steeling himself. It was one thing to accede to mass suicide while in thrall to Eleazar's rhetoric. It was another thing altogether to kill people he knew, men and women and, yes, God cleanse his soul, children, alongside whom he had lived, fought, and prayed for nearly three years. His heart pounding, he took a deep breath and touched the curtain with the point of the dagger. Then he realized it was heavy—and wet. He let go of it and stared down at his hand in the dim light, frowning at the dark stain. Then it hit him: The curtain was soaked with blood. He took another deep breath and pushed the curtain aside. What he saw took his breath away.

He had been at war continuously now for the past seven years, first in Galilee, then at the Siege of Jerusalem. When the city finally had fallen and almost the entire surviving population, reportedly some one hundred thousand Jews, had been put to the sword, he had seen the city's streets literally awash with blood. What he beheld now, in this tiny room, still managed to shock him. Simon, son of Giora, had apparently been the executioner. He had cut their throats. Judah counted, his lips moving silently. Ten people. The entire room, the walls, the low ceiling, the back side of the cloth curtain, and every square foot of the floor had been painted in arterial blood. The bronze stench of it nearly overwhelmed him, and he had to swallow hard to keep from gagging. Simon had taken an easier way out, he noted, stabbing himself in the inner thigh and then wrapping a prayer shawl around his head and face, unable to bear further witness to the horrifying thing he had done. *It is still an eligible thing to die after a glorious manner,* Eleazar had said—but this was not glory. This was simply slaughter.

Judah's eyes filled with tears at the horror of it . . . but Simon had done the thing, hadn't he. There was no need here for the Last Man, in this ghastly place. He sobbed out a quick prayer and backed out through the sodden curtain, the hair on his neck rising at the touch of it. He had personally separated more than thirty men's souls from their bodies with the fourteen-inch iron dagger he held in his right hand. He had killed scores more than that in the battles of the Revolt, most of them Romans or their allies, for whom he was beyond counting or caring.

This, though . . . My God, he thought, his mind trembling: They actually did it. The wind shifted slightly, and the smell from the interior room seeped through the curtain. My *God!* What have we come to?

A big, ten-mina ballista stone crashed short of the building and rattled by the back door of the anteroom, skipping neatly over the empty pools and out into the shadows behind the bathhouses. He was seized by a sudden burning desire to finish himself, right there, to end it before he had to confront any more scenes like the one inside. He held the dagger point up under his chin for a second, and then a quirk of the night wind carried the sound of laughter, Roman laughter, across the desolation of the mountaintop. He let the dagger point drop and glared out into the night. The laughter was coming from the burned-out siege tower. A coldness settled on his chest, and he went back inside the blood-soaked building to find their weapons. There was one long-range war bow standing in a corner, an old Parthian, by the look of it. He slipped his dagger into its thigh sheath, retrieved the oversized weapon and one arrow, and went back to the anteroom, steeling himself to look at all the grotesquely huddled bodies, to memorize this scene from hell.

He carefully wiped blood spatters off the heavy bow, then stepped through the curve to set the gut string, grunting with the effort. The bow had probably been "liberated" during the Siege of Jerusalem, most likely from the body of a Roman auxiliary. He crawled out of the doorway and around to the eastern wall of the bathhouse. There, protected from the sight line of the siege tower, he could stand up. There were some large, empty clay amphora stacked against the wall. He turned one upside down and used it to stand on, keeping his head just beneath the edge of the flat roof. When he heard the laughter coming again, he carefully lifted the heavy bow over the edge of the roof, fit the arrow with its three-bladed iron head, then stood up straight. The tower was nearly a hundred cubits distant. He was firing directly into the wind, so it was simply a question of range. Aiming dead center but over the tops of the tower, he drew and released in one fluid motion. He caught a brief glimpse of four helmeted faces, red in the backlight of the flames, then heard the satisfying scream as his unexpected bolt struck home.

He dropped the weapon, his shoulder trembling from the effort of pulling the heavy bow, and jumped down. He scrambled across the space between the bathhouse and the main storeroom building. Eleazar's wind sent spark-filled clouds of wood smoke across the ruined buildings of the fortress, enveloping him entirely. Zigging and zagging across the open space, he ran for the southeastern wall, where the bulk of the Zealots' living quarters were.

He made it down to the eastern casemate walls without attracting any more catapult fire from the siege tower. He scuttled through a small doorway and turned right, not wanting to push his luck with the Roman snipers. Fortunately, the ground sloped down from the ritual bathhouse, so he was not too badly winded by his sprint. Even so, he crouched down on the dirt floor for a moment to catch his breath. A ballista had punched a hole in the mud brick wall, so he could see out onto the open area. The flames were now visible only as a red glow behind the walls of the western palace building, itself afire in spots. Thanks to the slope, most of the heavy wood smoke from the smoldering wall fire was blowing overhead. The gloomy corridor formed by the casemate structure was no more than a man's height wide, filled with right-angle twists and turns to make it easier to defend against invaders. There were tiny oil lamps guttering in wall niches, their own wisps of smoke casting a visible pall along the ceiling. Once the Romans had managed to bring the heavy ballista catapult, capable of throwing the ten-mina stones, up onto the western slopes, most of the Kanna'im had moved their quarters into the eastern and southern casemate walls. The living quarters were little more than hovels, one or two rooms formed by poles and hides stretched partially across the corridor, leaving barely enough room for a man to squeeze by the improvised walls. There were larger, more permanent dwellings down at the southeastern corner of the fortress, where there was also a large rim cistern. Normally all the warriors would be holed up in the northern palace buildings, but on this night . . .

He took one of the tiny oil lamps and started down the corridor. Being taller than most, Judah had to bend forward to keep from hitting his head on the overhead beams. He could still hear the occasional cheering from the main Roman camp whenever a gust of the night wind carried the sound across the fortress grounds. The steady thumping of war drums pulsing through the night sounded like Death's own heartbeat. He could just visualize what first light would bring, a seething mass of metal-plated Romans swarming over the ruined ramparts, short swords and pila, the dreaded javelins, bristling as they fanned out to end this awful siege.

The walls seemed to echo his fatal mantra: *I shall be the Last Man.*

The first makeshift quarters he came to were empty. Holding the lamp high, he scanned the few possessions—cooking pots, jars for water and oil, some clothes hung on pegs. Three or four crude toys stacked neatly in a corner. A tiny fire pit against the inner wall, with a hole above to let smoke out. A tiny rug for prayers. No weapons. He felt a twinge of relief, but it was extinguished when he stepped back into the corridor and saw the pool of black blood that had seeped out from under the hides of the next cubicle. He drew his dagger and pushed aside the stiff flap of cowhide. Inside were three women, one young, the other two elderly. All had been killed by a deep slice across the side of both wrists. The short knife used to do the killing lay like a small obscenity out on the dirt floor. The women sat propped up against the outer wall, their heads and faces covered in shawls, their wounded forearms drooping like broken wings.

He pushed aside one shawl and then the other with the tip of his dagger. He knew them, as he knew almost every one of the nine hundred and sixty souls left on the mountain. This was the family of Jeshua, son of Matthias, veteran Kanna'i, from Galilee. Then he frowned. So where was Jeshua? There had been little children, too—where were they? He remembered something else: There had been an elderly aunt. She was also missing.

He whirled at a sound outside the inner casemate wall and brought up the long dagger. He was half expecting skulking Roman scouts. He listened hard, and this time he recognized the sound—a sob. It had come from outside. He stepped back out through the hide curtains and went down the corridor to the first bolt-hole, stooped down, and climbed out onto the rocky slope leading back up to the western palace and walls. A hundred years before, Herod had kept gardens out here. Now there was only rock.

There he found Jeshua, slumped in the shadows of a rubble pile, his back against the casemate wall. He was weeping. A coldness gripped Judah's belly. He was going to have to do it after all, despite his fervent hopes to the contrary. Jeshua had been a hero at Jotapata, where Josephus, that ultimate traitor, had gone over to the filthy Romans to save his miserable life. Jeshua's left arm hung uselessly, the result of a Roman pilum thrust deflected by his shield into the meat of his shoulder. Jeshua had been one of the few survivors of the slaughter at Jotapata. He had also been one of the final ten.

Judah commanded his feet to move toward Jeshua, even as his heart tried to hold him back. The old warrior saw him at last. He stiffened by the wall, his face a mask of tears. They looked at each other for a long moment. Then Jeshua spoke, holding up his bloody right hand, his eyes flaring under heavy, scarred brows.

"Come, Destroyer," he croaked. "I've done the hard part."

"Jeshua," Judah said, his own voice strangely weak. He swallowed to wet his throat. "Jeshua, I don't want to do this thing. Not to you, not to any of us."

Jeshua looked down at his bloody hand for a moment and then dropped it into his lap. He let his chin slump onto his chest. The expression on his face, barely visible in the dim light, broke Judah's heart. Never had he seen such utter despair.

"We are the accursed of God," Jeshua whispered. "Everything has been destroyed, everything, and we've been reduced to killing our own flesh and blood." He looked up at Judah. "With sunrise comes the end of the world, Judah. I can't bear it. I can't *bear* it!"

Judah stepped closer, trying to keep the long dagger out of sight. To his surprise, he found himself trying to determine how he would do this killing. Then Jeshua pointed with his chin to a small ballista, perhaps four mina. He kicked it over to where Judah was standing and then lay down sideways, face alongside the wall, the back of his head toward Judah.

Judah understood. He sheathed his dagger and picked up the heavy stone, and in one swift chop brought it down on Jeshua's head. The man grunted, twitched, then lay still. Judah knelt alongside and watched for a moment. Jeshua lived still, a pulse visible in his throat. He drew his dagger and opened the large artery on the left side, standing up quickly to avoid the spray. Then, his heart as heavy as the bloody ballista, he wiped the dagger on Jeshua's cloak and crawled back inside the casemate walls. The Roman drums boomed again as he pressed on down the dark passageway. There was still the question of Jeshua's missing children. Judah didn't want to think about what he would do if he found them. He mouthed a silent prayer that he never would.

After methodically searching all of the eastern casemates for bodies, Judah paused at the northern end of the mountain, waiting to make a dash for the huge granary storehouse that was next to the main, northern palace. Eleazar had exhorted them to burn their belongings and weapons but to leave all of the provisions—grain, oil, wine, and dried fruits—untouched, so that the Romans would know they had not been starved into the act of mass suicide. Nor was there any dearth of water: Even after two and a half years of siege, the great cisterns along the western wall were still more than half full, with water enough for years remaining.

He watched the open space between the end of the casemate wall and the palace storehouse. The eastern night sky was subtly changing in anticipation of morning twilight. Up here, though, on the higher northern promontory, the western wall fires were now sending sheets of eye-stinging smoke billowing across the open ground. The tops of the siege tower were just visible, peering over the smoldering walls like some war dragon whose eyes had been burned out by its own exertions. Twice Judah had seen what he thought were human figures slipping silently through the smoke out there along the palace walls. He could not afford to encounter a squad of Roman skirmishers at this late hour, as there was one final mission he *had* to perform once he knew that all were dead. He had to seal the great cavern.

There! Man-shaped shadows in the smoke, fifty, perhaps sixty cubits from where he hid watching at the end of the casemate corridor. He blinked several times to clear his eyes. He was tired, very tired. They had been fighting hard ever since the Romans had advanced the siege tower to the western gates, and Judah, an officer of some rank and much bloody experience, had been in the thick of it. When the great battering ram had finally been shoved into position, there had been desperate fighting indeed, with waves of screaming Jews charging across virtually open ground, dodging a hail of arrows and catapult bolts from the high tower, to swarm over the western wall and stab through curtains of armor and tinned hides at the tower defenders, while others flung pots of burning oil onto the ram crew, sending them shrieking back down the siege ramp, their garments aflame. This had gone on for three days and three nights, the tide of ferocious battle sweeping back and forth, until Eleazar took the desperate gamble and fired the walls themselves to burn out the siege tower and destroy the huge ram.

He stared hard into the swirling smoke but saw no more running shadows—and shadows they probably were, he thought. I'm imagining things out there. The Romans don't have to risk sending scouts. They know the dawn will bring an end to all this. He gathered himself to make the dash across open ground. He would aim for the double-door portal on the east side, the Lake Asphaltites side. Once inside he would make a final check of the palace before torching it. He knew what he was going to find there, because that was where most of the defenders had gone to execute the compact. With no family of his own, he had fled the palace when the killing began, unwilling to just sit and watch the slaughter, piteous children writhing on the marble floors, pouring out their lives through carmine mouths, mothers tearing at their eyes to blind themselves from the bloody spectacle, stone-faced warriors standing over the human wreckage, their faces and robes bloodred in the torchlight, stunned at what they had done, many of them turning their daggers into their own bodies with the hot shame of it.

Judah the Daggerman had finally had enough of slaughter. He just wanted it all to end. He had himself been a killing machine ever since those

37

dramatic days in Jerusalem, almost forty years ago, when the Romans, aided and abetted by fat Levites, had crucified an insignificant, deluded visionary from Galilee in a grotesque public execution, thereby igniting the fuse that led ultimately to the utter destruction of Israel. Just precisely as that ragged prophet had predicted, he reminded himself. He surveyed the war-ravaged grounds of what had been Herod the Idumean's pleasure dome. *This is the last of our works,* he thought, *and I shall be the Last Man.*

The smoke cloud thickened momentarily as he gathered himself. He could see nothing of the palace now and had to bend his face into the crusted shroud of his outer sleeve to keep his eyes from tearing in the acrid smoke. Then it cleared, and he made his run, staying low, not even looking toward the siege tower as he scrambled across the rubble as fast as he could go to the palace wall, where he flattened himself out of sight of any watchers in the tower. The smoke coiled upon him with a vengeance, and he had to inch his way across the stone wall, eyes clamped shut, until he felt the double doors, which were partially open. He bent low and took one last look around in the gloom for intruders, then slipped through the doorway and pushed first one and then the other man-high door shut behind him.

It was nearly full dark inside the storeroom

building, but Judah, like all of the warriors, knew his way around these corridors blindfolded. There were three main parallel passageways, off of which were the storerooms themselves. The building was attached to the northern palace, whose spacious throne room had that night become the communal killing ground. He moved quickly through the storeroom passageways, blinking back tears. Even here, in the storeroom building, he could detect another smell above the wood smoke. He knew all too well what it was.

He pushed open individual storeroom doors, looking for anyone who might have lost his nerve and hidden in the labyrinth of small rooms. There was no one. He slowed as he finished his survey of the third and last passageway, dreading what he had to do next.

What's the point, he asked himself as he stood in front of the connecting door between the palace complex and the storeroom building. They're all dead in there. Anyone left alive would *want* to kill himself, just from seeing the spectacle of death behind that door.

Because you promised, he told himself. You, Judah Sicarius, will be the Last Man, but not until you have made sure that none of them is left alive. Only the ten most senior officers among the Kanna'im even knew about the great cavern's existence, and only Eleazar, Jeshua ben Matthias, and Judah knew what was secreted there. At least, that's what Eleazar had told him, but who could know what rumors might have leaked out among almost a thousand defenders? It was tragic enough that the pagan bastards had burned God's Temple in Jerusalem, carrying off sacred scrolls, vestments, and the glorious golden fixtures to one of their tawdry triumphs for the mob in Rome. Nothing could be done about that. Perhaps one day, however, in the distant future, the Jews would establish a new kingdom, and if they did, what was hidden in the heart of the mountain might once again adorn a great Temple.

He pushed open the doors to the main palace and gagged at the stench. His stomach clenched, and for an instant he thought about stepping outside for a lungful of wood smoke—anything would be better than this horror in the darkened audience room beyond. Directly ahead was a short corridor and then a guards' room, and beyond— well, there were no words for what lay beyond. There were no lamps burning here, no more royal torches flaring in their iron holders.

He was supposed to fire the palace but not the storerooms. For that he needed flame. He went sideways down a small corridor to a complex of what had been offices in King Herod's time, beyond which was a second, larger guards' dayroom. He felt his sandals slipping on the marble floors and realized there were bloody footprints running down the center of the hallway.

Someone had fled the massacre inside. He stopped.

Was that someone still alive?

The hallway was too dark for him to see much other than the slick smudges on the marble. Slick, but also sticky. Not fresh blood, then. He reached the larger guards' room and saw what he needed, a small oil lamp burning high up in a niche on the outer wall. All he would have to do would be to roll a few amphorae of oil into the audience chamber, crack the seals, and ignite the oil.

There were windows in the guards' room, and it was definitely growing lighter outside than in. He could see the clouds of smoke rolling past, looking like huge amorphous ghosts on a mission of vengeance. The sound of the kettledrums penetrated this end of the palace. Very soon now, he thought.

He reached high and picked off the oil lamp. Turning around, he froze. The gaunt, soot-streaked face of another man stared back at him from the gloom of a corner in the room. Not just any face: It was Eleazar himself.

Judah raised the tiny oil lamp to make sure. *"You?"* he gasped. "How can this be?"

Eleazar was a lean and intense warrior who had led the defense of Masada from the beginning. He was not much younger than Judah, and he was a descendant of that Judah who had instigated a tax revolt against Cyrenius, which had in turn led to the formation of the Sicarii. Judah was suddenly furious that Eleazar, of all men on the mountain, had failed to keep the covenant, the one *he* had preached in the first place. He lifted the oil lamp higher, better to look into the leader's gaunt face. He noted that Eleazar's sleeves and shins were bloody, but there was no other mark upon him. When he thought about the sights he had witnessed in the outer precincts of the fortress, and the catastrophe that lay beyond in the great hall, he trembled with anger.

"It is still an *eligible thing* to die after a glorious manner?" he growled, throwing Eleazar's earlier words back at him. "And after we have slain them, let us bestow that glorious benefit mutually and preserve ourselves in freedom? *Glorious benefit?*"

Eleazar wouldn't look at him, nor would he speak. He stared down at the white tiles of the guards' room, his hands empty in his lap, his mouth set in a grim, flat line. Judah moved closer, his right hand closing on the haft of his dagger.

"*You* said these things," he spat. "*You* convinced them—you convinced all of us—to kill ourselves to spite the Roman beast. 'Where now is that great city that was believed to have God himself inhabiting therein?' you said. 'It is now demolished to the very foundations, where unfortunate old men lie upon the ashes of the

Temple, and a few women are there preserved alive, for our bitter shame and reproach'? Were these not *your* words?"

Eleazar still refused to look at him. "I couldn't do it," he said softly. He shook his head, slowly, from side to side, as if amazed at his own cowardice. "I could not bring myself to do it."

Judah drew the long dagger and pointed it down at Eleazar's wan face. Eleazar raised his eyes and made a gesture of resignation with his hands. In one swift movement, executed too many times throughout his career as a professional assassin, Judah stabbed down, impaling Eleazar just below the breastbone.

"'Let us make haste to die bravely,'" Judah roared, as he pushed the blade deeper, ignoring Eleazar's mortal, convulsive groan and desperately grasping hands. "'Let us pity ourselves, our children, and our wives, while it is in our power to show pity to them. Let us go out of the world in a state of freedom!'"

Eleazar's back arched in agony, the blood now running like a river from his open mouth, his feet kicking helplessly alongside Judah's legs.

"'Let us die before we become slaves under our enemies,'" Judah recited, as he twisted the blade, severing every vital link to life within Eleazar's body, "'and let us go out of this world, together with our children and our wives, in a state of freedom, so that we leave an example which shall at once cause their astonishment at our death, and their admiration at our hardiness.' "

Eleazar collapsed back against the wall, a great wheezing, bubbling sigh escaping from his mouth and nose as the blood slowed, his eyes fixed now in that rigid contemplation known only to the dead.

Judah withdrew the blade and straightened up, exhaling forcefully. His arm was shaking, and he found himself weeping. He had followed this man through the hell of civil war, the immolation of the Jewish state and most of its population, and finally the long and dreadful siege in this God-forsaken place, only to have Eleazar, the commander, the leader, the fiery heart of the revolt, lose his nerve? He could not abide it.

A gust of wind blew smoke into the palace, stirring once again the reek of mass death coming from down the passageways. The rumble of the drums seemed to be growing louder. The formations must be massing down below the ramp.

An hour at the most until dawn. It was time to fire the palace. Then he would slip down the Serpent Path to the great cistern. To his own end. Unlike Eleazar, he had no doubts that he could do what he must. He was anxious to die.

Judah had to lower himself on a rope over the eastern parapets, the gate to the Serpent Path having long been sealed by the defenders. He felt doubly exposed as he slid down, because this was the sunrise side of the mountain. The Zealots had seen Roman patrols on the Serpent Path, but always down toward the bottom. General Silva had allowed the path itself to remain open in hopes of encouraging defections from the mountain. He had closed it only after discovering that Jews were using it to *join* the defenders.

He crunched down into the loose sand and gravel below the walls and flipped the rope a couple of times until the special knot let go, dropping the full length of it at his feet. He gathered it up and trudged down the path, moving from boulder to boulder as best he could, stopping to listen for the tramp of Roman sandals. The air was fresher here, as the diurnal winds prepared to change. The smells were no longer of death and smoke but of brine and long-burned sand. He reached the tiny cave, dragging the coil of rope behind him to smooth out his tracks, and then stepped inside. There had been a rain two weeks ago, and the sand on the floor of the cave was still wet.

He stopped to rest, very much aware now that the opening of the cave was gray against the darkness inside. Soon the Romans would advance up the siege ramp. What a sight they would find! He had never found the missing children and the two women. Perhaps they had taken refuge in one of the dry cisterns at the southern end of the fortress. A few inconsequential survivors wouldn't be all bad, he thought. The Romans would find them and hear firsthand what had befallen their triumph. Then, unfortunately, they'd throw them off the ramparts.

It was time. He went to the back of the cave and began to dig away the sand until he exposed the hole into the great cavern. It was covered with a closely fitted wooden hatch, which he was able to pull up, turn on its side, and then drop through the hole. It took a frighteningly long time before he heard the crash of splintering boards below. The cavern was at least sixty cubits from the ceiling to the floor. Then he moved more sand, exposing the heavy stone slab that had been buried next to the hole. It was much too heavy for one man to move without levers, but they had prepositioned five small round logs under it to serve as rollers. On the top was an iron ring, bolted to an iron shaft that penetrated the slab. There was a smaller ring on the bottom side. He attached the rope to this underside ring. Then he rolled the slab over to the very edge of the hole, leaving enough room for him to climb through. He used his sandals to sweep mounds of sand right next to the hole and on top of the slab, so that the sand would fall in behind the stone and conceal it.

He sat for a moment on the edge of the hole. Once he lowered himself onto the rope, the slab would begin to move. He would have a few seconds to get beneath it before it rolled into the cambered hole, sealing him into the cave forever.

It was well and truly over. His entire life. Old as he was, he could still remember it all, even as far back as the heady days in Galilee when he'd joined the wild bunch, after having been expelled from his family and his village for mocking the religious pretensions of his older brother. The expulsion, when he was just fifteen years old, had come as no surprise, really. He had been a rebellious child from the first, a fighter and a scrapper and much more interested in hunting and trapping in the hills than in boring scripture and the study of long-dead prophets. Increasingly forced to endure endless lectures on how much better his older brother was, how much more worthy, devoted, scripturally brilliant, such a good son, all of it, he jumped at the chance to join the small band of ruffian teenagers who roamed the northern hills of Galilee, living off the land and the occasional stolen herd animal. His parents had renounced him and stricken his name, while his brother, the saint, went off to study with the priests and scholars about minutiae in the holy book.

He stopped to listen. Something was different. The drums. The drums had stopped. He closed his eyes and recaptured the images from the palace above and the desperate, bloody hovels in the casemates, the glorious defenders of Jewish honor and history reduced now to sodden lumps of carrion.

For a moment, his faith in the cause almost broke.

Implacable Rome. Vengeful Rome. Divine Rome. Conquerors of the whole world, masters of the visible horizon who even called the entire middle sea Mare Nostrum, *our* sea. Challenged by tiny, insignificant Judaea.

They had been mad to even imagine they could break the Roman yoke.

It was time to end it. The treasures were secure. The people's testaments were all collected at the bottom. The Romans were coming.

He sighed, grabbed the rope, turned sideways, put his weight on it, and slid down beneath the edges of the slab hole. Nothing happened for a moment, and then the slab responded, moving toward his face as he slid farther down beneath the rectangular opening, the wooden rollers dropping through, banging off his shoulders, and then the slab seating with a granitic, sandy thump, leaving him suspended in utter darkness. The roller logs crashed down onto the rock floor of the cavern a very long way beneath him. He listened and thought he could hear the whispering flow of sand covering the slab. Hand over hand, his fingers clutching the rough knots, he lowered himself into stygian darkness.

He continued to slide down the rope until his

sandals came up against the big knot at the bottom. He could see absolutely nothing; the darkness was profound. He tried to visualize the great sphere of the cavern but had no way to orient himself, so he began to swing, pumping the rope back and forth until he was swinging through the darkness, initially in one line but then in a sweeping circle, wider and wider, until he finally felt his feet bang up against the rock wall. He kept it up, expanding the arc, until one of his feet engaged the scaffolding wall they had erected. It was a lashed pole-and-crosspiece affair, rising from the floor of the cavern to the entrance of the side cave.

He lost it and then found it again. It took three more tries before he could hook a foot into the lattice of the ladder and stop his swing. He was puffing from the exertion and took a minute to regain his breath. He was now hanging like a hammock, his feet locked around the ladder structure while the rest of his body hung out over the blackness as he gripped the rope. He considered just letting go. It was some forty cubits to the floor of the cavern, certainly far enough down to smash the life out of him when he landed. There were two more things he had to do, however, and they had to be done in the cave.

He extended his feet through the lattice, hooked his knees, and then let go of the rope. He felt it swing back out into the center of the cave, his last connection to the world above gone forever. He raised himself on the scaffolding and began to climb in the total darkness, visualizing the ladder wall and the tiny cave entrance in his mind from the times before. Then there had been torches. When he got up to the top lattice of the scaffolding, he felt his way along it until the lip of the side cave entrance came under his hands. He stepped up onto the top of the lattice, swung around it, and crawled into the narrow tunnel. Keeping his head low, he eased his way up the tunnel on hands and knees until he felt the tunnel widen as it opened into the cave itself.

He stood up then and reached into the leather pouch at his waist. He carefully extracted the smoldering ember of wood he'd taken from the palace and blew on it. One end glowed red, revealing just the tips of his fingers. From a second compartment in the pouch he took a twist of lint that he had dipped in lamp oil. He pressed it to the ember and blew on it steadily until the lint flamed. Holding it upside down, he found the first of the oil pot lamps on the wall of the cave and lit it. Using that lamp he lit the rest, until he had a dozen flickering lamps going, their tiny lights throwing eerie shadows onto the walls. He walked across the sloping floor of the cave to the wooden altar where the Temple artifacts gleamed in the lamplight. Then he bent down and probed the sand beneath the altar with his dagger until he felt it hit something solid. He dug in the sand with his fingers and extracted a small, unadorned bronze wine bowl. Straightening up, he poured all the dry sand out of the bowl and held it in both hands, overwhelmed once again by a flood of memories. Holding the bowl in one hand, he picked up a piece of charcoal and began to write on the wall.

When he had finished writing his testament, the oil lamps were guttering. He stood up by the altar and faced the entrance to the cave. He bent down and positioned the haft of his dagger in a crack in the cave's floor with the blade pointed straight up. He took one final deep breath, stiffened his back and his arms, and fell forward like an old tree.

He never felt the floor of the cave smash him in the face. Instead he felt a white-hot lance of pain transfix his consciousness even as it paralyzed that final deep breath in his chest. He opened his eyes but could not see. So this is what it felt like, all those men he had killed. A roaring red haze gathered in his mind. His last thought was that he was dying exactly like a Roman general who has been defeated on the battlefield. For some strange reason, he found that amusing. He tried to laugh, to make one last time that most human of sounds, but he could not.

Part II

Tel Aviv, Israel

1

David Hall took a final standing stretch at his seat before sitting back down and refastening his seat belt. The beauty queen masquerading as an El Al stewardess had slunk through first class to tell each of the ten passengers individually and somewhat breathlessly that the captain would soon be turning on the seat-belt sign in preparation for landing at Ben Gurion Airport. David had paid close attention to her every word and the effect they had on her quivering superstructure. At these prices she better be a beauty queen, he thought, although one look back into the coach section upon boarding had confirmed the wisdom of electing first class. The crowd back there was somewhat eclectic.

It was early afternoon as the Airbus descended toward Tel Aviv over the eastern Mediterranean. Virgil's famously wine-dark sea glittered out the window, except that it was a deep blue, edged with precisely aligned, spidery whitecaps. The sea actually looked chilly. Well, why not, he thought. It was the first week in September, which meant that he would be visiting Israel four weeks before the major religious holidays of Rosh Hashanah and Yom Kippur, compliments of careful planning. Landing and getting through security, immigration, and customs would be the first hurdles, especially with some of his special equipment. He had all the proper paperwork, which was good because the Israelis were extremely thorough about entry paperwork. The portable computer and his scuba regulator pack should not be a problem. Some of the seismic sensor stuff might attract attention, but it was pretty well disguised as part of his underwater camera equipment. Besides, everything had made it through the equally strict El Al security inspection back at Dulles, so he was fairly confident he would get it past the security people here in Tel Aviv. Immigration would be relatively pro forma for an American tourist, and customs, well, who ever knew about customs.

He swallowed as the cabin pressure was adjusted. He caught the beauty queen looking at him. In her tight-fitting uniform she could adjust the cabin pressure just by sitting down, he thought. He smiled at her and she smiled back, but it was a professional smile and not any indication of interest, he decided. He turned away, looking out the window for a first glimpse of Israel, but there was only the sea, a bit closer as the big jet bumped gently through light coastal clouds. He'd been planning this thing for a year now, ever since Adrian had disappeared. It still made his spine tingle when he thought about what he was going to attempt here and what he might discover on that haunted mountain down at the literal bottom of the world.

· · ·

"He's here," the man with the pockmarked face breathed into the public pay phone, his face averted from the shuffling crowd of bleary-eyed tourists streaming past him from the customs hall.

"Anyone meet him besides his driver?"

"No. Shall I follow them out to the car, or are we done here?"

"You know the answer to that one."

"Just thought I'd ask."

"Shall I run that question by the boss for you?"

"Thank you, no." The man in the phone booth was silent for a moment. "I'll confirm him in the car, and again at the hotel."

"Yes, you will."

The watcher mouthed a silent insult, hung up, and hastened down the carpeted aisle of the customs area, keeping the big American and his driver in sight over the shoulders of the milling tourists. He thought this was all something of a waste of time: What did they think this American was going to do, jump in a *sherut* at the last minute and whisk off to Amman to see the king? According to his supervisor, they had the American's official Israeli government itinerary, his hotel, his driver—what the hell was the big deal? A nobody nuclear engineer turned whistle-blower who was now famous in Washington for winning a seven-figure settlement after suing his former employer for wrongful termination.

Coming to Israel to play amateur archaeologist, do some skindiving, and then go home. Ridiculous. Who could care? He wondered again whom he had pissed off to get a shit detail like this on a Friday afternoon.

The throng of tourists bunched up again at the row of glass doors leading out to the public transportation area, and the watcher turned to look out the windows when his subject stopped. The American, David Hall, seemed to take the delay in stride, indicating that the driver should put the bags down for a minute, let the crowds ahead clear out. The American carried one large, awkward-looking case, probably his diving gear. He also carried what appeared to be a portable computer. The driver was humping two large suitcases and an overnight bag on an airport cart. Hall was holding on to that portable computer like it was his baby.

Trying not to be too obvious about it, the watcher confirmed the briefed description: Caucasian male, close to two meters in height, late thirties, barrel-chested, eighty, maybe ninety kilos, black hair laced with some gray, square face, a Semitic nose that would make a rabbi proud, prominent chin, and the tanned complexion of an outdoors-man. This Hall fellow didn't look like an engineer at all, certainly not like the Israeli engineers and scientists the watcher had seen on the telly. This one had big, strong-looking hands, wide shoulders, and a lot of solid muscle under that expensive sport coat. In that regard he truly stood out from the rest of the tourists, who were mostly old and overweight. Hall: Was that a Jewish name in America? He certainly had the Moses nose for it.

The watcher took care not to stare directly. His instincts told him that the American appeared to be aware of his surroundings. He was definitely looking around in a manner that belied his informal, relaxed pose with the driver. The briefer had mentioned that there was an intelligence interest in this American, although what that was had not been explained. Even so, the watcher had been instructed to pay attention to his tradecraft, because there was always the possibility that this American had had some field training. The watcher looked at him again. No way, he thought. Guy looks like a rich playboy, with all that fancy luggage and his fashionably thin computer.

One of the ubiquitous airport security teams, consisting of a man and a woman in rumpled army khakis, strolled by, the noses of their shoulder-slung submachine guns pointing lazily at the floor. They looked like brother and sister. They gave the nondescript Israeli lounging against a concrete pillar, dressed in tan slacks and a cheap sport shirt, the once-over and then, recognizing him for what he was, looked immediately away and kept going. By then the crowd at the doors was thinning out and the American was helping his driver gather up the bags, and then they were pushing through the glass doors to the usual chaos outside. The watcher followed them from inside the terminal building, observing until they stopped at a shiny if elderly four-door white Mercedes.

The watcher waited for the American to get in the car, right rear seat, just like some stuck-up officer. Next stop would be the Dan Tel Aviv Hotel, unless of course they really were going to make a quick getaway and go underground to meet some CIA fiends. Right. Wanting a cigarette, he glanced at his watch. Four forty-five, almost Shabbat, so of course all the CIA agents would be bellied up to the bar at the Sheraton by now. The watcher was not religious, but he was definitely ready for a day off. This American was boring, like most of them. At least he wasn't fat, like most of them.

2

David Hall pulled back the sheer curtains of his twelfth-floor corner suite and admired the ocean view. The Dan Tel Aviv, one of the city's five-star hotels, was just across a small street from the Mediterranean, and the sea still looked cold, with rigid rows of whitecaps being driven in toward the beige, sandy beach by a chilly northwest wind. The sunset was bisected by the silhouette of the

Yamit Towers. He looked to either side, where horizontal rows of windows seemed to propagate in every direction. No other faces were visible. The street sounds of the diminishing Tel Aviv evening rush hour echoed quietly up the concrete and glass palisades of the Hayarkon hotel district. He'd specifically asked for a seaside room to avoid the noise of Tel Aviv's raucous traffic. He yawned and looked at his watch: seven o'clock here, one back in Washington. Why the hell was he sleepy, then?

So far so good, he reflected. All the gear had made it through customs, and he'd received no special attention from any security types, just what appeared to be routine surveillance in the terminal. Suspecting that the nonchalant man in the short-sleeved white shirt and tan pants behind him might be a watcher, he had stopped abruptly thirty feet back from the doors, ostensibly to wait for the crowds. White Shirt had stopped dead in his tracks to examine the empty space between the terminal windows and the ramps. Okay, so maybe the guy had been following him, or perhaps someone else in the crowd of tourists ahead of him. There was absolutely no way they could know what he was really up to, especially since he had made all of his cover arrangements with the help of the Israeli government. That was the beautiful part of his plan. Adrian's dream, but definitely his plan.

He realized he was hungry, but then yawned again and decided maybe he would send down for room service. Sundown on Fridays brought the official beginning of Shabbat. All the travel guides warned of interruptions in every kind of basic services extending until sundown Saturday. He yawned again. All his great plans for adapting immediately to the local time zone were being defeated by an overwhelming urge to go to bed. He flopped on the expansive bed and thought about what he would order for dinner. Or was it lunch? Maybe wait a couple of hours. Then get something.

The rattle of a room service tray out in the hallway woke him. He sat up in bed, groaned, and rubbed leaden eyelids against the bright daylight streaming in through the side windows. What the hell time was it? Nine thirty. In the *morning?* He had slept, what, fourteen hours? Many muscles protested. He looked again at his watch. Three thirty in the morning in Washington. Damn the jet lag. He felt like he'd been hit by a marshmallow train, and now he was really hungry, his earlier plans for room service having been swallowed up in a long if fitful sleep.

He dragged himself off the bedcovers and sat up. He needed coffee and a shower and then breakfast and then some more coffee. His eyes felt sandy, and his neck was stiff from lying on his back all night. He could not remember ever sleeping that long. This was Saturday, the day he had budgeted to get himself acclimated to the six-hour time difference before the game began. If his present mental fogginess was any indication, he would need Sunday, too. He headed for the bathroom.

Tonight he was to meet with a Professor Yosef Ellerstein for a drink in the lobby bar at six thirty. Ellerstein was his official point of contact at the Israel Antiquities Authority, the senior government bureau in charge of all archaeological sites. The Israeli cultural attaché at the Embassy of Israel, where Adrian worked, had gone to Columbia with Ellerstein, and they had remained professional and personal friends, even after Ellerstein had emigrated to Israel back in the early seventies.

Whenever Adrian had talked about her obsession, she'd said that getting access to the site was going to require a connection with a senior guy in the IAA. Her boss, the cultural attaché, knew a professor at Columbia who was still connected to Ellerstein, who was now on the board of directors of the IAA. After Adrian disappeared, and David had made the decision to pursue her life's dream, he'd called the attaché, who in turn had contacted Ellerstein, who eventually agreed to be David's interlocutor within Israel's archaeological establishment. David had corresponded with him for the past year while preparing for his trip, and the professor had suggested meeting Saturday night at David's hotel before David had to face his first meetings at the IAA and Hebrew University on Monday.

Finished in the bathroom, David went to the north window and stared again into the harshly bright sunlight. The whitecaps were gone. The glass felt warm against his face. So much for the cool breezes of fall, he thought. He walked around to the west windows and stared out at the sea again, trying to get his brain to function, but he still felt stupefied. He went over and sat on the edge of the bed, then realized he was going around in circles. Coffee time.

At six thirty that evening, David was waiting in the bar when his guest appeared through the double doors. The attaché had told him that Dr. Yosef Ellerstein was sixty-five years old. David spotted him at once from his corner table in the lounge and got up, waving the older man over. Ellerstein, looking more like seventy, was a short, round man who wore thick glasses over a prominent nose. His unkempt grayish white hair reminded David of Albert Einstein. The professor was wearing a rumpled white short-sleeved shirt over baggy dark trousers and plain shoes. The well-chewed stem of a pipe protruded from his right pants pocket, and there was actually a scattering of ash burns down the right seam of his trousers. The perfect image of the absentminded professor, David thought.

Ellerstein made his way through the crowded room, filling now with tourists and bustling hotel staff in about equal numbers. David had learned that, besides being on the board of the IAA, Ellerstein was also a professor emeritus at Hebrew University, which gave him a foot in each of the two most important archaeological entities in Israel. David was counting on him to help him navigate the intricate and time-consuming maze of the Israeli academic bureaucracy. Once the university archaeological institute and the IAA had given their preliminary approval, Ellerstein had helped David with the paperwork. After almost a year of making arrangements, David was still not quite sure who was in charge of the site—the academics or the IAA. Ellerstein had told him that the Israelis probably didn't know either.

The professor approached the table and offered his hand. "Mr. Hall, I presume," he said in a gravelly smoker's voice. "Welcome to Israel."

"Dr. Ellerstein," David said. "A pleasure to meet you in person after all those e-mails and letters." They shook hands and sat down.

"You don't look like an engineer, Mr. Hall," Ellerstein began, "and as for the accursed e-mail: a double-edged invention, that. In the old days, one had time to digest a letter, think about it, pretend you hadn't received it, or at least have time to formulate some elaborate excuses. Now these things come in showers, instantaneously. One loses his maneuvering room."

David laughed. Maybe not quite so absent-minded, David thought. There was a definite gleam of intelligence behind those thick glasses. "An American phenomenon, I think," he replied, signaling a nearby waiter. "We seem to want everything instantly."

A waiter scurried over to their table and looked inquiringly at Ellerstein. The professor peered up at him myopically. "Whisky and soda, if you please, young man. Not so heavy on the soda."

He gave David an appraising look. "As you will soon find out, Mr. Hall, instant gratification is not the norm here in Israel. Especially when you propose to put both hands on the flypaper of our bureaucracy. Instant stasis is more like it. Everyone frozen in a tableau of earnest intentions, but doing absolutely nothing."

David smiled, remembering the months of paperwork to get the permissions. He waited while the waiter deposited Ellerstein's drink with a flourish. When the waiter had gone, he raised his own gin and tonic in salutation. "To Israel," he proposed.

Ellerstein dutifully tipped his glass. "To Israel," he grunted. He savored the Scotch for a moment and then put his glass down on the table with a clumsy thump. The waiter hovered nearby, having set up a small order stand near their table.

"You speak excellent English, Professor," David observed. "I apologize for not knowing Hebrew."

Ellerstein shrugged. "And why should you know Hebrew? As for my English, I was born and raised in America—New York, to be precise. Came over here supposedly to do graduate study after taking a degree in mathematics at Columbia, but mostly out of curiosity. A long time ago, it seems now. Never went back. Actually, you will find that many Israelis speak reasonably good English."

He looked around the crowded room for a moment. "So," he continued, examining David as if he were an interesting specimen. "What is this really all about, hah? This business at Metsadá?"

David felt a small snake of fear slip through his innards. There was absolutely no way in hell they could know, he reminded himself. No way in hell.

"It's really no more than I've said all along, Professor. I'm an amateur historian, or perhaps 'student of history' would be a less presumptuous term to a real academic."

"I'm a mathematician, Mr. Hall," Ellerstein said. "Amateurs are not unknown in our world."

"Yes, well. I want to spend some time on the mountain, actually at the site. Something more than the typical tourist's one-day excursion to Masada, which I've been told results in about an hour's stay time up on the mountain. I want to spend three or four days there, maybe even go up at night and just keep watch. I want to soak it up, to get the feel of the place, to think about the terrible things that happened there, to perhaps commune with the spirits there."

The older man stared at him without blinking for a full minute before replying.

"Commune with the spirits," he murmured. "There *are* spirits on that mountain, to be sure . . . but all this to satisfy, what is it, your *hobby?*"

There was mild disbelief evident in Ellerstein's voice. Time for some elaboration, David thought.

"Well, it's a little more than that, Professor. I've been working in the nuclear energy world ever since college. It is, how shall I put this, a sterile existence for the most part. A total focus on the science and engineering of a nuclear reactor."

"A well-deserved focus, I should think."

"Yes, indeed. A reactor can be a very dangerous servant."

"I totally agree," Ellerstein said. "I worked in our own atomic energy program for a few years. As only a mathematician, you understand, but still. I know precisely what you are talking about. So how did you take up ancient history, then?"

"Met a very pretty girl," David said.

"Ah," Ellerstein said with a smile.

"I was doing a course at George Washington University," David said. "The company sent me there for some refresher training in digital communications systems. Met Adrian at a Friday afternoon happy hour."

"This Adrian, she was an archaeologist?"

"No, she worked at the Israeli Embassy," David said. "Ministry of Tourism. Her name was Adrian Draper, and we became—close. Masada and its history was one of her fascinations, as she called it. Obsession was more like it, I'm afraid."

"*Met*-sa-dá, Mr. Hall. You might as well pronounce it correctly while you're here. In Hebrew *metsada* means fortress."

"*Met*-sa-dá. Got it."

"So why is Adrian Draper not here with you?"

David sighed. "Her work for the embassy required a lot of travel within the U.S. About eighteen months ago, she left on a routine trip to the West Coast and never came back."

Ellerstein frowned. "She simply disappeared?"

"I expected her back on a Friday; when she didn't show up I called her cell phone, but it was no longer in service. On Monday I called the embassy. They told me she'd been summoned out of the country on short notice and that she was fine. Not to worry."

"She didn't bother to even call you?"

"You had to know Adrian. She was a very independent woman. Our relationship was never boring. Anytime I made marriage noises, she'd go off on a trip. I assumed maybe she was sending me a message, and by then I was up to my neck in a problem of my own causing."

Ellerstein lifted his glass at the hovering waiter, who quickly brought him a refill. He raised his eyebrows at David, who shook his head. The alcohol was already affecting his jet-lagged head.

"You mentioned that you were no longer working in the nuclear energy field because of a, what did you call it, 'whistle-blowing' matter?"

"Yes," David said with a wry smile. "My fifteen minutes of fame, in Washington at least. Short version or long?"

"Short, please."

"After GWU I was reassigned to the company's Washington office in the materials audit division. In the weeks before Adrian went walkabout, I uncovered what looked like a materials diversion scheme within the company. Went to management, who told me to forget about it. Talked to my uncle, who is a senior bureaucrat at the Nuclear Regulatory Commission. He opened an official investigation, confirmed my findings, and fined the company. That in turn got me fired."

"They can do that? Fire you when you find out something illegal?"

"Well, yes and no," David said. "I then was called to testify before the congressional committee with oversight of the atomic energy business. Having been fired, I held nothing back. After that, I heard there were some discreet meetings with other government officials, although I never learned what that was all about, other than it seemed to involve some kind of espionage case and heavy water."

"Heavy water? Deuterium oxide?"

"Yes."

"When was this?"

"As I said, about six weeks before Adrian left on her trip. She wasn't too happy about it, in fact. We'd been talking about our future together, and now suddenly I was unemployable in the nuclear industry. As the cop shows term it, I was officially 'radioactive.' It caused some tension."

"Perhaps she was having second thoughts, then?" Ellerstein asked. "Forgive me for presuming, but sometimes the prospect of permanence exposes fault lines that are not obvious in the bedroom. She was perhaps getting a case of the cold toes?"

David laughed. "Cold *feet,* remember?" He paused to finish his drink. "That's possible. She was a bit of a wild child. Very smart, quick, opinionated." He thought back to some of their arguments. Cold feet? By now he'd realized it had always been him bringing up the possibility of marriage, never Adrian. "I guess you had to know her. She was mercurial sometimes. Impatient with people who weren't as smart as she was. Loved to scrap, then make up. The name Astarte ring a bell?"

Ellerstein smiled. "Of course," he said. "Usually

71

depicted in stone or marble as a supremely lush female figure. Ancient goddess of fertility and motherhood."

"And war," David reminded him. "In my mind, Adrian was the reincarnation of Astarte, right down to that lush womanly figure *and* a fondness for combat. Anyway, after all the dust settled with the whistle-blowing flap, I was approached by a law firm who wanted to file a suit on my behalf for wrongful termination, for a percentage fee, of course. I was still angry with the company, Adrian was off on her trip, still treating me to hot tongue and cold shoulder, so I said yes. The company settled."

"How much?" Ellerstein asked. David told him, provoking a low whistle.

"So *that's* how you can afford the Dan Tel Aviv, a first-class airline ticket, and two weeks here in Israel. Well done, Mr. Hall."

"I'm not sure I'd claim to be proud of myself, but I did feel a certain sense of vindication. Adrian was right—as they say in Hollywood, I'll never work in that business again."

"And so: Now you're here."

"I am indeed."

Ellerstein nodded slowly, appearing to gather his thoughts. David thought he was about to ask him the obvious question: Why was he pursuing his ex-girlfriend's obsession with Masada? Instead, he shifted subjects. "Metsadá is an important site to

Israel," he said. "A mythic shrine, in fact. A symbol of a calamity in our history that every patriotic Israeli vows never to let happen again. Do you know what the army does there?"

"Yes, I do. They take all the new lieutenants graduating from each class of officer school up to the mountain for a night vigil, and then at dawn they retell the story, and all the new officers swear an oath that basically says, 'Never again.' "

Ellerstein pursed his mouth in surprised approval. "Just so. Of course, you know the history. The nine hundred sixty Jews who took their own lives rather than surrender to the Romans."

"Yes. It is an astonishing and sobering story. I think that's why Adrian was so mesmerized by the place. It was more than just a hobby with her. After a while she inspired the same interest in me."

"You know that you are asking for a degree of access to this site that is normally granted only to professional archaeologists, and few of them at that? By your own admission you are no such thing."

If you only knew, David thought. Access doesn't quite describe it. He nodded but said nothing. Ellerstein swirled his glass for a moment.

"I agreed to put your request forward," he said finally, "because I owed Professor Hanson a big favor."

David blinked. Had Ellerstein already known about Adrian's disappearance? He realized that the answer had to be yes. On guard, boyo.

Ellerstein sipped his drink and appeared to reflect again for a few moments. David noticed that the room was completely full, with standing room only at the bar. The ending of Shabbat apparently generated a very secular thirst.

"To answer your unspoken question," Ellerstein said, "yes, Professor Hanson had told me the gist of what had happened to Adrian Draper. Sorry, but I wanted to hear it directly from you."

"All right," David said. Play along, he thought. Remember the objective.

"Okay," Ellerstein said finally. "On Monday you will go to the Rockefeller Museum in Jerusalem, where the Israel Antiquities Authority head office is located. I will meet you there. There we will hopefully finish the paperwork. Then we will go over to the Hebrew University to meet with Professor Armin Strauss, who is chairman of the Archaeology Institute, and Professor Reuven Bergmann, a specialist who has cognizance over the Metsadá site. He will put you together with some other academics who will refresh your knowledge, and—you've read the Yigael Yadin exploration reports?"

"Yes."

"Very well. All of these people will discuss the current status of the site, ongoing excavations, and also explain where you may *not* go because of work in progress."

"I hope there won't be too many restrictions. I know the public can't go down to the lower palace terraces to see the mosaics, for instance, or to the cisterns."

"Only for reasons of safety. It is a four-hundred-meter fall if they make a mistake. And the cisterns, did you say? Do you have a special interest in the cisterns?"

David felt a spike of panic. Get him off this, right now. "No, but I remember the Yadin reports said that the cisterns had never been explored."

"Ah, well, they have been entered, but there was nothing in any of them except dusty rock. Basically, they're just dry holes in the side of the mountain. Cavities. No, for you, the only restrictions will be because of ongoing restoration work. Basically, we'll simply ask that you do not interfere, and, of course, no digging."

"I understand—and please, I really do appreciate the help. I know this is probably, no, surely, an inconvenience for you real scholars, as Professor Hanson constantly reminded me."

Ellerstein showed another brief smile. "How is my colleague George Hanson?"

"Fine and in pretty good health," David said. "He said you were at Columbia together. Why did you emigrate, may I ask?"

"I came over at an exciting time. I was a theoretical math mechanic and, of course, a Jew.

It seemed to me that I might be a bigger fish in this pond than in the United States."

"I see. Did it work out that way?"

Ellerstein smiled enigmatically. "After a fashion, Mr. Hall. Although I may have contributed to some of your country's nonproliferation efforts."

David laughed out loud. Ellerstein was telling him that he had worked at Dimona, Israel's atomic energy research facility down in the Negev Desert. He knew the old man would not elaborate, though.

"Look," he said, changing the subject, "I've engaged a car and driver. Would you like me to have him pick you up before we see the IAA people?"

"No, no, thank you, Mr. Hall. Some of my colleagues at the IAA are already teasing me about this, ah, project. A car and driver would only add to the fun and games."

David, feeling a twinge of embarrassment, nodded. His visit was indeed causing some discomfort. Remember why you're really here, he told himself. This is no time to waver.

"I'll try to get out of your hair as quickly as I can, then," he said. "I've scheduled some diving tours after the site visit."

Ellerstein shrugged again, as if to say, *There's nothing for it but to get it over with.* "You are established here?" he asked, indicating the hotel. "Your logistics are in order?"

"Yes, it's fine. I'm out of sorts with the time change, but I'll be okay by Monday. I hope."

"Yes, it is difficult. Too many Americans expect to function on the very first day. You are wise to allow two days. So, what will you do tomorrow—go see the Old City in Jerusalem, perhaps?"

"Yes, I thought I would. Any recommendations?"

"The usual things. Begin with very comfortable shoes: The whole place is made of stone, and it's very hard on the feet. Take a hat and some water, and first have your driver take you to the scale model of ancient Jerusalem at the time of Christ. It's at the Holy Land Hotel. It's worth seeing before you go into what remains of the Old City. Sets things in physical perspective." He finished his drink and pushed back in his chair. "So," he concluded. "Monday at the Rockefeller. Ten o'clock, yes?"

"I'll be there, Professor. Thanks for coming down this evening. It's been good to meet you."

"And you, Mr. Hall. Monday, then. Shalom."

Twenty minutes later the waiter who had been taking care of David and his guest stepped out the hotel's employee entrance and made his way to Hayarkon Street. He turned left down the sidewalk and started walking north. A few moments later a large black Mercedes sedan with deeply tinted windows pulled up alongside the curb, facing the wrong way in traffic. The waiter quickly looked around and then got into the left rear seat of the car, which pulled away from the curb with a clack of electric door locks. In the gloom of the backseat was an elderly white-haired gentleman. He was wearing a dark coat over a business suit, with expensive-looking black leather gloves on his hands. A black homburg perched on his head.

"Well?" the man asked. His voice was barely more than a hoarse whisper. It almost seemed to come from speakers hidden in the car's lush upholstery.

The waiter gave his report but did not look directly at the other man. The driver, a large, impassive young man with no apparent neck, stared straight ahead as he steered the heavy car across oncoming traffic to regain the proper lanes. The sedan's insulation muffled a chorus of blaring horns.

"Based on what I heard," the waiter concluded, "I think he is what he seems to be. A successful American, very full of himself."

"Aren't they all. Did he elaborate on precisely what he wants to do at Metsadá?"

"The lounge was pretty noisy, but basically, he says he's an amateur historian who mostly wants access to all the ruins and the time to take it all in. Says he wants to commune with the spirits."

"Indeed." The old man took a deep breath and then slowly let it out. "Hall. Not a Jew, correct?"

The waiter cast a quick sideways glance, but the old man's face remained in shadow. The waiter knew who he was but had never actually seen him before. Almost no one had. "No, sir, I wouldn't think so."

The old man lapsed into silence for almost a full minute. The waiter wanted another look but was almost afraid to take one. The stories were alarming.

"Commune with the spirits of Metsadá. Don't you just wish one or two of those bloody old Kanna'im would pop out at him with their throats gaping open. I wonder if he would survive the experience. Psychologically speaking, of course."

The waiter, a sergeant in the military intelligence organization known as LAKAM, swallowed. Colonel Malyuta Lukyanovitch Skuratov had an uncommon ability to evoke images of death.

"Did he indicate interest in any specific parts of the fortress?"

"He knew which parts are normally off-limits to tourists," the sergeant replied. "He mentioned, for instance, the lower palaces, the mosaic remains, and the cisterns."

"The cisterns? He mentioned the cisterns?" The big car swung right, away from the beaches.

The sergeant turned slightly in his seat, curious about the faint note of alarm in the colonel's voice. "Only in the context that the Yadin report said the cisterns had never been explored. He was using them as an example, I think, not as a point of specific interest. Or to show off, to prove that he's read Yadin. Professor Ellerstein took no particular notice, that I could see."

There was another long moment of silence, when the only sounds in the car came from the raucous noise of a bus momentarily alongside. They were passing through an area without streetlights, which enveloped the colonel's face in even deeper shadow. Then there was a splash of light coming from inside the bus, and the sergeant had to suppress a wince. Spiky, brush-cut white hair showing under the famous homburg. Starkly pink skin with the seams of the grafts visible as a mosaic of fine white lines. Deeply inset, hooded eyes, with bare wisps of eyebrows below a wide, gleaming brow. Long, bony nose. Thin, bloodless lips. His tight pink skin only emphasized his skull-like appearance, but it was the eyes that gave the sergeant a jolt: pale gray with glints of amber, projecting a gleam of what most people took for repressed fury. Colonel Skuratov of the Shin Bet, Israeli military counterintelligence, also known behind his back—a long way behind his back—as Colonel Lazarus. The Russian émigré who had risen from the grave called Gulag to a position of shadowy power in Israel's counterintelligence apparatus. With a start, the sergeant realized the colonel was looking right at him. He snapped his face away, focusing hard on the driver's head. Skuratov leaned toward him.

"Do not look at me, young man," the colonel whispered in accented Hebrew. "I'm not someone you want to know."

"Yes, sir," the sergeant replied, also in a whisper, his throat suddenly dry. The car made another right, heading south now. The hotel towers were just visible a few blocks away.

"You have done well tonight," Skuratov said finally. "Although this all is probably about nothing. Another insouciant American with more money than manners, imposing on the goodwill of a client state."

"Yes, sir," the sergeant said, feeling he had to say something. His watcher briefing had been cursory. A description of the American. A description of the professor. Eavesdrop. Report. The car was slowing. They had come full circle, a block away from the hotel. The car pulled over.

"That will be all, Sergeant," Skuratov said.

"Do you—?"

"No, no, we are finished with him, this American. Be careful when you open the door, Sergeant. You are on the street side now."

3

On Monday morning, David found his elderly but highly polished hired Mercedes 240D sedan waiting at the hotel entrance, right on time. His driver for the week was an intense older man named Ari, who appeared to be in his sixties. Ari was solidly built and presented the no-nonsense demeanor of an ex-military man. He spoke good English with what sounded to David like a faint German accent. He wore a loose-fitting sport coat over an open-throated white shirt and pressed khakis. Given the incipient heat, David suspected Ari was carrying. The option of having an armed driver had seemed prudent, considering the current state of tension in the country. Naturally, the hire car company had charged extra.

They made good time for about one minute down Hayarkon, and then traffic bogged down in a noisy stew of honking cars, smoke-belching buses, and Arabs on ancient bicycles, their djellabas tucked up around their knees and their heads hidden in multipatterned kaffiyeh head-dresses. There were knots of pedestrians on every corner, blocky, canvas-covered military trucks with soldiers dozing in the back, and a surprising number of ragged children darting in and out of the traffic. David had been advised by the concierge to allow an hour and forty-five minutes to get to the Rockefeller Museum in Jerusalem, and he wondered if even that would be sufficient now that he saw the traffic.

He was not entirely over his jet lag but doing much better than on the first day. He had spent Sunday playing tourist in Jerusalem, taking a hotel van up to the city from the hotel. He had taken in the model of ancient Jerusalem at the Holy Land Hotel, its waist-high buildings and walls giving an excellent perspective on Jerusalem at the time of Christ. He then walked through the narrow streets of the old walled city, stopping on the margins of tour groups whenever he overheard an English-speaking tour guide and stumbling onto the major tourist sites more by accident than by design. He had been conscious of the strategically placed soldiers, always in pairs, strolling throughout the Old City, or perched up on rooftops. There was much too much to see in just a one-day walkabout, and every time he stopped and asked for directions, he was pointed to yet another must-see holy place. By the middle of the afternoon he was hobbling, so he had a taxi take him to the Hadassah Ein Karem hospital to see the famous Chagall windows, after which he hired a *sherut*, or shared van, for a ride back to Tel Aviv.

"Are we going to make this in time, Ari?" he asked the driver.

"Yes, of course," the driver replied. "No

problem." David smiled inwardly. Adrian had once explained about asking yes-or-no questions in the Middle East. If any answer but yes might embarrass either the one asking or answering the question, the answer was always going to be positive. At least the car's air-conditioning was working, keeping at bay most of the brown diesel haze that served for an atmosphere in the city's streets. They did the stop-and-go dance for about twenty minutes before the traffic began to thin out.

The purpose of the meeting this morning was to obtain the final written approvals from the IAA, the government bureaucracy responsible for the preservation and study of antiquities in Israel. Professor Ellerstein was going to run interference at the IAA and also be available to handle any language problems. David would have to go in and sign some documents promising to respect any and all sites he visited and not to engage in any physical disturbance of them. In other words, as Ellerstein had reminded him, no digging. Well, that shouldn't be too hard: If things worked out the way he hoped, he might have to probe a little, but not dig. He was pretty sure all the pertinent digging had been done two thousand years ago.

Then back into the car and over to the Mount Scopus campus of Hebrew University for what would probably be a somewhat more ticklish session with the scholar archaeologists. He wasn't afraid of them so much as impatient with their endless condescension, which never seemed to be satisfied by his own frank admission that he was very much an amateur. Suffer through it and humor them, he thought. Remember the objective. He sat back and dozed.

"Almost there, Mr. Hall," the driver announced. David woke up to see that they were climbing the twisting highway that led up to Jerusalem from the coastal plain. The highway was bordered by dramatic ravines on either side, in which he could see the rusting hulks of armored vehicles, left there presumably to remind passersby of the intense battles for Jerusalem back in the 1948 war for Israel's independence.

"Good deal, Ari," he replied. He looked at his watch. They had made good time. He might actually be a few minutes early, which was probably a cultural offense in the Middle East.

Twenty minutes later they pulled up in front of the Rockefeller Museum. He was relieved to see Professor Ellerstein sitting on a park bench in front of the building, reading a newspaper and puffing away on his pipe. David got out, told Ari to find a place to hole up, and warned him that he had no idea how long this would take.

"Is government business? I will go for a coffee. You come out, I will see you. No problem, Mr. Hall."

David walked over to the park bench, where

Ellerstein was folding up his newspaper and knocking pipe ashes out onto the sidewalk.

"Good morning, Professor," David said. "Or should I call you Dr. Ellerstein?"

"Here at the IAA, doctor. At the university, professor. Ready to grasp the flypaper?"

"Ready as ever." David detected that the old man was a little less friendly this morning than he had been when they parted at the bar. Maybe it was the lack of Scotch.

"Okay," Ellerstein sighed. "We go."

Two and a half hours later they were back in the Mercedes and on their way to the university, with the professor this time accepting David's offer of a ride. David vowed that he would never again complain about the District of Columbia's bureaucracy, having now experienced the exquisite agonies of dealing with the Israeli variant. Flypaper indeed, but they had achieved their goals and now had a sheaf of vividly stamped documents to take with them to the Hebrew University. Doctor, now Professor, Ellerstein assured him that the academics were capable of every bit as much obfuscation and delay as the bureaucrats in the IAA, but the fact that he now had official documents in hand might ease his way somewhat.

"Besides, there will be a minder."

"Minder?" David asked. What was this?

"Yes, well, I think it is the price you will pay for your unusual access to this site. Both the IAA and the university people thought it would be appropriate that you have an escort while you are at the site. Someone who knows it well, who can answer your questions, and perhaps even direct your explorations. That sort of thing."

"I see." Boy, did he. This was going to complicate matters. Could they possibly be suspicious? Had someone gone through his stuff in the customs hall and found the geophones? Or worse, the encapsulated source charge? He dismissed that idea—there would have been immediate hell to pay if they'd found the explosive disk, tiny as it was. He had been prepared to confess the whole scheme if they found the source charge, knowing full well that the Israelis had zero tolerance when it came to security issues. The charge though, was encased in a stainless steel cylinder that fit precisely into the chamber of his spare scuba regulator. If they had opened that regulator, they would have found only a very thin steel disk. Hermetically sealed, so no vapors to alert dogs or bomb-sniffing machinery. Four ounces, just enough to make a noise, and the geophones had been inserted between batteries in his underwater sealed beam diving light. All of it should look perfectly innocuous, just like the rest of his diving gear.

"Who will this minder be?" David asked. "You?"

"Goodness, no. I suppose the joint committee will have picked someone. It will depend upon availability and schedules. You know how it is. It would help if you can agree to keep the visit short, say two, three days at the most. It will be difficult to get a faculty member for more than that. An imposition, in fact."

"I didn't ask for a minder, Professor."

"You asked for unusual access to Metsadá, Mr. Hall. That is the same thing. Of course, if you object—"

"Yeah, right. I can always go away."

"That is an option, as you say."

They traveled in silence through more heavy traffic for the next twenty minutes. I should have expected this, David thought. Except that I thought any minder would be someone who was already at the site. Archaeologists, security guards, tourism bureau people, but not an escort from the Hebrew University. I wonder what the hell changed to provoke this? Oh, well, his plan was flexible. This would just mean he would be doing his real explorations at night. If nothing else, he thought, the time zone differential would work in his favor.

"The committee will want to know what you already know about the site, Mr. Hall," Ellerstein said, breaking the silence as the car sped up a landscaped four-lane parkway toward what looked like the university buildings visible in the distance.

"A little examination, I suppose?"

"Yes, something like that. They assume you have studied the site. That you have read Yigael Yadin's final reports, and the relevant history—Josephus, Tacitus, for instance."

"Of course."

"Very good. There is much controversy surrounding Josephus, as you probably know."

"Colored somewhat by the fact that he went over to the Romans after Jotapata fell."

"There is that. We Jews have no tolerance for traitors. Still, he survived when no one else did. Without his so-called history, we would know next to nothing about what really happened at Metsadá."

You still don't know what happened there, David thought to himself. That was not a notion he wanted to advertise to these people, however. When he found what he had come to find there, *if* he found it, there would be time enough for bragging rights. Right now, the game was to reveal less rather than more about what he knew. Convince them he was just another amateur, a know-nothing with more zeal than real knowledge, and they would dismiss him and his one-man expedition as a trivial matter. Success, in fact, depended on that. The assignment of a minder showed that they weren't completely lulled yet. Then something occurred to him—maybe the minder had been Ellerstein's idea.

"You've been on faculty here since you emigrated, Professor?"

"No, no. For a while I worked for the government, doing research. Then I got tired of that and came to the university to teach graduate-level mathematics. Now I am emeritus, semiretired, on some boards. I am called in to consult on little projects like yours. Just here, driver."

He paused before getting out of the car. His eyes were distorted through the thick lenses of his glasses as he peered at David.

"Mr. Hall," he said, "we have arrived. To review: we will be meeting with Professor Armin Strauss, chairman, and Professor Reuven Bergmann, who holds academic responsibility for the Metsadá site. There will be two of his assistants present as well. Perhaps others, yes?"

"A regular crowd."

"Well, yours is a unique request. There are some details to be worked out, such as how long you will be at the site."

"Which is a function of how long the minder can be spared."

Ellerstein beamed. "Full marks. I assume you are ready to go right away? You are sufficiently rested from your trip?"

"Yes, I am," David said, mentally reviewing his equipment list. For the preliminary search, he had everything ready to go.

"Very well. I suspect that Professor Strauss will

offer a three-day stay, beginning as soon as tomorrow. That would give you Tuesday through Thursday at the site, with a return Friday."

"In time for the minder to begin the Sabbath Friday evening."

"Just so. If you are amenable to that schedule, this meeting can be brief. Yes? Okay?"

"Okay."

"Splendid. Let us proceed."

The conference room was spacious, with a central table, a stage and podium, and chairs for twenty people at the table. Ellerstein introduced David to the two senior professors and their assistants. David wondered briefly which one was the minder as he sat down with Ellerstein. Professor Strauss took the lead. He spoke in English with a trace of a British accent.

"Mr. Hall, welcome to the Hebrew University. Professor Ellerstein has asked us to assist you in your project of personal exploration at Metsadá."

"Thank you for your hospitality, Professor," David replied. "I am aware that my request is somewhat unusual, and I do appreciate your helping me out."

"Yes, Mr. Hall. We are aware that Professor Ellerstein has been interceding for you with the government authorities. May we assume you have obtained the necessary permissions from the IAA?"

David fished the collection of forms out of his

briefcase and passed it to the nearest assistant, who passed it over to the second professor. The chairman continued while his colleague inspected the paperwork.

"We also assume that you realize that this site is of profound significance to the modern state of Israel, Mr. Hall. The events that happened there in A.D. 73–74 have some dramatic analogies to offer our countrymen, even to this day."

"I am aware of that, Professor. Even though I am not a professional archaeologist or historian, I am equally aware of the requirement for me to respect the site and to cause no harm."

"Exactly, Mr. Hall. We are reassured to hear that. Which brings me to the matter of an escort. Has Professor Ellerstein explained to you that we will re—. Let me rephrase that, that we wish to appoint an escort for you during your stay at the mountain?"

David decided this was the time to take the initiative. It was imperative that he give no inkling that he might *not* want an escort. "He has, Professor Strauss. I would very much appreciate an escort. In fact, I would have asked for one except that I knew I was already imposing too much as it is."

David knew he had said the right thing when the old man almost beamed, although Ellerstein was now giving him a distinctly speculative look. The chairman had obviously been anticipating some objections. David decided to press on, aiming to neutralize all the contentious issues. "Professor Ellerstein tells me that you propose a three-day stay at the site, departing tomorrow and returning on Friday of this week, which also is most amenable and generous. I am prepared to leave for the site tomorrow morning."

"Wonderful, Mr. Hall. We will inform your escort."

"He's not here?" David asked, looking around the table.

"*She* is not here, Mr. Hall. We have appointed Dr. Judith Ressner, who is a faculty member of this institute with extensive knowledge of the site. In fact, I have excused her for the morning in order to let her prepare for your trip. I hope you will meet her at lunch today, as soon as we are completed here, if you will honor us with your company."

"The honor will be mine, Professor." A woman, he thought. Well, this was Israel. A good third of the soldiers he'd seen had been women. He shouldn't have been surprised.

The chairman conferred in Hebrew for a moment with the professor who had been inspecting the papers, then nodded.

"All of the papers appear to be in order, Mr. Hall. Now, I wonder if you would, for the benefit of me and my colleagues, review the nature of your request to visit this site." He pointed with open hands to the younger men at the table. "These gentlemen will be briefing you this afternoon on the current status of explorations and archaeology at Metsadá, and we are all somewhat curious, as I am sure you understand."

"Of course, Professor." David turned in his chair to include the two younger academics, then briefly gathered his thoughts while the Israelis waited politely. He thought he heard someone come into the room behind him but did not turn around. He had anticipated this question. Whatever he said now had to convince them that there was a genuine reason for his being here.

"I've been a professional engineer since college. My field is nuclear power, what we used to call atomic energy. I've been in that business one way or another until just recently, when my company, a major nuclear energy conglomerate, got into trouble with our regulatory authorities because of something I discovered and then revealed."

"Revealed?" the chairman asked.

"Yes," David said. "Are you familiar with the term 'whistle-blower'?"

"Oh, yes," the chairman said. "We have those in Israel, too. Lots of them, in fact."

"And everyone loves them forever after, right?"

The chairman laughed. David saw that Ellerstein was watching him, as a snake charmer watches his cobra.

"Well, I am currently an unemployed nuclear

engineer," David said. "So I decided to pursue a project that had been close to my girlfriend's heart for many years, involving Metsadá."

"She is here with you?" the chairman asked.

"Mr. Hall's girlfriend worked for our embassy in Washington," Ellerstein said. "Ministry of Tourism. She was ordered out of the country unexpectedly, and Mr. Hall decided to pursue her longtime dream in her sudden absence."

David nodded at Ellerstein, acknowledging his cue. "Her name was Adrian Draper. I met her while doing a course in Washington, and we became a couple. Among other things, she was fascinated by the history of the first century, and especially by what she called the Masada myth. *Met*sadá, excuse me."

The academics nodded but did not comment on his use of the word "myth." David had discovered that most archaeologists preferred to remain at professional arm's length as to the veracity of the story of what happened up on the mountain fortress—however dramatic and amazing—until there was more physical evidence.

"The Roman occupation of what they called Judaea is a particularly interesting nexus in the history of the ancient and the modern worlds. I'm a Christian, and for most Christians, as you well know, what happened here in the early first century remains a mesmerizing focus."

"So, Metsadá?" the chairman prompted gently.

Crunch time, David thought. He had to tell enough of the truth to convince them without revealing his real purpose.

"Sometime in the early fourth decade A.D., Jesus of Nazareth and his followers were declared to be revolutionaries. Jesus was executed, and his movement scattered. That should have ended the story. Yet from that point forward, starting underground, sometimes literally, the Christian movement evolved into a historical colossus. Thirty years or so after Jesus was executed, the Roman province of Judaea rose in revolt against Rome, a revolt ending five years later with the utter destruction of the ancestral city of Jerusalem, the Second Temple cult, and the annihilation of Jewish society. Except, of course, for those defiant survivors who holed up on Herod's mountain at Metsadá, where they withstood the siege of the Roman Tenth Legion for over two more years."

"I believe we know that history, Mr. Hall," the chairman chided. "In other words, what's your point, please?"

"My point is this: Adrian had always wondered what might have happened to the Jews as a nation and a religion if those Zealots, the warrior survivors of the Siege of Jerusalem, had *not* all killed themselves rather than surrender when the Romans finally breached the walls. In other words, was that a deliberate myth? What if they had fled from the mountain, instead, and gone underground? Like the early Christians."

The room went silent as they considered the question.

"It was probably not to be, of course," David continued, "and it's taken nearly two thousand years for another Jewish nation-state to arise here in Judaea. Now, I know it's a purely speculative question, one that a real scholar might dismiss, but it's a thesis that fascinated her for a long time, and once she left my life, I felt I had to come here. I wanted to spend some time on the mountain, more time than just a one-day tourist trip. I'm told that it's one thing to read about it, and quite another to stand among the stones and bones. So there it is."

There was a long moment of silence while the Israelis looked at him, and then at each other. Professor Bergmann, who had said very little up to this juncture, began nodding his head.

"The stones and the bones," he said. "As an archaeologist, Mr. Hall, I can understand that compulsion. When I was a young man, I was an unimportant member of the Yadin expedition for one season. Herod's fortress draws you. We academics like to think that we are always dispassionate, that we can stand back when we poke around in the graves of history; that we, too, can look at the stones and bones, as you term it, and remain completely detached. That place, however—well, one cannot remain dispassionate when one is actually there. It is a haunted place, Mr. Hall, and a revered place. And your question is more relevant to the profession of archaeology than you might think."

He looked up for an instant, his eyebrows lifting, as if he had become aware that he had said something seriously unorthodox. "You must never tell anyone I said that," he whispered conspiratorially, and everyone laughed and relaxed. Then the chairman looked over David's shoulder and stood up.

"Mr. Hall, permit me to introduce Dr. Yehudit Ressner."

David turned around and pushed back his chair. Judith Ressner was tall and slender. As he got up to greet her, he absorbed a quick impression of enormous dark eyes, thick black hair coiled on her head, and a remote expression on a classical Jewish face. She did not smile when he proffered his hand, but she did accept the gesture.

"Dr. Ressner, my pleasure," David said.

"Mr. Hall," was all she said, withdrawing her hand after a perfunctory squeeze. Her voice was soft, her English accented but her diction precise. She seemed perfectly at ease, willing to just be there, as if waiting for someone else to make the next move.

"Yehudit, thank you for joining us," the chairman said. "I think we can proceed to lunch now."

They left the conference room and walked down a long hallway and then down a flight of carpeted stairs. The university buildings were built on a series of terraces on a hill, so the floor below was actually at ground level. The faculty dining room was small but well appointed, and a large circular table in a corner had been reserved for the group. David ended up being seated next to the chairman. He noted that Judith Ressner took a seat diametrically across the table from him, so there would not be much chance for any direct conversation. She did not seem willing to make eye contact with him or with anyone else, for that matter. Oh boy, he thought. Isn't this going to be a wonderful little trip.

The lunch passed congenially, however, as the chairman steered the conversation away from David's project and on to his own opinions about the Masada myth. David kept an eye on Professor Ellerstein, who was talking quietly with Ressner as if they were old friends. She was a beauty, all right, but a wounded one. The two assistants listened, one more than the other because his English was obviously much better. Toward the end of lunch, Ressner said something in Hebrew to the chairman, nodded to the rest of them, and excused herself politely, again not looking directly at David. If the others thought that anything was unusual about her sudden departure, they did not comment. After lunch the assistants took David to a seminar room, where they had laid out several charts of the site. Ellerstein came along, but then excused himself after about fifteen minutes. The assistants took David through a review of the site's archaeological history.

4

Judith Ressner sat at her cluttered desk, quietly fuming. She thought she had been fairly civil, considering the imposition this idiot American was causing. Well, not idiot, perhaps, but certainly inconsiderate. As for his girlfriend's stupid theory? Well. Insult to injury. If Hall had learned anything at all about Roman siege warfare, he should know that no Jew would have escaped the final morning on the mountain, not after pinning the Tenth Legion for two and a half dusty years down on the Dead Sea, Lake Asphaltites to the ancients, and certainly not after the colossal bloodletting in Jerusalem. The besieged ones at Masada had only to look across the Dead Sea at the moldering knob that had been the fortress of Machaerus, still aswarm with wheeling cones of vultures, to know what was coming.

Machaerus, another of King Herod's bolt-holes, had actually surrendered. The Romans, unimpressed, summarily put thousands to the sword, making them kneel in yoked ranks on the hot sand while two centurions came behind, one to place a knee in the victim's back while grabbing a handful of hair, the other to slice open the prisoner's throat. Four-footed scavengers came from miles around to fight carrion birds for the bloody bones, not to mention the plain fact that, had Jewish warriors escaped in any numbers, they would have immediately formed factions and turned to fighting each other, making them easy prey for the inevitable Roman mopping-up operation. This American had no concept of the ruthless Roman Empire. He should study what happened to Carthage: Once the Romans finally took the city, they dismantled it, stone by stone, and then forced the remaining inhabitants to sow bags of salt across the entire area so that nothing could ever grow there again. To this day, nothing did.

She felt her pulse pounding in her temples and spun her chair around to look out the window into the courtyard, where the gray-greenery of a dozen ancient olive trees softened all those hard, modern angles of the academic buildings. Thirty-eight years old and already worried about high blood pressure. Five years now since Dov had been killed in the accident at Dimona. Five years of emotional and intellectual stasis. Five *long* years.

A knock on the door produced Professor Ellerstein, shambling as usual, his shirt decorated with a few stray bread crumbs from lunch and his hands already fumbling around with that wretched pipe.

"Do not ignite that abomination in here, Yossi," she warned, speaking in Hebrew.

"I know, I know, no smoking, anywhere, forever. Although I have this wonderful new Dutch tobacco—"

She silenced him with a glare. He regretfully stowed the pipe in his front pants pocket before dropping into the single visitor's chair. He looked around her cramped office, littered with papers and books. An oversized computer screen presided over the clutter on her desk.

"So, Yehudit," he began. "Fire away." He hunched himself down in the chair as if preparing to absorb a verbal fusillade.

She did not disappoint him. "What the hell is this, this *charade,* Yossi? And why me? This man is no more than a *tourist,* of zero academic consequence, and three days at Metsadá I do not need just now, thank you very much. Especially as a babysitter to some American with idiotic theories about the Kanna'im."

"As you say, Yehudit," Ellerstein replied. "It is not a serious matter. Still, the IAA has—"

"Sod the IAA. I googled this man's name. He caused an uproar in his profession when he disclosed what his own company was doing. Then he sues them and is awarded a fat settlement? And now we're accommodating him because his *girlfriend* left him? Come *on,* Yossi."

"I owed a favor," Ellerstein said. "To an American professor, George Hanson. He asked me to intercede with IAA and the university, and I did. This whole thing is harmless. I never expected Strauss to require a minder. Your involvement is my fault, not Mr. Hall's."

Judith gave him a long, hostile look. "You're not telling me everything," she said.

Ellerstein squirmed in his chair. "That is always possible."

"Well?"

Ellerstein shrugged. "That's a pointless question, Yehudit, as you well know."

"The ministry."

Ellerstein shrugged again and reached for his pipe.

Her mouth snapped shut. She had her answer. The university was being played. The government was behind this situation.

"Why, pray God, am *I* stuck with this baby-sitting mission?" she asked. "Strauss would not explain himself."

Ellerstein stopped shifting around in his chair and fixed her with an intent look. Suddenly gone was the shambling, absentminded professor. In his place sat a man with the grim visage of a judge. "Because it is time for you to end this self-destructive, self-serving so-called life you have been leading since Dov died. For one thing."

She felt a rush of fury. "How dare you," she hissed, but he silenced her with an abrupt gesture.

"Self-indulgent, self-centered, self-fixated, self, self, *self!* Dov is dead, Yehudit. You are not. You have been widowing now for what, five years? Believe it or not, your colleagues are worried about you. You fit the profile of someone suffering from clinical depression, and yet no one can get near you, talk to you, or help you."

"Rubbish," she spat. "Besides, if I wish to grieve, that's my business."

"Not when your work is not as good as it could be, even if no one here is willing to tell you that to your face."

"What?"

"Because if anyone presumed to try, you would wrap your widow's cape around you and stiffen your spine. From what I hear, Yehudit, you are becoming a royal pain in the academic ass."

"From what you hear? 'Not as *good*'? My work is sub*standard?* This is the first *I've* heard about it." Even as she said it, she could hear the note of shrill hysteria in her voice.

"My point, exactly," Ellerstein said.

She looked away from him, back out at the olive grove. No comfort there now; suddenly they were just trees. "So maybe I should just leave academia to fend for itself, then?" she asked. "It's not as if I had to work, especially for the fabulous salary."

104

"Then why do you work, Yehudit?"

"Because—because—"

"Because being a full-time academic fills your days, doesn't it, which means you only have to contend with the nights. If you quit, you get both the days and the nights to wrestle with, and still all alone, yes? No. You need to stop with the Lazarus routine and come back to life, Yehudit Ressner."

She twisted all the way around in her chair, turning her back on him. Damn his eyes. God damn them all. Damn Dov for leaving her alone like this. She wanted to scream at him, scream at them all. What did all these men know of the hole in her heart? Dov had been perfect for her— loving, bright, principled. The litany of if-onlys began to parade through her head, and she fought back tears. I will not cry, she thought, gritting her teeth.

Ellerstein was speaking again, his voice more gentle now. "Yehudit. We've known each other for a long time. This is friendly fire."

"I wish Dov had never become involved with you and that—that damned group."

"But he did. He believed as we did. He was a man of principle."

She sniffed but said nothing.

Ellerstein leaned forward. "Take this little side trip, Yehudit. Go with the American—he's inconsequential. He wants to see Metsadá, spend some time up there on the mountain, and think about things. Possibly even honor his missing lover. You should do the same. Let him poke around in the stones; you go find yourself a window in the battlements and examine your life, Yehudit. The Judaean desert has always been a good place for that."

Go find a window in the battlements and jump out is more like it, she thought. She turned back around. "Why is it necessary for anyone to go with him? If he's so innocuous, that is."

Ellerstein sat back in his chair. "Well. It is Metsadá, after all. If he was one of those treasure hunters, started digging or something, it would be a major insult to one of our most important shrines."

"Digging, at Metsadá? I've tried that, Yossi. You break your intellectual teeth and your shovel. Yigael Yadin went to bedrock at every important feature at the site. Now there's nothing but rocks and scorpions. Digging is the least of your worries."

"You know what I mean. Me, I'm just a glorified number cruncher, but you are an archaeologist. You know what can happen when amateurs interfere with a site. Plus, Metsadá is not the safest site in Israel: You can fall four hundred meters from three sides of that fortress if you misstep."

"That prospect is not all that unappealing sometimes," she muttered. "Perhaps I *should* do this thing."

"Yehudit, Yehudit, don't talk like that. Three and a half days. Time to reflect. Then you'll come back here, prepared to talk about it."

"*Talk* about it? Talk about what, my summer camp at Metsadá, or my future here at the university?"

"The latter, of course." Ellerstein got up, giving her a moment to absorb what he had just said. His voice became formal again. "Because the chairman has told me he wants to conduct a board of academic review, Yehudit. If you will not seek professional counseling, if you will not open up to the people who want to bring you back into the human fold, they will probably terminate you here."

She just stared at him. "My God, what have I ever done to that man? And why did he send you to tell me this instead of coming himself?"

"Come on, Yehudit, that's a silly question. He knows we go back, you and me. Officially, he sent me because I am emeritus here in another department, and thus not directly involved, and I'm on the advisory board of the IAA." He fixed her with that intense stare. "It's what you are doing to yourself, Yehudit, that is the issue. So stop your complaining. Accompany the idiot American, as you call him. Then come back next Monday prepared to deal with this matter, because the time has come."

Only when Ellerstein closed the door behind her

107

did she let the tears come. In her mind she stepped aside as two parts of her personality argued: He's right, all this blackness and wailing is just self-pity. Dancing with the demons, as Dov would have called it. And what, do you think you're the only widow in Israel? You don't read the papers every day? You're just afraid to face life again. The bastards never would tell me what happened. He just disappeared. I said Kaddish over a letter on the kitchen table, for God's sake. They said it was a radiation accident, but how do I know? No one knows what goes on in that awful place, Dimona: atomic bombs and possibly worse things. Israel's world-famous, worst-kept secret.

Dov would not have been a part of the bomb making: He had signed on to work only on the peaceful nuclear engineering projects. Power stations. Radiation against cancers. Safer X-rays. Someday, the ultimate dream: nuclear fusion for electrical power. He had made that clear to the whole damn government when he took part in the LaBaG protest that year. The headlines had been sensational: Government physicist joins anti-nuclear-weapons protest.

She took a deep breath as she remembered those tense weeks. For a while they both thought he might lose his security clearance, and thus his job, but slowly it blew over. Dov had kept his contacts with LaBaG but stopped throwing it in his bosses' faces. Yosef Ellerstein, whom he had met in the secret meetings of LaBaG, had counseled him to lie low, to subdue his activist profile. He was of more value to them inside the gates than outside in the protest marches. A year later Dov was dead. Snuffed out by a sudden pulse of energy that man had no business fooling with. She had never said it out loud but had always wondered if there had been a connection.

She stared into the olive trees, their foliage blurring now into a green mist, wishing not for the first time that she could just float out through the windows and merge with all that ancient greenness. Supposedly the trees were incredibly old, so old that the builders had carefully planned around the grove when they laid out the new university buildings on Mount Scopus. The olives were one of the spiritual hallmarks of this tortured land. Olives and blood. Everything, the stones, the trees, the warring religions, was incredibly old and drenched in the blood of forty centuries, if not more.

Masada was no exception, of course. Built as a palatial retreat by Herod the Great on the remains of a Maccabean fort, Masada had been both a desert villa and a place of refuge stocked with water, grain, and oil enough for years if the need ever arose. Herod, an Idumean appointed by Rome to rule the ungovernable Jews, had lived in dangerous times. Cleopatra VII of Egypt watched with acquisitive eyes from the Nile, and Rome, whose military power had spread over the known world, was engrossed with the transition from republic to imperium. Many of Herod's own subjects hated him with a passion he returned whenever the occasion permitted. Technically Rome's vassal in Judaea and a politician with no illusions, he built fortresses at strategic points all over ancient Judaea for both defense and personal refuge. All of the silly theories this American might conjure up would never disguise the fact that Masada was ultimately just like the rest of Israel—one more ancient killing ground.

She sighed, wiped her eyes, and gathered some papers into a dilapidated briefcase. She decided to go home early. After all, she had to pack for her great expedition. As for the meeting next Monday? That was serious—of this there was no doubt, not with Yosef Ellerstein being the messenger, which was a message in itself. So: for Monday? She sighed again. She would deal with Monday on Monday.

5

David dozed during the ride back down to Tel Aviv. Professor Ellerstein was beyond dozing: He was sound asleep and snoring forcefully. It had been an interesting afternoon, especially when David had had a better look at his minder. Tallish, maybe five eight in her stocking feet, athletically slim, and dark: black hair; pronounced, arching eyebrows; dark brown, almond-shaped eyes. He thought her forbears must have been Sephardic Jews, for she bore their ancestral features: elongated oval face, high cheekbones, dusky olive complexion, and full lips. All of it under a rigid control, emphasized by her stern demeanor and signs of a quick if impatient intelligence. Properly decorated, she would have been strikingly beautiful, but she appeared to have eschewed makeup of any kind. There had been a brittle edge to her that fairly shouted: This is a man-free zone; back off.

She had not attended the afternoon discussions conducted by Professor Strauss's two assistants but did appear briefly toward the end of the session to set up their rendezvous for the following morning. He had made a casual comment to the two assistants about her, and they both rolled their eyes. Very beautiful, yes, but a walled city, Mr. Hall. Which had not dissuaded a few of their more adventurous academic colleagues from making a run on The Ressner, as she was known in certain male circles. There was now an informal club of eligible males who called themselves the Shot-downs, after having made a pass with a singular lack of success. Okay, so she's exotic, if not exactly Miss Personality. A widow of five years, they said. Something going on there, but the two young assistants declined to elaborate.

111

The briefings had allowed David to focus on something besides academic politics as the two research assistants reviewed the Yigael Yadin expedition report and more recent excavations and analysis, then walked him through extensive maps and diagrams of the fortress. David had been secretly edified to find out that they had nothing new to tell him: His own research had been thorough and current, and Adrian had told him more than he wanted to know about the place. Even so, he had been careful to remain in the listening mode, not wanting to reveal just how much he knew about Masada. Professor Ellerstein had eased out of the briefing session after about twenty minutes, returning two hours later at five thirty when the assistants were finishing up. By then David was satisfied that any concerns the academics might have had about his project had long since evaporated. That had been his primary objective for the day's meetings. The only wild card in his plan now was Judith Ressner. He mentally kicked himself again for not having expected an escort.

When his hired car finally made it through the dense midtown traffic to the hotel, David woke Ellerstein, who looked around in momentary confusion.

"We're in Tel Aviv?" the old man protested. "I left my car at the Rockefeller."

David had forgotten that. He invited Ellerstein

in for a drink. "What's the hurry?" he asked. "In rush hour traffic you won't get anywhere fast. Ari can take you back, and it's been a long day. A Scotch will make it go away."

"Okay." Ellerstein laughed. "You have convinced me. Difficult, wasn't it?"

The lobby bar was much less crowded, and they took the same table they had shared Saturday night. After the waiter brought their drinks, David decided to probe a little about Judith Ressner.

"The briefings this afternoon were very useful," he began. "I think that the university is perhaps a little less apprehensive about my project now."

"Yes, I think so. You were clever to defuse their concerns about time and not to object to having an escort. Their whole tone was much different from just a week ago. Then they were trying to decide what to do with you and if they would even permit it."

"Yes. They seemed quite friendly when we left. Except for Miss Ressner, or is it Mrs.? I'm not sure I have her figured out."

Ellerstein chuckled. "Figuring Yehudit Ressner out, as you say, is not something that will be accomplished in a single afternoon, Mr. Hall. There is some background there you should probably know."

"I'm all ears."

"Well, she is a widow. Her husband was a physicist, working for the government. He died in some kind of accident—the circumstances are unclear—while working on a classified government project, about five years ago."

Ellerstein paused to see if David would make the connection between physicist and classified government project.

"Dimona?" David asked.

"Just so. Judith had recently completed her doctorate in archaeology when this happened, and it was naturally a very difficult time for her. She got an appointment to the HU faculty a few months later. The government may have had something to do with that, perhaps a form of compensation, yes? Well, never mind: She is very bright and entirely qualified."

David nodded, recalling the dark circles under her eyes and her habit of avoiding eye contact. "An accident? That word has a very defined meaning in the world of nuclear engineering."

Ellerstein shrugged. "A physicist. Who can say?"

A radiation accident, David thought immediately, but decided to let it pass. Dimona was a tightly closed book within the international nuclear community. "She's still grieving."

"That is correct, Mr. Hall. You saw her: She is very attractive, but suffering, I think, from severe depression. Frankly, we are all worried about her. She was a very businesslike young lady before this thing happened, but since then, it is like the human being is no longer there, just the academic. She has actually produced some fine work, especially on the Metsadá materials and the possible links with the Qumran scrolls."

"You seem to know her pretty well, Professor."

"Yes, well, I met her husband, and through him, Yehudit. That was some time ago. I had actually worked for the same government laboratory where Dov, her husband, ended up working. When he died, she became in a small sense a protégé of mine, but now she lives alone in every sense of the word. She is younger than she looks, and some of the younger men have tried to engage her socially, but, well—"

"I see," David said, remembering the Shot-downs. "So she's probably just delighted to be assigned this little babysitting mission."

"Babysitting!" Ellerstein smiled as if he knew a secret. "I like that, Mr. Hall. You are maintaining a realistic view of your situation here. Actually, and you must never mention this, the chairman probably had an ulterior motive. As I said, they are worried about her. Your little expedition will give her something entirely new to deal with, if only for a few days. Time to reflect, perhaps."

"Wonderful."

Ellerstein laughed again. "It is a small price for you to pay, but if you can get her to talk to you, she has some interesting insights on what happened up there on that bloody mountain."

The waiter came by and took their orders for a refill. "A melancholy focus for a melancholy lady," David mused.

"What, Metsadá? What those people did is considered a glorious act of defiance in this country. If, of course, it happened; there was never any physical evidence of a mass suicide found."

"Nine hundred sixty men, women, and children taking their own lives is not my idea of glory, Professor. Dramatic, yes, but horrendous is more like it. Josephus says that the Romans were so shocked by what they found that they were speechless."

Ellerstein stirred his drink with his right index finger for a moment before replying.

"Your Adrian's theory is—interesting, Mr. Hall, but you must keep in mind that Josephus was not there. Plus, Metsadá wasn't the only case of this."

"Yes, there was Gamla, wasn't there."

"Very good, Mr. Hall. Also Machaerus. With much larger numbers, we think. Basically, you must keep in mind what was in store for them if they were captured alive. All of the uninjured men would have been put in chains and sent to Caesarea, either to be worked to death in the galley fleet or to be torn to pieces by wild beasts at the hippodrome. Their wives and daughters would have been raped before their eyes, and the attractive ones taken away as slaves. The plain ones would have been flung off the ramparts, along with the young children and the wounded, all in full view of the surviving men. Remember, these people had defied the Roman Empire for almost three years."

"Even so, how, how in the world, could a father steel himself to kill his whole family?" David asked. "I mean, supposedly, that's what they did—each man slaughtered his own wife and children and then himself. Then ten men, who had been selected by lots, were assigned to kill any of the men who didn't kill themselves after what they'd done. It is almost unbelievable, and yet Josephus says that's exactly what happened."

"To an American it may be unbelievable," Ellerstein said with a rueful smile. "Americans, if you'll forgive my antecedents, have led a sheltered and very brief existence as a nation. Especially compared to the sweep of events in this part of the world since the beginning of human history, which, in itself, probably began here in the Middle East. Surely you acknowledge that."

"That's what Adrian maintained, too," David sighed. "I guess that's why I really need to see this place. That's what I meant by that 'communing with the spirits' remark. I must say, if this Ressner woman is suffering from clinical depression, Metsadá might not be such a good venue for reflection on her life."

"We Jews tend to see the glory, Mr. Hall, because we use it to remind ourselves that such things may be necessary again if we are to remain free as a Jewish state. The theory goes like this: They were the last men. If they could do such a thing, then so might we, but this time not without a fight to end all fights. That in turn sends a message to our enemies, who are legion. We Israelis take a certain cold comfort in the history of Metsadá."

David shivered. "Cold indeed, Professor, but thanks for the heads-up on Miss Ressner. I'll be careful with what I say. Right now, I'd better get upstairs and start packing. She's picking me up at five thirty in the morning."

"You will not be using your car and driver?"

"Nope. I offered, but she didn't want to be without her own car. She also said that she doubted we'd be there for the full three and a half days."

"Ah, so you did talk."

"Only for a minute, when I asked about arrangements. Apparently there's a hostel of some sort near the site. We'll be staying there. She said it was pretty Spartan."

"The fortress of Metsadá is at the end of the Dead Sea, Mr. Hall. It is literally at the bottom of the world. Even the Spartans would have had their reservations about such a place. There is grandeur, but it is stark beyond belief. I will be very interested to talk to you when you get back. Now I must go get my car. Thank you for the drinks. Good luck down there."

He stood up, and David did likewise. "Professor Ellerstein, you've been most helpful," he said. "Thank you for everything. I'll call you when I get back. Ari should be waiting outside. Send him home once he's dropped you off."

Up in his room, David began to lay out his gear, trying to suppress his growing excitement. After all the plotting and scheming, he was finally going to the mountain. He thought about going out for dinner, but lunch had been late and he wasn't really hungry. Besides, this might be his last night in a comfortable bed for a while; maybe he'd do room service later.

Ostensibly, he didn't have that much to take along: some changes of working clothes, camera, portable computer, and paper notebooks. He had brought along a collapsible knapsack so that he could hump stuff up to the fortress. Three days and no social amenities meant very little luggage, except for the special equipment.

He hauled his diving gear suitcase over to the bed, opened it, and pulled out his wet suit, regulators, underwater camera box, diving knife, BCD vest, and personalized mask—all the accoutrements of the scuba tourist. As part of the cover plan, he had booked a tour with a dive shop in Yafo to take him out to the submerged ruins of Caesarea during the second week of his stay here. He didn't know at this point if he would actually be making those dives, because the real function of the diving gear had been to conceal the seismic source device and the four miniature geophones, which he now went about extracting from their hiding places. He was a fully qualified, PADI-card-carrying open ocean diver, in case the question ever arose. The only diving he'd stayed away from was cave diving. That took special skills and more nerve than he could muster underwater.

He examined all the gear to see if he could detect signs that it had been searched, but everything seemed to be as he had packed it. The diving gear case was clearly marked as such, so a fluoroscope operator should have seen what he expected to see. Even so, he had prepared everything for a physical inspection. He disassembled the spare regulator and removed a shiny metallic disk, about a quarter of an inch thick, with two wire terminals soldered on to the top. It had been encased in shrink-wrap plastic and nestled at the back of the mixing chamber. He reassembled the regulator after removing the device, which he then transferred to a soap dish in his toiletries kit for the trip to the mountain.

The geophones were smaller but thicker versions of the seismic source, bright, shiny waferlike objects about a quarter of an inch thick. Each of the disks came with a single battery slot embedded in its side, and a tiny, telescoping stub antenna. These he had secreted in the battery compartment of his diving light. He retrieved the special batteries from his laptop computer case, made sure the tape segments were still in place over the positive terminals, and inserted them into the geophone slots. The receiving and data storage unit for the hydrophones was not much bigger than the hydrophones themselves, and this he had packaged into the plastic case that normally contained a spare battery for his laptop. The final part of the system was a sixty-foot-long roll of very thin wire, which he had taped to the zipper path of the portable computer's black carrying case. Along with a flashlight, the system was complete: source, ignition mechanism, geophones, data retrieval, and the portable computer to collate the data and draw the profile. Ready.

He finished packing the rest of his clothes, which included lightweight, long-sleeved cotton shirts for sun protection, khaki shorts, sturdy low-topped climbing boots, leather gloves, a windbreaker, three bottles of the hotel's bottled water, and a floppy sun hat. There were two empty notebooks, a legal-sized portfolio of grid-lined drawing paper, and, of course, his digital camera and spare memory sticks. Socks, underwear, the toiletries kit, and a small, basic outdoorsman's survival kit: a package of toilet paper, signaling mirror, GPS unit, some bandages, halogen pills, insect repellent, sunblock, a thermal survival blanket, and matches.

He then extracted the portable computer, a top-of-the-line Sony, and an international voltage transformer. He plugged the computer in to top off the battery charge. He stacked his gear in a corner of the room and then flopped down on the bed, his heart racing just a little. He stared out the partially cracked curtains at the darkening western sky. Tomorrow he was going to actually do it, assuming he could get away from his minder. He would probably have to go through the motions during the day and somehow get back up to the fortress at night to locate his objective. He would have to play a lot of things by ear, but if it was indeed there, as Adrian had just *known* it had to be, the hard part would be getting into it, not finding it. He shivered at the thought of a night climb up the thousand-foot-high escarpment. He would probably have to use the historical Serpent Path, a switchback footpath covered with loose sand and shale that ascended from the Dead Sea side up to the battlements at the top. Alternatively, he could take a long hike around the base of the mountain and come up on the Roman camp side, where the siege ramp, still in place after nearly two thousand years, led right up to the walls.

Time would be key. They would probably take the cable car over on the first morning, so maybe he would talk the minder into a hike back down the siege ramp to the hostel at the tourist center in order to find out how long that took. Maybe he would climb that instead. Keep it flexible. He needed to get up on the mountain, late at night, to do the seismic survey. The geophones would tell the entire tale.

Well, later for all that. He rolled over and called the concierge to make arrangements about keeping his room while he was gone. He had considered checking out, but the concierge told him that a room might not be available when he came back if he did that. He called the desk clerk to put in a wake-up call and then undressed and prepared to go to bed. What did the marines call it? D minus one. The whole thing might be a bust, he knew, but he really didn't think so. He thought again about room service but then drifted off. He wished Adrian could be here, and still frowned at the way she'd broken up with him.

6

It was almost fully dark when Professor Ellerstein parked his ancient Renault sedan at the curb about a block away from the restaurant and trudged back up the hill. It was a tiny place, with only six booths inside, but the owner-chef was a Christian Arab, and the food was an excellent blend of French and Middle Eastern cookery. Ellerstein, who lived in Rehovot, frequently took his evening meals there. He pushed through the single glass door and saw Gulder sitting in the last booth at the back of the restaurant in what Americans would call the gunfighter's seat, his back against the wall. Ellerstein walked over and pushed in between the booth partition and the table. The owner was busy speaking on the phone but waved to him anyway.

"An informative day, Yossi?" Gulder asked as Ellerstein sat down. Israel Gulder was the prime minister's executive assistant. He was a heavy-set, late-middle-aged man who looked totally undistinguished, with a broad plain face, glasses, and the beginnings of a double chin. His sleepy eyes implied a dullard, a feature that had fooled many political enemies into gravely under-estimating him, often to their ultimate dismay. There were rumors that he had occasionally undertaken certain duties that went well beyond the usual scope of being the PM's EA. He had a glass of mineral water and a bowl of pistachios in front of him, both of which looked untouched.

"Very much so, Gulder. I must say, this American can be pretty smooth when he wants to be."

A fat waiter trundled over, and Ellerstein indicated that he would have a glass of Carmel red. When the waiter had gone, Gulder raised his eyebrows in an unspoken question.

"Well," Ellerstein began, "he took the assignment

of a minder very much in stride when I broke the news to him. In fact, when the chairman, Armin Strauss, you know him I think, broached it at the meeting, Hall not only agreed but said he had been planning to ask for one."

"Clever, if true."

"Actually, I don't think he had been planning any such thing, but, yes, it was glib. Just saying it defused things. He was fully amenable to the time offered on-site. Apologetic for being an intrusion. Deferential to the academics, self-deprecating when the discussion came around to his own interests in the site, and, I think, generally candid about why he was really here."

"Ah. And that is?"

Ellerstein related the story Hall had told, including the tantalizing what-if question underlying his research. Gulder nodded slowly at the end.

"A fascinating question indeed. Except that we know the answer: There would have been no hope of escape. There was a circumvallation. Those thousand Jews would have been stinking carrion bait by the middle of the afternoon. They had kept the Romans at bay down on those delightful salt marshes for what, nearly three years? Even Josephus says that General Silva didn't even bother going up the ramp on the final morning once the walls had been burned through. Most likely didn't want to spoil his breakfast."

"Well, that's very probably true, Gulder. Still, my conclusion is that this young man is sincere, if, as he is the first to admit, somewhat uninformed. Anyway, three and a half days, and Yehudit Ressner will bring him back to Tel Aviv, and then we'll be through with it."

"Very well, Yossi. We, of course, appreciate your help in steering this matter."

Ellerstein noted the royal "we." He accepted the glass of wine from the waiter and ordered his usual evening fare, salad and a broiled fish. The waiter glanced over at Gulder, who shook his head. Once the waiter left, Ellerstein decided to take a small chance.

"I don't suppose you can tell me why you have taken such an interest in this man?"

Gulder didn't look at him for a long moment, and then finally reached for his glass and took a small sip of water. A couple of tourists peered into the windows. Gulder gave them his best terroristic stare. They recoiled and kept moving.

"Tell me, Yossi," he said. "How did Dr. Ressner react to her assignment?"

Ellerstein gave a mental shrug: So much for sharing, he thought. "Well, I went to see her while Mr. Hall was getting his afternoon briefings. She was less than overjoyed. She had been in the back of the room when the American was explaining why he was there, and she thought he was, what was her word, silly, yes. She has a low regard for men who are her inferior intellectually, and this poor fellow, nuclear engineer that he is, probably qualifies. He's in for an unpleasant journey."

Ellerstein had earlier decided to omit his more personal discussion with Ressner. He thought he saw the hint of a smile cross Gulder's face, but what he said next removed it.

"I may have made an error, though."

"What was that?" asked Gulder, his eyes alert now.

"Well, she didn't say anything while we were talking, but I told her it was the ministry who wanted the minder."

"Yes, so?"

"She may wonder, once she's had time to think about it, how I became involved. How *I* knew about the ministry's requirement for a minder."

"Ah. She made a connection?"

"Not then, as I said, but she was raising hell with me more than with her department head. She probably hasn't thought it through yet, but she may wonder: What's Yossi have to do with the ministry?"

"She doesn't know?"

"No. I dissembled."

"You are a competent dissembler, Yossi," Gulder replied, "and ignorance occasionally has its uses. If she asks, remind her that you're on the advisory board of the IAA. The IAA works for the ministry. Like so."

The waiter brought Ellerstein's salad, and he dug in, waiting to see if Gulder would amplify this remark. Instead, Gulder had another question.

"What is your opinion of Ressner's psychological state since her husband died?" Gulder asked, seemingly out of nowhere.

Ellerstein paused with his dinner, took a sip of wine, and thought for a moment. Given his own previous secret association with Dov Ressner and LaBaG, the anti-nuclear-weapons splinter group at Dimona, he wondered where Gulder was going with this, and whether or not Gulder knew what Ellerstein's role in LaBaG had really been. It was always wheels within wheels with Gulder, he thought, not for the first time.

"As I mentioned when we first met on this, I think she is declining," he said at last. "Spiritually, emotionally, I mean. She has never been an extrovert, but now she is almost a recluse. I actually think she is capable of suicide, except—"

"Yes? Except?" Gulder was focusing very carefully. Be careful, Ellerstein told himself.

"Except for a reservoir of anger," he said. "She never did find out exactly what happened to her husband, you know. No one did, actually, according to her."

"With whom is she angry?" Gulder asked, toying with a lone pistachio nut.

" 'Them,' " Ellerstein said. "The 'government.' "

Gulder nodded, sipped some mineral water, and

pried the nut's shell apart. Ellerstein waited, then gave up and concentrated on finishing his salad. After a while, Gulder spoke again. "I am a little surprised. This is the same government who has taken care of her since her husband died? That was partly your doing, was it not?"

"Partly, yes. I had met them both. Dov Ressner was an idealist, who perhaps didn't pick his political friends too carefully. By the time this happened I had moved to the university, so, yes, I spoke up for her. Although others must have helped as well."

"You perhaps had some high hopes, Yossi?"

Ellerstein actually thought he saw a twinkle in Gulder's eyes. A confirmed bachelor all his life, he waved the thought away. "She was a widow, for God's sake. Vulnerable. Confused. Grieving. And, of course, beautiful. Every man who saw her wanted her—but not then, not under those circumstances."

"Well," Gulder grunted, "others did help. Even *she* must have known that the government she's so angry with had a hand in getting her that appointment to the university. Not that she wasn't qualified, but there were other equally qualified candidates. And her widow's pension—that of a soldier, not a civil servant—that was a government decision as well."

"She apparently has some money of her own," Ellerstein said. "She lives in Rehavia, has her own car. One can't manage that on an academic's pay."

Gulder nodded. "Dov Ressner was a small pain in the government's comfortably large ass, but he had done valuable work. The government did the right thing, despite his association with the antinuclear left. If she has strong feelings about escorting the American, someone should perhaps remind her of these things."

Ellerstein was somewhat surprised that Gulder knew so much about the Ressners. He tried a probe. "He died in some sort of accident at Dimona, as I understand it. He was a scientist, so I always assumed radiation. Something like that. Did you perhaps know him?"

Gulder looked away for a moment before replying. "No, only through briefings," he said, deflecting Ellerstein's question. "There were not that many homegrown physicists in Israel back then. He was educated at the Weizmann Institute and in France. He got mixed up with some of that antiweapon, left-wing fringe crowd. You know, the LaBaG faction. People he'd probably met at university. Got into some kind of trouble, but then it was smoothed over. You know how that all works. The Dimona scientists all have *protectsia*."

"I guess I'm still a little bit confused about all this," Ellerstein said. "There's obviously something going on here . . . ?"

Gulder gave him a patronizing smile. "Yossi, let

me tell you a little something. These are dangerous times for our country. More dangerous than perhaps many people right here in Israel are aware. The prime minister has been—alerted, yes, that's the best word, I think. Alerted to something going on, something that frightens him."

"An attack?" Ellerstein asked. "The goddamned Arabs—"

"No, not exactly, although that's always possible. Hezbollah grows stronger every hour, thanks to the madman in Tehran, and Hamas is the legally elected government of the Palestinians. But look: I can't say any more. Right now, I will ask you to just keep your nose in. Monitor this American's little project. Keep an eye on Judith Ressner. Keep me informed. When the time comes, I will, if necessary, fold you into the situation. Hopefully, we are all wrong, and this other thing will just go away, and you can go back to your regular duties. Okay?"

"As you wish, Gulder," Ellerstein said immediately. His own bosses had warned him in no uncertain terms: Never cross Gulder. "But I'm not young anymore. I feel that I can do a better job when I know the parameters, yes?"

Gulder nodded. "Certainly, but trust me here, knowing those parameters could put you in some genuine danger." He stopped for a moment and pressed the button on his watch that turned the light on. Before Ellerstein could figure out why

Gulder needed the light, four large and very fit men appeared from nowhere. The restaurant owner quickly hung up the phone and scuttled out of the dining room. Ellerstein recognized them as guards from the prime minister's personal security detail.

"See, Yossi?" Gulder said, getting up with some difficulty from the tight quarters of the booth. "Dangerous times. Even I need minders these days, yes? I will be in touch. And thank you, again." He patted Ellerstein on the shoulder and left the restaurant, the guards closing in on him as he went out the door.

Ellerstein could only stare, his supper forgotten. What the hell was *this,* he wondered. Was it about the American? Ressner? Or something bigger? He signaled the waiter for a second glass of wine, something he rarely did.

Later that evening, Judith Ressner, dressed in jeans and an oversized army sweater, saw a large black Mercedes with tinted windows nose to the curbside in front of her small apartment building. Rehavia was a quiet, if densely packed, upscale residential neighborhood, fifteen to twenty rush hour minutes away from the Hebrew University. The area consisted mostly of two- and three-story garden apartment buildings. The streets were very narrow, with hardly enough room for even small cars, so the Mercedes was effectively blocking the street. The trees were beginning to lose their leaves as fall approached. The breeze coming down from the university precincts was cooler than usual, reminding her that Jerusalem was built on high ground. As she watched the car, she could hear the sounds of neighborhood domestic life subsiding into the darkness: dogs barking somewhere down the block, a few radios playing through open windows, and the muted sounds of traffic from the Road One.

A tall man, dressed all in black, even to his strange hat, got out of the car, carefully, as if in some pain. She fussed with her hair for a moment before heading for her front door. He had called her from the car twenty minutes ago. A Colonel Skuratov. That name was vaguely familiar. When he said he was an officer in the Shin Bet and the head of security at the Dimona laboratories, she had agreed to see him. Now she watched from behind a curtain as he walked up the steps to the building's entrance and rang the bell for her apartment. She buzzed him through the front door as the big car backed quietly up the street to double-park near the corner, its yellow emergency lights flashing silently. She drew the curtains and waited, listening to him climbing the stairs slowly, an old man's tread. Perhaps he had a heart condition. She had not been able to see his face, but that name— Skuratov. Definitely familiar. Stooped back, white hair, that hat. A homburg, that's what it was. And Dimona. She experienced a slight feeling of dread, but the exact memory continued to elude her.

She opened the door before he had time to knock, and then struggled to keep her expression composed when she saw his ruined face. *That* face. *That* night. He had been one of the men who had, who had—

"Good evening," he was saying, in a wheezing voice. "I am Colonel Malyuta Lukyanovitch Skuratov, Mrs. Ressner. We have met before. Under unfortunate circumstances." He took small breaths between sentences, but there was nothing frail about those bright gray eyes gleaming from the scarred face.

"Oh," was all she could manage, standing in the doorway like a dummy. Staring, while not wanting to.

"May I come in, please? It is late, but this will not take long. It concerns the American who wants to go to Metsadá."

"It does?" she asked blankly, showing her confusion. Then she recovered her manners. "I'm so sorry, yes, come in."

God, yes, she remembered him. That worst of nights. *There has been an accident. We regret to inform you.* She stood aside, trying to drown out the memories. Her legs were actually trembling. The colonel walked by her, putting the homburg down on a small table by the door. If he noticed her discomfiture, he gave no sign. His clothes gave off a faintly medicinal scent.

Recovering her composure somewhat, she asked if she could get him anything, tea, or coffee. She stood in the middle of the tiny living room, feeling totally lost. The old man found a chair that faced the sofa and sat down.

"Thank you, no, Mrs. Ressner. Thank you also for seeing me at such short notice. Would you care to sit down, please?"

She sat down on the edge of the sofa, knees and hands pressed together like a schoolgirl summoned to the principal's office. Through the doorway to her right she could see her bedroom, an opened suitcase on the bed. She was suddenly embarrassed by the state of the living room, with the academic paperwork mess overflowing off her desk and onto the floor. She saw him glance at the computer on her desk.

"They do not make a desk big enough for both my paperwork and the computer," she offered apologetically. *We regret to inform you. There has been a serious accident.*

"Nor for mine, Dr. Ressner. Our small country is beginning to drown in paperwork, I'm afraid. The ultimate sign of modernity."

She did not reply, choosing to look down at the floor instead, her mind still reeling with the memories. She waited for him to tell her why he was here. There was certainly no worse news he could bring her.

"I wanted to speak to you briefly about this American you will be escorting to Metsadá this week."

"Really," she said. "But why? What possible interest—?"

He raised a hand to interrupt her. "As I told you, I am associated with internal state security, yes?"

"I thought you were with security at Dimona."

He smiled sheepishly, as if caught out in a small lie. The smile deformed the scales of skin on his face. Part of it smiled, part of it did not. The effect did nothing to make his expression more reassuring.

"Quite right. Yes. I said that because I thought you might remember our meeting. At that sad time, when you and I last met, I was a military security officer at the Negev laboratories. Now, I am the director."

"I see," she replied, still baffled. *Regret to inform you.*

"This American has come to Israel with a rather unusual request. Did you know that it was the Ministry of Foreign Affairs who prevailed upon the Interior and Education ministries to accommodate him?"

She shook her head. Yossi had mentioned the ministry, but not which one. Foreign Affairs?

136

There were so many ministries. "Why?" she asked.

"I have no idea, Doctor Ressner," Skuratov said. "Now that he has arrived, I wondered if you did?"

She shook her head again. "My assignment as his minder came from my department chairman. Ministries are his province, not mine."

"Just so," Skuratov said. "Well." He paused again, as if to assemble enough air in his lungs to speak. "My interest is more direct, and has to do with Metsadá itself. You are an acknowledged expert on certain aspects of that site, but I wanted to remind you that it is a place of great reverence for the Israel Defense Forces. For the nation, as well."

"Yes, so I understand, Colonel," she said.

"I wish to make very sure that this—foreigner—does not have some hidden agenda, as the Americans say. Especially with all the stories of buried treasure out there in the caves along the Dead Sea."

She smiled for the first time and thought she saw him relax minutely.

"Professional archaeologists the world over fear treasure hunters, Colonel; they often do incalculable damage to the ancient sites. I don't think this man is a treasure hunter. More of a misguided amateur, with some very sophomoric ideas about the history of Metsadá."

"He is no scholar, then?"

"Hardly. He says he is pursuing this visit to

137

honor his girlfriend's long-term dream to explore certain historical theories about the site."

"Go on, please."

She described what David had told the committee.

"This woman—the girlfriend—she disappeared?"

"So he says. I have the feeling he's being a bit dramatic. She probably dumped him after he lost his job."

"What was her name, please?"

She told him Adrian's name and why Hall had lost his job.

"He is a nuclear engineer?"

She nodded.

"Did these indiscretions have something to do with nuclear matters?"

"I assume so," she said. "The press reports were a bit vague."

"Do you trust him?"

"I would say he is harmless, based on a very short acquaintance."

Skuratov nodded gravely. "I am glad to hear that," he said. "Still, I want to emphasize that you are the single person who will be in a position to make sure he does not go astray, Doctor. The Defense Ministry is especially interested in seeing to it that he does nothing to dishonor that place."

"I appreciate the significance of Metsadá, Colonel, to the IDF and to all of Israel. I don't understand why you of all people are talking to me about this trip. If IDF internal security is concerned, why don't you put some of your own people on the matter?"

He sat back and paused, as if choosing his words carefully. "The matter has been briefed. I mentioned to my superiors that I had met you, the designated minder, some time ago. I was asked to speak to you." He stopped for a moment and wet his lips. "As with all government offices in these times of budget austerity, we do not have unlimited resources. It has been a long time since the last war, you see."

She didn't know what to say to that, so she remained quiet. He nodded a couple of times to himself, and then heaved himself painfully out of his chair, fishing a card out of his suit pocket.

"I know this might seem a bit paranoid, but paranoia is our business, Professor Ressner. If you should become suspicious that he is not what he seems, or has intentions other than what he has told you and the university, would you be so kind as to please call me, right away, at the number on that card? My people can always find me, yes?"

She stood up and took the card without looking at it. This wasn't making much sense. Dimona and Masada? As he turned for the door, she remembered something. She stopped him.

"Colonel Skuratov. I thought you were a scientist of some kind. That day. When you . . .

when you came with Solomon Scheinfeldt to tell me about . . . Dov."

He picked up his homburg and unconsciously began to turn it around in his hands. She realized he was wearing gloves.

"At that time, I suppose you could say I was a bit of both. I am a nuclear physicist by training, and now a policeman of sorts. The kinds of work done at Dimona, well, this was a useful combination. As you probably can understand."

She moved around him, toward the door, so that she could see his face better. He seemed to shrink into himself, as if not wanting to be stared at. "Are you aware, now," she asked, "that I was never told what happened to Dov?" She surprised herself, bringing this up, but she was suddenly desperate to hear his answer. He had been one of "them," the people in authority at Dimona.

The colonel appeared to be momentarily embarrassed. He looked down at the floor for a few seconds before replying. "The authorities at Dimona assumed Dr. Dov Ressner's full discretion, Professor. Necessarily we also assume that the spouse of everyone working there knows what Dimona is all about. Certain aspects of Israel's nuclear energy program are Israel's worst-kept secret, yes? I need not elaborate. What happened to your husband was an accident. An operational laboratory accident, with severe radiation consequences. There were two others

140

who also died. Security was of course involved, to determine if this had been an accident or deliberate sabotage. There are two more widows like you."

"Who are they?" she asked quickly, but he shook his head.

"No, it is best that you don't know that. The incident and the program in which it occurred were then and are now highly secret matters. Everyone involved was and remains sworn to absolute silence. It was an accident, nothing more."

"*I* was never sworn to silence."

"Your husband was, and took his oath willingly, Mrs. Ressner," he replied quickly, and this time the smile was gone. His eyes projected the cold gleam of official power. She realized that she had made an implied threat when she said she was never sworn to secrecy. "Your husband died, Mrs. Ressner," he continued. "It was most unfortunate, but you cannot bring him back, no matter what you might do. Or say. Please keep in mind that the government did not put you out beyond the city walls after the accident, did they?"

She made as if to reply but then closed her mouth, understanding right away what he was talking about. An implied threat to counter hers.

He reached for the doorknob, slipping the homburg on his head. "I am sorry for your loss, Mrs. Ressner. Believe it or not, behind these official masks, even one as frightening as mine, we are also human. Nevertheless, some of us serve a higher responsibility than family, a responsibility that in the final analysis guarantees the very existence of our tiny nation."

"Your precious freedom is worth a few deaths, is that it, Colonel? The occasional operational accident?"

"*Your* precious freedom is indeed worth a few deaths, Mrs. Ressner. I would have to assume that Dov Ressner agreed with that proposition."

"Dov would not have worked on weapons, Colonel," she said. "That's what got him into trouble with LaBaG. Dov had principles."

"Did he indeed?" He looked at her for a moment. "Some principles are more important than others. I think your husband actually made an accommodation with his principles, Mrs. Ressner. Perhaps that bothered him."

"If he did, he never told me," she said. Her chest felt tight. The man was frightening her, but she resolved not to back down.

"Because he was not allowed to, you see. Many sincere men and women have had to put aside their principles and sometimes compromise their very souls to accomplish what has been brought forth out there in the desert. Do you know what some people call that place?"

"Dimona? Of course. The Third Temple. The weapons are called the Temple Weapons. The final resort."

"Just so, Doctor. So many names. The Samson Option. The Temple Weapons. A 'final solution' all of our own making, yes? Such irony. Only this time we will be on the delivery side of the equation. The thing is, those who work there believe these things. They think it is all worth it, the excessive security, the cost, and, yes, the occasional human loss. They are zealous, and if we can believe Josephus, that's what those Jews at Metsadá believed, too."

She looked down at the floor, unable to think of anything clever to say.

He stepped to the door. "Remember, please call me if something seems wrong about this American."

She nodded but did not answer him. He opened the door by himself, went out, and closed it behind him. After a moment she sensed that he was still standing outside the door and discovered she had been holding her breath. She made a noise putting up the security chain lock, and only then did he go limping down the stairs.

7

David came out the hotel's front door at five twenty the next morning and was surprised to find Judith already waiting for him. It was barely daylight, and the sun was not yet showing over the city's skyline. She was driving an elderly white

Subaru station wagon. David felt a momentary pang of regret for the spurned Mercedes. He lugged his gear around to the hatchback and stuffed it in. She had brought only one small bag and a portable computer. He got in the passenger seat and said good morning.

"Good morning, Mr. Hall," she replied in a cool tone of voice as she maneuvered out of the hotel's circular driveway. There was very little traffic, and she piloted the small car at a smart clip through the city's streets. David was dressed in khaki trousers, low-cut sneakers, and a long-sleeved white safari shirt with lots of pockets. He had aviator-style sunglasses and a sun hat. Judith was wearing jeans and a peach-colored sleeveless blouse. Her hair was pulled into a severe bun on the top of her head, and she wore oversized mirrored sunglasses that hid her eyes. She was bustier than he had remembered, but he quickly took his eyes off her figure.

"We need to stop for some petrol," she announced after a few minutes. Her English was accented, but not very heavily.

"For which I'm paying," he offered immediately, but she shook her head.

"I have a university credit card," she said. "Government discount. You can repay the university. Trust me: They will bill you."

"Okay." He tried to think of something else to say but couldn't, and she was not exactly a

144

bubbling font of conversation. She pulled into a sidewalk gas station and got out to take care of fueling the Subaru. David had been about to get out and do it, but she was acting as if he were not even there. He got out and bought coffee instead. He raised the small cup in her direction, but she shook her head emphatically. Right, he thought. Isn't this going to be fun.

In five minutes they were on their way. She told him the trip would take about two hours, and then lapsed back into silence as she concentrated on getting them out of Tel Aviv. She took the main highway up toward Jerusalem and then continued right back out of the capital city on Highway 30, which, according to the multi-lingual road signs, led toward Amman, Jordan. Once out of Jerusalem, the countryside changed rapidly, evolving from city buildings to high sierra desert almost immediately. On the rocky hills above the road there were occasional clusters of white apartment buildings, interspersed with rocky pastures dotted with goats. He assumed the distant buildings were the notorious West Bank settlements to which the Palestinians objected.

"Are there good roads all the way to Masada?" he asked.

"Metsadá," she said, correcting him. "Near the cities, yes. Along the Dead Sea, they are so-so. We'll take this road to Highway 90, and then we'll go south, past Qumran and Ein Gedi, right along the Dead Sea."

"Professor Ellerstein said you were a specialist on this site. Do you go down there often?"

"No. I haven't been to the mountain for years. My academic focus is not the site; I study the relationship between the scroll fragments found at the site and the scrolls of Qumran, actually."

"There is a relationship?"

She sighed impatiently. "There is a body of thought that holds that the so-called Dead Sea Scrolls were not created by the so-called Essene community, but rather that they are a collection of scrolls brought down from Jerusalem in the final days of the Second Temple."

"Just before the Romans destroyed Jerusalem, around A.D. 70."

"Of course." As in, yes, of course, dummy.

David put on his sunglasses. The glare from the surrounding countryside was growing with every minute of sunlight as the day began. Everything out there, sand, rocks, cliffs, seemed to be painted in dazzling shades of white. He figured that they were headed almost directly east, and evidence of human habitation was getting scarce. David recalled some lines from the Bible about scorpions, sand, and stones, and he could now appreciate the reality of it. It was also getting hotter by the minute as the sun rose. He glanced over at the console and saw a button for air-conditioning. She must have seen him looking.

"There is no air-conditioning at Metsadá, Mr. Hall, at the site, of course, or in the hostel. I recommend you acclimate yourself to the heat. And I hope you brought a jacket."

"I did. I've been in the desert before." She didn't reply, and he decided to quit trying.

He saw more road signs for Amman, Jordan, in Hebrew and English, and also for Ein Gedi and Qumran. After another thirty minutes of increasingly heavy truck traffic, the road finally bottomed out and they came to the highway that led south along the western edge of the Dead Sea. Fifteen minutes later she pulled off the road by a sign that said KHIRBET QUMRAN and drove up a dusty hill that led to a tourist information center. There were some low cliffs above and beyond the building, and when he saw the caves, David realized that this must be the site of the Dead Sea Scrolls discoveries back in 1947. He decided not to ask her if he was right. She pulled up next to the building.

"It's not open yet," she announced, "but the public toilets are always open. It's another half hour or so down to Metsadá."

She walked around one side of the building, and David went to the other side to pump bilges. When he came back out, an army jeep was coming down a dirt track leading from the bare cliffs and ruins behind the tourist building. The jeep wasn't going very fast, but even so it was raising an enormous cloud of dust. Judith came out from the women's room and waited for the jeep, which pulled up next to her. Two bored-looking soldiers sporting submachine guns spoke in Hebrew to her for a few minutes. From their bantering tone of voice and easy smiles, it was apparent they were a lot more interested in talking to an attractive woman than in any issues of security. One of them gestured toward David, and Ressner's reply provoked some more smiles. After a few minutes they broke it off, waved good-bye to her, and then turned the jeep around and headed back up the hill, followed by their trusty dust cloud.

Judith returned to the car without further comment and got in. David joined her. The sun was fully up now, and the little car had become an oven in the few minutes of their stopover. Once they were back on the highway, David wiped his brow and asked if there were army outposts all along the Dead Sea.

"Along this road, the army guards Qumran, Ein Gedi, and Metsadá, Mr. Hall," she replied. "Primarily the major tourist sites. It supposedly makes the tourists feel safer, and it also discourages the treasure hunters."

"Is treasure hunting still a big problem out here in the desert?"

"Yes, it is. The Bedouin do most of the poking and digging, as they have been doing for centuries.

It was a Bedou shepherd who discovered the original Dead Sea Scrolls. Also, there is a thriving market for antiquities in the cities."

David wished he had positioned the water bottles in the backseat instead of in the way-back of the car. He hoped there was a concession stand at the Masada visitors center, because he was also getting hungry, a hunger accentuated by the fact that there was absolutely nothing out here in this shimmering wasteland except the coppery expanse of the Dead Sea on their left and lots more sand, stones, and scorpions on the sterile escarpments to their right.

The Dead Sea was appropriately named. It was in reality a salt lake that was roughly four hundred square miles in area, lying in the northernmost reaches of Africa's Great Rift Valley, between Israel and Jordan. At over 1,300 feet below sea level, the Dead Sea was the lowest topographical point on earth. There were no fresh and cooling breezes coming in from the water, only the stink of sulfur and assorted halogens, a residual, he surmised, of the destruction of Lot's wife and the cities of Sodom and Gomorrah. The biblical legends took on a little more substance when you could actually smell the lake. The Jews of old had called it Lake Asphaltites, because it threw up gobs of bitumen from time to time.

"Tell me, Mr. Hall," she said, speaking up over the wind noise from the opened windows. "How much do you really know about the history of Metsadá? The place, not the events."

David had been expecting this question. He had even prepared enough of an answer to satisfy her that he was not totally ignorant, without revealing the true extent of his knowledge.

"The name Masada—Metsadá—means 'fortress,'" he recited. "It was built upon a huge outcropping of rock at the southern end of the Dead Sea, half a mile long and an eighth of a mile wide, in the shape of a broad spear point. On the Dead Sea side, it rises about twelve hundred feet from the water. On the other, western side, it is about four hundred feet to the bottom of the uphill gorge. It was probably first occupied by Alexander Jannaeus, and then King Herod added to it with palaces, storehouses, and a curtain wall with battle towers all around the top rim. When the first Jewish revolt began in A.D. 66, a band of Zealots seized the fortress from its Roman garrison and began guerrilla raids around the countryside. When Jerusalem fell in A.D. 70, the remnants of the city's defenders and their families fled south to join their allies on the mountain.

"The Romans followed the next spring and began a siege that lasted for over two years. Since the mountain was impregnable to direct assault, and well stocked with water and supplies, it should never have been taken, but the Romans built a dirt ramp on the uphill, or western, side of the fortress and then moved a siege tower into position on the ramp to break down the walls. After a protracted fight, the defenders realized that they were going to be overrun, so they elected to commit mass suicide rather than surrender to the Tenth Legion. Of about nine hundred and sixty defenders, only two women and five children survived. The fortress fell in either A.D. 73 or 74, and the Romans occupied the site for the next several decades before finally abandoning it. There were Byzantine settlements on the mountain a couple of hundred years after that."

She nodded thoughtfully. "What primary sources have you studied?"

"Well, I've read the Yigael Yadin final reports of the Israel Exploration Society's archaeological expedition in the early sixties, and of course I've read Flavius Josephus's first-century A.D. history of the Jewish Wars. The Roman historian Tacitus."

She nodded again. "You are limited to American English, I presume?"

"Yes, I am. Limited."

She gave him a quick glance. "I did not mean anything critical by that, Mr. Hall. It's just that there has been a lot more written about Metsadá than the sources you mentioned, primarily in German but also, of course, in Hebrew. In my experience, nonacademic Americans are usually not literate in other languages."

David chuckled. "Have you had a lot of experience with Americans, Mrs. Ressner?"

"Not really, Mr. Hall. I have not traveled outside of Israel except for university and a brief honeymoon trip to Cyprus. Most of the Americans I have seen are tourists."

He nodded. "I live in Washington, D.C. We have thousands of tourists there every summer, and the crowds can be a royal pain. The reason I asked is that you seem to dislike Americans."

She was silent for almost a minute, negotiating a series of curves in the highway. When the road straightened out she answered him.

"Not dislike, Mr. Hall. Resent, perhaps. We all know Israel is a client state of America, and dependency does not engender affection. We, too, feel that the hordes of tourists are a royal pain, as you put it, but we desperately need their money. The problem is that our two countries' appreciations of the political realities here in the Middle East are quite different, but yours often governs, does it not?"

"Well, I can understand that this trip probably falls into the category of a royal pain, too, Dr. Ressner. I hope you know that I did not request a minder."

She shrugged.

"What are your instructions, if I may ask?"

She looked at him again, although he could not see her eyes behind those mirrored surfaces.

"I'm not sure that is any of your business, Mr. Hall. To keep you from doing any harm to the site would about sum it up, I suppose."

David grimaced. On one hand, he needed to keep this woman at arm's length and in the dark about what he was up to; on the other, he disliked the fact that she was being so standoffish, if not outright hostile.

"Doctor—may I call you Judith, by the way, since we're going to be together for nearly a week?"

"Mr. Hall, I would prefer Doctor, or Mrs. We Israelis are quite informal, but our relationship is going to be very much business, not personal, okay?"

"Fine, Mrs. Ressner. By all means, let's not get personal. I'm sorry you're so insecure about American informality."

"I am not insecure about anything, Mr. Hall."

"Given that you got tagged with being my babysitter, that necessarily must not be true," David snapped and then regretted it.

What the hell am I doing, he thought—the more formal their relationship, the better chance he would have of getting away from her. You wouldn't have said that if she were a he, he told himself. The "she" did not reply, concentrating instead on her driving.

He gave up. After a little while they passed a sign for Ein Gedi, but she drove right past it. He wondered why they hadn't stopped there instead of Qumran. Then they rounded a corner and he could finally see the mountain fortress of Masada looming up above the Dead Sea some ten miles distant.

It was as impressive in real life as in any of the many dramatic photographs Adrian had shown him. From their vantage point northeast of the mountain it looked like the looming bow of a stone ship, frozen in passage up the west coast of the Dead Sea, its sheer walls rising straight up over one thousand feet above the dunes and bromine marshes. At this distance he could not yet make out the ruined palaces of King Herod that he knew were perched on descending, stepped terraces facing them. To the right, or west, were the shadowed recesses of the Wadi Masada, a four-hundred-foot-deep ravine dammed up now by the bleached bulk of the siege ramp the Romans used two thousand years ago to conquer the fortress. Farther west and slightly above the ravine was a sloping plateau, which David knew contained the outlines of the main Roman camp's walls, with other perfectly square outposts scattered on the plateaus overlooking the fortress, or in the ravines beneath it. He remained absorbed with the mountain as she sped down the dusty two-lane road, deciding that he would talk to his minder only when it was necessary.

The Masada visitors center was a single-story

glass and metal building, which also served as the boarding station for a cable car that went up to the summit. A two-story barrackslike building was set off to one side. There were expansive parking lots, empty at this hour, except for two army vehicles. The sky was still clear in the glare of the morning sunlight, but David sensed that it would soon develop a blistering haze. A large thermometer mounted next to the front entrance gave the temperature in Centigrade. It was showing 39.

Judith parked the car, and they got out. It was just after eight o'clock, and there were signs of life in the visitors center and even the smell of coffee.

"The cable car will not start running until the first tour bus arrives, and that is another hour or so away," she announced. "We can go in and see to our rooms."

"Fine."

She led the way up the steps from the parking lot and into the visitors center, which was basically a ticket lobby for the cable car, with a small restaurant on the side nearest the mountain. There was no one at the ticket counter, so Judith went into the restaurant and found the hostel clerks having breakfast. David could see through the restaurant's doors that one table was occupied by six Israeli soldiers, their ubiquitous submachine guns all slung over the backs of their chairs. An annoyed-looking clerk followed Judith back out to

155

the lobby, wiping doughnut sugar off his chin as he opened a booking register.

"Papers, please," he said to David, who handed over his travel documents.

"Where is the hostel?" David asked.

"Through there, in the annex," the clerk announced in a bored voice, pointing with his chin. "First floor or second?"

"Ground floor," David replied immediately.

"Second," Judith said.

"Individual or group?"

At the moment they were the only visitors, which meant that they had a choice of individual or the cheaper group bunkrooms. They both requested individual rooms. The clerk briefed them on the hours of the restaurant, pointing out that it was not open at night, closing when the last tour buses left in the afternoon. David realized that this meant his main meal would be at midday. He would have to stash some fruit and bread in the room for the evening. The clerk also pointed out that bottled water was for sale, and he recommended laying in some for their rooms.

"The well water tastes like the Dead Sea smells," he announced. "You must, of course, pay for your drinking water."

He gave them room keys. They unloaded the car and took their bags across the visitors center lobby, through a connecting passageway to the hostel. David's room was all the way at the end of the first-floor hall, right next to a set of fire doors. Judith disappeared upstairs, carrying her portable computer along with her bag. Good, maybe she would want to stay in and do her homework. David's room was small, no more than ten feet square, with a single screened window giving an expansive view of the familiar sand, rocks, and scorpions. There was a single metal bed that looked suspiciously like an army hospital bed, a single chair, and a small wardrobe. He had passed the communal bathroom and showers halfway down the hall in the middle of the hallway. He opened the wardrobe and found a shelf with a single extra blanket and four wire coat hangers. He dumped his gear bags on the bed and went down the hall to wash up. When he returned, he took out his notebook and camera, changed from sneakers to his trail boots, slipped a tube of sunscreen into his pocket, and went out, locking the door behind him. He headed for the restaurant.

He was finishing his second cup of coffee and a breakfast roll when Judith showed up. She was still wearing the same outfit but had taken off the mirrored sunglasses, which she now had hanging from a button on her left shirt pocket. The soldiers gave her a frank group appraisal as she came into the room but politely lost interest when she bought a cup of tea and a sweet roll from the counter and joined David. In addition to the roll,

David had breakfasted on some small squares of what tasted like cream cheese, and two hard-boiled eggs.

He gave her a curt nod when she sat down and then resumed his inspection of the mountain. The cable-car wires originating from somewhere above the restaurant dipped lazily across the parking lots before rising in a sweeping arc to the plateau on top of the mountain. David could make out the ruined battlements and casemate walls along the southeastern rim, and what looked like the vague outline of a switchback path leading up from the ravines below the parking lots to the casemates on the east side of the fortress. He was pretty sure that was the so-called Serpent Path.

"Is it necessary that we wait for the cable car?" he asked.

"Are you really fit, Mr. Hall?" she countered. "Do you perhaps ski?"

"Actually, yes to both. I work out on a home exercise machine daily and spend about a third of the year hiking and climbing."

"I ask because the army patrol gets annoyed when they must rescue tourists whose legs have turned to jelly halfway up the Serpent Path. That is a forty-degree slope."

"I see," David said, swallowing. Wow, he thought. Being a skier, he knew full well how steep that was. Forty degrees. It didn't look it.

"The switchbacks are deceiving," she observed, as if reading his thoughts, "but it is a very interesting climb, and there is history to the Serpent Path, of course. During the siege, the Romans apparently left it deliberately unguarded, although not unwatched. They wanted to keep it open as an avenue for defections, as a way of diminishing the garrison. They only closed it when they realized that Jews were not deserting but coming *in* from what was left of the country to join the garrison. The climb will take you an hour or so if you keep moving. You will need to rent a stick and take some water. You have a rucksack, I believe?"

"Yes, I do. Why the stick?"

She gave him the first inkling of a smile he had seen on her face. "For the serpents, of course. Possibly to lean on occasionally. Should your legs become tired, that is." Her eyes were laughing at him, almost daring him to make the climb. "I will wait for you by the eastern casemate gate."

He realized then that she would be able to take the cable car and get there ahead of him, even if he left immediately. So much for ditching the minder.

"You won't come along, then?" he asked innocently.

"I wouldn't dream of trying that climb, Mr. Hall. I am definitely *not* in shape for that slope."

He considered making a gallant reply to that comment but decided against it.

"Okay," he said. "I'll go get my stuff. See you up there in an hour or so."

8

An hour? In your dreams, Mr. Hall, she thought, as she watched him set out across the parking lots for the base of the mountain. The soldiers made some funny comments as they watched him go. What a silly, silly man, she mused. Well, maybe not silly, but certainly impulsive. It must be an American trait. She had caught his surprise when she told him that it was a forty-degree slope, so he must know enough about mountaineering to appreciate the challenge, and yet, almost like a teenaged boy showing off, he had plunged ahead. But showing off for whom, Yehudit? Certainly not you. You've been about as cold a fish as could come out of the sea. Nothing new there. Since Dov had died, she had gone cold inside and out.

She thought back to her childhood days in an Ahuza neighborhood on Mount Carmel above Haifa as an only child. Her father's parents, both wealthy medical doctors, had made aliyah from Europe before World War II, and her father taught European history at the exclusive Reali School. Judith had grown up as something of a solitary person, shy in adolescence from being too tall, eternally awkward, nearsighted, and uncommonly bright in school, characteristics that guaranteed a certain degree of ostracism by her more boisterous classmates.

Her mother had died of breast cancer when Judith was twelve, devastating both Judith and her father, who proceeded to cocoon himself from human relationships until he died seven years later. Judith had later realized that her father had been simply marking time for those seven years until he could join his wife, but at the time, his self-imposed isolation left her alone at a terribly vulnerable phase of her life.

With both parents effectively gone, she had thrown herself into academic achievement, excelling in high school and scoring a thirty-four out of thirty-five on the matriculation exams. Upon completion of her army service, she had gone first to Hebrew University, and then to Cambridge University in England to study with a Scrolls scholar. Like many Israelis, she had met her future husband, Dov Ressner, in the army. It turned out that Dov was something of a clone to Judith in terms of personality. He was a physics and mathematics major, extremely shy, near-sighted as she was, devoted to his academic career, and entirely inexperienced in the field of human relations, especially if they involved young ladies. It had taken a while, first because Judith had money and Dov did not, which caused a certain amount of awkwardness while she figured out how to get around his stubborn pride. Dov had lost his mother and father in an automobile accident, and the growing recognition that he and Judith had shared similar childhood experiences, combined with their mutual passion for academic achievement, blossomed into a marvelous year of catching up across the full spectrum of postponed adolescent love.

Sitting now in the dusty restaurant of the Masada tourist center, her eyes open but unseeing behind her glasses, she could still conjure up the images of the first awkward, tentative, and ultimately wonderful time they had made love, in the back of his cousin's ancient Volkswagen van just like a couple of American hippies. That they were going to be married was almost a given, with the only obstacle being the requirement for him to study abroad in France for two years. Upon return from Europe, he completed his graduate studies at the Weizmann Institute and later took a job at the government research facilities down at Dimona. They got married as soon as she finished her own graduate degree in ancient languages.

Their time together, even once married, had been all too short. Because his work involved shift hours that often went through the night, he lived in a bunkroom at the site during the week. She had plunged directly back into graduate work, aiming now at a full Ph.D. in archaeology. Deferring as ever to the singular goals of academic achievement, they had put off having children until she completed her Ph.D., which ended up taking four years because of all the summer site work. Their marriage worked, although she had begun to appreciate, toward the end of her graduate program, that the enforced separation might have been shielding both of them from some of the more normal stresses and strains of marriage. Then Dov had begun to change, not so much in his personality but in his attitude about the work at Dimona. It was no secret between most of the married couples connected with Dimona what the site was really all about, although Dov never once told her anything that could be considered a violation of security. He became increasingly frustrated the year before he died, and Judith sensed that he was having trouble sustaining his passion for the pure science in the face of the product it was serving. It was a topic he avoided, however, and because it caused him to be more rather than less affectionate in his love for her, she had decided not to rock that particular boat, even after he became secretly, and then not so secretly, involved with the LaBaG faction.

Then the terrible night five years ago, when his laboratory supervisor, gray-faced and tongue-tied, along with the cadaverous Colonel Skuratov, had appeared at the apartment, hats in hand, a military driver standing nervously down in the lobby, to announce that Dov Ressner was dead. A sudden catastrophe at Dimona, mumbled words about an accident, a matter of urgent security according to Skuratov, and, worst of all, the news that he had been already interred. Judith had been raised in a mildly religious family, casual in the sense that they respected the tenets of the Jewish faith but were not overly zealous in observing every aspect of it. Besides, quick burials were a fact of life in the Middle East. Still, it had accentuated her sense of loss and grief never to see him again, even in death, or to be able to go to the place where he was buried. The scientist had told her as gently as he could that in all probability no humans could ever go near that place. Just like the stone-cold empty place in her heart, which no man would ever get near again.

"I say, miss, are you quite all right?" Judith looked up, her eyes blinking as she came back to the tourist center. The tourists had begun to arrive, and an elderly British gentleman was standing next to her table, looking at her with concern. Without knowing it, she had removed her glasses, and there were tears in her eyes.

"Yes, thank you," she said hastily, blinking her eyes rapidly. "I was—I was far away, that's all. Yes, I'm quite all right."

He nodded, apologized for intruding, and sat back down at his table. She wiped her eyes, put the glasses back on, and scanned the sunlit side of the mountain, finally spotting the dogged American chugging his way up the Serpent Path, something that even dear Dov, outdoors enthusiast that he was, would probably never have tried. She stood up, shook the sorrowful cobwebs out of her mind, and decided to be nice to the dummy on the hill. He was harmless.

The climb took closer to two hours than one. It had been technically simple but extremely demanding because of the punishing heat and the nature of the trail itself. David had seen no serpents, remembering halfway up that the Serpent Path was called that because of the way it snaked back and forth across the face of the ancient scree. The trail itself was no more than a footpath, all loose dirt, shale, stone rubble, and sand. It was not so much treacherous as fatiguing, since every step demanded he first find a secure foothold before the other foot could be planted. The view out across the Dead Sea and into distant Jordan was stupendous the higher up he went, and his appreciation for the fortress's natural defenses improved as he climbed closer to the casemate walls guarding the rim. He could not imagine anyone trying to come up this slope in the face of archers, or even a crowd of women with a good supply of big rocks. Every time he looked up at the walls above he had to plant the stick behind him to overcome the sensation that he would topple over backward and go tumbling down the slope in a cloud of sand and dust, pursued no doubt by a sand-slide of scorpions.

He had not bothered with the rucksack, choosing to stick the plastic bottle of water in a pocket. After twenty minutes on the slope, he had shucked his shirt, tying it around his waist, and built up a pretty good sweat by the time the cable car rumbled overhead with its first load of tourists. He had heard and then watched the initial squadron of tour buses come down the coast road from the cities. He wondered if Judith would take the first run up the mountain or watch from her vantage point in the air-conditioned restaurant until she saw him getting close to the top. He was breathing strenuously because of the heat but felt fine otherwise except for a stinging in his calf muscles.

Judith Ressner, he thought. A strange woman. His first impression of her remained intact: physically very attractive, with that exotic sabra face and those mile-long legs. Smart, but distant. No, more like preoccupied. Or maybe just plain sad. Ellerstein had said that she had not recovered from the loss of her husband, the physicist. As a "nuke" himself, he wondered briefly if her husband had worked directly in the not so secret Israeli nuclear weapons program. Right now, though, he needed to focus on the mission here, and not get involved with The Ressner. She was actually doing him a favor, because he needed that distance. He especially did not need to aggravate the woman. So keep your trap shut, he reminded himself. Maybe she'll stay down at the tourist center.

As it turned out, however, she was waiting for him as he climbed wearily through the stone gates at the top of the Serpent Path. He was pretty well soaked with sweat and puffing when he climbed up the last one hundred feet, which were much steeper than the rest of the path due to the erosion over twenty centuries. He walked unsteadily up the rounded stone steps that led inside the casemate walls, stopped briefly in the cool shadows of the guards' chamber to regain his wind, and then emerged into the bright sunlight of the fortress enclosure. Judith was sitting on a low stone wall, facing the guards' chamber and reading a book. She had her mirrored sunglasses on again but now had changed from jeans to abbreviated khaki shorts, and David took a moment to admire the scenery. She looked up at last.

"Welcome to Metsadá, Mr. Hall. Did you enjoy your climb?"

"I don't know if I'd say I enjoyed it, but I certainly have a better appreciation of the defensive strength of this place."

"Well, that's why it wasn't the side the Romans attacked, of course. I brought you some water in case you might have run out."

David's single bottle of water had run out a third of the way up the mountain, and he reached for the cool plastic bottle gratefully. Their fingertips touched for an instant.

"Thank you very much," he said, drinking half the bottle in one gulp. "The climb would be a whole lot easier without that sun."

"The Bedouin call it the Hammer of Allah; now you know why. During the siege, all of the traffic up and down that path was at night."

A trio of very blond and pretty girls came by, one of them giving his sweaty torso a frankly sexual appraisal. He decided to put his shirt back on. Judith turned and shot them a pointed look, and they strolled away, giggling in what sounded like a Scandinavian language. He sat down a few feet away from her in deference to his aromatic condition and looked around. The top of the mountain looked to be about three football fields long and about one and a half wide, in the rough shape of a large, broad spear point, just as all the books described. The sharp end of the spear pointed north, up the Dead Sea, and, like a spear point, the offset spine of the mountaintop was ridged slightly higher than the surrounding edges. Sitting near the eastern gate, he looked up a gently rising stone slope to a collection of ruined buildings that appeared to be about eighty yards away near the western rim. To his right, the ground also sloped upward toward a much larger collection of ruins situated behind the remains of a smooth fifteen-foot wall.

All around the rim were the remains of casemate walls, which consisted of two parallel fortification walls spaced about eight feet apart and which originally had been covered by a ceiling to allow defenders to get anywhere around the rim without being exposed to enemy fire. The walls were much reduced now, and the ceilings were, for the most part, long gone. The open ground space between the ruined clusters of masonry was hard-packed sandy dirt or bare stone, reminding him of the flinty surface of the Acropolis in Athens. The rubble of buildings and fortifications gleamed bone white in the glare of the late morning sun. The eastern gate he had come through was just north of the middle of the plateau, and the cable-car landing platform was close by. Small knots of tourists were scattered here and there across the plateau. One group had a guide who was giving his tour in French. His voice carried crisply across the stones.

"The main palace-villa complex is on the north end," Judith said. "I assume you know something about the layout, and that there are several periods of history represented by the various buildings."

"Yes, I've studied it a bit. As I understand it, the mountain was probably first fortified during the Hasmonean period, say 167 to about 37 B.C. Then came the Herodian period, from 37 to 4 B.C., which is when the bulk of all this was built up as a summer palace and potential refuge for the king. Then Judaea became a Roman province, and there was a Roman garrison up here until a band of Zealots took the place away from them around the beginning of the Jewish revolt, in either A.D. 66 or 67. The Romans took it back in 73 or 74, left a garrison here for about fifty years after that, and then later there was a Byzantine monastery up here until the late 400s or so, after which it fell into complete ruin. In brief."

"In brief, that's pretty good," she said. She seemed somewhat friendlier since he had made his climb up the Serpent Path. Perhaps her earlier frostiness was some kind of initiation. Be careful, he told himself—don't show off. She'll become suspicious if you can name every building up here, which he could.

"If you would like, and if you're ready to walk again, I can give you a tour of the major ruins. Unless, of course, you would rather go off on your own."

"No, I'd appreciate a tour. I know that the complex up there is the storeroom for the northern palace, and that one is the so-called western palace, and that the siege ramp should be right behind those buildings up there, but beyond that—"

"Very well. If you are ready, then . . ."

"Just raring to go, Miss Ressner," he said, "but let me check with hobble central." In fact, he could barely make his legs function for the first twenty feet, a fact of which she seemed to be aware based on the slow pace of their walk. Big mistake, he thought, that sitting down for even a few minutes. He was in good physical shape, but a twelve-hundred-foot climb up a forty-degree slope under the fierce Judaean sun was still a major expenditure of muscle power. He would definitely not volunteer for any walk *down* the damn hill.

He shifted mental gears and began to focus on his real reason for being here. He took note of the slope of the slate-hard ground as they walked up toward the northern end of the fortress, upon which stood the curtain wall, and behind that, the remains of Herod's elaborate northern palace complex. If Adrian's theory was correct, what he was looking for would lie behind them, in the vicinity of that eastern gate, because that was the point toward which any surface rainwater would run down whenever it chanced to rain on the mountain.

The view beyond the reduced casemate walls was stupendous. They could see for at least twenty miles in every direction except west, where the bare Judaean hills were silhouetted against glare-drenched metallic sky. They entered the northern palace ruins through a narrow gate cut through reconstructed man-high stone walls. She explained that the maze of large rooms immediately in front of them had been storerooms for the palace-villa complex, containing enough grain, oil, and wine for several years' survival on the mountain. The rooms immediately beyond the storeroom complex were the public rooms of the palace—an audience chamber, offices for officials, and a living area for palace functionaries. David knew from his studies that the northern palace complex occupied nearly one hundred thousand square feet.

Beyond the ruins of the main storehouse buildings they came out onto a courtyard area that provided the most spectacular view from the mountain. Standing in the courtyard was like standing in the bows of a very large ship. On either side of this northern point of the mountain, the cliffs dropped away over a thousand vertical feet to the desert floor. At the very point of the bow was a low stone wall, over which could be seen the remains of the ornately terraced palaces below, accessible by stone stairways cut into the living rock on the left-hand side. Here King Herod had carved two notches into the descending spine of the mountain and erected what looked like a cascade of gardens, baths, open terraces, and porticoes that dropped down a few hundred feet from the summit plateau. The view from the terraces would have been magnificent and utterly private, offering cool breezes to ward off the oppressive desert heat rising from the bare, baking rocks far below.

"Can we go down there?" David asked after a few minutes of staring at the view.

"Not today," she replied, looking around as if to see if some of the other people standing at the wall were eavesdropping. "I must make arrangements to get through these gates. The villa terraces are kept locked away from the general public—the steps down are not safe, and there are some rare frescoes and mosaics down there we wish to preserve. Tomorrow perhaps."

"The main cisterns are down there to the left, under the terraces, aren't they? I seem to remember reading about how Herod's engineers made the water flow uphill."

She smiled behind the mirrored sunglasses. "An illusion. Not exactly uphill, either. We will go down the siege ramp, and I will show you how they diverted water from Wadi Metsadá into the cisterns."

"One of the historians said they had three years' supply of water up here; the cisterns must be enormous."

"That they are. The largest of the three main cisterns can hold one hundred forty thousand cubic meters of water. They are just great big holes in the rock now, of course. Like cavities in a tooth. There are more, smaller cisterns along the rim. Mostly on the south and eastern side. One big one. Again, all empty holes in the rock."

"Yes, of course. It looks like there's been a good

deal of reconstruction done up here," he said, changing the subject. The cisterns were vital to his objective, but he must not attract her attention to them with too many questions. Especially since he already knew all the facts she was quietly describing. Be impressed, he said to himself. Drop some oohs and ahhs.

They spent the next two hours walking through the remains of the western palace, which the archaeologists thought might have predated the more luxurious northern palace. The palaces had been reconstructed only up to the point of piling the wall rocks back up to the height of five or six feet, enough to show the overall scope. Of roofs, audience rooms, and Roman-style baths there were only outlines. In the intense white sunlight, the stones gleamed with age, and David felt like he was walking through the bones of some enormous ossified museum. Judith pointed out the outlines of the Byzantine-era church and the small monastery and noted that the time sequences had a lot to do with the scale of the ruins. They walked back over to the parallel lines of the casemate walls, which on the western rim were barely two to three feet high. They looked down into the deep ravine four hundred feet below the western rim, where they could see the sloping ramp of sand and stone the Romans had used to finally defeat the fortress's natural defenses. The ramp had eroded over the intervening span of nearly two thousand years, but the core was still there, pointed precisely up from the other side of the ravine at a forty-five-degree angle, like some enormous stake still stuck in the heart of the Jews' final bastion.

"Amazing, it's still here, after all these years."

"Large things endure in the Judaean desert," she observed. "The ruins up here were jumbled, but everything described by Josephus in the first century was basically still here when Yadin came digging."

"What do you mean jumbled? By the battle?"

"Not exactly. By time and occupation. Herod used the mountain until 4 B.C. His son Antipater used it into the Roman provincial days. Then it fell into disuse, with only a small Roman garrison stationed up here, perhaps a demicohort. They occupied only a part of the buildings, and probably took materials from other parts to furnish the place as they wanted it. When the Kanna'im took it from them in A.D. 66, they did the same thing: rearranged buildings, closed off various parts of the palaces to make the mountain more defensible, and strengthened the casemate walls. Once the siege began, the Romans used artillery, you know, ballistae?"

"Yes, I've studied their weaponry. Mobile catapults throwing big round rocks, two-, three-hundred-pounders, against defensive masonry. Pretty damned effective."

"It wasn't effective here until they built the

siege ramp and brought a siege tower up within range of the top. Then it must have been devastating. Yadin found several dozen ballistae stones embedded throughout the ruins. Once the Romans could get the catapults and a battering ram within range, it was the beginning of the end."

"Not quite the end, though, right? The Zealots tore down the big wooden beams from the palace structure and built a bulwark of sand and wooden beams on the outside of the walls, which cushioned the impact of the ram."

"Very good. You have done your research. Then, in the final attack, the Romans came up the ramp with Greek fire and set the wooden beams afire."

"Yeah, but the wind changed halfway through the attack, and the fire blew back onto the siege tower, setting it afire, driving the Romans off."

"And—?"

"And then when nightfall came, the wind changed again, this time driving the fire back into the walls, consuming the beams. That's when the defenders knew."

"Yes. Without the casemate walls, the Tenth Legion would swarm over the rim at dawn and overwhelm them by sheer numbers. There were nine hundred and sixty defenders, according to Josephus, but probably more than half of that number were women and children. We estimate the Romans had between three and five thousand.

Look there, and you can see the main Roman camp."

David could see clearly the outlines of the Roman headquarters camp, a precise military square drawn on the plateau across the western ravine, almost within a long arrow shot of where he stood. He knew there were other camps surrounding the mountain, and that the Romans had connected all the camps with a circum-vallation to seal their objective area. Oblivious to the small knots of tourists climbing through the rocks and ruins, they both stood in silence on the ruined casemate wall, looking down into the deep ravine, thinking their own thoughts about that final night and what these amazing people had done. Finally Judith glanced at her watch.

"It's going on two o'clock," she said. "We should go down to the tourist center now and have a meal before it closes. I need to talk to the security people before they go home, about tomorrow."

"Great idea." David realized suddenly he was very hungry. He had been sufficiently absorbed by the fortress and its sanguinary history to have been paying no attention to the time. "Join me in a stroll back down the Serpent Path?" he quipped.

"No way, Mr. Hall," she said, but there was a much friendlier note in the "mister" term.

The ride down in the cable car gave them another stunning view of the eastern wall of the mountain, where David could see the dusty, tortuous footpath he had climbed that morning. It was now partly in shadow as the sun dipped toward the Mediterranean beyond the Judaean hills. The ramp, he thought. The ramp will have to be my route. Tomorrow I have to get her to let me hike back down to the center from *behind* the fortress. Go down the siege ramp and walk back around the southwestern corner of the mountain to the visitors center. I have to know how long that takes.

The cable car groaned and clanked as it settled into its lattice structure above the visitors center. The parking lot was about half full of tour buses and cars, and there were people still waiting to go up.

They went back to the hostel briefly to clean up and made it into the restaurant by two thirty. The food was a mixture of Arabic and Israeli fare. David had what Judith had, willing to eat a whole goat by that point, and then finding out that he was doing so. Judith reminded him to stock up on some fruit, bread, and more water when the waiter announced that the place was closing for cleanup. By that time the tourists had thinned considerably, and the security guards in the center were getting a head count over the radio from their counterparts up on the mountain.

"How do they make sure everyone's off the mountain?" David asked.

"There is a guard in the cable car. He tells the tourists that the last cable car leaves at five; anyone not down by then has to walk down the Serpent Path with the guards."

"That ought to do it. So the guards actually walk down after the last cable car?"

"Yes, they do. It's a fitness requirement, and there might be someone stranded on the path who is too tired to continue. As you can see, the path is in shadow by late afternoon, so the observation point can't see it. Down is actually harder than going up, I'm told."

David nodded absently and then looked around to find that observation point. After a few minutes, he realized that it must be on top of the cable-car landing. Casually, he looked. There was a tiny room up there, more like a pillbox, with slotted windows that had a panoramic view of the mountain. He wanted to ask if it was manned at night, but that would have been pushing it. He thought he saw a spotting scope sticking out of one of the slots. He still could not figure out where the security people were based. There must be an army camp nearby. Perhaps up the road at Ein Gedi; he had seen army vehicles there, but in Israel there were army vehicles everywhere. He made a show of looking at his watch.

"I think I'm going to call it a day," he said, stretching. "My legs are informing me that there's a wheelchair in my future if I don't lie down pretty soon, and I have some notes I want to get down on paper. Eight o'clock tomorrow okay with you?"

"That will be fine. There is usually someone here by then so you can get a coffee."

"Great. Well. Good evening, then. Thanks for the tour."

"Yes, Mr. Hall. Good evening."

He walked back through the tourist center lobby to the hallway leading to the hostel rooms before remembering to get some water and snack food. When he had acquired his supplies, he saw that she was still sitting in the restaurant, pensively now, looking out the big picture windows.

9

It was full dark when David's wristwatch alarm went off. He groaned and turned over in the uncomfortably small bed and pushed the dial light: 10:00 P.M. He sat up and swung his aching legs over the side, shivering in the sudden cold. As his eyes adjusted, he could see starlight coming in from the single window, but no moon. He shook the mental cobwebs out of his head and recalled the moonrise data: This was Tuesday, so there would be a quarter moon, waxing, at around three-thirty. Tonight it wouldn't matter that much. For the next two nights it might. He yawned, got up, and slipped into dark corduroy pants, a dark red flannel shirt, thick socks and hiking boots, and his black windbreaker. He let himself quietly out the door and went down to the bathrooms. The hostel was silent; to his knowledge, no one else was staying here except Judith, and she was berthed upstairs, sound asleep. He hoped.

He'd had no trouble going to sleep. The combination of some residual jet lag disturbance, a carbo-load meal, and the climb up the mountain had sent him into a deep sleep as soon as he hit the rack. The only problem was that he was too long for the bed. His feet had hung over the end of the mattress, a detail that bothered him for about ten seconds.

Leaving the bathroom, he walked quietly down the hall to the fire door on the south side of the building, away from the hallway that led into the tourist center lobby. He checked for alarms, but there didn't seem to be any, just a standard bar handle that allowed someone to exit from the building but not to enter. He wedged a small wad of wet toilet paper into the strike-plate hole to keep the door from locking behind him and stepped out into the desert night. There was a stunning canopy of stars overhead, glittering with that unusual brilliance found only in the desert or on high mountains. He shivered again; it was colder than he had expected.

Okay, he thought. First order of business: See if that security observation checkpoint is still manned at night. He walked around to the back of the two-story hostel building, his boots crunching quietly in the sand. Even in the cold night air the stink from the bromine flats a half mile away was strong enough to annoy him. He thought he could see steam clouds rising down on the salt flats from some geothermal pool. He walked across the back of the hostel, past darkened windows, including his own, and paused at the corner. From that point, he was almost under one of the legs of the cable-car suspension towers and in deep shadow. He could see the back and bottom of the observation box but not the window slits. Have to get higher.

He turned around and walked diagonally away from the corner and up across the slope of rocks and sand behind the hostel building. As he climbed up the hill he suddenly realized that one window on the second floor had a light on. He crouched down on the hillside, about fifty feet away from the back of the building. Could she see him from in there? Probably not. With her light on, she should be night-blind looking into the darkness of the hillside. He was about to continue up the hill when she passed in front of the window, studying some papers in her hand. She was wearing a shirt and what looked like white bikini underwear. Even at this distance there was absolutely nothing wrong with those legs, he mused. Too bad she had taken herself out of play; he could understand the anguish of the Shot-downs.

He turned away and continued up the hill, reaching a low ridge that was about level with the roof of the hostel building. There were some large boulders along the ridge, and he used these for cover as he worked his way back toward the fortress end of the tourist center building. From this elevation he had a clear view of the observation box. The view-ports appeared to be completely dark. He sat down on a flat rock in the shadow of an adjacent boulder and waited. Damn near every male in this country was a smoker, it seemed, so if there was someone in there, he would eventually see a match or lighter flare. Up on the hillside, the stink of the Dead Sea was less evident. He took a deep breath of the cold desert air, which was so pure he could almost taste it. A heavier jacket would not have been unwelcome, but later, when he went up the mountain, the light jacket would be more practical.

He looked over at Judith's window again, but now it was dark. Good. He did not need her coming downstairs to check on him. Then he smiled in the darkness; the thought of that sad woman coming downstairs and knocking on a strange man's door at night was laughable. He watched the observation box and reviewed his plan. Tomorrow she would tour him around the rest of the fortress: the terrace palace ruins, the big cisterns under the northwestern palisade walls, the siege ramp, and possibly the Roman camp to the west of the mountain. He wanted the camp to be last, because then he wanted to walk down the wadis that ran down along the west and south sides of the mountain, to see how long that took. Something scrabbled by in the sand beneath his feet, and he jerked his feet off the ground, but whatever it was disappeared. He was pretty sure that reptiles would be immobilized by this cold night air, but the scorpions were probably out hunting.

He needed to arrange the day so that he got back to the tourist center at about the same time they had returned today, three, three-thirty. Get a meal, replenish water, go to bed, and get up around eleven. Maybe earlier, depending on how long the walk down the wadis took. Add a half hour because he would be climbing back up, two hours' stay time on the top, time to get back down an hour before false dawn. So ten.

He rubbed his eyes and stared at the pillbox. He concluded that there was nobody in that thing. He was sure of it. Well, pretty sure. Last thing he needed was a guy in the box with an infrared scope nailing his ass when he left the cover of the ridge and started up the gully. He decided to wait some more, shifting his position slightly to get out of the clammy night breeze coming off the Dead Sea.

A shiver went up his back when he thought about where he was and the fantastic history of this area, going back well before the time of Christ. The Bible's description of the destruction of Sodom and Gomorrah, the Pillar of Salt, the petrifaction of Lot's disobedient wife. He stared up at the darkened rock of Masada itself and considered again the bloody story of the Jews' heroic self-immolation on that last night. He tried to picture it: high on the mountain, the wooden walls around the western rim ablaze in the night, illuminating the scorched top half of the huge siege tower perched at the top of the ramp as it catapulted huge stones across the flaming sky; the nine hundred sixty Jews, huddled inside the wrecked palace walls, knowing that it was over, as they took their last desperate counsel. They would have been listening to the massed cheering shouts of the bloodthirsty legions as they worked themselves up into a frenzy for the coming assault, waves of hard-bitten male voices hurling Roman war cries up the mountain slopes.

The final decision to commit mass suicide was chronicled in Josephus's history of the revolt, which in itself was an astonishing piece of writing. Josephus, a scion of the priestly Levite class, had been one of the Jewish leaders of the revolt in Galilee, but when the city he was charged to defend fell to Roman assault, he surrendered to Vespasian and saved his own life by prophesying Vespasian's ascent to Caesar's throne. When Nero was killed in Rome some weeks later, Vespasian's legions proclaimed him the new emperor, and prophet Josephus had won himself a permanent new lease on life. Since there were other claimants and the prospect of a civil war, Vespasian turned over the Judaean campaign sideshow to his son Titus so that he could begin the politico-military campaign that would lead him back to Rome months later as Emperor Vespasian.

Titus allowed Josephus to join his campaign staff as an adviser, and Josephus apparently became a willing ally of the Romans, not so much to subdue his own people but to convince the Jews to end the revolt before things went too far. He was present for and participated in the siege that culminated in the catastrophic destruction of Jerusalem, the Temple, and the core of the Jewish nation. He tried in vain to talk his countrymen into surrendering the city, but to no avail, and was reviled in Jewish history as a turncoat. In his later years, Josephus, now *Flavius* Josephus, having taken the family name of his royal sponsors, lived in Rome as a ward of the Flavian aristocracy and wrote several histories, including the one titled *The Jewish Wars*. Even though he had not been present at Masada, he had told the story as if he had been, writing in vivid detail about the final attack and describing the exhortations of Eleazar ben Jair, the leader of the Zealots on Masada, that death was far better than the dishonor of surrender and slavery. David knew that Josephus's account of what the Jewish defenders thought and did up on the mountain was mostly made up, and yet his descriptions of the siege and the final Roman assault had been verified by the Yadin expedition two thousand years later. Now David was here to prove, if Adrian had been right, that even the illustrious Yadin had missed the truth.

He looked at his watch. Eleven ten. He was getting cold just sitting here and had seen no signs of life in the box. The entire tourist center was in shadow, with only the sounds of the onshore wind and the occasional cry of a night bird from the salt marshes stirring the darkness. He was about to get up when he heard the sound of a vehicle coming up from the south. He scrambled around the large boulder and crouched down beneath its overhang as an army vehicle pulled off the coast road, slotted headlamps dimmed, and drove up into the parking lots in front of the tourist center. It pulled all the way to the edge of the lot nearest the mouth of the wadi leading up behind the mountain and stopped, its engines and lights subsiding.

David waited, but nothing happened. He glanced back up at the box to see if someone would be climbing down, but there was still no movement. There was the flare of a cigarette lighter in the left front window of the truck, but no other signs of life. Twenty minutes later, as David was trying to decide how to get back down the sand slope to the fire door in the hostel, he heard another sound, this one coming from the mouth of the wadi. He crouched lower, aware that he was exposed to anyone coming down that darkened ravine. He stared hard at that darkness, then froze as a single file of soldiers emerged from the shadows, their footfalls tramping small puffs of dust. He couldn't make out many details of their uniforms or faces in the dim starlight, but the unmistakable shape of submachine guns slung from shoulders confirmed who and what they were.

Shit, he thought. An army patrol. So this place was not unattended after all. Now the question was, where did they patrol? Did they go up on the mountain, or just into the hills around it? What were they looking for? Arab terrorists setting up some atrocity at the tourist center, or Bedouin thieves bent on making off with ancient artifacts from the mountain? When did the patrols go out? He looked at his watch again but decided not to illuminate the dial. Had to be closing in on midnight, though. Was there a relief patrol in the truck? Or had they already been inserted somewhere else?

He watched as the silent gray figures filed past him thirty yards away and converged on the truck. There was some milling about, the further flare of cigarette lighters, and then they started climbing into the back of the truck. He could hear murmurs of conversation, and then the truck engine started up. David withdrew around the corner of the boulder to avoid any headlamps that might sweep the hillside. He listened as the truck drove back out of the parking lot and on down the coast road.

When the noise of the truck had died away, he made his way back along the ridge of rocks, staying in the shadows and stopping to listen every twenty feet or so. When he was satisfied that there was no one about, he walked down the sandy slope to the fire exit door and let himself back in. Once back in his room he got undressed, set his watch for seven, and then lay back on the bed. Tomorrow he would play boy archaeologist with the widow Ressner. Tomorrow night he would go up there on that mountain and find what he had come here for.

10

The following morning dawned bright and sunny, with a slight dust haze in the air carried in by a brisk breeze from the northwest across the tops of the Judaean hills. David met Judith in the restaurant as planned for coffee, where she surprised him with the suggestion that they walk up the southern ravine to the Roman siege ramp. "The cable car won't start up for another two hours; we might as well see some things in that time," she said.

This was the reverse of David's plan, but it

served his purposes even better, allowing him to gauge the time required to go *up* Wadi Masada. They set out twenty minutes later, passing the ridgeline where David had kept vigil the night before. The sheer walls of the mountain rose about six hundred feet on the right, or north, side of the ravine, which was about a hundred yards wide at its mouth. As they climbed, the ravine narrowed down to about thirty yards in width. On their left rose the sheer rock walls of the southern plateau, which was actually higher than the rock of Masada. The wind kicked up dust devils along the ravine floor, and the going was much more difficult than David had anticipated due to the soft sand, hundreds of small rocks, and leg-deep fissures carved in the old stone by centuries of flash floods. The occasional scream of a hawk punctuated his grunts and quiet curses as he forced his way up the gradually more demanding slope. He was very grateful she had reminded him to bring his stick. She led the way, dressed in jeans, army boots, and a sleeveless sweatshirt. She wore a floppy sun hat and her mirrored glasses and had a plastic water bottle sticking out of her fanny pack that bobbed incongruously as she climbed ahead. He realized that she was puffing a little more than he was, but she put her head down and pressed on, and so did he. After forty-five minutes of climbing in the wadi along the southern edge of the Masada escarpment, they reached a ridge from which the ground fell away in a steep hillside into a second ravine, this one pointing north along the western edge of the mountain until it ran smack into the right side of the Roman siege ramp about a quarter mile away. Judith paused to take a water break and to point out some of the engineering features of the fortress.

"This is the western branch of Wadi Metsadá, the ravine used to fill Herod's cisterns. You can see that it runs down from the hills on our left and along the western wall of the fortress."

"Yeah, but the cisterns are on the north face."

"North*west,* actually. Before the Romans built the ramp this wadi ran all the way along the west side of the mountain and down to the Dead Sea around the northern tip. Herod's engineers dammed it up just beyond where the Romans eventually put the ramp. They then dug channels into the stone palisade that forms Metsadá's west face. In the winter, storms occasionally sweep in off the Mediterranean and turn this wadi into a torrent. You may have seen the pictures in Yadin's report. The water would back up at the dam and overflow sideways into the channels, run down along the channels, around the corner, and into the cisterns on the north face."

"Ingenious—but of course the Romans destroyed the impoundments."

"The very first thing they did. In a desert siege,

of course, water is the key, but the fortress had been collecting water for decades. Even after it fell, people lived up there on what remained in those cisterns for nearly fifty *years*. There were other cisterns, too, of course, up along the rim, but they were small compared to the palace cisterns."

"How did they get the water up to the top from the palace cisterns?"

"I will show you, but basically, water slaves carried it up in buckets. Shall we go?"

They started down the side of the Wadi Masada, slip-sliding in the loose sand and dirt until they reached the bottom, and then traversed the ravine from side to side as they made their way north down the slope to the base of the Roman siege ramp. Although they were in the shadow of the mountain, it was getting hotter by the minute, and it seemed to David that the dry desert wind was sucking the moisture right out of him. The ramp, a huge pile of sand, dirt, and stones, rose four hundred feet from the bottom of the gorge, bridging the wadi between the western plateau on the left and the western rim of the fortress. Having been built across the ravine, it made its own dam, and there were signs of some violent erosion over the centuries.

David knew that the main Roman camp was up on that plateau above them to the left, and Judith indicated that they would first have to climb up the left side of the ravine to get to the beginning of the ramp. David could see that the sides of the ramp itself were much too steep to climb without axes. The ravine at that point was about two hundred feet deep, so it took them another thirty minutes to get up to the base of the ramp. David was winded when they climbed over the top and stood at the base of the siege ramp itself. Judith was red-faced and completely out of breath. He realized they had been slowing down for the last thirty minutes. It was the heat, he told himself. At night he should be able to do better than this.

"For someone not in shape, you're doing all right," he said.

She could only nod and smile weakly and mop her forehead with a handkerchief. He looked at his watch. To the base of the ramp had taken an hour and a half, including the rest stop at the top of the cross ravine. He would have to allow two hours in the dark. The going would be slower, but he should be able to make better time without her. He looked up to the fortress walls, hundreds of feet above them, and then at the ramp.

"How in the hell did they build this thing? The defenders could hit anyone exposing themselves out here just by throwing rocks."

"We have no firsthand facts," she replied, between inhalations. "Historians surmise that initially they took some casualties. Then they probably went back to the remains of Jerusalem and gathered up a few thousand women, since all the men had been killed. The Jews on the mountain probably could not bring themselves to kill Jewish women who were being used as slaves. They built it by carrying baskets of earth and sand and throwing them into the wadi. Eventually they filled it in and then piled more on until the ramp reached the summit and the engineers could bring up the siege tower."

"Good Lord."

"Yes, even then it was a very bad thing to lose a war. Beyond the hard labor, since there was no water here, each woman was forced to carry an amphora-sized jar of drinking water from Jerusalem to the Roman camp. By night they would have been used by the legion. You can begin to understand how the defenders might choose death over what they saw befalling their countrywomen. The Roman camp is over there. Do you wish to see the ruins?"

"No, I think not. I saw the outlines yesterday from up there, and it looks like only wall foundations. My focus is on what's up there. Besides, I'm just dying to climb some more."

She gave him a look that said she was just plain dying, but then hefted her stick, and they set out up the ramp. Damn, he thought, maybe she's human. He stumbled in the loose sand. This is *in*human, he thought then. Just hard slogging, up another forty-degree slope of hard-packed sand and rocks. They paused halfway up to catch their breath, and David wondered aloud about the siege tower.

"On this slope, how could they pull something like that up close enough to the walls? Those towers were fifty, sixty feet high."

"The slope was probably not this steep; there is evidence that the ramp started closer to the Roman camp than the edge of the wadi. They would have taken the siege tower up the ramp in pieces: the base on wheels, the tower sections one at a time. The soldiers would have pulled it up the ramp using ropes. They would have used a testudo to protect the soldiers—do you know what that is?"

"Yes," David nodded. "The tortoise back: Several dozen soldiers put their shields over their heads and advance in close formation. From above they present an impermeable shield wall. Still . . ."

"Yes. Those men? Now *they* were in shape, and implacable."

David nodded soberly. Implacable indeed. He could only imagine the growing despair on the mountain as that siege ramp took shape and then the antlike columns of soldiers began pulling a siege tower into position to begin the bombardment that would batter down the casemate walls.

By silent agreement they set out again to walk up the final few hundred feet to the top of the ramp, where they encountered a steel and concrete stairway that took them up to the western gate.

David looked around for indications that the gate was locked at night but did not see any signs of chains or other securing devices as they went through the gate, climbed the casemate ramp, and encountered the first group of tourists.

They spent the rest of the morning walking through the casemate wall that surrounded the entire rim of the fortress, where she pointed out the locus of individual archaeological finds including some coin hoards, weapons, the skeleton of a man apocryphally believed to have been Eleazar ben Jair himself, and a small stash of scroll fragments similar physically to those found in the caves of Qumran, the so-called Dead Sea Scrolls.

"Were any of them legible?" he asked.

"One they were able to recognize right away, because the text was visible on the outside of the scroll. It was the Vision of the Dry Bones, from Ezekiel."

"Now there's a lovely metaphor, especially here."

"Indeed."

In the early afternoon they met with a security guard who admitted them to the narrow stone stairway leading down to the terrace palace ruins. Two terrace palaces had been built below the northern prow of the mountain, descending two hundred feet down from the main plateau in two stepped levels. The view out over the Dead Sea was breathtaking as they maneuvered carefully down the worn and very steep steps. Judith explained that the first terrace, confusingly called the middle terrace, had had a circular pavilion surrounded by a colonnade, and the lower terrace a rectangular, nearly square hall called a triclinium in the center surrounded by porticoes on all sides and a bathing area. Sheer stone and mortared brick walls dropped away from the marble balustrades on either side.

Down below the left, or western, side of the middle terrace Judith showed him the water channel that had once routed storm water from the wadi to the very large cisterns cut into the northwest face. The channel was about three feet wide and two feet deep, cut along the face of the cliff, aiming back along the western palisade to a point now buried by the Roman siege ramp. Fifty feet back along the channel was a large, irregularly shaped hole in the cliff, with several smaller holes behind that one, all in a line across the cliff face.

"May I?" he asked, pointing to the hole.

"With great care, please," she answered, reminding him that there was no railing on the outside edge of the water channel. It looked to be about four hundred feet straight down from the channel to the bottom of the gorge. He stepped off the stone stairway and walked back along the water channel, whose bottom was polished smooth. He tried not to look over the side. A

197

sudden updraft tugged at his shirt. He did not have a big problem with heights, per se, but this was pretty exposed.

He reached the first hole, knelt down, and peered into it. He was at the top of an enormous spherical cavern, perhaps eighty to one hundred feet across and the same dimension in depth. Beams of sunlight coming through the hole projected his silhouette on the smooth lower walls. Descending from the hole was a set of steps that had been cut out of the rock, spiraling down the side to the very bottom of the cistern. There was no railing there, either. The walls of the cistern were water polished, and there were two large pillars of rock that had been left in the center to support the ceiling. He wanted to walk down those steps, but it was pretty clear that the cistern was completely empty. It was just a big dry hole in the rock. As worn as the steps were, it would have been very easy to fall to the bottom of the huge stone cavity. Judith came up behind him to join him at the entrance.

"The steps leading back up to the top palaces are called the water steps. Slaves would have to come down here continuously to collect water in jars and then carry them back up to the main level, where they would fill smaller cisterns, which in turn piped water throughout the palace for the baths, hypocausts, and fountains. There are other cisterns farther back along the channel."

He looked beyond the entrance and saw the second hole, smaller than this one. "Same thing—dry hole?"

"Yes. Once the Romans breached the dam and raised the ramp, no more water ever came into these cisterns."

"Yet, if they were full when the siege began, and these things are, say, sixty feet to eighty in diameter, then each one would have held nearly three-quarters of a million gallons of water."

She looked at him. "Did you just compute that?"

He smiled, trying to cover his sudden error. "I'm an engineer, remember?" he asked. "Volume of a sphere; pretty simple calculation." Pay attention, dammit, he thought. She doesn't need to discover she's telling you things you already know. Especially about the cisterns.

He looked over the edge of the water channel again. Some birds sailed through the wadi a few hundred vertiginous feet below them. He gave a small shudder. Judith turned to walk back to the relative safety of the water-slave steps. They went up and then turned left and down the terrace steps to the lowest level, where she showed him some of the remaining fresco fragments and speculated about what the buildings looked like. He remembered the drawings in the Yadin reports and said so.

"Very speculative, but at this distance in time, as

good as any," she replied. "Truly, there is much we do not know."

A warm breeze swept across the ruined terrace, bearing just a sulfurous hint of the Dead Sea far below them. They stood and looked out over the panoramic view, which from this elevation covered nearly thirty miles in every direction except due west, where the Judaean hills blocked out the metallic sky. Those hills looked to be about as dead as the sea over which they kept silent watch. From the lowest terrace, the main Roman camp, approximately a quarter mile distant, was at about eye level.

"Do you suppose the Zealots came down here?"

"They did for water, depending upon how much remained in the rim cisterns. We think they took some of the stone works from down here to reinforce the outer casemate walls once the Romans began the siege ramp. As you can see, the foundations are all here, but there is a lot of material missing—and, of course, no wood fragments."

"Right. The wood went into the walls at the end of the siege. This was a tough fight."

"Yes, with very high stakes. If you have studied Roman military history, you know that once the Romans sank their teeth in, there was usually only one outcome."

He gazed out over the western hills, shimmering in the early afternoon heat, and tried to imagine what it had been like up here for the Zealots. They would have watched with growing desperation as the inexorable Romans built first a wall around the entire mountain, the circumvallation, and then the ominous ramp, and finally the siege tower. The fighters among them must have known as they hunkered down on this impregnable rock, day after day, month after month, how it would have to end: an entire Roman legion fastened onto the flanks of the last Jewish stronghold, inching ever forward and upward. She seemed to sense his thoughts.

"When you actually stand here," she said in a soft voice, "it is perhaps easier to appreciate why they did what they did. Two years and more, day after day, fighting off the daily probes, all the while watching the ramp grow. How many times must some of them have come down here to the lower palaces to look out at the Roman camp, watching and wondering: when? What they finally did may have come as a release of sorts."

"Yes. Now you can understand why I wanted to come here. The books don't convey that feeling. Adrian had been here, and she was fascinated with the place."

"I forget. Was she a writer?"

"More of a dreamer, I think. Why?"

She smiled at him, a full smile this time. It illuminated her face. "Writers must above all have feelings," she said. "For the atmosphere of places, for people's emotions, a sense of tragedy if that's appropriate. I am an antiquities historian more than anything else. We have feelings, too, but our passion is for cold facts and the truth more than for the people who made the history." She paused for a moment. "This terrible place tends to confuse archaeologists, because the feelings intrude so forcefully."

At that instant he was seized with the urge to tell her why he was really here. The intensity of this impulse surprised him, this sudden need to share with her, with someone, the enormous concept that had brought him here, but he knew he dared not do that. He would have only one chance, and that was probably going to be tonight or tomorrow night. One shot, yes or no, Adrian had been right or utterly wrong. He needed to keep his minder here well out of that picture until he *knew.* He looked at his watch. Almost three o'clock.

"Yes," she said, looking at hers. "We must get back to the base. Do you want to walk back the way we came, or shall we take the cable car?"

"That's a no-brainer," he said.

She smiled again. "No-brainer? I haven't heard that expression before, but I presume it means we ride, yes?"

After their meal together in the restaurant, they again bought some fruit, bread, and bottled water for later that evening. On the way into the hostel to stash their supplies, David suggested they take a walk down to the beaches of the Dead Sea. At first she seemed reluctant, but then agreed, and they met fifteen minutes later out in the parking lot. The sun was well down in the western sky, and the day's heat had begun to break, the ovenlike air giving way to the first hint of an evening breeze. The east side of the mountain and the southern ravine were in deep shadow, with only the rim of the fortress reflecting a golden light off the ruined casemate walls. There were still some tourists up there, but for an instant David imagined he was seeing the long-lost defenders.

They threaded their way through the parking lot where half a dozen tour buses were loading up a gaggle of Japanese tourists, each of whom appeared to be carrying his body weight in camera gear. The bus engines were running at high idle to maintain air-conditioning inside, and the billowing exhaust gave the two of them an incentive to break into a light jog out of the parking lot, down the access road, across the coast road, and into the crystalline dunes.

David admired the determined way she walked along the hard-packed sand. He found himself walking slightly behind her, conscious of the poise and strength of her stride across the difficult ground, and the way those long legs moved. She had the body of an athlete, which made him curious: She didn't seem to be the type who worked out, and yet she had managed the climb up the southern ravine at a pace almost equal to his, and he had been training for this trip for nearly a year. His thoughts were interrupted when she looked back over her shoulder and caught him looking.

"Tired already, Mr. Hall?" she asked with a teasing smile.

"I was just enjoying the view," he replied, without thinking, and then colored. "I mean—"

"Yes, the *light* is interesting at this time of day, isn't it?" She turned back around and kept walking.

He caught up with her, trying to cover his embarrassment, but she simply looked away across the water, as if suddenly fascinated by some distant object on the Jordanian shore. He kicked at a lump of solidified phosphate.

"This isn't like any beach I've ever seen," he said. "Certainly not like our ocean beaches."

"You were one of those 'surfer dudes'?" she asked.

He laughed. "No, not at all. I grew up in Washington, D.C. My father was a scientist at the National Bureau of Standards. We kept a summerhouse on the Delaware beaches. I was something of a natural water baby. My father was not thrilled."

"He expected you to be a scientist as well?"

"Well, he didn't expect me to grow my hair long

and spend every waking hour down on the beaches with a bunch of surfer dudes, as you put it. I discovered scuba and girls when I was fourteen, and that didn't help."

"Scuba is an expensive sport for a fourteen-year-old, I should think," she observed.

"So were girls," he said. They had to walk carefully now, picking their way through a scrub of cactus and razor-sharp crystal stalagmites. "My Uncle Jack lives for outdoor sporting activities. He's the one who actually taught me scuba. Do you dive?"

"My husband was the fanatic with the scuba," she said. "At first I did the diving just to be with him. Then I became an enthusiast. It is popular here in Israel."

"Yeah, well, in the summers I went to work in a dive shop to pay for all the pricey toys. I love to dive; I'm going to do Caesarea Maritima when I'm through here."

"I would think a parent would be afraid, a fourteen-year-old doing scuba."

"Part of a general pattern, I'm afraid. Teenaged boys in America often do precisely what most disturbs their fathers. I had a much better relationship with my uncle than with my father. Fortunately, I had a younger brother who was everything Dad wanted. Outstanding student. Career oriented from the age of about eight months. I think Dad kind of kissed me off once he figured out that Larry, that's my younger brother, was going to turn out closer to the mold."

"Yet still you became a nuclear engineer?"

"That was the funny part. My mother realized before I did that I had more brains than I was letting on, especially in math and science. She steered me into the right courses, the ones I could do in my sleep—math and science. That left me more time for other interests."

"Your uncle sounds interesting," she said, stopping to dump small stones out of her shoes.

"He is. He works at the Nuclear Regulatory Commission in Washington. He always told me to go to work for the government."

"For the security?"

"Not quite. He used to say he worked in order to play. You know, the fat man who lives to eat versus the thin man who eats to live? He once told me that he worked for the government because, if you wanted it that way, it was just a job, not really a career. Do your job, eight to four-thirty, and then resume your real life. Careerists bring it home with them."

"And university?"

"Went to my local state university in Maryland. Took a degree in chemical engineering, minor in physics. Uncle Jack got me a starter job at the NRC. *Damn!* This place stinks."

"Yes, it gets stronger in the late afternoon. There is geothermal activity along here. Cooks the chemicals. There are big salt mines farther south. Did you have to do national service?"

"No. It's not like here, where *everyone* must serve. I thought about it, but they told me I'd have to serve in nuclear submarines, and I didn't want that."

They entered a clearing where suddenly the stink of chemical salts went away, and they stopped to breathe clear air. He looked back at the looming mountain fortress, which was subsiding into even deeper shadow as the sun went down.

He kicked a rock down onto the beach, where the sand was so hard it skittered all the way to the water. She had certainly warmed up this afternoon, but he wanted to stop talking about himself.

"You called yourself *Mrs.* Ressner," he said. "What does your husband do?" Having spoken to Ellerstein, he already knew the answer, but pretended not to.

She looked away. "I am a widow, Mr. Hall. My husband died five years ago. I have never remarried."

"I'm sorry," he said automatically, feeling like a heel.

"For what? You haven't done anything. Or do you mean you feel sorry for me?"

Oh, hell, he thought, here we go. Miss Attitude is back. "It's just an American expression. Of sympathy. Someone loses his or her spouse, we presume they're sorry, too. How long ago did you say?"

She took a minute to reply and turned around to start walking back toward the hostel. "Almost five years. And, yes, I am sorry. Perhaps too much so. My life has not been very good since then, and that has created some problems." She told him about the chairman's ultimatum and the reasons behind it. David frowned. Ellerstein hadn't mentioned any ultimatum.

"Wow," he said. "Decision time. All this because you elected to withdraw from social life for a while? To live alone? I should think that was your option."

"Thank you, yes, so did I. Apparently I've overdone it. I've kept myself immersed in my work, which is easy enough to do. Historical linguistics is an introspective business, but I think I have given cultural offense to the collegial community."

"What about the rest of your life?" he asked. "Do you get out at all, or are you just holed up in an apartment somewhere and calling it life?"

She gave him a curious look, her head tilting to one side. "Who have you been talking to, Mr. Hall?"

"Nobody, Mrs. Ressner," he said. "I've met people in your situation before, although I must admit they were all men. What happened to your husband, if I may ask?"

She sighed. "He died in an accident of some kind at the place where he worked. He was a scientist."

David took a gamble. "An accident of 'some kind'? That sounds as if you don't know exactly what happened."

She turned to face him. "He worked at Dimona. You're a nuclear engineer from Washington: You know what Dimona is, don't you? Israel's so-called atomic power research center?"

He smiled at her. "So-called, indeed. Yes, I know what Dimona is. By reputation, anyway."

She nodded. "The implication was that it was a radiation accident," she said. "I—I never saw him again. He is buried out there at the site, along with some radioactive waste, no doubt. Okay? Don't ask me anything more about it, because I don't know anything more about it. One morning he left for the site and I was a wife. By that night I was told that I would never see him again, and, oh, by the way, now you are a widow. We have lots of those in Israel."

She turned and walked away, her face and posture suddenly stiff. Startled by her bitter outburst, he hurried to catch up with her. He remembered Ellerstein's equally vague description: some kind of an accident. Something bad enough that the body had not been returned to the widow. He conjured up the image of a lead-lined body bag at the bottom of a green-glowing moonpool somewhere. He understood her anger a little better.

He closed the gap and then walked by her side as they picked their way through curious crystalline formations that stood along the shore like stumps from some petrified chemical forest.

"Five years," he said, after a few minutes. "That's a long time to grieve. Or is that customary for the Jewish culture?"

She looked sideways at him again, as if to see if he was being sarcastic. David shook his head. "I meant that question sincerely. I've heard that there are some Middle Eastern cultures that do not permit a widow to remarry. I guess I'm trying to figure out why someone as attractive as you are hasn't rejoined the world by now."

"I forget how direct you Americans are," she said, with a hint of exasperation in her voice. "Really, Mr. Hall. This is hardly any of your concern. Whether or not I am an attractive woman, if I choose not to rejoin the world, as you put it, that's my business, is it not? You would not say that to a man, would you?"

"Touché," he said. "I would not. Although I would probably still ask the underlying question. It's always interesting to know why people do what they do. Besides, sometimes it helps to talk about it."

"I don't feel any particular need to talk about it, Mr. Hall. Especially with a stranger."

"Well, forgive me, but I sense that you do. Need to talk about it, that is. If nothing else, what you're facing on Monday morning compels you to at least *think* about it, and it's safer to discuss such things with a stranger, especially one who will be gone in two weeks. As opposed to a colleague, for instance, who might have a stake in the outcome? I don't know. If you just crawl into a hole and pull it in over you, you become compost, you know?"

She kept walking, not answering him, her head down now, concentrating on picking her way through the scraggly underbrush in the fading light. Finally she stopped.

"What of you, Mr. Hall? You were in love, yes, with this Adrian? Then she disappears. Are you 'back in the world'?"

"Well, I'm here," he said. Once again he suddenly wanted to tell her the real reason he was here.

"So you are," she said.

He pressed on. "And, yes, we're having this conversation because I'm interested in you. You're a beautiful woman, still young, and smart enough to hold a Ph.D. from a prestigious university."

More silence. Then, finally, softly, "So—what about Adrian? She is, what, forgotten now?"

He swore, loud enough to startle her. "We're in the same boat, Mrs. Ressner. You don't know what happened to your husband. You do know that he is—gone. I don't know what happened to Adrian, but the probability is that she decided our relationship was over and just—left."

"So now, what? I am potentially her replacement?"

"Oh, for God's sake," he exclaimed. This was getting too hard. A voice in his head was warning him to shut up, go back to the hostel, and leave this poor woman to her own devices, but he couldn't help himself. "What I'm saying is, why not get on with your life? There must be a hundred guys right there at the university who would jump at the chance. Why waste your life?"

"In your humble American opinion."

He laughed. "Yes, in my humble American opinion."

"A waste."

"Yeah, a waste." He tripped over a rock trying to keep up with her and nearly went sprawling. She turned to face him.

"Is that what *you* did, Mr. Hall? When your Adrian did her disappearing act? Did you jump right back into life? Did you go find another woman? To avoid the *waste?*"

Again her vehemence startled him. "It's not quite the same," he began, somewhat defensively. He couldn't see her face in the shadow of sunset, but her voice was trembling.

"You said it was. We were in the same boat, you said."

"Well, I guess we're not, are we? I kept hoping, believing when no one else did that she was coming back. That she would call. E-mail. Something. When I finally realized she'd dumped me, I finally accepted it."

"And then?"

"And then, I did nothing, for a while. Then my friends started to invite me to parties or outings where there was always an unattached woman. I went through the motions, but . . ."

"Me, too," she said, surprising him. "Same thing. But . . ."

"Well, it's not like I haven't seen other women since then. I just haven't met the right one to marry, that's all. At least I'm looking. I finally recognized that you have to *do* something to make something happen."

She gave a snort of derision. "That's what it is about you Americans, I think," she said. "You think that every situation can be, I don't know, what's the English—*fixed?* Fixed as long as you *do* something. You people go all over the world fixing things, doing things, whether or not you should, whether or not the people involved even want them fixed. Iraq. Afghanistan. Who's next, I wonder."

"Ah," he said. He turned back toward the hostelry and started walking again, forcing her to catch up with him this time. He had to acknowledge, though: Her life right now might be precisely what *she* wanted.

"Ah?" she echoed. "What does this mean, this 'ah'?"

"Never mind, Mrs. Ressner," he said. "I guess I'm just another ugly American. You were right: I've been making assumptions. Please forgive me."

That silenced her, and she remained silent as they picked their way through the reeking patches of solidified alkaline wastes back toward the road. He got to the road first and waited for her. The tour buses were all gone, and the security floodlights up at the tourist center pointed hot white eyes at them. Her face was a white blur in the darkness along the empty road. He turned to head up toward the hostel.

"Please go on," she said. "What assumptions?"

"Are you mad at me?"

"Yes!" A moment. "No. Please."

"It's the romantic in me, I guess," he said, trying to keep it light. "I assumed you were looking for love."

"What do you mean by love, Mr. Hall?"

He smiled in frustration. Damned woman. Now she did want to talk. "Well, the older I get, the more I feel that love is an accommodation more than a pursuit. Two people who meet and like each other. As friends first, and then as lovers in the physical sense. Who grow to care for each other. Who can give each other affection. Who have enough similar interests that they can enjoy doing things together, but don't get upset over being apart occasionally. Who've outgrown all those unreasonable expectations we had when we were starting out. Grown-up love."

She didn't reply for a moment. "Yes," she said finally. "That sounds like love to me. Except perhaps for the being apart bit."

"Well, if you live entirely alone, dwelling on or in the past, you are by definition being apart." He paused and then said, "The folks I've known who kept themselves apart from life usually ended up on the bottle, or drugs, or in frequent contemplation of a premature exit."

He heard her sharp intake of breath as she stopped in her tracks and then turned to face outward toward the sea. He mentally kicked himself. He had touched a nerve. He stopped behind her, close enough to reach out and touch her shoulders, but kept his hands to himself. He looked out over the purpling waters. He could just detect the scent of her hair on the evening breeze. What are you *doing?* a warning voice in his head asked.

"You have to be out there for love to happen, Judith Ressner. Memories are simply not enough to sustain life, not until you get very old."

She didn't reply for a minute, and when she did it was in a very soft voice. "They are very good memories."

"Want to tell the ugly American about them?"

Surprisingly, she did. She sat down on a flat-topped boulder, and he did likewise, startled by the residual warmth in the stone. He noticed that, sitting together, they were the same height.

She told him about her short life with Dov Ressner: the way they were so evenly matched intellectually, he the physicist, she the linguistics historian, not having to protect each other from the sharp edges of their own intelligence; their casual, almost bohemian existence after he finished his schooling and went to work for the government, while she worked to achieve the Ph.D. She described their mutual love of the outdoors and diving, their expeditions to Eilat and Caesarea, and the many recreational dives they shared along the Mediterranean coast of Palestine and in the Red Sea.

Then she talked of how, as time passed, he had become disillusioned about what was really going on at Dimona, struggling to live up to his promises of keeping the government's secrets but making it clear that he felt he was being used to facilitate something truly awful.

"I probably should not be speaking about that," she said.

David knew a great deal more about Dimona than he was willing to let on. "Well, you're right about Dimona," he said casually. "I mean, that's hardly a secret anymore. Everyone assumes Israel has a nuclear weapons capability, which is the whole point of the exercise. Nuclear weapons are basically useless except as a deterrent. If people don't think you have them, then having them is pointless."

"Yes, but there is a difference between your assuming it and a government scientist coming right out and stating it as a fact."

"Your husband did that?"

"Not . . . precisely, but he did take part in an anti-nuclear-weapons demonstration once. That caused a lot of trouble, for both of us. We even argued about it before he did it—and after. The site management took it as a major security breach. We had to spend some time with some very unpleasant officials. I thought we were going to lose everything, and I had not finished my Ph.D. yet. Our income, our apartment, everything depended on his job. Yet . . ."

"For him, it was a matter of principle?"

"Yes, exactly, and one of the most appealing things about Dov was that he was a principled man."

"How did you fix it?" he asked.

"Fix it. That word again."

"I'm sorry, I—"

"No, actually, 'fix it' is an Israeli concept, too. Dov had a friend in the LaBaG who became something of a mentor, really." She looked sideways at him. "Your interlocutor, Professor Ellerstein? He emigrated from America. He is a mathematician.

He actually worked at Dimona for a while. He was sympathetic to LaBaG's cause, but the fact that *he* was a member of LaBaG was a secret. I think that's why he left Dimona, finally."

David's brain was churning. He knew some of this, courtesy of Ellerstein, but didn't want her to know that he knew.

"Anyway, he 'fixed' it. Dov had to make amends, had to do some publicity work to restore the peaceful image of Dimona. Still, for several months, it remained very difficult for us, both at work and at home. Dov kept telling me that the program out there had gotten out of hand. That they were reaching for something they did not need. In the end, though, they needed him, so they kept him on."

"Some of the frustration must have come because he realized that someone else's survival depended on his keeping a paycheck coming. Namely you. That all those lofty principles of his might have to be compromised, because to persist might be putting his wife in danger."

She turned to look at him. She has truly beautiful eyes, he thought, as she registered pleasant surprise.

"You are perceptive, David Hall," she said. "Yes, that was exactly correct. He made amends. He did insist that he would only work on peaceful uses for atomic energy: power plants, medical research, things like that. Never weapons.

218

Dov was good at that: taking a position, but then making people come around to his point of view by his obvious sincerity. I think there were other scientists out there who felt the same way, but Dov was the one who *did* something. Sometimes I think that the work he was required to do might not have been so clear-cut. I always had the sense that he had uncovered something else, that he knew more than he would tell me, but I also knew better than to ask. Our life was happy again, with just this one strange thread woven through it. Then one day"—she stopped and took a deep breath—"he was just . . . gone."

David wondered fleetingly if something bad had happened to rebel scientist Dov Ressner. Something bad that had nothing to do with radiation accidents. He could just imagine the kinds of people who might be working security for Israel's nuclear program. The modern-day descendants of the Masada Zealots? What was their security organization called? Mossad? Bad MFs, from everything he'd read.

"And ever since then, nobody's quite measured up, has he?" he asked, trying for a safer direction.

"Yes. No. I don't know, really. That's always an unfair comparison. We were just extremely well suited, that's all. In every way. Marriage to Dov was so very easy. The only tension we had between us was physical, and the solution to that was wonderful. That's what I mean about the memories."

"I have similar memories. Adrian was . . . difficult, but resolution was spectacular."

"Difficult how?"

He let out a long breath. "She was too smart for her own skin. Everything I said was a challenge. For a while, it was interesting, exciting even. Then, truth be told, I got tired of the eternal sparring. I asked her once if she was always 'on,' and what it would take to have her turn all this intellectual fencing off."

Judith smiled. "How did that go over?"

"A week of silence."

"What then?"

"A week of the best sex of my life."

She smiled again. The transformation of her face was amazing, but then it faded.

"What?" he asked.

"I could never do that," she said.

"At some point, you must," he said. "Even if you find a new guy, you must."

"A new 'guy,' as you put it, would not be interested in my lost husband," she retorted.

"The *right* guy would," he said. "The right guy would have to accept your former marriage as a part of you. If he couldn't do that, then he wouldn't be the right guy."

"Then what would I do, Mr. Hall?"

"Hell, look for another guy."

She smiled. "How very American. Always a solution: *Do* something until you get your way."

He laughed. "Well, yeah, persistence is an American trait, I suppose. That's what we do. We want something, we go for it. It may take several tries and an expanding tolerance for failure along the way. We call that growing up, but we typically will give it a shot."

"You Americans are not embarrassed by failure, then?"

"Sure we are. Just look at the state of politics in America right now. But some of us are even more afraid of regrets, as in, the thought of having never tried in the first place."

"Even if you think that what you are seeking may not ever happen again?"

"Like you'll never find another man as well suited to your love as the first man was? Well, what if he *is* out there and you never go looking? Do you really want to go out to the end of your life and then have to regret that you never even looked?"

She stared down at her sandals.

He remained silent, marveling that she had opened up. He was also surprised at himself. He could not figure out if he was attracted to her just because of her looks or because he was responding unconsciously to her need for an emotional bridge of some kind, a need that seemed to be missing absolutely in every female he'd met in Washington over the past few years. Get a grip, he reminded himself. You can't afford to get involved with this woman. That's not why you're here. *Focus,* dammit.

"It's getting dark," he said. "We'd better get back."

She nodded without replying, her silence implying that she was probably having second thoughts about revealing so much to this foreigner. They retraced their steps to the hostel building without talking. He was conscious that they had stepped beyond some barriers. Jesus, he thought, if she only knew . . .

11

At a quarter to one the next morning, David paused halfway up the siege ramp to catch his breath in the crisp night air. He bent over to ease a cramp in his side. The fortress loomed above him in the darkness, the edges of the ragged casemate walls tipped with gray starlight. The hike up through the ravines had taken slightly longer than two hours. He had slipped out of the hostel at ten, watched the observation point for a few minutes, and then walked down to the parking lot, from which he would have a clear shot up the southern ravine, retracing their steps of the morning. After an hour of steady climbing, he had reached the top junction, where the southern ravine met the western ravine. Which is when he had remembered that the army patrol had returned to the tourist center at midnight, emerging *from* this same area. It being just after eleven, he realized that the patrol might be headed back in toward the hostel even as he stood there on the slope about to start down into the western ravine, assuming they followed the same routine every night.

He decided to find a clump of boulders and settle into the sand, after first poking around with his walking stick to run off any venomous wildlife. He shrugged his arms out of the backpack to give his back a rest for a few minutes while he waited. There was no way to tell if they would be coming through again, and, when he thought about it, it was doubtful they did follow the same routine every night. Dumb tactics if you were looking for bad guys. Predictable routines made for easy ambushes. On the other hand, this was the army: Dumb tactics were not entirely out of the question, although the Israelis were supposedly pretty good on the ground. He decided to wriggle his way down into the sand, in case they were using infrared scanning or night-vision devices. The deeper he was in the sand, the less the heat contrast. It was warmer, too.

After twenty minutes of sitting in the total silence of the desert night, he started to fall asleep. Then he decided that they weren't coming. He got up, brushed off the sand, remounted the backpack, and set out again for the ramp. His decision had been helped along by the fact that he had not heard any signs of the truck returning to the tourist center below. Besides, he was losing precious time—he needed at least an hour on the summit to set up and use his equipment.

Now, poised on the steep slope halfway up the siege ramp to catch his breath, he almost couldn't believe he was so close. After all the months of preparation, tonight might bring proof of the real reason why the defenders had chosen death over surrender. From his vantage point on the ramp he could see all the way down the widening mouth of the western ravine to his left, to the edges of the terrace palaces. A ghostly night bird called from somewhere up in the shadows of the ravine, and there was a slight stirring of the night air. He shivered. If ever a place was haunted, this place surely must be. Nine hundred sixty fugitives from seven years of brutal civil war had offered their throats to the knife rather than face capture, an act of desperation made more horrific by the fact that it had been fathers slaughtering wives and children. He could well imagine that tendrils of human energy remained behind after an event as horrifying as this one. He felt ghostly eyes watching him approach their ruined battlements.

He stood up, wobbling a little with the effort of balancing the backpack, and continued up the slope to the western gate.

• • •

Judith jerked up in the bed with a muffled shout, her eyes wide open but momentarily unseeing. The nightmare had been terrifyingly vivid, ending with the sight of Dov, his back to her, slowly opening a large steel door, heedless to her shouts of warning as he was exposed to a green cauldron of radiation boiling over in a flare of unearthly light that first put him in silhouette and then showed him as a skeleton, transfixed in the doorway, and then as nothing more than a humanoid wraith, leaving her shouting his name over and over but unable to move or make him hear.

She gulped several breaths of air and then subsided back onto her pillow. The glowing door had been replaced by the blank wall of her room. Never before had she experienced a dream like that. Her chest was trembling, and her T-shirt was damp with perspiration. What on earth had brought that on? She thought back to her talk with the American. Maybe talking about Dov had evoked some long-hidden subconscious pain. She wanted to switch on a bedside lamp, but the austere hostel rooms had only the one overhead light. She rolled over and looked out the window, but there was only the shadow of the sand hill behind the building. A breath of cooler air came through the partially opened window. She decided she needed some fresh air.

She got up and slipped on her jeans and sandals, considered and discarded the idea of a jacket, and went out into the corridor. She went downstairs and headed for the side door, not willing to take a chance on encountering some night owl from the hostel staff in just her damp T-shirt.

The side door was a fire door, with a steel bar across the middle, and she looked for signs of an alarm system, but there were none. She opened the door into the cool night air and felt instantly relieved. Not wanting to be locked out, she fished in her jeans for something to stuff into the bolt receptacle, only to notice that there was already a piece of paper wadded in there. Frowning, she stepped back into the hallway and let the door close, then pushed gently on the door itself. It opened. Damned careless, this, she thought. She would have to speak to someone at the desk in the morning. For now, she took advantage, and went outside to get some fresh air and clear away the lingering images of her frightening dream.

The night was dark, but there was good starlight, enough to see the ground. She walked out behind the building, glancing casually back at the hostel to see if there were any lights on, but the place was fully dark. The darkened mass of the fortress mountain loomed before her. The cable-car wire actually glinted in the starlight. A gentle breeze blew in from the western desert, pleasantly obliterating the sulfurous fumes of the Dead Sea.

She sighed as she walked slowly over to the sand bluffs overlooking the parking lots. This was, what, Wednesday night. One more full day here on this ridiculous assignment, babysitter to David Hall, American philosopher, and then back to Jerusalem on Friday. In time for another glorious Sabbath, alone in her apartment. Alone in her life. As she stood on the sand, she pondered her unusual openness with this man. She had talked to him about Dov and the emptiness of her life as she had talked to no man, to no one, actually, in the five years of living alone. Why was that, she wondered. Because he was a foreigner and was soon, as he had pointed out, going to leave, to go back to that strange planet called America? Or because he seemed to be a sympathetic as well as an attractive man?

She shivered in the darkness as she looked up again at the fortress. It had been different when she had been down here on digs. The hostel had not existed. There had been little more than a guard shack, with no cable car or even parking lots for tour buses. They had camped in semi-permanent tents up on the western plateau next to the main Roman camp, courtesy of the army engineers. Their water had come through an oil company's makeshift pipeline, and the weather had been atrocious, but there had been good times, too: nights around the fire like in the kibbutzim. Stories, academic gossip, deep intellectual arguments. The comradeship of the profession.

The symbolism of the expedition had been hard to avoid. Even Yadin had commented on it in the reports from his earlier excavations. With their camp cheek by jowl with that of the Roman army, and the IDF's temporary cable lift for tools and machinery mounted on the siege ramp itself, the parallels were hard to miss: They were the new besiegers, digging in the dust of the centuries to find—what? Proof of Josephus's tale? Artifacts? Treasure? Some indication of how those miserable men, as Josephus called them, could have steeled themselves to do what they had done rather than surrender. Was this what the American had come to find out, too? The whole grim story had remained lodged in myth until the Yadin expedition had found what looked very much like the ten lots described in the story of the Last Man, told in meticulous, bloody detail by Josephus, the turncoat. The Last Man, who would go among the dead and dying, to "extend the privilege" to anyone who might require it, before then thrusting his sword through himself with all his strength.

She shook her head, as if in defiance of all the brooding sadness up there. Israel: Your history is written in blood like no other nation's, and from the beginning of time, too. She had begun to wonder lately if she should get out of the archaeology business altogether, go find a job as a secretary or librarian, something that would lift her nose and her spirits out of the sanguinary past and into contemporary life before she became a complete ghost. Hall had said it, as only an American would be brash enough to say it: You are wasting your life, Judith; you're compost in a hole. Not even Dov would want you to exist like this.

Her breasts were cold with just the undershirt. She decided to go back in. Try again for sleep, and pray that the terrifying dream did not come back. That was part of her problem, she knew: not knowing what had really happened to Dov. And what had that security man with the skull-like face said? That she would never know. As she went through the door, she reached down for the piece of paper jammed in the lock but then thought better of it. She would leave it there, rub the manager's fat face in it in the morning. What kind of security was this, anyway?

At one fifteen David stood just outside the ruined walls of the western palace, the backpack at his feet. He studied the gradual slope of rock that seemed to converge, like a very shallow amphitheater, on the small cluster of stub walls and rubble down by the eastern gate. From this elevation, he could see over the eastern casemate walls, across the glittering Dead Sea, and into the lumpy, dark foothills of Jordan on the other side.

The question was this: If it rained up here, where would the runoff go? The top of the mountain was not flat. The major portion of the area between the southern fortifications and the entrance to the northern palace-villa, nearly five acres by David's estimate, consisted of a shallow, bowl-like—no, he thought, more like a shallow, tilted dish. He bent down to the backpack, and extracted a tennis ball. From his crouching position, he launched it gently down the slope and watched to see where it would go. The white ball, barely visible in the starlight, bumped across the rough surface, hitting some small stones but rolling in almost a straight line directly to the mound of rubble surrounding what looked like a shallow pool about fifty feet back from the entrance to the eastern gate. He went down there, retrieved the ball, and repeated the exercise three more times from different positions at the top of the slope. Each time, the ball ended up near or in the same mound of rubble.

Okay, that computes, he decided. Now, if that's where the water would go, and I'm right about all this, there should be another cistern, something a hell of a lot bigger than that pool, somewhere under this slope. It can't be too close to the gate, or the Yadin expedition would have found it. They had found and mapped all of the rim cisterns that pitted the eastern and southern wall of the mountain. What had attracted Adrian's attention a long time ago when she had begun studying the mystery of Masada was that none of the rim cisterns would have tapped the biggest catchment area of the mountaintop. There had been speculation that the top of the mountain had been under cultivation in Herod's time, but David did not accept that this had been farming in the traditional sense. Ornamental gardens and parks in the palace precincts, yes, but even two thousand years ago, there would have been no real topsoil up here on this barren wedge of rock. He knew that an inch of rain on a flat acre accumulated twenty-seven thousand gallons of water. So five, maybe even six acres of rocky slope would have produced a fairly decent runoff of water down there by that gate. He had seen no signs of drainage holes or channels when he approached the eastern gate from the Serpent Path, and he had been looking. More than ever, he was certain that they had not wasted that bounteous runoff. Adrian had been convinced that there had to be one more cistern, probably a natural cave system of some kind. Time to find out.

He scooped up the ball, went back over to the backpack to extract the survey equipment, and then checked his watch. Twenty until two. He smiled as he began laying out the equipment, remembering the salesman's curiosity as to why a nuclear engineer would want to buy a geologist's seismic survey pack. He had told the man that he owned property up in the Shenandoah Valley and wanted to search one of his fields for caves. The salesman had recommended a refraction survey set, which consisted of a small explosive sound source, four geophones, a data collection unit, and a software package that would draw a vertical profile of the area under the geophone array from the data collected. Since he was doing a vertical survey, he placed the seismic source as close to the middle of the open area as he could figure, then placed the four geophones in a rough square around the source at a radius distance of about one hundred and fifty feet. Before placing the source, he scuffed the ground to expose bare rock and then found a large stone building block from one of the casemate wall sections to put on top of the source disk. Once he had the source positioned, he used his hat to gather sand from around the area to bury the source charge in order to deaden the sound.

Returning to his backpack, he extracted a small coil of wire and made connections to the terminals on the side of the source disk. He stretched the wire out to its full extent, about sixty feet, and left it there while he went around to the four geophones and took the tape off their battery connections. He repeated the precaution of clearing away any sand or loose soil to ensure that the geophones were in contact with bare rock, raised their tiny stub antennas, and then placed a small stone on top of each one to maintain firm ground contact.

Working quickly now, he set up his portable computer, using the backpack as a cushion, and then ran a cable between the computer and the data collection device, which he perched on a rock so that it was in clear line of sight of all four geophones.

He stood up and surveyed the layout. Geophones equally spaced around the source, the seismic source tamped with a good-sized rock, the data collection block in position to receive the signals from the geophones, the computer on and hooked up to the data collection block. Good. He took the spare battery for the computer over to where the end of the wire lay in the dirt and put it down. Then he walked around the geophone pattern and energized each one, getting a tiny green LED light in response showing readiness to record and transmit. He walked back to the data collection block and turned it on, checking to see that it was receiving a carrier wave on its first four channels.

All right. He went back to the computer and brought up the data display program, which on-screen looked like nothing more than a piece of graph paper, with X and Y axes. Ready.

He looked at his watch again. Two ten. Still feeling a nagging sense of concern about that army patrol, he walked all the way back over to the western wall gate, stepped down through the casemate stairs, and peered out over the siege ramp. He could see both ends of the deep ravine, but there were no signs of activity down there in the shadows. He wondered how many slave skeletons were buried under that ramp. The rubbled walls of the Roman camp were etched in gray spidery lines on the plateau opposite, adamantly foursquare after two thousand years.

He walked quickly back up the stone steps and across the open space to his computer. Checking one more time that the device was ready to receive data, he went over to the end of the wire. He hooked up one conductor to the negative terminal of the battery, and then, pausing to take a deep breath, he touched the other conductor to the positive terminal. There was a flash of dull red under the big stone as the sand was blown out, and simultaneously a thump. He was glad he had piled the sand on top of the source charge: Otherwise that noise would have carried for miles in the still desert air. The rock had not moved, though, which meant that the bulk of the energy had gone down into the rock.

He disconnected the wires, slipped the battery into the backpack, and walked back down to the source, rolling up the wire as he went. He picked up the large stone, scuffed out the black smear under it, picked up the scorched disk, and carried the stone back over to where he had found it. Then he went around and picked up each of the geophones, turning each one off and ejecting its batteries into the backpack. Finally he returned to the computer, kneeling down on the hard ground to examine the screen. He punched a few keys, confirmed that data was available, and then, again holding his breath, hit the DISPLAY command. His heart sank when the NO DATA message appeared on the screen.

There had to be data. He hit the HELP key, which dropped a box of instructions. Do it again, he told himself. Slow down on the keyboard. Be precise. Then his heart started to pound when he saw the dancing cursor, beginning at the top of the virtual page, begin to scrawl fine, densely packed horizontal lines across the screen.

One line.

Five lines.

Seven lines. Straight as a die, indicating solid rock.

C'mon, c'mon, he thought. Don't tell me this has all been for nothing.

Then, on the eighth, a partial line, a space, and then a completion. He held his breath to see if it was simply a data anomaly. No—the ninth line, the cursor did the same thing, only the space in the middle of the line was infinitesimally bigger. As was the tenth.

He felt a rush of excitement as the display continued to show, line by line, a large, very large cavity in the rock below. She'd been right, by God!

No more theories: There it was, and it was big, as big as, if not bigger than, the northern wall cisterns. He stared down at the left-hand scale as the cursor descended down the screen, outlining a huge spherical cavity. When it had finally reached the bottom of the screen it was showing one hundred and eight feet vertical height on the cavity, with one end shallower, at about eighty feet. One edge of the cavity image was missing; he would have to figure out what that meant. There was no way of telling precisely how wide across it was, because the shot had provided only a single vertical acoustic profile. The geophones had a maximum separation of three hundred feet, so at least that wide. This damned thing wasn't big: It was *huge!*

He rocked back on his heels. The main thing was that it was indeed there, and, even better, it looked like the top of the cavity was within only a few feet of the surface somewhere over there, near the eastern wall. Precisely where, in relation to the sound source, was not possible to determine from the screen, but his experiments with the rolling ball gave him a pretty good idea.

He closed his eyes, trying to visualize the huge cavern. At last, he thought. Adrian had studied and thought about the incredible history of this place for years, and here was the dramatic final piece of her theory. The story he'd told the academics was a cover. The truth was that Adrian had never been able to swallow the theory that the Zealots had died only to defend their personal honor. These were the survivors of the Roman holocaust at Jerusalem. These people had been the defenders of the last, great Second Temple. They were the Zealots, the wild-eyed Daggermen who had instigated the revolt against Rome in the first place. These had been men who had started a civil war with the superpower of their day over the issue of the Romans bringing graven images of their own pagan gods into the Temple precincts. They had been first and foremost fighters, not philosophers. She'd been convinced that there had to have been more to this tragedy, something else that drove them to their incredible mass suicide. She was certain they had been protecting a great secret, and now he had direct evidence of the place where they might have hidden it.

From her study of the history, Adrian had been convinced they would have brought out holy objects from the Great Temple, religious scrolls, or even perhaps some of the fabled Temple treasures described in the Copper Scroll of Qumran, and they would have brought these things *here,* to Masada, the last stronghold, which they believed to be impregnable to direct assault and impervious to a siege. Her theory was this: When they finally realized that the Romans were, after all, going to take the place, they elected a dagger in the throat to ensure the Romans would never parade the sacred final relics of their god's holy Temple in front of the barbaric mobs of faraway Rome.

So why hadn't the archaeologists found them? The Romans had never found anything of value, because Flavius Josephus, their principal apologist for the Jewish wars, would have mentioned it. Adrian had shown him pictures of existing Roman coins that depicted a triumphant soldier standing next to a palm tree, against which sat a despondent woman, surrounded by the inscription JUDAEA CAPTA. Adrian felt that these coins celebrated the destruction of Jerusalem, not Masada.

Adrian had fixated on a single line in Yigael Yadin's final report: *The cisterns have not been explored.* Subsequent digs *had* gone into the cisterns, but nothing of real interest had been found. He himself had looked into the main cisterns yesterday morning, and they were indeed, as Judith said, big dry holes, impressive feats of ancient engineering, undeniably, but still empty. On the other hand, if Adrian had been right about all this, there was a good chance that he might find their secret hoard in this enormous undiscovered cistern. The one she felt had to be there, because, otherwise, all that runoff water would have been wasted. The one that appears, he exulted, to be right where she thought it would be!

He stood up. Time to get back to the hostel. Tomorrow he would come back up here, minus

Judith, if he could manage it, and search for a way into the cistern. He hoped that if he found it, there would be steps cut into the walls like in the northern cisterns. If not, he had come prepared to lower himself on a wire, using his diving harness, if he had to. Assuming he could find the entrance during the day, he would stick to the schedule of going back down around three and going to bed early, and then he would come back up here tomorrow night to explore the cistern and see if he could discover what the Zealots had been protecting. He might find another empty hole, but his excited heart told him otherwise.

He gathered up all the equipment, checked again to make sure that any signs of the seismic source explosive were gone, slipped into the backpack, and headed for the western gate. It was almost 3:00 A.M.; moonrise would come in about an hour. He wanted to be most of the way back to the hostel before then. He let himself through the western gate, went down the steel platform steps to the siege ramp, and paused for a few minutes to survey the ravines on either side and to listen. There was only the sound of the night breeze whistling gently through the lattice-work supporting the steps. The ramp stretched down in front of him like a competition ski jump.

His adrenaline was pumping, but, by God, she had been right! All the professional explorers had missed the fact of another cistern, and a huge one at that. Much bigger than the ones on the northern face. Maybe too big to have been made by human hands: Probably it was a natural cavern and not a cistern at all. Maybe it had been unknown to even the Herodian occupants.

He sighed. "Don't get ahead of yourself," he muttered out loud.

He retrieved his stick and set off down the ramp, trudging in short, sliding steps down the loose sand and gravel to keep his balance. Except for the strain on his thighs, it was still a lot easier than climbing up had been. He turned left off the bottom of the ramp and slid down the western edge of the ravine until he scrambled all the way to the bottom in a shower of sand and small rocks. He rested again for a few minutes and then set out to make the climb up the western ravine. It took him forty-five minutes to get to the junction at the southwest corner of the mountain. He was more tired than he had expected to be.

Physical reality was setting back in, especially now that the excitement of discovery was wearing off. He topped the western ravine and stumbled over the crest, where, unbalanced by the pack and unexpectedly soft sand, he sat down hard and slid halfway down the slope of the south-side ravine, losing his stick. Pursued by a silent avalanche of sand and small rocks, he fetched up hard against a large boulder that knocked the wind out of him. What little wind was left, he thought. When everything stopped moving, he shrugged out of the backpack and flopped over onto his back in the sand to rest, after first making sure he hadn't landed next to a snake. It was dark down here, but his eyes were fully night adapted and the starlight was much brighter. Amazingly, the sand was still warm, and he scrunched down into it.

Which was when he heard the murmur of voices.

He froze in the shadow of the rock, not daring to even move his head.

It sounded like the voices were above him, up on the top edges of the western ravine. They were speaking softly, but in the desert air, every word was clear, if totally incomprehensible. Israeli soldiers? Bedouins? An image of hooded men with knives popped into his mind. He squinted, listening hard. It sounded like Hebrew, but he didn't know either language well enough to be sure. Then came a surge of panic when he realized that they should be able to see him.

All his fatigue vanished. Don't move, he thought. Don't move one muscle. Don't turn your white face up the hill. Meld in with the sand and the rocks. With any luck they were just finishing their patrol, anxious to get back down to the truck, and not carefully probing the sands for sign of human passage, or sweeping the slopes of the ravine with infrared devices. Or just looking for tracks.

He tried hard to control his breathing, aware that a light cloud of dust probably still hung in the air around him from his slide down the sand hill. There had to be a big furrow down that slope, too, more evidence of his presence. Hell, they *had* to spot him.

He could hear their steps crunching through the sand, along with an occasional clink of hardware. Hardware: Then these had to be soldiers. It *had* to be the Israeli patrol. Then the voices were passing above him, rising in volume and number until a short, barked command brought silence. David held his breath. Discovery? Or was the sergeant reimposing some tactical discipline? He waited, his throat and mouth dry, trying to figure out which way they were going, hoping against hope that it was *up* the western ravine toward the plateau that held the Roman camp. He did not want them going down the ravine and finding his tracks at the ramp. Except that he and Judith had walked that way, so maybe tracks weren't that important. *Shit!*

After a few more minutes, the sounds of the patrol died away, and he relaxed again. Wait a while, he thought. Make sure they don't double back. He yawned mightily, releasing the tension in his face. Not too long, though: You've got to be back in the hostel in an hour or you'll be caught out in the moonlight. He closed his eyes and tried to regain control of his breathing.

Fifteen minutes later he jerked awake. He swore out loud and then abruptly held his breath, listening to see if anyone had heard. He couldn't believe it: He'd gone to sleep! Yet it was incredibly comfortable down here in the warm sand. Only with a great effort did he manage to rouse himself for the trek back down the ravine to the hostel.

12

Thursday morning David got his wish: Judith agreed to his taking the cable car back up the mountain by himself. She seemed to be somewhat distracted, and when he left to go upstairs to catch the first cable car, she was having an animated conversation in Hebrew with the hostel manager. A group of German college kids had arrived for an overnight stay in the hostel, creating some noisy confusion around the front desk.

As he rode up in the cable car he tried to keep from yawning. He had made it back to the room by four-thirty and had dropped off into a sound sleep after only a few minutes of excited speculation about what he might find once he located a way into that cistern. He had reviewed the data image on his computer before going down to meet Judith for breakfast. Whatever it was, natural or man-made, it was truly huge, and he wondered again if by some slim chance the defenders had not even known about it. He quickly discarded that notion: Water was the single most precious commodity in desert siege logistics. Someone would have had to realize that all that runoff was going somewhere. He had written down the coordinates of the image in one of his notebooks, and then, after a moment's deliberation, he had deleted the image from the computer before leaving it unattended. That way, if his secret project was uncovered before he had time to find the cistern's entrance, no one would know what he had found. The image on the screen, with its brightly shining edges, remained fixed in his mind even as he sat with Judith for breakfast and babbled on about spending a day in the casemate rooms.

"What is the attraction of the casemate rooms?" she had asked.

"That's where they lived," he replied earnestly. "The Zealots. During the siege. The palaces had been abandoned, and they'd even used some of the building materials from the palaces to reinforce the walls. The Yadin expedition found hearths, middens, and living quarters all throughout the casemate system. I want to get a feel for that."

"I see. There is much that we do not know about the Kanna'im, your so-called Zealots. Or perhaps you do *not* know. There is much controversy. "

"I thought most of the controversy was over the Dead Sea Scrolls."

"There is plenty there as well, and far too much

secrecy, especially with foreign scholars holding tight to their discoveries. The problem is that we do not know for sure who these Zealots were. Yadin calls them Kanna'im, fanatics. Others call them Sicarii, the Daggermen. More like mercenaries for hire than patriots. Political activists, agitators, Roman haters. There is even speculation that there were Essenes here."

"My guess is," he said, after a moment's reflection, "that they were mostly all survivors from the end time up at Jerusalem."

She had thought about that for a few minutes while they finished their coffee and watched the first tour buses roll into the parking lot.

"I have often wondered about that," she said finally. "Speaking personally, not professionally, I would have expected Yadin to have found some evidence of that, some *things* taken from the city in its last hours. If most of the defenders here had come from Jerusalem, that is."

He had almost stopped breathing. Had she figured it out? Was she hinting that she knew why he was really here? He watched her out of the corner of his eye as he pretended to look out the window, but there was nothing in her face to indicate that she was playing games.

"I would agree," he said, trying to keep his voice casual, "but if they had, they would have been valuable things. This place has been exposed for two thousand years. Valuable things . . ."

245

"Yes, of course. Long gone. I have work to do. You had better go upstairs or you will miss the first cable car."

As the gondola bumped gently into the landing dock, he told himself to put Judith Ressner out of his head. As long as she had not caught on to what he was really here for, his job now was to focus, focus, focus.

Once on the mountain he walked down the steel steps near the eastern gate into extremely bright sunlight. Twenty tourists followed him down and then collected around their guide, who launched noisily into her spiel. David walked casually away from the group, moving slowly toward the southern end of the plateau, where, in comparison with the palace ruins and the spectacular views on the north rim, there was very little to see except the badly deteriorated casemate walls. He calculated that there was about a sixty-foot net drop in elevation from the western palace down to the eastern gate, and as he walked along the eastern wall, he kept his eye out for any signs of where the water would go. There was always the chance that the collection point was in the casemate wall, and, in fact, there was one cistern shown cut into the southeastern rim on the Yadin maps, about one hundred fifty yards away from the eastern gate area. That ball had come down here, though, not to the gate, even when he released it from three different points up by the

246

western palace walls and the remains of the Byzantine-era church.

When the tourist group moved off toward the northern palace complex, he turned around and ambled back over to the area between the eastern gate and the cable-car landing. The two young security guards who had come up on the first run were following the tourists, attracted no doubt by some of the more nubile German girls who were dressed for a day in the hot sun. David had on his sun hat and cotton khakis and was ready to get out of that direct sunlight.

To the right of the eastern gate were the remains of one of the Byzantine buildings. Not much survived: low walls, exposed foundations, and piles of rubble that were identified here and there by tour placards. Near the easternmost point in the wall system, in an area the size and general shape of a baseball diamond, there was a strangely shaped low stone wall that paralleled the casemate wall for about sixty feet and then cut in toward the center of the flat area to the right of the eastern gate complex. At the lowest point was a hollow depression that might have once been a shallow pool.

David studied the wall and the saucerlike depression. The wall did not seem to be part of a building foundation, more a curtain wall of some kind, delineating an area rather than providing security for it. There was a tourist information sign down by one end of the wall. He walked down to the sign.

ORCHARD AREA, the sign's title read. "In this area is believed to be the location of an olive or fruit tree orchard, sited here because the low ground would capture the occasional rainwater that came once or twice a year to the mountaintop. Several other parts of the plateau were believed to have supported cultivation in ancient times."

Well, now, David thought. So the archaeologists confirmed that rain runoff, however infrequent, would end up down here. That pool, however, would not hold much water. Why had they surmised an orchard of some kind and not a cistern? He tried to recall the data image. Where he was standing should be very nearly right on top of the eastern edge of that cavity, with the bulk of the cistern actually lying under the amphitheater-shaped ground that rose behind him toward the western palace. He turned around and looked up the slope. From here, the focus point, the slope was easily discernible, especially in the bright light of day. So if there was a cistern under here, where would the inlet be?

He looked around to see if anyone was watching, but the tourists had all moved up the hill, panting security guards in tow. The cable-car wheels were rolling again, meaning another load was inbound. He walked over to the casemate walls and stepped through a hole in the crumbling brickwork, down into the shadow of the corridor running down between the inner and outer walls. Here the roof had been reconstructed. Once the next load of tourists had disembarked and the car started down, he walked back out into the sunlight, notebook in hand, studying the ground. From the sounds of them, these tourists were Americans. He turned his back on them, hoping no one would come over, and ambled slowly around the area. He looked to see if there were any traces of the explosive source, but nothing was visible in the hot dust.

There had been no hole in the bottom of the dry pool, and there was nothing but rubble, battered square stone building blocks, patches of gravel, slate-flat stone, and the foundations of the Byzantine-era buildings. The only anomaly was that strange low wall that hooked out from the casemate walls.

He walked over to the wall again and, after looking around first, kicked at it absently. Solid, ancient rock. If sheets of rainwater were flowing down this hill, he mused, what would this wall do? It would keep that water away from the casemate wall foundations, which he suddenly realized were slightly lower than the surrounding ground. Okay, he thought, I can understand that, but it means the water would be diverted to, well, to the foundations of the Byzantine enclosure and that damned pool.

He walked back over to that ruin and stepped over the foot-high foundation walls. The enclosure was about seventy feet by thirty, shaped roughly in a rectangle, except that the wall on the southern end of the rectangle was curved and was also incomplete, as if to allow vehicles or perhaps animals to be driven inside. He realized he needed to see it from above, so he walked over to the cable-car platform, past a pile of steel scaffolding pipes, and climbed up the twenty steps to the loading and unloading platform. Looking down the drooping cable, he could see a small crowd getting into the car at the tourist center, a half mile distant. He pretended to be sketching in his notebook in case anyone was watching from the tower down below.

He turned around and looked down at the Byzantine enclosure, confirming the notion that the southern end was open for a reason: There was no hint of a foundation wall in the smooth rock surface at that end. Staring up the shallow slope, he tried again to visualize where the water would go. It would sweep across and down this hill, divert along that odd-shaped low wall, into the shallow pool, and then—what? Where would it go? He suddenly realized, from his perspective above the ruins, that the water would then sweep all the way *around* the Byzantine enclosure, which he saw now was shaped like a drain. It would have to end up *inside* that building, if indeed it had been a building. Maybe there had been another pool of some sort, not like one of the fancy Roman-style baths up in the two palaces but a watering hole, perhaps for livestock.

He climbed back down off the cable-car tower and walked back over to the casemate walls on the eastern side of the Byzantine enclosure. It was getting really hot now, the sun blazing over the Dead Sea like a malevolent furnace. There were several smaller cisterns cut into the eastern and southern rim of the mountain, so maybe the water filled the pool and then was diverted to a central channel to fill them. Studying the ground, he finally found what he was looking for: two dirt-clogged drain holes, about a foot square, leading under the inner casemate wall. He walked back to the opening he had used before, turned left, and went back down the casemate corridor until he found the two channel openings. There were no channels in the floor. Pipes, then? He looked harder. The floor was discolored. He poked at it and discovered that there *were* two channels, long since packed with hard dirt, running across the corridor and through the external wall. The dirt was packed hard enough to look and feel like stone.

Looking over his shoulder again, he walked over to the nearest arrow-slit aperture and looked out and down. Below was the steep slope up which the Serpent Path cut its zigzag pattern. He could see where the runoff channels came through the outer wall, and beneath that point there was an erosion notch in the hillside. Was there a rim cistern down there?

Excited now, he walked north along the rim, staying inside the casemate corridor, and back to the eastern gate. There he paused, standing in the shadow of the gate vestibule. He scanned the surrounding area to see where the two security guards were. They were still tagging along behind the German tourist group, now talking to three of the girls. David slipped out the gate and walked down the stone steps, stepping down onto the flat area on the hillside that ran directly beneath the fortress walls. The Serpent Path stretched away in the first of its switchbacks leading down the mountain. Overhead the cable car squeaked and groaned as it neared the tower landing at the summit. He waited close by the walls until the empty car had started back down. He realized now he had to be in full view, or almost so, of the observation post below. Actually, not quite: A shoulder of the hillside would block their view of him as along as he stayed close to the bottom of the exterior casemate wall. Fifty feet down the Serpent Path, though, and they would be able to see him, but he didn't need to go down: He needed to climb *across* the base of the wall to that notch.

Proceeding very carefully, he did a hand-over-hand act along the bottom of the crumbling wall. The stones were already hot to the touch. With no path, the footing was very treacherous, and twice he felt himself starting to tumble down the hillside, only to stop the incipient slide by grabbing one of the scraggly bushes growing along the wall. It took him fifteen minutes to eke his way over to the notch, and he had to scuff a small level area in the dirt and sand so that he could stop there. He took one last look down the escarpment to confirm he was still out of the guard tower's sight line. Then he knelt down and looked inside.

When his eyes adjusted to the shadows, he saw a small cavelike opening in the base of the wall. Looking at the walls, he realized it was a man-made cave, probably the remains of a rim-wall cistern. It was bone dry, like all the other cisterns, and no more than twenty feet in diameter. He could tell that it was man-made because of the obvious tool marks in the stone near the entrance. The floor of the cavity was almost level with the opening in the hillside and sloped down from back to front. There was a small patch of grayish light coming from a tiny aperture up above, no bigger than a handhold. There were no steps per se at the opening, but the dirt and gravel that had fallen through the opening provided a loose ramp, and, looking around one last time, he let himself into the cistern.

Judith was just about to declare victory in a software fight with her portable computer when there was a knock on the door.

"Yes?"

"Phone call for Dr. Ressner. From Tel Aviv."

"Thank you." She looked at her watch. Eleven o'clock. As good a time as any to break. The room was starting to heat up. David Hall had been smart to take a first-floor room. She energized the screen saver and went downstairs.

The sole phone for guest use was next to the front desk. She looked around at the lobby, crowded noisily with milling tourists, and asked if she could use an office extension. Forbidden. She sighed and picked up the receiver, putting a finger in her ear to silence the noise coming from the cable-car machinery room.

"This is Judith Ressner."

The ghostly voice of Colonel Skuratov answered. "Good morning, Dr. Ressner. Skuratov here. Calling to see if everything is going smoothly. With the American."

"So far, yes."

"Very good. He is what he seems to be? A privileged tourist?"

"Yes. That is my impression. He has studied the history."

"And he has covered the ground? Seen everything he wanted to?"

"I think so. We're not done yet, of course." She had a sudden, alarming thought: Should she tell the colonel that Hall was up on the mountain by himself?

"You are always with him in his excursions, yes?" Her throat went dry. Instinctively, she stalled.

"I'm sorry, Colonel. I'm standing in a crowded lobby. Many tourists. Can you say your question again?"

"Are you with him in his excursions?" The colonel's voice was cold and very clear. "He is escorted when he is on the site, yes?"

"Oh, yes, of course," she lied, suddenly afraid. She had just assumed . . .

"Very good. Remember, call that number if there are any false notes. I may not be here, but my people will find me. You still have my card?"

"Yes, I do, Colonel." She hoped. Somewhere, anyway.

"Very well, Dr. Ressner." The dial tone appeared.

She put the handset back onto its cradle and walked slowly over to the restaurant. All the tables were taken, but she threaded her way through the crowded room and peered out the big picture windows at the mountain. Should she go up there? It would be so damned obvious that she was checking up on him. There were the security guards, of course. Maybe call them, ask if they could see him, wandering around the site? He was going into the casemate walls, though. They would have to go search. Make a big deal. She decided to leave it alone. The old colonel was a little crazy to think this American was some kind of spy or something. That was nonsense.

The temperature inside the cavelike cistern was a good twenty degrees cooler than the outside, and the sunlight streaming in over his shoulder from the hole looked like the beam of a movie projector in a dusty theater. He slid across a mound of loose sand and wiggled his way down to the bottom. Maybe fifteen feet to the roof and twenty feet from front to back wall, and nothing in the hole but dry sand and a stinking substance he finally identified as bat guano. He looked up at the ceiling but did not see any bats.

He tried to recall the diagrams in the Yadin report. There had been several of these small cisterns shown along the eastern and southern rims, which was topographically the lower, or downslope, edge of the plateau. In some cases the defenders had built well structures above them to service their living quarters in the casemate walls, but this was certainly not the giant cavity that had shown up on his screen last night. In fact, this cavity had not shown at all. Well, okay, he thought, that was a vertical refraction shot. The side edges of the big cavity hadn't shown up, either. He walked around, looking for any signs of there being anything here but a dry hole, but there was nothing but soft sand on the bottom. He stood still in the middle of the bottom area. The water came down off the hill, collected in that shallow pool, which probably slowed it down, and then funneled into the Byzantine building, perhaps into a small bathing area, or a stock lagoon or other agricultural impound, and then the overflow went through the two channels across the floor of the casemate wall system, out the aperture in the wall, and down here into this cistern.

Okay, so where did the overflow from here go? His research had shown that the rains in this end of Africa's Great Rift Valley came only in the winter, but when they came, there was sometimes a deluge. The Yadin books had a picture of a flash flood going down the normally bone-dry western wadi, looking like a churning brown Niagara Falls, so he knew what quantities of water might come down across that hill. Yet there was no water in here. He looked back at the hole. Okay, so perhaps over time the rains had washed out the front opening used by the cistern diggers. The cavity would fill with rainwater, and most of it would spill out the opening, leaving a pool in the back to evaporate over the intervening eleven months.

He climbed back to the main opening and saw that indeed there were traces of a gully below it.

A gully meant erosion, which meant water. All right, that computes. So where was the entrance to the big cavity? He had a distressing thought: Maybe the cavity wasn't a big cistern after all, but simply a hollow cave in the mountain that had had nothing to do with water. In which case, there would be no entrance. He swore, then crawled back down the sand, squatted at the back bottom of the bowl-shaped cistern floor, and tried to reconstruct the image from last night. Except for the ammonia stink of the bat guano, the deliciously cool air in the cave felt like air-conditioning. He wondered if anyone had seen him slip out through the eastern gate. He also wondered if Judith was going to be coming up here to see what he was doing, but he doubted that. She said she had some translations to work on, and she also seemed to be a lot more relaxed about his intentions for this visit.

He caught himself in a giant yawn. Up all damn night. Stumped, he decided that this was a perfect place for a nap. He stared around at the bottom again, making sure there were no hostile creatures with the same idea, and then looked at his watch. Eleven-thirty. Grab an hour or so of sleep, putter around up top some more, and then go back down. Have to come back tonight when he would be free to explore the surface buildings again. Maybe a flashlight would reveal what could not be seen in the light of day. He simply *had* to find the entrance. Assuming there is one, his internal Doubting Thomas reminded him.

And if there isn't one? He quashed the thought. It wasn't as if he had all the time in the world. All he could do was to keep trying. The big difference now was that he *knew* the big cavity, cistern, cave, or something, was there. He yawned again, pulled up a small hill of sand for a pillow on the front slope of the cave floor, positioned his hat, lay back, and closed his eyes.

He awoke with a start to the sound of voices, nearby voices. He sat up, disoriented for a moment, before remembering where he was. He realized the voices were speaking German. That mob that had come to stay in the hostel. Bunch of gung-ho German kids. They had probably climbed the Serpent Path. He shook his head and looked at his watch and did a double take. It was almost two-thirty in the afternoon. So much for an hour's nap. Time to get down the hill before Judith got suspicious. Then he had a bad thought: You better hope she hasn't been wandering around the surface, looking for you.

As he straightened to get up from his sandy bed he realized suddenly that his buttocks were wet. Wet? He felt the seat of his pants. Definitely wet. Noxious, too, he discovered as he smelled his hands. Ammonia, or worse. Bat urine? Oh, wonderful. He had bedded down in a

259

bat manure pile. He stood up, reluctantly brushing off his backside, but when he looked down he stopped brushing. There, in the depression made by his buttocks, was the sheen of water. Standing water.

Whoa, he thought.

I wonder.

He squatted down and dug at the depression, pulling away sand until he had a hole slightly more than two feet deep, which immediately filled up with water. He was about to give it up when his fingertips felt something hard—and smooth. The sun had long since gone over to the western side of the mountain, so he couldn't see much in the dimming light of the cistern. Definitely should have brought a flashlight. Whatever it was, it was smooth, almost like polished stone. Maybe even metal.

He stood up again and looked around. He was standing in the lowest point of the chamber, toward the back of the cave. He had to get down to the visitors center, reestablish contact with Judith, tell her all about his stimulating hours on the mountain, eat the one substantial meal of the day, take another nap, and then get back up here again tonight. This cave *had* to be the way in. The big question remained: Into what? He stepped up the slope of sand and out into the light of day. Once outside he sat down in the dry sand, squirming around to see if that might disguise the fact that he had soaked the back of his pants. There was, he realized, no disguising the aroma. Pray for an empty cable car down, and time to get to his room before he ran into Judith.

13

At 9:00 P.M. David lay in bed, fully clothed, recalling the hasty descent from the mountain earlier in the afternoon. He had hoped to shuck the eau de bat-crap without running into anyone, and, for the most part, he had succeeded, although some of the American tourists had commented about the smell in the cable car. He had planted himself at one end of the gondola and kept his mouth shut, not wanting them to know he was an American. He was painfully amused by their immediate assumption that he could not understand what they were saying, but did not delay in getting to his room and changing the offending trousers, which he washed out in a deep sink in the bathroom.

Judith had been waiting for him in the restaurant and was pleasantly conversational about his day on the mountain. She did manage to steer the conversation around to the subject of when they would go back.

"I'd like to go up one last time in the morning," he had replied. "Stay until about noon, maybe one o'clock, and then we can hit the road, if that's okay. I'll hike up the wadi to the ramp, maybe before sunrise."

She agreed, although she cautioned him that it was not permitted for anyone to leave the hostel before full daylight. He promised to observe the rules. After their meal, they walked again down to the shores of the Dead Sea and talked mostly about the history of ancient Israel and how many parallels remained with contemporary times. Their walk was cutting into his naptime, but, refreshed by his rest in the cistern cave, he was content to walk with Judith and listen to her talk. She seemed to need to talk now, he realized, and after her personal revelations during their last walk, she was much more at ease. He had learned the value of being a good listener from Adrian, who'd always been surprising him with the range of things she knew something about. Besides, he liked being with Judith. She was so damned serious about everything that he was itching to poke a little fun at her, get her to lighten up a little, but he had sensed that if he did, she'd get offended and go back into her prickly shell.

They had walked up and down the grainy multicolored sands, stepping around salt-encrusted pools reeking of sulfur and halogen compounds. About a half mile south of the fortress, out of sight of the hostelry, there were some windowless concrete buildings, two squat steel tanks, and one tall tank, all surrounded by barbed-wire fencing. Clouds of steam were rising from vent pipes on one of the buildings. Judith explained that there were many mining operations along the Dead Sea, some of which used the heat from geothermal vents to concentrate minerals before the final extraction process. There was almost no vegetation growing along the seashore itself, and only sparse, stunted trees and thorn bushes populated the edge of the coast road. The sea itself was purplish in color, only grudgingly reflecting the hues of a glorious sunset shaping up over the Judaean hills. David was surprised to observe seabirds soaring here and there and wondered what they ate in this lifeless part of the world. Judith prattled on about the difficulties of getting things done in an academic bureaucracy while he mentally rehearsed tonight's expedition back to the fortress.

He would have his backpack and the flashlight this time. He needed something to dig with, to clear the sand away from the bottom of the cistern cave, but he thought he knew how to solve that problem once he got up there. He also had to take his diving harness and the wire rope in case there were no steps down into that big cavity. A good bit of weight to hump up that damned ravine, but tonight he needed real equipment, and a camera, in case there was something in there. In case, hell. There *had* to be.

Now, what about La Ressner? She was the closest professional archaeologist. He had just about decided to include her in the project, assuming he found something other than a big empty hole. Adrian had been totally convinced that the whole point of the Masada legend was that they'd been protecting something incredibly valuable, some religious artifacts being more likely than a heap of gold. He promised himself he would tell Judith if he did find something and then let her call in the pros. She, hell, all of them, would be furious with him for going up there on his own, for doing precisely what he had promised not to do—intrusive exploration, sneaking around at night, and, worst of all, digging, the cardinal sin of archaeology: an amateur putting spade to ground. Even worse than worst, finding something important. That said, he suspected that if the find was big enough, all would be forgiven in the excitement of the discovery, as long as he let the professionals *exploit* the discovery. If he had been wrong all along, and the cavity on the screen was just an empty cave, well, he would fold his tents and steal away into the desert night, or rather, back to Tel Aviv, do some diving at Caesarea Maritima, and then slink home to Washington.

A sudden assault by biting sand flies forced them to retreat to the hostel. The German kids had been organizing a picnic fire outside the building near the edge of the parking lot, and now David

264

could hear soft singing coming through his single window. The night outside was still moonless, although tonight he would have to be more careful coming back down, as moonrise was around two. There had been no sign of the army patrol trucks when he had come up to his room. He peered out the window to see if the yellow rectangle of light coming down from Judith's room upstairs was still visible, and it was.

Ten minutes later he decided to make his creep. He rose from the bed, slipped the backpack on, and headed out the door and down the hallway toward the fire door. Besides the gear in the backpack, he carried a bottle of water and his walking stick. He paused to listen for sounds of someone in the bathrooms, then quietly walked to the fire door, opened it, and wedged another piece of wet paper into the bolt hole. He crept down the outside stairs to the ground and stopped. He listened again for sounds of anyone coming around this side of the building, but all he could hear was the sound of the kids' party out front. With his eyes not yet night adapted, it was much darker out here than he had expected. He walked around to the back of the hostel building but this time went straight up the hill behind it, trying to keep out of the field of view of that observation post. He did not stop until he was over the first sand ridge and able to hunker down below the line of sight from the building.

He peered back over the ridge and could see Judith's window still lighted, but she was not in view. There were five other rooms with lights on the second floor, and three on the ground floor, but otherwise the building was dark. The observation box under the cable-car tower was also fully dark, but that didn't mean it wasn't manned. He waited for fifteen minutes, watching the box for the telltale signs of a cigarette, but there was nothing. There were still no army trucks in the parking lot, either. The flicker of light on the palm trees from the kids' bonfire was the only movement around the hostel building. He decided to go for it and, crouching behind the sand ridge, began the hike up the southern ravine.

Judith put down her pen and rubbed her eyes. It was close to ten o'clock. She realized that she had been listening to the German kids singing out front instead of concentrating on her work, which was a sure sign that it was time to quit. She wasn't really all that sleepy, but she really hadn't been concentrating for the past half hour. Besides the distraction of the voices and guitar music out front, she couldn't shake the building apprehension about going back to the university to face the chairman and his questions.

She decided to go downstairs and perhaps sit out on the front steps of the hostel for a while. Get some fresh air and enjoy a little human contact. She smiled to herself as she reached for a sweater. Between her sojourns on the desolate beach with David Hall and talking to random tourists, security detail soldiers, and the kids staying at the hostel, she had had more social interaction in these few days than she had normally in a year at the university. She had almost forgotten the diversity of the human race, dealing as she did with the same small coterie of professional academics day in and day out. She stopped by the bathroom and then went out the hostel lobby corridor to the front steps.

The kids were arranged in comfortable-looking clumps on blankets around a small bonfire. Two girls were strumming guitar, and another was playing a harmonica. Judith thought she saw some wine bottles being passed around and wondered where they had obtained wine at this desolate spot. They're students, she remembered; silly question.

She sat in the shadows of the front steps for nearly an hour, her mind a blank screen across which images of times past flowed: growing up in Haifa, her own time at university, her days with Dov . . . and nights. Don't forget the nights. What was it her next-door neighbor, a widow of the Yom Kippur War, had said: You never know, when they go out the door in the morning; you just assume they'll be back at dark. David Hall, the

American, was right, she mused. Going through the motions is no life at all. Leave it to an American to come right out and say it.

She considered going back inside and down the hall to his door, to see if he might want to join her out here, but then dismissed the idea. He would think her much too forward. Besides, while he was obviously attracted to her, he seemed at the same time to be holding back. Attracted and interested were two different things. Yes, but to be interested there has to be at least an indication of a two-way street. She wasn't sure she knew how to manage that anymore.

The night air was cool and soft, and the bonfire, though subdued, warmed the night with its timeless, comforting light. She did not want to look up at the mountain, looming in the darkness over her left shoulder. Up there everything was dead. Down here there was life. She contented herself with just sitting there, if only on the edges of it.

It took David just under two hours to reach the western gate. Buoyed by a growing excitement, he had climbed steadily, passing now familiar landmarks along the way, waiting a few minutes at the top of the southern ravine to see if there were any patrols stirring but then pressing ahead. He had stopped again before ascending the ramp, just to make sure no one was advancing up the ravine or across the plateau of the Roman camp. There was only the night breeze, and the black shadow of bloody King Herod's haunted mountain looming before him.

He went up the ramp, crossed through the northern precincts of the western palace, and stood in a ruined archway for a moment, recovering his breath and looking down across the starlit stone slope. The battered white walls, scattered in haphazard clumps around the plateau, lay like bones in the starlight. Two *thousand* years ago. The Vision of the Dry Bones. He shook his head at the enormity of it and then walked down the slope to the eastern gate, where he dismounted the pack near the pile of scaffolding pipes and checked his gear. He wanted to switch on the flashlight, but once out that gate, even a small light could be seen for miles. So he switched off the Maglite, and it was darken ship until he was inside that rim-wall cistern. He walked over to the supposed olive grove site next to the Byzantine structures and found the historical marker sign, which he grabbed and worked out of the hard ground. One makeshift shovel, he thought, holding the sign in both hands. All he had to do was move some sand.

He retrieved his pack, went through the gate, and carefully made his way across the top of the Serpent Path to the cistern entrance. He could not resist sticking his face around the corner of the shoulder of rock that protruded just enough to hide him from the observation post. Far below was the tourist center, its empty parking lots looking like ponds, but there was no sign of the campfire in the picnic grove. Good. Party's over; the entire place should be asleep by now.

He scrunched his way through the loose sand to the cistern entrance hole, passed the pack and the sign in, and then climbed through himself. The faint stink of ammonia lingered in the air. He flicked on the Maglite and scanned the ceiling and the upper walls of the cistern for bats, but there were still no other visible creatures in the cave. He hoped there were no desert adders lurking just under the sand.

The small depression he had dug was still there, with his tracks all around it. He set the light flat on his pack and, using the sign, began to shovel away the sand from the low point of the cistern. At first it was easy, but then the sand became progressively wetter and more difficult to move. After fifteen minutes he had cleared an area four feet square, down to a depth of nearly two feet. The reek of ammonia was very strong now, and even with a handkerchief tied across his nose and mouth, he had to step away every few minutes to get some fresh air near the entrance hole. After another fifteen minutes he had dug past the layer of bat guano, and the atmosphere cleared considerably. The sand was really wet, almost saturated. He stopped when his improvised shovel hit something hard.

Reaching into the hole, he pushed the wet sand aside and uncovered what looked like a flat rock or paving stone. He ran his fingertips over it and was thrilled to see that it was artificially smooth, not like the wind- and sand-blasted rock walls of the fortress above. Man-made, he thought. Smooth—and wet. Vestiges of the last rainfall here, he thought. Probably back last winter. The almost constant temperature in the cave would slow evaporation, especially once the water level subsided into the sand. He cleared away more of the stone, looking for an edge. He found something better than that. Two feet to the right side of the hole he encountered a depression in the stone, into which had been fixed an iron ring about three inches in diameter. The ring was rusty and did not lift under his prying fingers, but there would be only one purpose to such a ring: to lift the stone.

By God, he'd found it! He experienced a strong yearning to have Adrian with him.

He rocked back on his heels, letting the Maglite shine into his face. He remembered the fateful words that had triggered Adrian's theory and his own search: *The cisterns have never been explored.* Now he had some real work to do, and not much time to do it in. He set to shoveling sand again.

Thirty minutes later he had uncovered the entire slab, which was actually a crude rectangle, four feet by about two and a half, with the ring embedded on the centerline about a foot from one end. There was a quarter-inch seam all around the slab, with the bedrock of the cistern forming the outer edge of the seam. The stone of the slab was a different color from the bedrock. He studied it, running his knife blade along the seam, loosening bits of sand. Depending on how thick it was, this probably was not something he could just lift out of its hole, unless there was some kind of counterweight mechanism, which he doubted. Besides, this stone looked like it had been here for a very long time.

His knife was a bosun's knife, and it had a four-inch stainless steel fid, or spike, on one end. He pried the spike under the ring and began to work it, but the ring's hinge joint seemed to be welded in place. There were no hinges visible on the slab. He put the knife down, climbed up the sand ramp to the entrance hole, and slipped outside. He had to wait a few minutes to get his night vision back but then found a good-sized rock, which he took back into the cistern with him.

Using the rock as a hammer, he banged on the ring until he thought he saw it move as his hammering broke through the crust of rusty metal. This time he was able to lift the ring into a not quite vertical position. He sat back again, not even trying to lift the slab. If it was even two or three inches thick, it would weigh a couple hundred pounds, if not more. He needed some leverage. A pole. Maybe one of those steel scaffolding pipes up above—that would do nicely.

He climbed back up into the fortress and removed one of the steel pipes, which was two inches in diameter and about twelve feet long. He took this back down into the cistern, realized he needed a fulcrum point, and returned once more to the fortress to look around. He finally decided to hump loose building blocks down to the cistern until he had a solid fulcrum point on which to set the pipe. Then it became obvious that if the blocks were resting on sand, they would just settle when he tried to lift, so he had to dig some more sand away and then go get some more building blocks.

It took him an hour to get the thing set up, with two poles now and a second stack of rocks instead of just one, after he realized he would need something to wedge the slab open once he got it lifted. *If* he could get it lifted. He looked at his watch. Almost two. Moonrise in ten minutes. He would need two hours to get back to the hostel, assuming he didn't have to hide from a patrol along the way. Sunrise was at around seven-thirty. Twilight an hour before that. So he could stay here no more than two more hours. This had better work right away if he was going to have time to explore the cave underneath.

He went around to the lever end of the steel pipe, which was sticking up about six feet above the sand, its other end wedged through the ring. He draped his arms over the pipe and then pulled down. Nothing happened. The pipe flexed slightly over its fulcrum of stacked stones, but the big slab didn't budge. He took a deep breath and hung his entire body weight on the end of the pipe. At first it simply flexed again, threatening to crimp, but then there was a noise of crunching sand and the edge of the slab came up out of its hole, rising about ten inches above the edge of the hole before becoming wedged against the end of the pipe.

Now what, genius? Cursing, David let the pipe back down again and went over to reset the pole and the second stack of stones. It did him no good to just open the slab while he was twelve feet away suspended on the lever arm. He had to wedge it open so he could go see what was down there. He obviously needed to be able to reach that second pipe once he had the slab raised.

He succeeded after two more tries and another trip to the rock pile up above. This time he was able to tip the big slab sideways a few inches onto a pile of building stones, leaving about a foot of daylight between the slab and the rim of the hole. He grabbed the Maglite and crawled over to the hole, being careful to keep his head and hands out from under the precariously perched slab. Holding his breath, he pointed the white beam down into the hole under the slab. There was another large, rusty iron ring attached to the bottom of the slab. That wasn't what got his attention, though. To his astonishment, the light beam shone back at him from what looked like a bottomless pool of black, motionless water.

14

Judith awoke again at two in the morning. This time it was not a nightmare but rather a suffocating sensation, the feeling of a huge dead-weight on her chest and lungs, accompanied by a lingering sense of some unspecified dread. The room was hot and stuffy, and she realized that she had again not opened her window before going to bed. Still, the aftereffects of that dreadful feeling clung to the edges of her consciousness like some night horror that was crouching behind her, remaining just out of her peripheral vision. Her face felt greasy with perspiration, and her mouth was dry. She swallowed a couple of times and then got up to find a bottle of water. She opened the window, and immediately a cool draft stirred the air by her legs.

She was getting a little tired of this. What was it about this place that gave her bad dreams and night sweats? She felt almost as if she had a hangover. Reluctantly wide-awake now, she threw on a robe and sandals and went down the hall to use the bathroom. She thought about going outside again but decided against it. Against the rules and a dumb idea besides. But the thought reminded her of the embarrassing scene that morning, when she had taken the hostel manager to the fire door to show him the piece of paper jammed in the bolt hole, only to discover it was gone. The manager, a fat man in his fifties, had given her one of those patronizing looks men reserve for semihysterical women while she insisted that the door had been blocked open the night before.

Now, as she headed for the stairs, she decided on the spur of the moment to check the door again. She stopped in front of it, ignored the operating handle, and gave the door a tentative push. To her amazement, it flopped open. Squashed into the bolt hole was another piece of wet paper. This time she pried the wad of paper out of the hole and reset the door lock. She unfolded the paper and found that it appeared to be a fragment torn from the hostel rules and regulation pamphlet.

Who the hell was doing this? Was someone leaving this door unlocked so that someone else could get in during the night? Two college kids, out for a lark at night? Thieves, perhaps, or, worse, hooded Palestinians bent on blood work? Then what had happened to the piece of paper that morning?

She went back to her room and tried to think it

through. The answer finally hit her like a bucket of cold water: The most likely explanation was that someone was leaving the hostel at night, secretly using the fire door, and coming back before morning. She knew in an instant who that someone had to be: the goddamned American.

Easy way to find out. Go and knock on his door. What if he was a sound sleeper? Knock louder. Beat the door down, if you have to. As she remembered, most of the German students were all up on the second floor with her, but not all, she realized. If he comes to the door? Tell him the truth; explain about the fire door.

She hesitated. What would the man think of this story, of her coming to his bedroom door at two-thirty in the morning with some wild tale about a piece of paper in the lock? She felt in her bathrobe pocket to make sure she still had the fragment. She almost couldn't bring herself to do it, until she remembered that man, that Colonel Skuratov, who had called her earlier. Checking up on the American. To whom she had lied. Why did he care? What the hell was going on here?

At that moment, she heard the noise of a vehicle laboring up the coast road. A truck or a van. The army. She remembered that the army conducted random night patrols all along the coast of the Dead Sea historical sites. Some of the soldiers had been complaining about the night treks when she chatted them up in the restaurant. She waited until she heard the engine slowing down as it came closer to the tourist center. Breathing a sigh of relief, she quickly got dressed and headed for the lobby to talk to the patrol leader.

Water? David rocked back on his heels. Water. The damn thing was full of water. Well, Einstein, you thought it might be a cistern, didn't you? So congratulations: You were right. But how in the hell . . . He wondered how long that water had been there. Since the Roman times? It was possible—the Romans would have found the smaller cistern on top, and its source of water would have been perfectly clear. There would have been no reason for them to suspect the much larger cistern underneath. He suddenly had this terrible feeling that Herod's builders had probably created the little cistern out of a grotto in the first place, never suspecting the presence of the bigger one underneath.

No, wait. Wrong. There was the slab.

So someone *had* found it, as evidenced by that ring. Which meant that Adrian's theory about something being hidden down there might still hold water. So to speak, he thought with a small grin. Who—the Zealots? King Herod? If it had been the Zealots, the secret would have died with them. He grew even more excited: This had been her premise all along. He looked at his watch. He was out of time. There was no way in hell that he was going to find out tonight.

Change of plan. *Big* change of plan: He would have to leave here tomorrow, no, make that today. Go back to Tel Aviv. Right on schedule. Tell his minders that he was going to spend the second week in the country as advertised, on his diving expedition to Caesarea Maritima. All finished with mighty Masada, pardon me, Metsadá, thank you very much. And scuba diving he would go, but not, as advertised, just down to Caesarea Maritima. Oh, yes, he would go through the motions for a couple of days, in case there were still watchers. Then, somehow, he would get back down here, only this time with his diving gear. For the dive of his life.

Time now to cover his tracks here. Using the poles, he reset the stone slab, slipping it sideways back into its opening. Then he used the sign to move all that sand back, smoothing it as best he could. He looked at his watch: Time to boogie, he thought.

He mounded a pile of the guano-laced sand right next to the entrance to deter any casual explorers who might come along. He buried the building stones, the harness, and the climbing wire under the sand for future use, then thrust his backpack, the sign, and the two steel pipes out of the entrance hole. He swept his tracks with a broken bush as he backed out of the hole. He rested for a moment in the chilly air outside, bathed now in bright moonlight. There was no looking away from the spectacular panorama almost a thousand feet below, the Dead Sea glittering in the moonlight, and the mysterious hollow hills of Jordan on the other side. From his perch outside the entrance to the cave, he could not see the tourist center, nor did he want to poke his head around that outcropping of rock. Leaving the sign, he gathered up the poles and his pack and headed up the slope to the eastern gate. Once inside the fortress he replaced the poles and then went back for the sign, which he used again to smooth out the line of his footprints that diverged from the Serpent Path toward the cistern. He replaced the sign by the Byzantine ruins, shouldered the back-pack, and then headed across the plateau toward the western gate.

An hour later he had reached the top of the western ravine and stopped to rest. It was now almost four. He thought he could afford about ten minutes here. The sides of the western ravine were brightly lit by the moon, leaving deep shadow along the bottom of the rocky gorge. Up here on the top, however, there was none of the cover he had enjoyed coming up. Every rock, stunted bush, and undulation in the gullies along the main ravine stood out in clear relief in the crystal-clear desert air. He sat on the back side of a sand dune that formed the intersection between the western and the southern ravines.

Coming up he had stayed in the bottom of the southern ravine in deep shadow. Now it didn't really matter, because in this moonlight there was no cover. He just had to hope that he wouldn't run into a patrol halfway down the ravine. He assumed the patrols would not walk down along the bottom. The military guys always favored high ground.

Like way up here, at the head of both ravines. He stopped breathing when he heard a small sound.

He turned his head slowly and found himself nearly surrounded by ten motionless figures wearing gray desert camouflage uniforms, their helmeted faces in shadow in the bright moonlight, but the glinting muzzles of their submachine guns astonishingly visible. One of the men lifted his night-vision visor up onto his forehead.

"American," he ordered. "You come."

"No problem," David said in a weak voice, his heart sinking even as his hands were going up in the air. La Ressner was going to be seriously pissed.

David breakfasted in splendid isolation that morning while enduring uniformly hostile looks from the hostel staff. Apparently everyone knew, and after the angry confrontation with Judith in the parking lot an hour before dawn he did not expect her to join him for the familiar cup of coffee.

Once back in the parking lot, the army guys had actually seemed underwhelmed by the enormity of his crime. With Ressner standing mutely to one side, the sergeant appeared to be mostly irritated by the stupidity of some American tourist's trekking around the Judaean hills in the middle of the night. If we had just collided we might have shot you, he had pointed out. We don't ask questions out there in the night, you know? It was only luck that Dr. Ressner here had come down and told us you might be sneaking out at night, so in fact we went looking for you. What if you had fallen in one of the ravines, or been bitten by a snake? Who would have found you then? That's what the rules are for, to keep you safe, eh? More along that line. Lots more.

David had been studiously contrite and extremely earnest in his assurances that he wouldn't do it again. One of the soldiers had said something in Hebrew, and the sergeant asked him what was in the backpack. David had quickly opened the pack and shown them the bottle of water, the flashlight, and the jacket, assuring them again that he had only wanted to go up there at night, to see what it was like.

The sergeant appeared to be getting progressively bored with it all and kept looking at his watch as if they still had a long trek ahead of them, which would be in hot daylight now, thanks to this idiot. He made a production of lighting up a cigarette and chewed David out some more, but with diminishing enthusiasm, and then they had grouped up and headed back up the ravine, leaving him to the not-so-tender mercies of Judith Ressner.

They faced off in the empty parking lot. From the look on her face, David had decided very quickly that a proactive defense was probably the best defense.

"I trusted you," she began, visibly controlling her temper.

"Now wait a minute," he interrupted. "I haven't done anything wrong. Stupid, maybe, but it's not like I was up there digging for buried treasure or something. I just needed to go up there, at night, without the tourists. To imagine what it was like. To imagine the fire lights of the Roman camps all around the mountain. To wander among the ruins, seeing them as the palaces they once were. It's beautiful. Sad but beautiful."

"It is not allowed," she replied. "It is not *safe*. Don't you understand? If something had happened to you they would have come after *me*. I will have to report this, you know. To the institute. I could lose my job. I don't suppose that crossed your mind at all?"

"I am sorry. I think they will blame me for

taking off in the night, though, not you. You can't be everywhere, twenty-four seven. I didn't go down anywhere dangerous, like the northern terraces. Just on the top. Remember, it's what I came here to do."

She rolled her eyes. "So this is what you mean by, what was your phrase, 'going for it'? Regardless of any consequences?"

He had felt a flush of embarrassment cross his face. His fine words on the beach sounded hollow, coming back like this.

"Tell me something," he said, scrambling for cover. "Did you never do that, when you were down here on one of the digs?"

She had tossed her head and groaned in exasperation, but then she had turned her face away, as if he'd uncovered a painful memory. "Yes," she sighed impatiently, "but not by myself, and not without someone knowing I was up there. What you did was foolish *and* an affront to our hospitality."

He had stared down at his feet. "Well, again I apologize. It's just that there was no way I could capture the spirit of that place during the day, not with all those half-dressed girls cavorting all over the place. Kids on a lark where nearly a thousand people committed suicide. It's what I really came here for, Judith. I'm done now. We can leave in the morning. I guess I mean today."

She had fixed him with a steady stare. He

couldn't tell if she believed him or was still trying to pick a hole in what he was saying.

"Yes," she said at last. "You are done here. We will leave at nine this morning, after I have had a little talk with the center manager—and, of course, after I make some phone calls to the authorities in Jerusalem."

"I understand. I didn't take anything, though. No souvenirs, no bits of rock, nothing. I just looked. Do you want to search my pack? My room?" She was obviously taking this personally, and he was feeling rotten about that. The look she was giving him confirmed it. She was really angry with him: She had trusted him, opened up to him, and he had gone sneaking around behind her back at night. Finally she turned away.

"Nine o'clock, Mr. Hall," she said over her shoulder. "Be prompt, please." Then she had stomped away, back into the tourist center, leaving him standing in the parking lot. As he watched her go, he felt the first inklings of real regret. It was more than the fact that she had trusted him. She had made the first tentative moves back toward life, something she probably needed very much to do. He might have inadvertently sabotaged that.

Now, waiting in the cafeteria, he stared up at the mountain basking indifferently in the early morning sunlight and thought about that giant cistern. Full of water! He had just assumed it would be bone dry, like the rest of them, but this one did not depend on the wadis or man-made dams. This one depended only on rain, twenty *centuries* of rain. He wondered again how old that water was. Once the cistern had filled, everything else would have sluiced off through the bat cave and down the hillside.

Thank God I brought the diving gear. What had been part of his cover story was now going to be the main event. If they don't throw your ass out of the country first, he reminded himself. He kind of doubted that they would, not for just walking around. If they had caught him up there in the cistern, he might be headed for an Israeli courtroom, but sneaking out of the hostel, walking around the wilderness at night, was, as the sergeant had pointed out, more an issue of stupidity than criminal trespass.

Fortunately, he had his dive expedition reservations all set up. What he had to do now was some detailed planning and forget about the lovely Ressner. That should be easy enough, he thought, remembering her final acid look in the parking lot.

Judith called in to the institute at eight-thirty, this time from inside the manager's office, courtesy of one of the cafeteria workers. The manager did not normally come down from Jerusalem until nine. She had explained the problem to the chairman's assistant, who promised to relay the story to Himself, as the chairman was known to his staff. Judith had the impression that the assistant was not as upset about the American's nocturnal walkabout as she was. She hung up, thought about calling Ellerstein, but then realized he would hear about it from the chairman's office soon enough. She went upstairs to throw her things together.

While she was packing, she remembered Colonel Skuratov. Her heart sank. The chairman and the rest of the academics might frown on what the American had done, but the security officer would be another problem. She could just see the fanatical gleam in that scary old Russian's eye. In a way, though, his instincts had been correct: The American obviously had planned to go out at night right from the start, as the pieces of paper in the fire door lock proved. The late afternoon meal and then a "nap." She had made a big deal out there in the parking lot about one night up on the mountain, but now she realized that he had probably been up there twice. *Damn* the man. Damn all Americans!

She fished around in her briefcase and found the card. International Planning Division, Ministry of the Interior. M. L. Skuratov. No Colonel. No hint of the security world. Planning indeed. Just another government phone number. She went back down to the office. She still had about ten minutes before the manager showed up.

"International Planning," a man's voice answered in Hebrew.

"I need to speak to Colonel Skuratov."

"He is not available. Your name and message, please?"

She hesitated. "This is Dr. Yehudit Ressner. He will know the name."

"Yes, Doctor? The message, please?"

"Tell him the American went out at night on his own. To the site. Probably twice. An army patrol found him this morning coming back along the Wadi Metsadá. We are leaving the site for Tel Aviv this morning."

There was a minute of silence.

"I have it. Where can he reach you tomorrow night?"

"Tomorrow night?"

"Yes. He will be unavailable until then."

"At home." She gave him the number, dreading the fact that she wasn't finished with the colonel. Wonderful. *Damned* American.

"Thank you, Doctor." The connection was broken. She was left standing there, the phone in her hand, when the fat manager came bustling through the door and started to upbraid her about being in the office.

"Oh, sod off," she hissed at him in Hebrew and stamped out of the office, leaving him speechless.

15

On Saturday morning David awoke back in his hotel room to the sounds of maid service carts rattling down the hallway. He opened one eye and looked at his watch. Well, maybe no longer morning. It was just noon. He got up and went over to the windows and pulled back the night curtain, revealing a bright, sunny day.

He frowned as he recalled the Friday morning ride back from Masada. Judith had treated him to a frosty silence for the entire trip, meeting his two weak attempts at conversation with curt, monosyllabic replies. When they arrived at the hotel she had turned in her seat. "I have called Professor Strauss with respect to your nocturnal excursions at Metsadá. Both of them, yes? The committee will meet on Sunday to discuss what actions they might take. They will also inform the Israel Antiquities Authority."

"Beyond unauthorized walking about the site at night, what's the charge, Officer?" he had asked, trying to keep it light.

"Charge? You misrepresented yourself and the true nature of your so-called project. The government made special accommodation for you, and you took advantage of them. Us. The IAA may not take that as lightly as you do, Mr. Hall."

Her expression and tone of voice revealed that

the "us" was just as angry with him as the government might be. Misrepresented myself, he had thought. Jesus. If they only knew.

"Well, again I apologize," he said, "but I did no real harm up there. Hell, you let me wander around up there unattended all day on Thursday."

"That was different. The security staff was in place. There were people about. If something had happened to you, there would have been help available. But to be wandering around out in the wadis at night, climbing that ramp, even walking the casemate walls in the dark—there are no railings, remember? Four hundred meters straight down? And that patrol: You were very, very lucky there."

"So what's next?" he replied, tiring of the harangue, trying hard to ignore the ass-kicking his conscience was all too ready to hand him.

"That will be up to the committee and the IAA. I suspect that if you want to play tourist next week, they will not object, as long as you are supervised by an approved tour operator. However, you are no longer welcome in official Israel, Mr. Hall."

He had tried to think of some smart reply, couldn't, and just nodded instead. He got out of the car and grabbed his gear from the backseat and put it down on the sidewalk. He stuck his head back into the car window.

"Well, so long, Mrs. Ressner. Despite the way it

ended, it was still a pleasure to know you. Good luck with the rest of your life."

He frowned now as he remembered the vexed expression that crossed her face when he made that last comment. Shit. Well, remember what you're here for, he reminded himself, for the umpteenth time. Focus. Think about this: If they were pissed at your taking a walk at night, they'll go positively ape-shit when they find out what you're planning next. They damn well better *not* find out about that.

That thought led to the consideration of next moves: If he was lucky, they would not throw him out of the country. They would check the site to be sure there were no signs of digging or missing artifacts. They might detect the missing building stones, but he doubted it. He also doubted they would go down into the rim cisterns: Nobody had been in there but the bats for a long time. Besides, as far as the archaeologists were concerned, the cisterns were all just dry holes. Hell, that reeking pile of bat guano he had put by the cave entrance ought to do the trick if nothing else.

On the other hand, after this "incident," whoever had sent the watcher at the airport might just keep him under surveillance here in Tel Aviv for a couple of days. Just to make sure. The Ministry of the Interior owned the archaeological sites, through the Israel Antiquities Authority. The ministry probably had ties to state security organizations. He thought about the guy in the airport. Maybe he was overdoing this—it was more likely that the guy in the airport was just another layer of airport security.

So: Today he would hole up, recovering his energy after the busy nights down on the mountain. Saturday meant Shabbat until sunset, so the country was essentially shut down anyway. Sunday things would be open again. He had his hired car and Ari turned back on, starting tomorrow. He would go over to Yafo Sunday morning to the dive shop and get set up for the expedition to Caesarea Maritima. Monday he would go make the first tour dive. Monday afternoon, he would drive around, see some other sites, and watch his back. He needed to convince any watchers that he had reverted to being boy tourist, going diving up on the coast in the mornings and touring the historical sites in the afternoons. No longer interested in things archaeological, and certainly not in Masada.

He would also spend some time here at the hotel, ostensibly transcribing notes from his trip down to the fortress. If they were really mad at him and got, say Shabak into it, they might even search his room. He should probably provide opportunities for anyone who might be interested to take a look into his computer. After recording the dimensions of the hidden cave in an other-wise innocuous file, he had erased all the seismic data files and even the program that computed the display. He would make a bunch of notes in a clearly labeled directory and then leave the computer unattended in the room. Just for the hell of it, he decided to activate a counter routine in the boot files that would tell him if the machine had been turned on in his absence. He would trash the four geophones, the data concentrator, and the wire today, which would eliminate all physical traces of the seismic survey. The devices were excess baggage now that he had confirmed there was another cistern and had found the way into it.

His diving gear, which now he needed in earnest, would also be on prominent display. Well, he was going to do some diving, right? Assuming he was going to be watched, the trick was to live the cover story, building up a pile of evidence to support it. From years of reading cloak-and-dagger books, he knew that if one wanted to get out from under a surveillance operation, the best way was to ensure that the watchers' logbooks became filled with perfectly ordinary entries. The objective was to shape the outcome of the meeting at which the watchers decide whether or not to continue the surveillance: the cost of overtime personnel versus what the surveillance reports were indicating. Give them nothing out of character to hang their hats on. Theories were theories; budgets were real. Get them to say the hell with it and go on to something else.

Then, of course, the hard part: deciding when the surveillance had been called off, so he could make his move. Two days? Three days? Assuming someone even gave a damn about David Hall, scuba tourist. He might be wrong about this, but better safe than sorry, considering the magnitude of what he was planning next.

He went back in to shower, shave, and mentally massage his new plan. He would arrange three days of dives, starting Monday. While playing tourist, he would surreptitiously arrange to rent a four-wheel-drive vehicle and some basic camping gear. Tuesday, same routine: morning dive, tourist ops in the afternoon. On Wednesday he would call into the dive shop, tell them he wasn't feeling well. Cancel Wednesday's dive. He would collect the rental car and his gear at midday and then make a late afternoon trip back down the Dead Sea road to the vicinity of the mountain. His objective would be to avoid detection long enough to get himself in position to make one more night expedition to the fortress. He would need to set up a base of operations. Maybe use the rim cistern itself?

The logistics would be daunting. He needed to think about that aspect some more. Humping all that heavy diving gear up the mountain would be really hard, not to mention evading the damn patrols. That sergeant had probably had *his* ass chewed for not catching him the first time, although thankfully no one had asked him if there had been a first time. Judith had figured it out, though, hadn't she?

Then there would be the matter of actually making the dive. The thought of that one curled his hair a little bit. He would be breaking every fundamental rule of diving: You never go down at night; you never go down alone or at least without surface backup; you never go into something without having the first damned idea of what's down there—how big it really is, how deep, what the water temperature is . . . all fundamental stuff. It would also be cave diving, the most dangerous kind of diving. He'd read books about it, and at the end of each one he'd sworn he'd never even try that.

As he stood in the shower, his better sense was fairly shouting at him not to go through with this harebrained plan. He should call Judith, tell her what he'd really been doing and what he'd discovered. She might not believe it, but once she told the archaeology world what he'd found, especially the slab, someone would mount a proper expedition.

He took a deep breath and then put off making his decision. Right now, it was time to get into character as an innocent tourist. He wondered what Adrian would have thought of all this. He could almost hear her: *Go for it!*

Judith was attending to her laundry when Professor Ellerstein called Saturday evening. Half expecting Skuratov, she had almost not picked up the phone. Hearing Ellerstein's avuncular voice was a relief.

"Yehudit, how are you?" Ellerstein began, his voice solicitous. No hint of condemnation.

"I'm back, Yossi. I suppose you've heard what happened down there?"

"I have indeed. Armin Strauss called me. It seems we now have to have a meeting tomorrow. As much as I love meetings, I can hardly wait."

"What are they saying?"

"*They?* Himself wrings his hands, as is his custom. The IAA is waiting for the security people at Metsadá to verify that no harm was done."

"I think that will come out all right," she said, trying to keep a hopeful tone out of her voice. The American better not have been digging. "They took a quick look around for me Friday morning. Nothing seems to have been disturbed."

"Yes, that is what Strauss reported. That you felt the man really was just wandering around up there, communing with the spirits, exactly as he said he wanted to do. I think this is not all that serious. The man probably simply succumbed to the mystery of the place."

She hesitated for a moment. "I'm not sure Colonel Skuratov will see it that way."

This time it was Ellerstein who hesitated. "Colonel Skuratov? Who is this Colonel Skuratov? How is he involved with this matter?"

"He is someone important in the military security services at Dimona. He came to see me the night before we left for Metsadá. He told me that the IDF was concerned about what this American was doing, going down there."

Ellerstein cleared his throat. "Oh, yes. I think I remember him. Odd-looking Russian. Some extreme history there. But Dimona? What on earth—"

"Yes, I had the same question. All he said was that they wanted me to watch this American for them."

"*Them?* What them? You mean Shin Bet? Why would they care?"

"I have no idea, Yossi," she said. "I—I had met this Skuratov before. He was one of the people from Dimona who came along the night they told me Dov had been killed. He is . . . memorable."

"Yes, that's the one. I remember now: The military cops called him Colonel Lazarus. A Russian Jew. They say that thirty years ago he escaped out of the Gulag and managed to walk out into Turkey. In the dead of winter. So *he* was interested in our Mr. Hall?"

"He came here to tell me to keep a good eye on him. Some good eye, hunh?"

"Does he know what happened?"

"I called his office yesterday morning, after calling the chairman. He had given me his card and asked me—well, ordered me, actually—to call if anything went out of the ordinary. I left a message. I assume he knows by now. I'm expecting his call." Judith found herself looking out the window for that big black car. "I can hardly wait."

"Yehudit, don't worry about it," Ellerstein said quickly. "These security people poke their noses into everything. You did what was expected of you. Don't let this man browbeat you. It's not as if you work for him. Forget about it. He calls, gives you grief, you tell him to call Strauss. You don't work for those people."

"Okay, Yossi. I'm glad you called. Now: What happens Monday?"

"That is a separate issue, Yehudit. Despite what happened down there. You can rest assured that what the American did has no bearing on that discussion. I trust you took some time to do a little soul searching?"

"Yes, I did. Believe it or not, Mr. Hall and I even discussed it. He offered to serve as a neutral sounding board. As he pointed out, he had no stake in the outcome. He was a good sounding board, actually. Americans. They are so damned . . . direct."

"Ah."

"Ah?"

"Your anger about his little adventure makes more sense now. You began to trust him a little, yes? Enough to talk to him, to talk about yourself. Then he deceived you."

A long silence. "Yes, I suppose that's partly true."

"Let me change the subject a bit, back to Metsadá. What parts of the site did he seem most interested in?"

She had to reflect for a moment. "Parts? No one part, really. He found the whole thing of interest. As I told the chairman's office, he spent one day up there by himself. The guards said he wandered all over the place, taking some notes, but not doing anything out of the ordinary. Although—"

"Yes?"

"One guy said he appeared to be surveying the middle ground. Between the western palace and the eastern gate."

"Surveying?"

"Well, sort of measuring it. Pacing it off. Of course, there is nothing there. Only empty space between the major ruins."

"I see," Ellerstein said.

"You do?"

"Well, no, not really. I mean, that doesn't sound significant, does it. Who knows what he was thinking. Is he going home now?"

"No, he's going diving, at Caesarea. Underwater tours."

"Yes, okay, that's good. All done with Metsadá. Well: Back to Monday. I think there is a way you might be able to short-circuit that whole problem. I mean, by taking the initiative right at the beginning."

"What: Confess my sins? Rend garments? Offer to anoint some feet?"

"Not sins, Yehudit," he replied, gently ignoring her sarcasm, "but perhaps explain that you realize that you've been wrapped in the widow's shawl for too long. That you have thought the matter over, that you will work on coming out of your shell. That you will perhaps seek some professional counseling. That you will agree to engage in some collegial projects again."

"Why should I offer to do these things?"

"Listen to you," he said, laughing. "Have you forgotten your academic politics?"

"I don't understand."

"Because, if you can do this, you will take the pressure off the chairman. *You* will have raised the problem, instead of making him do it. *You* will propose the solution, the measures that must be taken. This relieves them from having to do *anything*."

He was silent for a moment, and Judith saw the logic. No academic ever wanted to "do something" when it came to personnel issues.

"Then all they have to do is nod their heads enthusiastically, talk supportively. Talk, not act.

These are academic bureaucrats, yes? Solve their problem for them, Yehudit, and all this talk of termination goes away."

"These sound like terms, Yossi."

This time it was Ellerstein who said nothing, letting his silence do the talking.

"Okay," she sighed. "I get the picture. Actually, I think I *can* say all those things. I have no idea if any of it will work, but I think I am ready to change course. Or at least try."

"That's wonderful, Yehudit. It sounds to me like talking to the American must have been therapeutic."

"I suppose," she sniffed.

"Ah, yes, well, one step at a time. I have to go now. Oh, one last question. Please forgive the further intrusion."

"Yes?" Now what?

"Will you be seeing the American again?"

"I should think not!"

"Right. As I said, forgive—"

"Now who's being a nosy old man, Yosef Ellerstein?"

"Just so, Yehudit. Shalom Shabbat. And don't let that Skuratov guy get to you."

She hung up the phone, but not without a small smile. A nosy old man, indeed, but with a good heart. Yosef Ellerstein had been a valuable contact at the IAA, and she had sought his advice even before that. An American transplant, he had an amazing network of friends in academia and in the government, and a tremendous reservoir of political wisdom to share. She had thought at first that he might be interested in her as a woman, although he was very much older, but he had never directly shown it if he was. He lived alone, and even though he was not an archaeologist, he was a leading light in the currently very disputatious field of the origins and ownership of the Dead Sea Scrolls. Right now he would undoubtedly be calling the chairman back to relay the message. You can relax, Armin. The Ressner will play ball. The meeting Monday should now be pro forma.

She felt relieved as she gathered up the clothes basket. But then you'll have to go through with it, you know, she thought. She stared out the kitchen window at the white brick wall of the building next door. Like a blank sheet of paper. A good metaphor for the rest of her life, perhaps? Well, maybe it *is* about time, she thought. She looked around the apartment. You know what? I'm going to move house. I'm going to find somewhere new to live. New life, new house. Maybe get out of Jerusalem with its crowds and tension. Money was not that big a problem. Maybe she would go back to the Carmel. Buy a real house this time, with a garden. A place for what—solitude? No. That way lay madness.

From now on she would have to avoid solitude.

Joining group projects, as Ellerstein had suggested, would be one way. She hated group efforts, feeling that the product too often was only as good as the least intelligent voting participant, but she could understand how that attitude probably infuriated her colleagues. Beyond that, she knew the hard part would come when, by her new behavior, another signal went out to the community of men at large. That she was socially available. Back in the marketplace. A new loaf of bread in the window. Well, maybe not so new, but still, like some kind of commodity. She knew already how some of her compatriots on the faculty, the so-called Shot-downs, would react to that news. She wondered if she could still attract a man beyond the allure of her physical looks, to the point of having a relationship. She shook her head. She recognized that her heart was not yet in this transformation project. I'm just going through the motions, and anyone who gets close will realize that. That will keep me safe.

Except that Mr. David Hall had been attracted. At least she was pretty sure he had. She'd kept him at definite arm's length, and yet he had persisted. Even yesterday, in the car.

She took the laundry basket into her bedroom and began to put away the clean clothes. Her enforced solitude had kept Dov too much alive for her to just go out with the first man who asked her. She sensed that David Hall had been ready to ask her, but even as she thought about that, she felt another flare of anger at his deception.

Then again, was it really such a big deal? He was, after all, an American, a man with money, a nuclear engineer, and someone used to a little bigger picture than the million pettifogging rules and regulations of tiny Israel. He probably felt they were all being a little bit ridiculous. Masada had survived the physical ravages of twenty centuries of sitting totally exposed under the relentless sun of the Judaean desert. What did it matter if one man took a walk at night, among the stones and the bones, as he put it. Even old Ellerstein had picked up on it: *Will you be seeing him again?* There was no way, of course. Not after what had happened, and especially after the very cold shoulder she had given him on the way back. Which he richly deserved. She finished putting away the laundry and then went to make a sandwich and to ponder the prospect of starting life over again.

She dismissed all thoughts of Colonel Skuratov.

Ellerstein hung up the phone and reached for his private phone book. He found the special number and dialed it. A man's voice answered after one ring.

"Israel Gulder's office; may I help you?"

"This is Ellerstein."

"Yes, Professor."

"Tell him I have spoken to Yehudit Ressner. There is nothing to worry about. The American is harmless."

"He has been told there was a problem. Some unauthorized excursions."

"It was no more than what the American said he came here for. To go up there and be alone with the spirit of the place. Unless they report something missing or disturbed, I think it was nothing. However, there is one discordant note."

"Which is?"

"I have found out that a Colonel Skuratov, supposedly of the Dimona laboratories, came to see Ressner before she went down to the site."

There was a silence, and Ellerstein gave the man time to take his notes. "Yes, go on?"

"He told her the IDF was concerned about this American. Gave her a lecture on the sanctity of Metsadá. Asked her to keep close watch on him. Gave her a card, asking—no, ordering—her to call him if anything went astray. Which, in a manner of speaking, it did."

Another moment of silence. "I have that. Did she call him?"

"She says she did. Left a message. He hasn't contacted her, and the thing's blowing over anyway. The American is supposedly going diving at Caesarea. Still, for what it's worth . . ."

"I have it. Anything else?"

"I can't think of anything. I'm going to assume

we're done with this thing, unless I hear otherwise. Will he want to talk to me tonight?"

"I couldn't say, Professor."

The man hung up, as did Ellerstein. He sat at his desk for a few minutes, wondering if indeed the American was harmless. Yehudit had sounded angry, or, more likely, a little bit hurt, which meant that they had struck a personal spark of some kind. He frowned when he realized that he had hoped they might do just that. The American had better not be playing games, especially with Yehudit's heart. This was a terribly vulnerable time for her, a fact of which this American oaf was probably unaware.

The man had wanted to conduct a vigil up there at night. That was perfectly understandable. Ellerstein had done the same thing as a young army officer candidate, and the majestic tragedy of what had happened there made the vigil a soul-stirring experience. He didn't know what this Skuratov's problem was with Masada, but he did not want the Russian picking on Yehudit. He shook his head. Skuratov was probably Shin Bet, and they were all anal-retentive nitwits. He looked up the chairman's number to give him the good news about Monday's meeting. As he was about to place the call to leave his message, the phone rang.

"Shalom," he intoned. "This is Ellerstein."

It was the voice from Gulder's office. "He wants

to see you. Right now would be nice. We're sending a car."

An hour later Ellerstein was waiting in Gulder's outer office, on the first floor of the Knesset building in the government district known as Hakirya. There was a surprising number of people coming and going in the prime minister's executive office suite, especially so soon after the conclusion of Shabbat. These were anxious times, he supposed. He'd been given a cup of coffee and a place to wait but had not yet seen Gulder.

"Professor? Come with me, please?" A lovely young woman was standing in the doorway, indicating he should go with her. Anywhere, he thought.

They went down a tastefully decorated hall, past offices where middle-aged men in short-sleeved shirts were talking softly on their phones. At last they came to another, even fancier reception area, where Ellerstein saw armed guards. Gulder was waiting and took him into the prime minister's office.

Once Ellerstein got over his surprise at being invited into the PM's office, he took a look around. The PM sat behind his desk, looking tired. He got up to shake hands with him and then indicated that he and Gulder should sit down. The beautiful young lady closed the double doors and left them in privacy.

"So, Professor Ellerstein," the PM said. "You

have been a consultant to Shabak for how long now?"

"Too many years, Prime Minister," Ellerstein replied, thinking back to his days as an undercover agent at Dimona.

"Israel Gulder here tells me that you are one of the best we have. That you are the soul of discretion, unencumbered by a wife or children, and therefore in a unique position to help us with a truly serious problem."

"I am ready to try, Prime Minister," Ellerstein said, somewhat apprehensively. Shabak was Israel's loose counterpart to the American FBI, an internal security investigative service that was aimed more at protecting the state from criminal operations than at gaining foreign intelligence, which was the role of Mossad. Shabak had regular, full-time agents and also a corps of so-called consultants, professional men and women, lawyers, doctors, professors, scientists, financiers, in strategic niches of Israeli society whose attachment to Shabak was a secret, and who could be called upon from time to time to help out with narrowly focused inquiries. Many of the consultants were foreigners who had made aliyah, or immigrated to Israel. The organization liked to recruit these people early on, when their patriotic fervor was at its height, and also because native-born Israelis tended to have a healthy disrespect for the numerous Israeli security organs. Ellerstein had been recruited while still a mathematician at Dimona, to penetrate the anti-nuclear-weapons faction calling itself LaBaG, where, in fact, he had first encountered the Ressners.

The PM sighed. "Good," he said. "We are grateful. Our little country is beset these days, by both friends and enemies, it seems. The Americans pressure us to make peace with people who really want war. The Iranians are centrifuging uranium hexafluoride twenty-four hours a day. Hezbollah stockpiles rockets, while helping Syria destabilize the Lebanon, again. Hamas is dabbling in nerve gas, with the help of those same European nations demanding we make peace. And I, of course, have one or two political problems of my own in the Knesset, yes?"

Ellerstein matched the PM's tired smile with one of his own. He did not know how or why these politicians did it. They were just driven, he supposed.

"However, those are not the problems we want your help on, Professor Ellerstein, and what I'm about to tell you is most secret. It is doubly most secret if it's true, but still most secret even if it's false, because the idea itself is a very dangerous idea. Am I making sense here?"

"No, sir," Ellerstein said.

The PM barked a laugh. Not too many people would say that to his face, apparently, Ellerstein thought. Gulder was looking hard at his shoes.

"Just so. Of course I'm not. Well: Here goes, then. Israel, *you* tell him."

Gulder cleared his throat. "You will recall my telling you that our interest in Judith Ressner was related to a serious problem, yes?"

Ellerstein nodded, remembering. In the restaurant.

"Well, here it is: There are rumors, the barest straws in the wind, mind you, that there is a small group of people who are calling themselves the Kanna'im, the Zealots."

"The Zealots? As in Metsadá?"

"Yes, just like that. They apparently believe that the government is getting close to giving away the store, as the Americans put it. That we are making too many concessions to the Arab side. That we, the government, are selling out our nation's security to the Americans, in return for their aid money, with which we buy votes. That the very existence of Israel has been called into question by the attitude of this new American president, who favors the Muslim side and who may even be a Muslim himself. That we, the government, have become far too accommodating."

"There are many people in Israel today who think those things," Ellerstein said. "Perhaps not in such strong terms, but—" He shrugged.

Gulder's face went red. Ellerstein looked back at the PM, who was giving him an exasperated look. He realized he might have overstepped the bounds of propriety, but it was true. People did think that. Hell, *he* thought that. He sidestepped. "These latter-day Kanna'im—they are military?" he asked. "They plan what, a coup?"

He saw the PM shake his head. Gulder said no, then looked over at the PM as if to ask how far he should go with this. The PM nodded.

"The group is inside Dimona. We think they may have engaged in the diversion of nuclear materials. What material, and to whom, we do not know."

"My God."

"Exactly," the PM said, "and to answer your question, we do think there are military people involved, and perhaps even scientists."

Ellerstein started to say something, but then the enormity of it sank in: Dimona. He took a deep breath and let it out slowly. There would *have* to be scientists involved. He could fully understand military types embracing the Zealot myth, but for a scientist to do it was something very new. "For how long?" he asked.

"Good question," Gulder said, "and the answer is: We don't know. This is supposedly a very small group, which makes things really tough. We do have one name. Unfortunately it is some kind of a code name. It is Lazarus."

They both looked at him to see if he would recognize who they were talking about. He did not. Then he remembered: Skuratov, the skull-faced Russian. Colonel Lazarus. Head of security at Dimona, who had paid a call on Judith Ressner.

"Colonel Skuratov," Ellerstein said quietly. "Head of security—"

"At Dimona," Gulder finished for him.

"Yes," Ellerstein said. "At Dimona."

Gulder nodded at him and fished a folder out of his briefcase. "I have a snapshot biography right here. Let me read you some excerpts." He pushed his glasses back up on his nose and read out loud. "Malyuta Lukyanovitch Skuratov. Probably an assumed name. Born in the former Soviet Union, trained as a physicist, and worked in the Russian atomic energy program until his aberrant political views attracted the attention of the KGB. Defiance at an interrogation and the fact that his mother was a suspected Jew brought him banishment to the Gulag. Served sixteen years at hard labor in a coal mine before making an incredible dead-of-winter escape out of Russia through the Caucasus Mountains. He survived this ordeal, but at the cost of having his face, feet, and hands badly frostbitten. Picked up by the Turkish Army border patrol. They promptly threw him in jail as a Russian spy, and it was not for another year that he was able to win his freedom and emigrate to Israel as part of a spy-swap exchange between our government and Turkey. After nearly a year in physical rehabilitation, Skuratov was invited into our weapons program at Dimona."

Ellerstein remembered something. He had

actually met the Russian by chance, at one of the small outdoor Sunday chess clubs in Beersheba, where some of the scientists working at Dimona lived. Like many of them he often frequented such informal clubs for intellectual companionship that was untainted by laboratory politics. The older Russian with the hideous face and black-gloved hands had established a fearsome reputation for something approaching grand-master-level play, and Ellerstein, much younger then, had tried him on. The Russian swiftly defeated him in four straight games, but then Ellerstein managed to check the fifth game into a draw. The Russian had given him a wintry smile and made some comment about persistence being worth ten times its weight in intelligence.

"After two years, it became apparent that Skuratov had been imprisoned too long to be of much use in the swiftly evolving world of nuclear physics. His training as a nuclear physicist, however, made him a technically qualified counterintelligence officer, and he was picked up by Shin Bet. As the PM has indicated, he is now head of the Dimona Shin Bet office."

"How old is he now?" Ellerstein asked.

Gulder consulted the file. "He is sixty-eight years old this month but apparently looks closer to eighty. He's never really recovered from the years of hard labor, malnutrition, and illness in the Soviet slave-labor system. His Shin Bet personnel file states that he has what the Americans call black-lung disease from the coal mines. He is also suffering from arthritis, severe loss of hearing, rising glaucoma in both eyes, a malformed knee joint from a rock fall during his escape into Turkey, ice-maimed hands, and the loss of all but ten of his original teeth. Recently he has been flying to a cancer clinic over in Cyprus once a week."

"And this is one of the conspirators?" Ellerstein asked, wondering why they were worried. The man sounded like walking death.

"What he lacks in physical capacity he apparently more than makes up for in nationalistic ardor. Let me quote you what he told one of our people: 'This country has gone soft since the Americans smashed Saddam Hussein's armies. Israel used to be serious about internal security. Now we act like little lambs. We make *peace* with the likes of that rat-faced, syphilitic Palestinian cur. We release known terrorists from our prisons by the hundreds while scabrous Arab teenagers bomb our school buses in broad daylight. While Shiite Iranian dogs in Lebanon send Katyusha rockets into the kibbutzim by night. And the goddamned preaching Americans, always coming over here, sending *women* to speak to us, bleating *peace, peace, negotiate, negotiate.* Soon we will fall like the Soviet Union fell, because we've stopped paying attention, while fat-choked

Americans overwhelm us with hamburgers, cell phones, television, Coca-Cola, filthy Hollywood movies, their hideous rock and roll, and computer game arcades. The Soviet Union collapsed like a rotten cabbage under this assault, and so shall we.' And more to that effect. Much more." Gulder closed the file.

"An old security fanatic, Professor," the PM said softly. "Living on borrowed time. A man with perhaps little to lose. A man who misses his homeland more than he recognizes. The Russian in him coming out of its cave one last time, yes?"

"This is something we *know?*" Ellerstein asked. "That he's involved in some scheme to what, steal bombs?"

The PM looked at Gulder, who cleared his throat. "What we know and what we suspect are intertwined, Yossi. But since it is our intention to put you onto Skuratov, the less you know about what *we* might know, the better, hah?"

Ellerstein thought about that one. How on earth could he watch a man like Skuratov? The other way around made more sense. Gulder was one step ahead of him.

"There's no way you can achieve surveillance on the head of security at Dimona. We know that. We want you to stay close to Judith Ressner, because we think there's something going on, some connection. Skuratov has put surveillance on Ressner *and* the American, who is now back in

Tel Aviv. All we're asking you to do is to keep tabs on Ressner, especially if she and that American get together."

"That's not very likely," Ellerstein said. "She's mad at him. He deceived her."

"Well and good. This is a precautionary step, then. Still, the army guards at Metsadá said they took long walks together. So: If they do get together while he's still here, and Skuratov is watching them, there must be a reason for that, and *that's* what we're interested in, okay?"

"No active measures, then?"

"Absolutely not. We have Shabak regulars available when the time comes. *If* the time comes. Skuratov has been interested in the visiting American since he arrived. An American nuclear engineer. Coincidence? Do you know what the American did back in Washington?"

"He said he'd been a whistle-blower."

"Yes, he was. He exposed a quiet little business deal that a certain country close to all our hearts had going with the American conglomerate that operates half the power plants in the United States."

"What kind of business deal?"

"It had to do with heavy water," Gulder said. He looked at Ellerstein to see if he understood.

"Heavy water?" Ellerstein said. "Why would that be a big deal?"

"Think back to your own days at the laboratories," Gulder said. "What do you do with heavy water at a place like Dimona?"

"Well, it's a moderator, for one thing. Keeps neutrons in the can when you're trying to maintain criticality. And then, oh—"

"Oh, indeed," Gulder said. "The other use. The reason why all those Western nonproliferation agencies watch it like a hawk. Why some of the American agencies think that Iran is closer to a bomb than anyone guessed."

Ellerstein nodded slowly. You could make tritium out of heavy water. Tritium was a substance that helped turn an A-bomb into an H-bomb, among other things. The Iranians might be using heavy water in just their reactor process, but if they already had a bomb, then their active quest for heavy water on the black arms market had an altogether more sinister significance.

"Is *that* why Skuratov is watching the American?" Ellerstein asked. "Because of his involvement in a proliferation exposé?"

They both looked at him expectantly until he figured it out. "Ah," he said. "It was Israel who was buying. And now he's here."

The PM smiled at him like an approving schoolmaster.

"How does Ressner fit into all this?" Ellerstein asked.

"We have no fucking idea, Yossi," Gulder said. "Skuratov is watching them both; we're watching

Skuratov. By happenstance, you are close to Ressner. That's all there is to it."

I doubt that very much, Ellerstein thought, but to hear this from the PM himself . . . Well. The matter must be serious indeed, even if there probably was a lot they weren't telling him. The PM rose to shake his hand again. Dismissal time.

"We never do this, you know," the PM said. "Bring a consultant in at this level. Right now, though, you're suddenly a possible way into these modern-day Kanna'im. Think about it, Professor: a small cell of military men and weapons scientists diverting—something. What outrage might they be planning? Especially if they feel they're patriots? Zealots even?"

Never again, Ellerstein thought. "I will do my best," he said, not wanting to think about the possibilities.

"They tell me you always do, Professor," the PM said with a strange, sad smile, as if having people around him who were doing their best was a mixed blessing.

Back in Gulder's office, Ellerstein wiped his forehead. He hadn't realized he had been perspiring in there. Gulder threw the Skuratov file down on his desk.

"You didn't have to say that, you know," he said.

"Well, he should hear it anyway," Ellerstein said. "The king has no clothes and all that. Obviously you guys are sheltering him too much."

"It's been hard, Yossi," Gulder said. "Harder than you know. He's buying time, okay? We know, or at least we think we know, what the other side will accept, but Iran and this other business . . ."

"You think it's true?"

Gulder sat down and cleaned his glasses with a tissue. "There are strict controls," he said. "Strict accountability of all materials. Of course, if it's the people who execute those controls doing the diversion . . ." He shook his head. "If they get the army or the air force on their side, then they could do something."

"Only if they had a weapon," Ellerstein pointed out, but then he thought about the time he had spent at Dimona. As a theoretical mathematician, he hadn't been involved in making weapons, only in design work. Everything was compartmented there at the laboratory, so he had no idea how hard it would be to divert components, especially if they had had some time. Maybe not that hard.

"So this is why you had me watching this American's little project?"

"Yes."

"*Quis custodiet ipsos custodes*?" he murmured. Who shall guard the guards themselves?

"Exactly, which is why we must take care, because Skuratov has people out there, too. Believe it or not, we're using some Mossad assets. We hope the Shin Bet people won't know them, as they do Shabak."

"Good God," Ellerstein said. "Mossad. Shin Bet. Shabak. We'll be tripping over one another. Tell me, please: What is the objective here—we want to identify the cell members, roll them up?"

"First we want to know if it's true. Then we want to know *what* they've diverted, and where they are hiding it."

Ellerstein thought about that for a moment. "Could Skuratov know that I'm a consultant to Shabak?" he asked.

"Probably not," Gulder said. "The consultant list is compartmented information, even within the internal security ministry. Even the PM does not see the whole list."

"PMs come and go, don't they," Ellerstein observed.

"Exactly. Look: You just stay close to Ressner as long as the American is still in the country. Once he goes home, your work is over. Your involvement is purely precautionary. A pop-up opportunity. *If* Skuratov is involved. *If* there is a cell. If, if, if . . . you know, counterintelligence work, Yossi."

"To whom shall I report?"

"To me, of course. Your bosses have been informed you are active on special detail. It's important that you keep up with your outside life while you observe Ressner. That's all you have to do. As the Americans say, piece of cake, eh?"

16

On Sunday morning David had breakfast in the hotel dining room and then went back to his room to contact the diving club with which his travel agent had made arrangements for the Caesarea Maritima expedition. He had spent Saturday afternoon seeing some more of Old Jerusalem in company with a tour group from the hotel. The Old City had been relatively empty, with only tourists making their way through the ancient streets. His group had spent most of the day in the precincts of the Temple Mount, which David, having read Josephus's account of the final days of Jerusalem, found particularly interesting. It had taken some time for the Romans to subdue the city, and David was convinced more than ever that some of the defenders would have had time to get through the siege lines, make their way down to the Zealot stronghold, and probably take some valuables from Herod's magnificent Temple with them. Not the vast quantities of Temple treasure rumored to be buried all over the Judaean desert, but possibly sacred artifacts or scrolls. The Temple Mount itself was riddled with tunnels, aqueducts, and caves, so it was all possible.

Despite the immensity of the history that practically oozed from every ancient stone, he had remained distracted during his day of playing tourist. While physically in the Old City, his mind had been increasingly focused on the dive into the big cave beneath the rim cistern. He was anxious to get back in there and had to keep reminding himself that it was critical first to establish his cover. He would never get the chance for a second expedition if the authorities began to suspect there was something afoot. He had to assume they were still suspicious, so he had trudged obediently along behind the tour guide, listening absently to her patter of historical facts and fictions with the rest of the herd.

He got back to the hotel by four o'clock Sunday afternoon, after a successful day of making arrangements and going through the motions of being a tourist. He had gone first to the dive shop in Yafo where he met the tours manager and some of the guides, all of whom were attractive young women. This dive shop owner was no fool; most of his foreign diving clients were men. They spent an hour walking through the dive expedition plan for Caesarea Maritima and establishing the level of his diving expertise. He had shown them his diving log for the past five years and was able to talk equipment with them with a degree of familiarity that established him as a knowledge-able and experienced diver.

"We get all kinds in here, Mr. Hall," the shop manager said, handing over the site charts for David to study. "We get people who have never dived, people who try to fake it, all the way to experienced divers like yourself."

"I'm impressed with your shop's technical currency, Mr. Bergman. I keep forgetting that Israel is very much a modern state."

"Yes, well, most of our custom is European. It was the French who invented scuba, after all."

David swallowed the mild reproof and asked for some additional maps of the Mediterranean coast. He also said that he might want to rent out some extra tanks in case the chance arose for some side dives in the Yafo area. That would be no problem. The manager assumed aloud that he would not dive anywhere by himself, and David had just raised his eyebrows as if to suggest that no one would be that dumb. Right, he thought. Wouldn't think of it. He tried to suppress the image of that cold black rectangle of water at the bottom of the bat cave, looking like a side entrance to the Underworld. Cave diving. He swallowed at the thought.

When he was finished in the dive shop, he dismissed the driver for the day and spent the next three hours on foot, walking down the coastal beaches to the ancient seaport. He wandered aimlessly through the warren of streets like the rest of the tourists, browsing in the shops and having lunch in a tiny seaside café, and very discreetly watching for a tail while staying in character as boy tourist. He couldn't look too hard; he knew that surveillance pros could always tell if their subject was onto them. Leaving the café, he nearly collided with an overweight woman in her fifties, who teetered dangerously until he caught her elbow. They apologized simultaneously, revealing American English. David then had to endure the where-are-you-from, oh-really-I'm-from, etc., drill until he could extricate himself.

The trip to the dive shop should have established his planned itinerary for the next three days in case anyone came in later asking questions. The only semicovert thing he needed to do was to make sure he got the two extra tanks. If the dive shop asked too many questions, he might have to find a second shop. He figured he needed a total of four fully charged tanks for the cistern dive. He also needed to rent a spare underwater light and some batteries—that water would be blacker than black: the total darkness of a cave dive. It might also be cold, maybe as low as fifty degrees Fahrenheit. For that temperature he would have preferred a dry suit, but that would have been the wrong equipment for the Caesarea dive. His wet suit would have to suffice.

The depth was going to present yet another problem. The computer graph had shown depths ranging from seventy-five to a hundred fifty feet. Stay time even at seventy-five feet was going to be limited, and the temperature, if it was as cold as he expected, compounded the stay-time limitation. He could not know, from just one seismic shot, how wide the cave really was, or what the sides looked like, or whether or not there were stairs, terraces, or even side caves. He did know that the diving rule for multiple dives was always to make the deep dive first. Then he would have to calculate residual nitrogen, establish a surface stay and recovery time, and calculate how long he could stay at the shallower depth on the second dive. For depths of a hundred ten feet, which was the recommended maximum, no-decompression stay time would be only sixteen minutes. Because of the expected temperature, he had to cut that back to probably thirteen minutes. Then at least an hour and a half back on the surface to let his body eliminate cellular nitrogen. After that he could make a fifty-foot or shallower dive to survey the sides of the cistern. Because of residual nitrogen, he would only be able to stay down on the second dive for about forty-five minutes.

He had seen three car rental agencies on his seemingly random walking tour, and he had borrowed the use of a phone at an antiques shop to make a reservation with one of them for a four-wheel-drive vehicle, for pickup Wednesday noon.

The final objective for his Sunday walkabout was to find a camping supplies shop. He would need to set up a base camp at Masada from which to mount the dives, and after considering the empty and exposed terrain around the fortress, he had settled on using the rim cistern itself. It was not a place into which any tourists were likely to stumble, certainly not without a flashlight. The downside of this choice would be the need to hump the four heavy air tanks up that slope. The Yadin reports had mentioned a road, created by the army, cutting in from the coast north of the mountain and reaching up to the western plateau, where the ruins of the main Roman siege camp lay. If that was still there, he could maybe find a hiding spot near that for the vehicle. Then he would only have to haul the heavy tanks up the four hundred feet of the siege ramp instead of up the twelve hundred feet on the other side. Either way, he would need some tarps, a portable camp stove, water and food for forty-eight hours, and things like a sleeping bag, a camp shovel, toilet paper, and a first-aid kit. The usual stuff.

By three he had located a trekking supplies shop after consulting a tour agent's brochures. He placed a phone call from yet another tours shop. He told them what he needed and that he would be by to get it Wednesday afternoon. American Express? We can do that, Mr. Hall. We can deliver, if you want. For a small additional fee, of course. He told them to do that and gave them the name of his hotel.

Throughout the afternoon, he kept one eye peeled for any signs that he was being followed or observed. A couple of times he thought he saw a familiar face in the crowd, or the same vehicle, but he couldn't really be sure. Until he saw that overweight American woman again, across the street from the tour shop. He turned quickly and went back into the shop as if he'd forgotten something. From the shaded front windows he watched her go into the nearest shop, come back out, then walk quickly up the street.

He sat down in one of the waiting room chairs and fanned his face, pretending that the heat had gotten to him. The pretty clerk behind the counter brought him a bottle of water, which he accepted gratefully.

Sneaky bastards, he thought. Not a guy, nor a prowling government car, but a woman who looked like and sounded like another American tourist. He'd walked for a couple of hours at a pace that no fat lady could match, and yet here she was. Right across the street. Fancy that. Probably making the call right now—I've been made. He shouldn't have made that quick turn back into the tours shop. Oh, well, he thought. Stay in character. The fat lady would have a backup.

"International Planning."

"Eyes Nine. I think I've been made. Eyes Thirteen is in place. Tell Skuratov."

"He's an operative, then?"

"I don't think so, but . . ."

"What has he done all day?"

"Nothing, and he's worked hard at it. The perfect American tourist. But . . ."

"But."

"Yeah."

"Okay, got it. Go home."

On Sunday David had refined the front end of his plan. Assuming that any tails would have had enough after watching him be a duller-than-dogshit tourist for two days, he would go on the dives to Caesarea Maritima Monday and Tuesday, renege on Wednesday's tour, and then, after picking up the car and packing out, decamp for Masada on Wednesday afternoon, timing his drive down to arrive on the Dead Sea coast road just after dark. His plan was to hide the car near the mountain, get all the gear up to the rim cistern during the night, then go back and sleep in the car until daylight and the first tour buses began rolling in. He would drive out to the coastal road, fall in behind a tour bus, park in the lot, join the gaggle of tourists, and take the cable car directly up to the fortress, hopefully keeping clear of the staff people in the hostel. Blend in with the tourists and wander around for a while, then check out with the site guards for a hike back down the Serpent Path. That would take care of the guards' head count, and then he would simply disappear into the rim cistern.

What about the rental vehicle? He would leave a note on the front seat of the car saying that it had broken down and that the rental agency had been notified and would be coming for it soon. He, the driver, had hitched a ride on a tour bus back to Jerusalem.

From there, well, he would have to improvise. If the cistern contained artifacts, then he would need to get out and contact Judith to start the official explorations. Either way, he ought to know what he had by Thursday evening.

He chafed at the thought of staying away from Masada for three more days, but he had to let all the bureaucratic dust from last week settle. The one thing he could not stand would be someone on his tail when he skipped town Wednesday. This was Sunday afternoon. Any way he looked at it, he had three more days to wait.

He decided to have an early dinner and then study the Caesarea dive maps and refine his calculations for the dives in the big cave. He thought again about Judith as he rode the elevator downstairs. He still had her business card in his wallet. He was assuming that she'd come running if he found something dramatic in that flooded cave, but what if she became outraged and brought ministry cops instead? Maybe you ought to work on that problem, he told himself, especially since you have three days to kill before you make your move. Like what? Like call her up, see if you can make amends for what happened down there. At least make friends again. That way, when you do call her, you'll have a chance of convincing her to come down there and see for herself what you've found. He knew exactly how to make her come to him: He'd tell her that she would be the archaeologist who saved the discovery from the amateur.

He laughed as he walked out of the elevator doors, provoking some strange looks from the people waiting for the elevator. Now that's really cynical, he thought, as he crossed to the lobby bar. You've tromped on her feelings once already, and now you want to set her up again. Well, maybe I just want to see her again. Yeah, right.

He needed a drink.

At ten-thirty Monday morning, Judith filed out of the chairman's conference room behind Professor Ellerstein. The meeting had been blessedly short, thanks mainly to her taking the initiative as Ellerstein had suggested. She had almost laughed at the visible relief spreading over the chairman's face as she covered the points. She would take on more teaching assignments, resume going along to support the digs, participate in the institute's book projects, and even attend the dreaded international conferences. Ellerstein sat unmoving in his chair, his impassive face revealing no knowledge of how much of her little soliloquy had been prestaged.

When she had finished, the chairman had been practically effusive in his praise, saying that he was just so delighted to have her rejoin her academic family and promising everyone's support.

Ellerstein wished her luck as they reached the corridor leading to her office. "I'm going to be on the campus for a few days," he said. "I'm as delighted as the chairman, Yehudit. I know you probably don't know exactly how you're going to manage all this, but maybe just pretend you're starting out all over again, and do the kinds of things a new faculty member would do."

"You make it sound so easy, Yossi."

He nodded sympathetically. "For a while," he said, "you'll simply have to go through the motions. Stop thinking about everything, and go live life. Spend time with people. See new people. Date attractive men. Sleep with some if you want to. You will think you are just going through the motions, but perhaps the motions will bring you back."

Judith was suddenly weary of all this personal exposure. Bring her back to what? "As always, I appreciate your support, Yossi," she replied, a little more formally than she intended. Ellerstein smiled.

"If you need more advice, you call me," he said. "My advice is always free, and thus probably worth exactly what it costs you. By the way, what about the American?"

She just looked at him. "What about the American? Surely you don't think—"

He put up his hands. "New things, Yehudit. New directions. If he calls to apologize, don't just cut him dead is what I'm saying."

"No, I won't," she said. "I'll yell at him again."

"Okay, okay," he said, "but have a drink with him first. *Then* yell at him."

She smiled dutifully over her shoulder and went on down to her office, where she shut the door, dropped into her elderly leather chair, and then let out a big sigh. Yossi was precisely correct: It was one thing to announce that she was back among the land of the interested living. It was quite another to actually plunge back in. Go through the motions. Date some attractive men. Sleep with some. Really! An image of David Hall crossed her mind, and she felt herself blushing. Ridiculous. She decided a good place to start was with her messages. There was one: from the university parking office, reminding her that her campus sticker was expiring in three days. Ah, she thought. The important stuff.

David returned to the hotel at three o'clock Monday afternoon, tired but exhilarated by the morning dive at Caesarea. It had been two months since he had been in the water, and it had been a joy to dive again.

He dumped his diving gear bag on the floor, extracted the wet suit, and went in to take a shower. His individual tour had turned into a group dive at the last minute, but he hadn't minded. The undersea scenery had been spectacular, and there had been enough sunlight to really see. Besides, he would have happily followed their dive guide anywhere she wanted to take him. The submerged Roman port had been made into one of the world's first underwater museums, with numbered sites marked across the entire area. Divers were given a tablet that had a map explaining the numbered sites. They had seen the base of Herod's enormous seawall ashlars, immense stones weighing hundreds of tons and submerged by a third-century earthquake, extending in a great curve out into the dim sea. There were columns and statuary fragments everywhere and other evidence that many artifacts still lay beneath the swirling sands below. After the tour they had lunched in the restaurant called Herod's Palace, with its second-story terrace and views of the sea and the walled Crusader city. The sea had been sparkling and lively enough to keep everything underwater moving.

It won't be like that in the cistern, he realized, a thought that diluted some of his enthusiasm.

He cleaned all his gear with freshwater and then flopped down on the bed in a big sprawl and relaxed. Then he remembered to check the computer for signs of intrusion.

He had put the laptop, stored in its briefcase, in the second drawer of the hotel room's chest of drawers, nested in his underwear. Besides setting the counter to zero in the boot files, he had placed three grains of beach sand on a top corner of the outside case and then very carefully closed the drawer. When he opened the drawer, the grains were gone. Well, well, well, he thought. The maid snooping, or somebody else?

He pulled the case out of the drawer, extracted the computer, and fired it up. He interrupted the boot sequence by pressing a function code key while the cursor was still blinking on the right side of the screen, then commanded the counter to display the count: 002. Once for this boot up, and once for the previous boot.

Bingo. Someone had indeed taken a look.

I wonder, he thought. Maybe the security people at Masada had found out that he had been into the rim cistern. If so, this wasn't going to work at all. How could he find that out?

Judith Ressner.

Judith would certainly know something about a development like that. So call her—and ask her what? For that matter, would she even talk to him? You are no longer welcome in official Israel,

Mr. Hall. Well, how about unofficial Israel? He thought it over.

So maybe call her and just ask her to meet him for a drink. Don't even bring up Masada. If there was a shit storm brewing, she wouldn't return his call, or she might just to yell at him. Even if nothing was happening, she still might say no.

Or she might say yes.

Damn. More false pretenses.

He got up and placed the call to her office. The department secretary, whose English was apparently limited, got the general idea of his name and the hotel number, but David didn't hold out much hope for the rest of his message: Would she care to join him for a drink at the hotel this evening? He would send a car.

When he hung up he felt even guiltier. Yet the part of his plan where he summoned her to the site and let her take over the discovery process made more and more sense. He had come here to make a discovery. He was halfway there. After that, he knew, he wasn't qualified to exploit it properly from an archaeological standpoint. He remembered the pictures of the human remains found by the Yadin expedition. Scraps of bone and hair and disintegrated sandals embedded in the dirt and dust of centuries. A vital find that an amateur like himself might have trampled in his ignorance.

Calling her in would be a dicey move, because

somewhere along the line he was going to have to confess what he had been doing all along, since the very first day. She would be more than angry with him. All he could hope for was that the excitement of the discovery might overwhelm all that anger. By taking over, she would become the *archaeologist* who had discovered the secret of the mountain, at least within the fiercely competitive context of professional archaeology. It would be like the Dead Sea Scrolls: The shepherd boy who actually found the scrolls was rarely named in all the books about them.

Or she might just call in the Israeli police. Accuse him of violating one of Israel's most treasured monuments and pack his ass off to jail. Wahoo.

Judith was surprised to find David's message when she came back to her office after a seminar with three Ph.D. candidate hopefuls, none of whom showed much promise. She wondered immediately if *Mr.* Hall was familiar with the Jewish concept of chutzpah, then marveled at Yossi Ellerstein's clairvoyance. She turned the message note over and over in her hands, thinking about it. Six o'clock. His hotel was down in Tel Aviv, and she lived in Jerusalem. If she was going to do it, she had to leave now to get home and change. First, though, there was a second message, this one from the hostel manager down at Masada.

She decided to return the Masada call first.

"Dr. Ressner, Assad Ghanin. This concerns your friend, the American. The site security people confirm no signs of unauthorized activity on the part of your Mr. Hall."

"He's not *my* Mr. Hall," she said acidly.

"He was under your charge," the manager responded primly. "Not ours."

"Now you listen," she began, but he interrupted her.

"I've also checked with the army border patrol district headquarters at Ein Gedi—they're the ones who supervise the patrols out here—and they said the incident report just says that the American was walking about in the desert at night. So I think this matter is closed, yes?" She could picture the fat little man wiping beads of perspiration off his face. On the other hand, this was good news.

"Very well, Mr. Ghanin. That was our impression all along. I will pass this information to the IAA and to the institute."

"Okay, Professor. Shalom."

She hung up and then left a message with the chairman's office relaying the gist of Ghanin's report. *Your Mr. Hall* indeed. Well, they had been down there together, so it was not an unnatural assumption. She had to admit that the man was at least interesting. So: You're going to start a new life here? Then go have a drink with him. It's not like he's propositioning you, and you're all finished with Herod's dreadful Masada. He leaves Israel in a week, so what can happen? It would also allow you to make a first move back into the social scene without involving a colleague. If he was contrite, she would spend some time with him. If he was an ass, she could always spend a little time with him, smile sweetly, pour a drink in his lap, and then cut him dead right there at the table. She placed a call to his hotel.

The message light on his bedside phone was blinking when David got back to his room. He had gone downstairs to check out the hotel dining room to see if it might be a suitable place for dinner. It was Judith, saying she would meet him in the lobby bar for a drink at six-thirty.

He put the phone down and sat back on the bed. Now he really had mixed feelings. Okay, smart-ass, you called her, and now here she comes. So chances are nobody found anything worth shouting about. So who is doing the surveillance, and why? Just someone being very careful? But who?

On a personal level, he did want to see her again. What man wouldn't? She was smart, single, and eminently streetable. Still, there was no getting around the fact that it was going to be, once again, under false pretenses. Maybe the thing

338

to do was to shut it off with her after a drink in the bar. Except, of course, there was his need for an archaeological lifeline once he came back out of the cistern. So a quick drink and dinner wasn't an option, unless she was coming here just to fang him again for the first deception.

He groaned out loud. Damned woman had him going in circles again. Wonderful.

He went back down to the hotel front desk and retrieved his passport and then called the rental car agency on a lobby phone to give them his passport number. They told him to be sure to bring it when he picked up the car, along with his American driver's license. When he was finished he stopped by the dining room and booked a table for two for seven-thirty, in case things worked out. If not, he still had to have dinner somewhere. He went back to his room, belatedly remembered that Judith lived in Jerusalem and not Tel Aviv, called her back, obtained her address, and dispatched Ari and the Mercedes to pick her up.

17

At six-fifteen, David was sitting at a table in the lobby bar, facing the door, a glass of white wine in front of him. He had changed into slacks and an open-collared, short-sleeved shirt under a white linen sport jacket.

Judith came in a few minutes later, creating a

small stir. She was wearing a blue open-front linen jacket over an ankle-length, gauzelike multi-layered white skirt. Underneath the jacket she wore a bronze-colored blouse that looked to David like the top half of a bathing suit. With her hair styled and a hint of makeup, the previously stern and serious college professor had cleaned up extraordinarily well. Judith in war paint was a stunning woman and definitely a female, David thought, remembering only at the last moment to stand up as she approached the table.

"Professor," he said, holding out a chair. He caught the scent of a tantalizing perfume in the air as she sat down.

"Mr. Hall," she replied solemnly.

"Oh dear," he said, sitting down. "So it's back to Mr. Hall, is it?"

"Are you drinking alone?" she replied, raising her eyebrows at his glass of white wine. He laughed and signaled the waiter. She ordered a white wine by name, and the obviously smitten waiter bustled away.

"I appreciate your sending a car to pick me up. Now tell me: Why did you ask me to come have a drink with you?"

"I wanted to see you again," he replied evenly. "Why did you accept?"

"I am practicing. Today I agreed to become a normal human being again."

"Ah, yes, the dreaded Monday meeting. With

the committee of ultimatum givers. How did all that go?"

"Quickly. I preempted them. I told them that I would give up the widow's weeds and rejoin the scintillating fold of academia."

"And will you?"

"As soon as I figure out precisely how, yes, I probably will. I remembered that handful of pills you mentioned. The thought did not appeal." The waiter returned with her wine.

"Well, I'm glad to hear that. The new you definitely does appeal. You look absolutely smashing."

He watched her as she considered the compliment. He could see that she was suddenly at a loss for words. It must indeed have been a long time. "I've booked a table in the dining room for seven-thirty," he continued. "Can you join me for dinner?"

She turned her head to one side and gave him a speculative look. "You're awfully sure of yourself, Mr. Hall."

He shrugged. "*I* have to have dinner somewhere. So do you, and you're thirty miles from Jerusalem. I promise not to duck out to investigate any ruins during dinner."

She gave him a reproving look. "That was not an intelligent thing you did down there. On any level."

He understood at once: We were doing pretty

well until you pulled your stupid stunt of going up on the mountain at night. If you liked that, he wanted to say, you'll positively love the next act.

"I admit that wasn't too bright," he said. "On any level. It's just that I tend to be a focused man. I came here to Israel to see and *feel* Metsadá. For the final defenders, the climax to that story came at night. I needed to experience that."

"Focused. Another American euphemism?"

He shrugged. "It's how I achieve things," he said, looking directly at her. He paused for a second. "Sometimes I focus to the extent that the consideration due to other people gets pushed into the background. Nuclear engineering is an unforgiving business."

"Especially when you become a whistle-blower, yes?"

"Especially then. The power companies desperately need for the public to believe they have the dragon firmly in the cave. Anyone intimately acquainted with the dragon knows better."

"As the Japanese just found out."

"Yes," he said. "A monster earthquake overwhelms the design; then a tsunami drowns the backup systems."

"The Japanese are a very clever people," she said. "One would have expected a better outcome."

"At some point in commercial power, your shareholders force you to balance cost versus redundancy. The Japanese got it wrong."

She gave a wry smile at that. "My life is a matter of balance, I suppose," she said. "Lately I haven't done a very good job of that, either. Hence this morning's meeting."

He nodded. "Believe it or not, I'm going to have to do something very similar. When Adrian disappeared my personal life was suspended."

"Except that, in your case, she might come back."

He nodded. "No closure," he said.

"Closure is overrated, Mr. Hall."

"Maybe," he said, "but in my case, the lawsuit resulted in my never having to work again. The truth is, however, that after this trip I suppose I'm going to have to do what you're doing: get back into the swim."

"The industry would let you back in?"

"No chance," he laughed. "I could possibly go back to working for the government, except for the fact that the bureaucracy just *loves* a whistle-blower."

He got a real smile that time. He could still detect a bittersweet aura in her face and lips, but it was a smile worth waiting for. She saw him looking, and looked down at the table, embarrassed, and then smiled again, a more gentle expression this time. Behind her, David saw the bartender grinning widely at him. *Go get her, tiger.*

"Tell me about your work, Mr. Hall. What does a nuclear engineer do?"

"First, it's time to call me David."

"Perhaps."

"No, it's David."

She spoke his name, softly, still looking down at the table. He leaned back in his chair and saluted her with his glass. "See?" he said. "That wasn't hard. What shall I call you?"

"*Dr.* Ressner?" she suggested, her face a study in innocence.

He told her about his engineering career over dinner, up to the point where he opened the can of worms on missing nuclear material.

"Where had it gone?" she asked.

"The funny thing is, I only got as far as proving that there was a large quantity of heavy water unaccounted for. Once the NRC got into it, I discovered that I was no longer in the loop, as we say. Once the company terminated me, I was really out in the cold. I have no idea where it went."

"In the loop. Out in the cold. I have much to learn about American idiom."

"If you could hear us talking in the office, it would sound like alphabet soup."

She sipped her wine, an iced Carmel white, letting her lips linger on the rim of the glass. She held the glass in both hands, her elbows on the table, which accentuated her lush figure. A tiny drop of condensation was forming on the bottom of the wineglass, gathering heft and curvature, threatening to drop strategically into that heavenly cleft, and he found that he was having trouble staying . . . focused, yeah, that was the word. He had noticed that her manner had changed during the course of dinner, the stoic, ultraserious academic blossoming into an entrancing woman who might be making up her mind about something. Or him.

"Anyway, it worked out, in the end. The big problem now is what to do next."

The drop finally let go, but she tipped the bottom of the glass forward just enough to keep from getting wet. It still took an effort not to follow the drop.

"Have you never wanted to do something more, I don't know, adventurous?" she asked.

Now he had to really control his face. He wanted to laugh out loud. Or cry. Part of him was once again dying to reveal what he was actually doing here. Why? To impress her? He realized he wanted this woman to like him.

"About the only adventure I get is through diving. Didn't you tell me you were a diver?"

"Yes, but not for some years now. Nothing too challenging: shallow-water dives off the coast. Things like the Caesarea Maritima dives you are doing. Back when . . . when I was still married. Dov was an excellent diver. I was technically competent, but not addicted, like Dov. He went everywhere to dive."

"I've become something of an addict. Did it scare you?"

"I was not so much frightened as uneasy. I felt we did not belong down there. Too much imagination, Dov said. So once he was gone, I put my equipment away. Looking back, I did the scuba mostly to please him, to be with him, I think."

Equipment. Another idea surfaced in his mind: Tell her now and take her along. Then he shelved the notion just about as fast as he'd thought of it.

"Yes, well, I understand that feeling," he said, finishing his wine, "and sometimes things come into view down there that reinforce the notion of whose place it really is. That's the adventure, I suppose. We live in such a controlled environment these days that we almost have to create risks to experience life."

She nodded slowly, but her eyes were no longer quite focused. He started to say something but then held back, keeping quiet while she communed with some comforting reverie from the past. Then, with a start, she came back.

"Sorry," she said, putting down her glass and fidgeting with her napkin.

"I understand," he said. "Really, I do. Listen, I was thinking: As you said, I'm going to spend two more days diving at Caesarea. Would you want to come along? I realize tomorrow's short notice, but perhaps Wednesday?"

She gave him a mildly surprised look across the table, a look that said, *Why are you asking me?*

"Look, I hope I'm not being insensitive. You just told me that diving was something you did with your husband, but you're also trying to make a break with that past, to start doing things *despite* the fact that your husband is gone. Not to mention the fact that I would very much enjoy your company. Everything's arranged. You still have your gear—why not?"

"Well, I do have a job, Mr.—David. I'm a professor, remember?"

"Sure, but you go see your chairman and tell him what you're doing, and why. There's no way he can tell you no. Especially after I call and offer him generous bribes."

She smiled again, eyes down. He was getting to really like that smile. Then she nodded. "Okay. I'll see what I can do. They'll have to refresh my qualifications."

"I'll have the dive shop take care of that. Bring your PADI card. They'll do a quick review and then check you out in the harbor at Caesarea—it's usually flat water. The weather's supposed to be great, and we're not going beyond ten meters down anyway. Do you have a buoyancy control device?"

"No, those came along after I stopped. We used weights."

"I'll have them bring one out. This is great.

Now, how about we get our check and maybe take a walk on the beach. I think I ate too much."

The waiter slipped out of the dining room long enough to make a quick call on his cell phone. A man's voice answered.

"International Planning."

The waiter gave his name. The man told him to wait, and then he was connected with his controller.

"They have just left," he said, turning his head as a couple of tourists came out of the dining room and walked right by him. "I think they are going for a walk on the beach."

"Together?"

"Yes, together; what do you think?"

"I think they could be going separately. How the hell would I know?"

"You haven't seen her. That would tell you quick enough. You have people out there?"

"Thanks for the call. Go back to work now."

Fifteen minutes later they walked down between two swimming pools to the beach itself. He got her to open up a little more about her own life, her childhood in Haifa, college, and then the long haul to the Ph.D. She ran aground slightly when it came to talking about Dov, how they met, and their first few years of marriage, but it seemed to get easier as she talked. He was enjoying the way passing men looked at her but remained painfully aware of the underlying deception.

"I just folded in," she was explaining. "I felt profound loss, and then, of course, the absence of completion. There was no funeral, no grave, no memorial I could visit. Because of the security I couldn't tell my friends at the university anything except that Dov had died in an accident. Everyone assumed a traffic accident, of course."

"Then the government made some things happen? A pension, an insurance policy, perhaps, and maybe a little influence with the appointment?"

"Yes, they did all of those things. In return for my silence, I suppose. There was this scary-looking man, a Russian émigré, someone who was involved with security matters for the Dimona laboratories, who laid it all out for me. In fact—"

"What?" he asked.

"I probably shouldn't tell you this, but he came to see me just before this trip to Metsadá. Our trip."

A mental alarm bell started ringing in David's head. "A security officer from Dimona?"

"Well, actually, I don't know. Those people are all so mysterious and elliptical. We have so many secret agents here in Israel, who can keep track? Anyway, part of my job down there was to make sure you were, how did he put it—that you were what you said you were. It didn't make too much sense."

It did to David. The watcher in the airport, and now evidence of someone looking into his computer. He could understand perhaps the Ministry for Internal Security, but Dimona? What the hell was this?

"No wonder you were mad at me for wandering off the reservation," he said, to cover his own confusion. "Did that get you in trouble, by the way?"

"Apparently not," she shrugged. "Although now that I think about it, Yosef Ellerstein seemed to be interested in what you were doing as well, but I think that was only because he was part of the committee. You know."

"Yeah." David kicked some sand. The beach was well lighted from all the hotels, but the sea itself was dark. Only the sounds of a small surf breaking in lazy curls against the sand revealed its presence. There were other people out walking, their faces pale blurs in the light coming down off the main street.

So there was more to this minder business than just the professors. A state security officer from Dimona, and also Ellerstein, his interlocutor? He sighed. "I apologize again. If I'd known there were security people—"

She shrugged it off. "Israel is full of security people. Mossad, they are the spies, of course. Shin Bet is counterintelligence. Mishtara, the national police. Shabak, like your FBI. Aman, the military intelligence. Then there's Mishmar Hagvul; they're the border police, part of the army, I think. The customs. The immigration. The army and the navy and the air force security. We seem to have security people in inverse proportion to how much real security we have."

As she was speaking, two border patrol men came strolling up the beach, Uzis slung over their shoulders. To David they looked like high school kids dressed up as soldiers, their uniforms sloppy and their hair modishly long. Judith greeted them politely in Hebrew, and they waved and walked on.

"Against the PLO from Gaza and the Hezbollah from the Lebanon," she explained. "Sometimes they send small teams of terrorists in rubber boats to shoot up the beach resort areas."

"Lovely. So those two guys are supposed to catch them?"

"Oh, I think not. I think the foot patrols are out here to reassure the tourists. The real guys are probably up there on the tops of all these hotels, with night-vision devices."

"Ah, so heaven help the lovers."

She gave him a sideways look but said nothing. They had wandered down the beach hotel strip for nearly a mile and had started back again. They continued in silence until they reached their starting point, where they encountered the same two border patrol troops eating ice cream cones. As they walked back up a boardwalk to Hayarkon, he toyed with the idea of inviting her to the hotel bar for a nightcap but thought better of it. So far she'd gone along with everything he had suggested: coming down for drinks, dinner, joining him at Caesarea, and the beach walk. Quit while you're ahead, he thought.

When they reached his hotel's entrance he checked to make sure the car was there. She turned to say good night.

"It has been very pleasant, David Hall. Thank you for inviting me."

"It has been very pleasant indeed, Judith. There's Ari."

"Thank you especially for the use of your car and driver."

"Jerusalem is too far away for a night drive. The least I can do. I'll call your office to confirm the arrangements for the dive on Wednesday. If you have any doubts about equipment, I'll get the dive shop to call you. I'm looking forward to it."

"I think I am, too," she said. "Although it has been a long time."

"It's like riding a bike or making love: Once you know how, you know how."

That provoked an amused look on her face as Ari pulled the Mercedes into the hotel driveway. David opened the door for her. One last dazzling smile, a flash of those glorious legs, and then she was gone. He stood in the driveway for a moment after the car pulled out.

Riding a bike or making love? Where had that come from? As he turned around he saw the bellhop giving him what looked suspiciously like a sympathetic look.

"Can't catch 'em all, sport," he said and went in.

Judith sank back into the cushions of the Mercedes after confirming that the driver knew where he was going. So: first outing for the new Yehudit. She had followed Yossi's advice and deliberately kept her mind blank for the last half of the evening, compliantly letting David take the lead, even saying she would go on a dive with him. Everything was so new. Putting on a sexy cocktail dress. Wearing makeup. Paying the slightest bit of attention to how she looked. Meeting a strange foreigner—well, not strange, but not a longtime friend, either—in a hotel bar. Having dinner with him. Talking about Dov. Walking on the beach like lovers. If he had proposed that they go back to his rooms for a nightcap she might well have done that, too. Well, maybe not.

She tried to assess her feelings but couldn't manage it. She stared instead out the windows of the car, her eyes unseeing as the suburbs of Tel Aviv raced by. Going through the motions. In truth, she could go through the motions forever, as long as she did not look over that wall and see her former life with Dov, the times when neither one of them had been going through the motions, those first years of love and marriage and romance and fun and contentment. Even when he had begun to get politically involved, it had been exhilarating to watch him get swept up in a cause and, when their jobs were threatened, to prove to him that she was with him even if it all went wrong and they had to start all over again. That was the problem, wasn't it: She simply did not believe that she could ever bond that hard to another human being again. No matter how long she went through the motions. Not even with this attractive American.

The road darkened as they headed up the long climb to Jerusalem. A lone taxi followed, one discreet kilometer behind.

18

Yosef Ellerstein was unpacking after his overnight trip to Amman when the phone rang. He looked at his watch. Ten-thirty. Late for phone calls.

"Hello, yes?"

"Professor Ellerstein," a raspy voice whispered. "I apologize for the late call."

"Who is this, please?"

"This is Colonel Malyuta Lukyanovitch Skuratov. I am the chief of security at Dimona. Would it be possible for me to stop by for a few minutes?"

Skuratov! Ellerstein thought. He didn't like this at all. "Well, Colonel . . . Skuratov, is it? It is very late. Perhaps in my office?"

"I am close by, Professor. Actually in the neighborhood. It won't take but a few minutes, and it is rather urgent, I'm afraid." Ellerstein put a hand over the mouthpiece and looked through the curtain of his front window. A large Mercedes was double-parked in front of his two-story apartment building. A white-faced figure was barely visible in the right rear window, raising a black-gloved hand at him.

"Well—"

"Thank you, Professor. I'll be right up."

Ellerstein put down the phone and saw that his hand was trembling. How should he handle this? Had Skuratov found out his attachment to Shabak? If so—what? He heard footsteps coming up the stairs outside. More than one person was coming. He stepped into his bedroom, brushed his hair, and put on a dressing gown over his trousers. The doorbell rang.

He went to the front door and peered through the peephole. There were three men outside. Skuratov he recognized from his own time at Dimona; one did not forget that face and the strange hat. The other two looked like bodyguards. He unlocked the door and opened it. Skuratov offered a gloved hand.

355

"Professor Ellerstein. We meet again."

"Yes, Colonel. Chess, wasn't it? Come in."

The two large men remained outside as Skuratov came through, trailing a faintly medicinal smell. He was a head taller than Ellerstein, but stooped and walking with an effort. He was wearing a dark suit. He took off his hat and proceeded directly to one of the two leather armchairs in the living room, where he sat down with a sigh of relief. He did not unbutton his suit jacket, and it hung in limp folds from his thin chest.

"May I get you something—a cognac, perhaps?" Ellerstein asked. He recognized that he was stalling for time but wasn't sure why. Maybe it was just that ghastly face.

The colonel stared up at him with those unusual gray eyes. "A cognac would be very kind," he said, touching his lips with a handkerchief.

Ellerstein went to the bar and poured two snifters of VSOP. He handed one to the colonel, gave a small salud, then sat down.

"So, Colonel Skuratov?"

"This concerns an American engineer, one David Hall, who is visiting Israel just now."

"Ah, yes," Ellerstein replied, sipping his cognac. He decided to say as little as possible. Israel Gulder was going to sit right up when he called this little visit in.

"It is my understanding that you have met with this American and helped him to arrange his trip

356

down to Metsadá. Along with Professor Ressner."

"Yes, I did. At the request of the ministry. May I ask, Colonel—of what interest this is to the security apparatus at Dimona?"

"No, you may not," Skuratov said, keeping the twisted smile on his face, the smile that did not quite reach those gray eyes. He took a birdlike sip of cognac. "Forgive my bad manners, Professor. What I meant is, of course you would ask, but I am not at liberty to make an answer. Tell me something: Did the American tell you much about himself?"

Ellerstein considered the question. He had to be careful here. What had Gulder said—piece of cake? He did not want to become Skuratov's piece of cake.

"We had drinks, once, no, twice. He said he was a nuclear engineer and that he had worked both in industry and for the government."

Skuratov took another small sip of cognac. "Did he tell you about a scandal he precipitated in Washington?"

"He said he'd gotten into trouble with his company for being a whistle-blower."

"Yes. A whistle-blower. Such a quaint expression. Did he explain what it was that he was blowing his whistle at?"

Ellerstein sat back in his chair. "Not really," he said. "Or if he did, I wasn't paying much attention. He did say his company fired him and then there was a lawsuit. Now, as I understand it, he no longer needs to work for money."

"Now he is here. This man who does not need a job anymore."

"Well, what of it, Colonel?"

Skuratov put down his glass. "Here's the thing, Professor," he said. "We think there is a chance that this American is, how to put this . . . connected? That he is involved in the American intelligence apparatus somehow. They do that, their CIA. They have what they call . . . consultants."

Skuratov was looking at him intently. It took everything Ellerstein had to keep his face impassive.

"So?" he asked. Consultant. He wanted to swallow but did not want Skuratov to see him do that.

The colonel blinked once, twice, and then changed gears. "Are you aware that the American and Mrs. Ressner are seeing each other?"

This time Ellerstein let surprise register on his face. "Really? I would have thought she was still angry with him. How do you know this?"

"Let's just say it's my business to know. Frankly, Professor, we are worried about this American. These are delicate times in our relationship with the United States. There are seismic shifts occurring in the balances of power here in the Middle East, and our own nuclear deterrent is a factor in those balances. We find his Metsadá quest somewhat unbelievable, and therefore we are asking ourselves what his real purpose for being here is."

Ellerstein shrugged again and drank his cognac. The professional spooks always assumed the royal "we" when they were fishing for information. He decided to probe a little. "You think David Hall is a spy?" he asked. "If he is a spy, what the hell is the connection between Metsadá and Dimona security, if I may ask. Oh, sorry, I forgot."

Again, the smile that was not a smile. "He went out at night, yes? Twice?"

"Up to the fortress, yes."

"How does anyone know that, Professor? The up-to-the-fortress part, I mean?"

"I don't understand."

"Dimona is only forty kilometers from Metsadá, Professor."

"So, what? He drove down to Dimona in the middle of the night? And did what? Did someone find a vehicle? Did he take pictures—better picture than their satellites can take? I rather doubt that, Colonel."

Skuratov continued to stare at him, as if he were some kind of specimen under a microscope. Then he put down his glass. "You are close to Professor Ressner, yes?" he asked, changing tack again.

Ellerstein felt another tingle of alarm. "Yes, she is a good friend. I have helped her at the university."

"I think you can help us, Professor. It is like this: We would like you to keep an eye on Mrs. Ressner for as long as she is seeing this American. Oh, I don't mean chaperone them or anything like that, but see if you can find out what they talk about, what questions he asks, if any, especially about Dimona. That sort of thing."

Ellerstein shook his head in wonder. This was exactly what Gulder wanted him to do: keep an eye on Yehudit Ressner. "Look," he said. "I can arrange to see her often enough. I can even make a casual inquiry about the American, but beyond that, well, you don't know her. I can't just pry like that."

Skuratov heaved himself to his feet, grunting with the effort. "That would be sufficient, Professor. You know how we security people are—professionally paranoid. The American may be exactly what he says he is. A fool for history. However, if *she* has doubts? Concerns? Anything about his behavior? These are things I need to know, and quickly. There is much I cannot tell you, of course."

There always was, Ellerstein thought as Skuratov handed him a card. "We ask these things as a favor to the government, Professor. We don't want you playing spy or counterspy. We'd just like some informal feedback. Information. That's the key. Pieces to a puzzle."

The colonel was smiling again. For some

reason, Ellerstein couldn't resist. "Like a distant consultant, then, Colonel?"

Skuratov's smile held in place. "Exactly, Professor. Like a consultant."

Once Skuratov and his bodyguards had left, Ellerstein poured himself another cognac. He shouldn't have said that, he thought. He sat down to call Gulder but then wondered if his phones were tapped. Skuratov had watchers on Yehudit and the American, Hall. He could be watching Ellerstein as well. Or listening.

Gulder already knew that the colonel was watching Ressner and the American, so he would call Gulder in the morning, from a random office phone at the university, and tell him about Skuratov's nocturnal visit. On the face of it, he could see why Skuratov had come to see him. Then again, it could also mean that the old Russian sensed movement in his backfield, and perhaps suspected that the government might be aware of the new Zealots. He might even suspect that Yossi Ellerstein was a government agent himself. What better way to neutralize him than by enlisting his support? Ellerstein was in no position to say no to Skuratov without revealing his own mission. Even the government did not know the breadth and depth of this new conspiracy. Or did they?

He sipped his cognac. Wheels within wheels

here, he thought. Or maybe more like a bunch of scorpions in a bottle. Then he wondered how he was supposed to sleep tonight, and, more importantly, how he was going to protect Yehudit Ressner.

As the big Mercedes pulled out of Ellerstein's neighborhood, Skuratov placed a secure call. The ringing stopped, encryption tones synchronized, and then a voice answered.

"Shapiro."

"Ellerstein was evasive. We need to do something."

"Your orders?"

"Scare the American. Scare him hard. Make him want to go home."

"Got it."

The connection was terminated, and Skuratov sat back in his seat. He needed to think.

"Drive around," he told his driver. "Anywhere there's no traffic."

19

After the second dive on Tuesday morning, David completed his logistical arrangements, including getting his hands on the two extra air tanks. Now, having invited Judith to go with him to Caesarea, he couldn't disappear on Wednesday as originally planned. It would have to be a Thursday getaway unless there was some convenient way of getting her out of the picture right after the dive tomorrow morning. He would have to postpone the run down to Masada until the following afternoon. The good news was that if there was still security on his tail, it gave him another day. His hooking up with Judith ought to make a pretty good argument for calling off the dogs. He was still trying to figure out why a security officer connected to Israel's atomic power facility would be interested in his visits to Masada, though. The scandal in Washington? That was a reach.

He had booked the rental Land Rover for Wednesday. He told the agency he would pay for it even if he didn't pick it up until Thursday. The camping gear had been a simpler matter, and now he had everything he would need on the mountain stashed in his hotel room closet, including four filled air tanks. The agency didn't seem to care one way or another, as long as they had that Amex card.

After making the morning dive, he had spent some time wandering over the landward remains of Caesarea Maritima, marveling at the twin aqueducts that rose out of the dunes and marched across the beaches to the crumbling Crusader walls. He had walked around the now eerily silent, sun-drenched arena of Herod's great hippodrome, trying to imagine the bloody spectacles played out on the now simmering sand. As he strolled through the ruins, he wondered about the wisdom of seeing Judith again. She had called to confirm the dive on Wednesday, agreeing to meet him at the hotel by eight that morning. Since he had a private dive guide set up, it didn't really matter if they took some time to make sure Judith still knew which end of the regulator to breathe from before going out to explore the now submerged Roman seaport. He planned to have lunch with her after the dive and then get her back to town. That might still give him time to slip away and begin the expedition to Masada.

As he thought about it, though, he realized that wasn't likely. It didn't really matter if the project slipped a day. Moreover, if he waited until Thursday to make his move back to the fortress, it would mean he would be diving into the cistern on Friday afternoon. Given that the Sabbath began Friday evening, the fortress would be empty of tourists and the site security guards for at least the next twenty-four if not thirty-six hours, which would significantly reduce the chances of his being caught.

What was more important, he realized, was that he was not so willing to let this woman out of his sights just now. As he sat in his hotel room, what he really wanted to do was call her and invite her back to Tel Aviv for dinner again. Take another walk on the beach. This time go have that drink.

Instead he went down to have dinner by himself

in the hotel and then went back upstairs to recheck his dive calculations for the cistern. As he got ever closer to his objective, he couldn't figure out why he felt like some kind of shit. Yes, you can, he admitted to himself.

David couldn't remember a nicer diving day: The weather was perfect, the seas calm, the underwater light clear and bright, and the drowned ruins of a Roman-era seaport spectacular. Judith had had no problems with her dive gear or her quick refresher course, and David's biggest problem now was keeping his eyes on the underwater scenery and not on the two heavenly bodies swimming ahead of him. Judith was in a peach-colored, clingy maillot, and the tour leader, a twenty-something beauty, could just as well have left her suit behind.

With Herod's colossal breakwater now in ruins on the seabed, there was a current running, strong enough to swirl the sand. Their little threesome was not the only group out there. There were single individuals and even larger groups, including a gaggle of snorkelers that created a moving shadow across the underwater area. Having already done the tour dive once, David had told the guide he might wander off the prescribed route of the underwater museum. She had been okay with that but told him not to get out of sight.

As the two of them kicked down to look at the Roman shipwreck, David threaded his way between two tilting ashlars. The giant blocks of stone had been spilled onto the seafloor sometime in the first century A.D. by an earthquake, which had ended Caesarea's usefulness as a protected seaport. David ran his hands over the surface of the stones, where one could still feel the marks of the chisels, even after nearly two thousand years underwater. How had they moved them onto the breakwater, he wondered. He'd learned earlier that the Romans had used a special hydraulic cement, made from volcanic ash from the fields beneath Vesuvius, to tie the blocks of stone together.

He felt a slight pressure wave above him and looked up. Another diver was about fifteen feet overhead, swimming just over the tops of the ashlars. He was in a full wet suit, all black, and he appeared to be carrying something. David couldn't see his face, but the man waved at him when David looked up. David waved back and went on with his exploration of what he was calling the ashlar canyon as he threaded his way between the cubes of stone littering the bottom. In some cases he had to make ninety-degree turns to make his way through the maze. As he was coming around one of these tight turns he felt something touch his neck. He stopped and tried to look to his left, but the stone face of the ashlar was too close.

There was definitely something above him, something big enough to block out the ambient light.

When he finally managed to turn his face he was startled to see a stainless steel cylinder, the size of a shotgun shell, pushing toward his neck. Just beyond the cylinder he found himself looking into a face mask, and the dark eyes behind the mask looked like the eyes of Death himself.

Before he could register his shock, another diver came through the tight channel between the huge stones going the other way and literally collided with David's face mask. The diver was a largish woman who put up her hands defensively when she banged into David. At that instant, she looked up and behind David, giving him a full view of the expression on her face, which was suddenly one of total surprise, then fear. A large bubble escaped her mouthpiece as a black-suited arm reached over David's head and pushed the cylinder on the end of the stick against the side of the woman's face. There was a nasty thump and then the side of the woman's head dissolved in a cloud of bone, blood, and a pink galaxy of bubbles.

David recoiled down into the sand at the base of the stones, trying instinctively to turn upside down so he could defend himself. When he finally succeeded, he was face-to-face with the swimmer in the black wet suit. Then the other man reached down and clawed David's face mask right off his head.

David was blinded instantaneously by the sudden loss of his mask as he felt the man kick upward. Then he was gone. David caught just a blurry glimpse of a black swim fin disappearing over the top edge of the ashlar, some fifteen feet above him, pursued now by the expanding cloud of blood and bubbles streaming from the sagging, inert body in front of him.

David's head began to pound, reminding him to suck in a deep breath from his mouthpiece, and then a couple more. He was still trying to comprehend what he'd just witnessed. He could breathe, although the saltwater was stinging his eyes. He knew what that stick was—it was called a bang-stick, used normally as a last line of defense against an attacking shark. Two to three feet long with a 12-gauge shotgun shell contained in a small, waterproof power head at one end. You made sure the head was in solid contact with the shark and then you fired it. Then you got the hell out of there before his buddies showed up for lunch.

He examined the woman's body in front of him. It was hovering just above the bottom, arms and legs outstretched and relaxed, fingers trailing in the sand, and still leaking profusely. She was quite obviously dead. He immediately wondered if there were sharks in the remains of the harbor.

No reason why not, he thought, and levitated himself smartly out of the ashlar canyon to go find Judith and the tour guide. He kicked hard to get over to the shipwreck where they were still kneeling down on the bottom, sifting the sandy bottom with their fingers, apparently looking for artifacts. He reached the guide and made the emergency/distress signal, then the follow-me signal. Once the guide saw the woman's body down between the massive breakwater stones, she went right to the surface and popped a signaling device.

An hour later David and Judith were in a police van parked on the beach, talking to two detectives, while the crew of an Israeli navy launch retrieved the unfortunate woman's body from the harbor. All the other excursions in the harbor had been canceled. While waiting for the cops to arrive, David had tried to make sense of what had happened down there. Had the killer been hunting him, specifically, or was he some kind of terrorist who just wanted to shoot a tourist? A bang-stick was a one-shot device—once he'd fired it, the killer could no longer do anything to David unless he wanted to get into an underwater knife fight. He'd done the next best thing—ripped David's face mask off, which then gave him time to swim away. As the detectives approached, David thought fast. His whole plan to go back to Masada would be in jeopardy if he told the cops that it looked as if *he* had been the intended victim. He'd decided to leave that little bit of information out when he told the cops what he'd seen.

Man in a black wet suit, swimming above me. Waved like any other tourist. I waved back. I was down on the bottom, looking at the big breakwater stones, which form a sort of canyon down there. Next thing I know there's a woman in front of me, and we bump into each other. Then she looks over my shoulder and—bang! It all happened in deep shadow between two enormous blocks of stone. The bang-stick was probably a 12-gauge, since it didn't have a long pole on it, and then he ripped off my face mask. That's what I saw.

You recognized this bang-stick, as you call it?

Sure; I've never used one, but I've seen the training videos. Used to protect yourself from an aggressive shark.

The two detectives asked him to go through it all again, then told him to remain in the area while they went to talk to the tour guide. David and Judith walked over to the seaside café nearby, where David ordered a brandy to steady his nerves. Judith hadn't actually seen the woman's body down between the giant stones, but she was still pretty upset at what had happened. They watched as the cops tried to get the attention of the recovery boat. They saw their tour guide in the back of the boat, and she looked just a little hysterical. A TV news-van crew was trying to talk its way through the entrance; they didn't seem to be making much headway with the big cop at the gate.

"Well, didn't this turn out to be a great date," David said, shaking his head.

"Out of nowhere," Judith said. "That's a state park, the ancient harbor. How does an armed man just swim into a state park, with all those people around?"

"There were lots of people visiting the park. He could have been with the snorkel group, or he just came around the breakwater. That poor woman. Talk about wrong place, wrong time. God!"

He hadn't told Judith that the man first threatened him with the bang-stick, and he wasn't going to, either. He was beginning to think that it *had* been a threat, or otherwise he would never had the chance to turn around—the bang-stick was in contact before he even knew what was touching him. Judith was asking him something.

"You don't think this was some kind of accident? An undersea hunter, shooting in the dark?"

"It wasn't like a spear gun, where you shoot from a distance," he said. "It was a bang-stick. First you have to press it against the predator's skin—*then* you fire it. This was no accident. He meant to kill that woman."

"Did the police say who she was?"

"A tourist is all they know right now," he said, wanting another brandy but deciding not to have one. Their lovely outing had been ruined, and all he wanted to do was get the hell out of there. Like he'd told the cops, he'd never fired a bang-stick, but he'd seen a training video where a diver used one against a fifteen-foot tiger shark, giving it a shot to the gills. The huge creature had been killed instantly.

The detectives came back over to them from the beach and told David he could go back to his hotel. They cautioned him not to leave the country just yet as there might be more questions. Judith asked about the victim's identity, but the cops just shrugged. A tourist, that's all we know.

They got back to his hotel an hour and a half later, where David prepared to send Judith home in the hired car. She surprised him.

"You've had a bad shock," she said. "You should not be alone just now. Let's have Ari drive us around. We can go to the Carmel, where I grew up. It's very pretty up there, and there are some interesting historical sites. The fortress of Acre is just beyond. You should definitely see that."

The last thing David wanted to do was go sightseeing. He still wanted another brandy, and then he wanted to crawl into a hole somewhere. He couldn't erase the way that guy had looked at him while pressing the bang-stick into his neck.

372

The killing had been bad enough. That look had been even worse.

"Come on," she insisted. "Ari, can you take us to Haifa?"

Ari gave David raised eyebrows, and he reluctantly nodded. Maybe she was right. Movement, activity, was probably better than being alone in the room, still seeing that horrible cloud.

They stopped for a late lunch up in Haifa, where he had a glass of wine and she actually ate lunch. Then she gave him a quick windshield tour of her hometown and the higher precincts of Mount Carmel. After that they went up the coast to the looming fortress of Acre. David had always thought that the fortified town right on the Mediterranean was a Crusader-era fortress, until he saw the plaque in the main entrance tunnel that listed the Conquerors of Acre, with one of the first ones being Ramses II. After a while, he got back into the groove and began paying attention to all the things she was showing him. They then spent a quiet trip back through late afternoon traffic on the coast highway, during which time she fell asleep on his shoulder.

David had been very glad he had hired the car and driver, because when they got to his hotel, she had suggested they go to dinner at a small place near her apartment in Jerusalem. He was more than amenable. He dropped off his diving gear, showered, and changed clothes, and then they went up to Jerusalem. When they got to her apartment, he quietly told Ari to pick him up at midnight. She changed, and they went out to a nearby restaurant and came back to her apartment a little after ten o'clock. She broke out a bottle of wine, and they sat out on the tiny balcony overlooking the garden enclosure. For a little while they simply sat there, not talking. David felt unusually comfortable doing just that, except for the residual horror at what had happened earlier in the day. He'd been squeezing it out of his mind all day.

"You were pleased with the restaurant?" she asked. He could see her face in the soft night light. Her dark eyes were luminous and concerned.

"Absolutely," he said. "With one major exception, the whole day was delightful. Thank you for sharing it with me."

"Thank you," she said. "I haven't done so many different things for . . . for a very long time."

He heard the hesitation and realized that she was still on pretty shaky emotional ground even spending time with him. The tragedy in the harbor hadn't helped. While he had been opening the bottle of wine and looking for glasses, she had touched up her makeup and refreshed her perfume. He was edified that she bothered, and very pleased to see that those dark shadows under her eyes had diminished, but knew better than to make any physical moves, much as he wanted to. He did not want to admit to her how badly the incident at the harbor had scared him. More than that, however, he was grappling with an overwhelming urge to tell her what he'd found on the mountain.

"It will come," he said quietly, not looking directly at her. A man's voice rose in argument somewhere below them, answered quickly by a woman's angry retort.

"Ah, marital bliss," he said with a smile, and she laughed. They went silent again as the argument got louder; then a door was slammed and the drama ended. They'd had the TV on earlier to see if there was news of the incident. The broadcast was, of course, in Hebrew, but Judith said they were calling it a spear-fishing accident. The TV was muted now, but light from the screen was flickering against the windows.

"I have a confession to make," she said. He turned his head to look at her.

"I have not made love with a man since Dov died. When I was with you, today, at Caesarea, I suddenly wanted to. Make love, I mean. My body ambushed me, I think." She stopped then, and he saw that she thought she had embarrassed herself.

"But?" he asked gently.

"But," she repeated, "my thinking mind was shocked. I felt so very guilty, as if my body had betrayed me into thinking impure thoughts."

He smiled at her in the darkness. "I have to say that those are not necessarily bad thoughts."

"Oh, no, I didn't mean it that way," she said all in a rush, her hand at her mouth. "I mean, it wasn't—I didn't mean that you—"

He put up his hand. "I know, Judith. This isn't about me. I find you extremely attractive. I think you know that. And of course, I would like to make love with you. What man wouldn't? But I would be astonished if you just hopped into bed with anyone right now, me or anyone else."

She sipped some wine, unable to meet his eyes. "This is so embarrassing," she said. "I can't believe I said that."

"Look," he said, "we're grown-ups, right? We're not two college kids trying to figure out who makes the first move. I like you. I like being with you. You're easy on the eyes, and you're smarter than I am. For me that's a very appealing combination. I'm satisfied to spend time with you and let whatever will happen just happen. So you relax, okay? Be yourself. I'll be myself. For right now, that's good enough."

She took a deep breath and let it out. "Thank you, Mr. Hall."

"Thank you, David."

"Yes, okay. David."

Then he asked her what lay ahead in her career at the university, and she began to talk again. It gave him time to quell his own tumbling thoughts.

Leading her on like this, he was beginning to feel like a true jerk. He had meant it when he said he would like to make love, but he knew that as long as he was lying to her about what he was really up to, that wasn't going to happen, no matter what *she* did. He was using her and on another level, abusing her growing trust. He had to think of a way to break this off. No, you need her for the endgame, he reminded himself. Now someone had threatened to kill him, and he didn't dare tell anyone. He was beginning to think that he had vastly overestimated his James Bond skills. *Shit!*

You have to tell her, the voice in his head declared. You *have* to.

"Where did you go, Mr. David Hall?"

Startled, he looked over at her. He hadn't realized she'd stopped talking. "Is there any more wine?" he asked, stalling for time.

"Certainly," she said, giving him a perplexed look before getting up to fetch another bottle. She came back, refilled his glass, and sat back down. Given that he was about to come clean, he wondered if they should move inside to the living room to spare the neighbors some reciprocal noise.

"Now I have a confession to make," he said finally. He was glad that it was fully dark now. He didn't want her to see his embarrassment.

"Oh, dear, now what?" she asked with a wan smile.

He drank some more wine. "I'll tell you on one condition," he said. "You say nothing until I'm finished. Then if you want to yell at me, you can."

"Why on earth would I want to—oh, no, not the Metsadá business again?"

He held up his hand. "Hear me out. Please."

Her smile faded. His heart sank. Oh, well, he thought, in for a penny, in for a pound.

"It begins with Adrian, the woman who started all this, who fired up my desire to come here, to go to Metsadá. You remember the story I told at the first meeting? About her theories concerning the Zealots?"

She nodded.

"That wasn't quite true," he said. He sipped some more wine while trying to assemble his thoughts. Incongruously, a bird began warbling its song from one of the trees below.

"That the Kanna'im had escaped the mountain?" she asked. "Regrouped somewhere else?"

"Yes. Her theory was actually this: They chose suicide not to spite the Romans but to keep a secret. To protect something hidden there."

She sighed. "Oh, Mr. Hall," she said. "You are telling me you're just another treasure hunter after all?"

He couldn't think of anything to say.

She put down her own wineglass. "This is not exactly an original theory, you know," she said. "People have been looking up on that mountain for years. Decades, even. Archaeologists looking for evidence of nine hundred sixty skeletons somewhere. Treasure hunters looking for the gold described in the Scrolls. The results are always the same: There's nothing there. Nothing but the mountain and the myth."

He lost his nerve. She was too much the skeptic about the entire story. Hell with it, he decided. He was in too deep now to turn back. He'd make the dive. If there was nothing in the cistern, then there was no point in making a fool of himself now by telling her about the cistern in the first place, or how he'd found it.

"Mr. Hall?"

"Sorry. It just seemed so plausible."

"Is that the reason you went up there at night? You were looking for treasure?"

He nodded. "It wasn't the only reason. I did want to get a feel for the place and contemplate the history. The myth, as you call it."

"Not just me, Mr. Hall. Most professional archaeologists would call that story a myth. Until someone finds real evidence, it will remain a myth."

"Won't find it if no one is looking," he said.

"It's been two thousand years," she said. "If someone finds a cave with nine hundred sixty skeletons, then, yes, we will all look a little foolish."

Right now, I'm the one looking a little foolish,

he thought. He looked at his watch and began making as graceful an exit as he could manage. He got out his rented cell phone and texted Ari to bring the car up.

They stood by the doorway as he waited for the car. Kiss the pretty girl good night? He looked into her large, dark eyes and saw the expectation. He kissed her then, lightly, tentatively even, and then again with a little more feeling. She broke it off after a few moments and smiled at him as she opened the door.

"Good night, Mr. Treasure Hunter," she said.

"Can I see you again?" he asked, surprising himself.

She cocked her head to one side. "You are not yet officially shot down, David Hall. We shall see."

As Ari drove him back to his hotel, David wondered if this whole project wasn't getting a bit out of hand. The incident in the harbor had unsettled him, despite Judith's all-day attempts to push it away. Would that guy have shot him if the woman hadn't blundered into the frame? Had one of Israel's many security organs deduced what he was up to? He'd found the cistern that no one knew about—was that enough? Why make a very dangerous dive into a black hole? Why not simply tell Judith and let the experts do it right?

He became aware of headlights behind them as

380

they went down the winding highway back to Tel Aviv. It looked like the other car had his high beams on.

"We being followed, Ari?" he asked the driver.

"Some asshole with his bright lights on," Ari grumbled. "I will slow down, make him pass."

Ari began reducing speed on the four-lane, and after a minute or so the other vehicle swung out and went past. David could see that it was some kind of nondescript van. He half expected a window to come down and bullets to start flying, but the van disappeared around the next bend in the road as Ari resumed highway speed.

Getting a little paranoid here, David thought. He turned around to look out the rear window and saw another set of headlights behind them, about a half mile back. This vehicle was on low beam. Was it a box trap being set up? He'd seen one in a movie, where the car ahead dropped back and the one behind sped up, and then the two of them pushed the target vehicle off the road and over a cliff. He looked sideways. There wasn't a cliff, but there was a pretty deep ravine. He peered past Ari's shoulder to see if he could spot the van, but there were no lights ahead as the road straightened out and the lights of the city hove into view ahead.

Get a grip, he thought. I'm gonna do it. I'm going to prove them all wrong about what happened long ago. Adrian might have dumped him after he got himself fired, but she had well and truly infected him with her unswerving belief in her theory. It was his theory now; nothing was going to stop him from validating it, one way or another.

"No traffic now," Ari called out from the front seat. "Fifteen minutes, tops."

20

He missed the turnoff onto the military road just north of the mountain, catching only a glimpse of it as he drove by in the darkness along the Dead Sea road. He slowed, stopped, turned off the head-lamps, and then carefully turned around to find the entrance again. It was nearly 10:00 P.M., and he could just see the security lights of the hostel and tourist complex shining down onto the tour bus parking lot three miles down the road. He hoped no one had seen him coming.

The main road veered east toward the Dead Sea shore just north of the fortress mountain, so his headlamps should not have been pointed directly at the tourist center. On the other hand, he had seen no other vehicles out here for an hour. He spotted the entrance again and veered left onto a gravel road that wasn't much wider than the Land Rover itself. He pulled a hundred yards off the road and shut the engine off, got out, stretched, and then walked to the back of a boulder to take a leak. To his left, two miles distant, the fortress loomed atop its sheer stone cliffs. The pale bones of Herod's marble palace-villas, perched out on the descending step terraces, shone through the darkness. He shivered in the rapidly cooling desert air as he looked up at it. Ahead the desert track led up toward the western plateau where the main Roman siege camp had been set up. He got back in the Land Rover and started up the track, now using only his parking lights. There would be no moon for several more hours, but the starlight was adequate.

A quarter mile in from the Dead Sea road he passed through the remains of the circumvallation wall, which now was just a two-foot-high pile of weathered stones disappearing in a ragged line into the darkness. The wall, a standard feature of all Roman sieges, was the first thing General Silva had erected after the main siege camp. It had then been an eight-foot-high rock wall thrown up around the entire circumference of the mountain, bolstered by outpost camps whose outlines could still be discerned from the mountaintop, and patrolled by sentries for the entire course of the siege. It had been designed to keep anyone from coming down off the mountain at night to escape the siege.

The track rose steeply now, and he had to drop the Land Rover into a lower gear to make the climb. He heard the equipment shift behind him as the boxy vehicle tilted upward. The army had bulldozed this track up to the western plateau so that the Yadin expedition could get their equipment and tents closer to the fortress. He thought it ironic that the Israelis had sought the same ground General Silva occupied two thousand years ago.

Once he got up onto the plateau he passed by the rubble of the main Roman camp's wall. He pulled the Land Rover up to four old Israeli Army Conex boxes that stood next to the remains of a mining cable-car tower. The army had erected the cable tramway using two towers back in the early sixties, one at the base of the siege ramp and the other up at the top of the mountain on the western parapet walls. The tramway was no longer operational, but they had not seen fit to dismantle the towers other than to take down the actual cables and the tower top on the ramp. The corrugated steel Conex boxes were the World War II variant of modern-day seagoing containers, some twenty feet long, eight feet wide, and seven feet high. They had been used during World War II to move cargo and then as shelters for small field headquarters or radio communications stations once at the battlefront. The U-shaped cluster of boxes made for a perfect place to nest the Land Rover, which should keep it out of sight of anyone looking down from the mountain and, he hoped, any patrols passing along the western rim of the Wadi Masada. He doused the lights, got out, put on his windbreaker, and then sat down on the steps of one of the Conex boxes to listen and watch for a while.

There was a light breeze blowing up here on the bare plateau. Surrounding the boxes and the tramway tower were small rocky enclosures that had been the foundations of the Roman army storehouses during the siege. The place was eerily beautiful in the starlit darkness. He marveled at the logistics of the siege. The Romans had had to bring everything they needed for subsistence down from the wreck of Jerusalem, including drinking water, because the Dead Sea was nothing more than a mineral stew. Water for the three thousand men of Silva's army had been carried for two and a half years all the way across the Judaean fastness by women prisoners of war. They used Roman amphorae, the ubiquitous two-handled clay jars that could hold up to three gallons and weighed fifty-seven pounds. Once the women arrived with the jars, they were put to work building the siege ramp. When they became exhausted with the routine of filling baskets with sand and then carrying them up to the base of the mountain, they would be rounded up and marched back to the springs of Ein Gedi to bring more water. Those who could still walk, anyway.

He had left a message on Judith's voice mail saying that he was feeling out of sorts after what had happened in the harbor and that he'd be in touch in a couple of days. He'd deliberately called early so that he wouldn't have to speak directly to her. It seemed the least harmful lie he could tell her, especially considering the larger lie of what he was attempting down here. If they caught him this time, the best that could happen would be immediate expulsion from the country.

After watching for a half hour, he began unloading equipment from the Land Rover. He had brought two large cotton laundry bags, into which went all his gear. The four filled air tanks were belted into dual-tank harnesses on luggage wheels. There were two additional bags with camp food, water, and other necessaries.

He took one more look around. No way around it, he thought and began humping the gear up the siege ramp. Thank God he'd asked for lightweight tanks.

It took him four hours to get everything up to the top and then over to the bat cave. Knowing that moonrise was going to be at just after three in the morning, he had first taken everything up the ramp to the casemate wall and then worked to move it across to the cave. That way, if there was a patrol out there on the wadi, he would not still be exposed in full view out on the ramp. The Land Rover was a potential liability. It was hidden, sort of, between two of the Conex boxes. If they did find the Land Rover, they'd know something was going on, but by then he'd be hidden in the cave. Even then, it could still all go wrong. They could trace the Land Rover to his rental information; the moment that news penetrated the archaeological network, there'd be an angry crowd on the mountain looking for him. Dogs could find him quickly.

After getting everything into the cave, he had taken a look down at the visitors center lot. There were four vehicles parked in the lot and, surprisingly, one darkened tour bus. By this juncture, he had modified his own plan slightly. He would take a quick nap through the remaining hours of darkness and then go down to get the Land Rover just before dawn, when any patrols should be on their way to breakfast. He would drive the Land Rover back to the main road and go *north* instead of south, until he got to Qumran. Then he would turn around and come back to the Masada visitors center, arriving as if he were an early tourist. With a floppy hat and some wrap-around sunglasses, he should be unrecognizable, especially if he waited for the first tours to arrive. He would get something to eat and additional water, then take the first cable car to the top, or perhaps the second, which would be more crowded. After that, he would play tourist until late morning and then get in line for the downhill cable car. At the last moment he would pretend to have lost something, drop out of the line, and make his way into the casemate and from there to the bat cave.

He planned to do the first dive right away, so that if he did make a discovery, he would still have time to get down the mountain and call Judith before everything shut down for the Sabbath. That would also allow him to resolve any head-count discrepancies at the end of the day down at the visitors center. He didn't need the security force getting all spun up over the possibility that a tourist was missing on the mountain, and he especially didn't want soldiers searching the Serpent Path.

He looked at his watch. It was just after 4:00 A.M. on Friday. He shone his flashlight around the musty cave, making sure he kept the light away from the small entrance hole. The ammonia stink was still there, although there was no fresh bat sign. The water remained at the same level as before, right up even with the bottom of the slab ledge. He shone his flashlight down into it but saw nothing except the refracted beams. He would rest for an hour and a half and then go back down the ramp.

21

Judith got to her office at a little after nine Friday morning. She went through her e-mail and voice messages, hoping that there might be word from the American. Despite their intimacy, that was how she still thought of him in her mind—the American. Mr. Hall. David. She couldn't quite bring herself to call him by his first name. His message about not feeling well had really disappointed her, more than she had expected. He had kissed her, a gentle, opening gambit kind of kiss. So very nice. She paused, staring at her e-mail screen without seeing it. She hadn't slept for two hours thinking about her day with him and that kiss, but of course, anyone would still be upset after witnessing what he'd seen.

There were no other messages. Nothing. She thought about calling him at the hotel, just to cheer him up a little. The phone rang. The departmental weekly meeting. She groaned and gathered up her portable and coffee cup.

She did not get back to her office until after lunch. There was still no word from the American. She decided to call his hotel in Tel Aviv after all. The desk rang her through to his room and then to voice mail. She left a brief hope-you're-feeling-better message and hung up. Then she wondered. Had the police come back? Was he waiting in some interrogation room at headquarters? Or maybe he'd eaten something last night that had made him ill—it happened to visiting Americans all the time. What if he'd been hospitalized? She called back, asked for the concierge, and explained the situation. The concierge put her on hold and came back a few minutes later. No report of Mr. Hall being ill or being taken anywhere; shall we check the room? Yes, please. Fifteen minutes later the concierge called her back. The room appears to be in order; his things are still there. No signs of trouble—is it possible that there's a different interpretation? As in, he's decided not to call you, Mrs. Ressner? Instantly embarrassed, Judith thanked him for his trouble and hung up.

What the hell, she wondered. Had she totally misread the American? That he'd failed to "score" that night in her apartment and had decided to just move on? She frowned. Not at all, she thought. That good-night kiss. There'd been a gentle promise there. She thought about it. Then she remembered he had originally been planning some more diving expeditions, although that was unlikely after what had happened at Caesarea. She fished in her purse for the receipts from the dive shop and made one more call.

David was suited up and ready to go into the cistern just before noon. Everything with the Land

Rover and the morning ascent to the fortress had gone as planned. As long as he got back down before the entire place shut down for Shabbat, he could make sure the security people got a correct head count. Stupid tourist just wandered off somewhere.

He checked his gear for the umpteenth time, switched on his headlamp, activated his dive console, and then lowered himself into the black rectangle of water at the bottom of the slab opening. He had pulled two of the steel staging pipes across the opening so he would have something to grab when he came back up. He'd also attached a hundred-foot-long rope to one of the pipes and then tied a spare handheld battery lamp to the end of it and added a few rocks in a catch bag. He switched the lamp on and then lowered eighty feet of the rig into the water, paying out line until it hung straight down. This would give him a reference point within the cistern to lead him back up to the hole. From the surface, he could not make out the light down below in the black water.

He'd measured the water temperature and found it to be warmer than he had expected, sixty-two degrees. Although this was far from warm, he calculated that this would give him an extra two minutes at maximum depth. He'd split the difference in his calculations and set the bottom time for fifteen minutes, with bottom time defined as the time from beginning of his descent until beginning of his ascent. If he came up to a lesser depth sooner than that, he'd gain an extra few minutes at the lesser depth, but not much. He was using the rules for recreational diving and trying to be conservative.

He sat there on the edge for a moment. What are you waiting for? he asked himself. The image of that wet-suited figure hovering above him looked back at him from the black surface. Was he really ready to go back underwater? He'd been mentally skating around a grimmer possibility regarding the incident in the harbor. Had someone tried to warn him off what he was doing? If so, that someone had to know what he was up to, and if that was true, the someone might decide to take even harsher measures now that he'd come back to the mountain. He shook his head like a wet dog to clear away the dark thoughts and then dropped into the water.

He adjusted his mask and regulator and let go of the pipe. He was now neutrally buoyant, not floating anymore but definitely not sinking. He arced over and began to swim down into the cistern. The water was not exactly clear, but it wasn't murky either. He turned periodically to sight in on the reference line with its dangling light, which was more visible now that he was heading down into the cavern. Of the walls he could see absolutely nothing, and he experienced a moment of vertigo as he stopped, suspended in a volume of water, his headlamp sending refracted beams of light into the void. He was absolutely, positively breaking all the rules here: a deep dive, by himself, no backup on the surface, and into a cavern about which he knew nothing. Brave? Yes, but not very bright, as he had heard his Uncle Jack say all too often.

After three minutes, he finally reached the bottom and hovered upright, paddling upward with gentle flapping motions to stay near the bottom. Then he bent over to touch the bottom and found, to his amazement, that it was littered with what looked like crusty, earthen half-sized bricks. There was a film of superfine silt along the bottom, and his efforts to inspect the bricks immediately enveloped him in a brown cloud. He swam sideways away from the silt cloud until the water cleared. He looked around for the reference light and found it behind him, not where he expected it to be. He looked straight up to assure himself that his bubbles were going up, not sideways or even down. They were. His wrist depth gauge indicated one hundred and four feet. He looked at his dive console compass and then started swimming due west, which should take him to the interior wall of the cavern. After a minute and a half he came up against it, a smooth rock surface that appeared to be natural, not man-hewn like the cisterns in the fortress's side walls.

Suspicions confirmed, he thought; much too big to have been man-made. He turned right, or north, and swam along the wall, ascending now to eighty feet, looking for steps or a ladder of some sort cut into the wall, but there was nothing. He did notice that there was a thin, boiling cloud of silt trailing behind him.

He kept an eye on the glow of his reference light out in the middle and realized that after a minute or so, it was moving to his right, which meant the cavern was indeed spherical, with a continuously curving wall. When he got to what should be the north side, he checked his time and found he had about eight minutes left, based on a hundred-and-ten-foot dive. He kept checking his compass, and when he was swimming in a southerly direction he ascended to seventy feet, some thirty-five feet off the floor of the cavern. Here there were no more silt clouds. The bottom must be layered with very fine mud particles. He kept going until he was headed west again, which meant he had reached the southern curve of the sphere. Still no features worth mentioning, just smooth rock walls, with the occasional vein of quartz gleaming back at him.

He stopped when he was pointed north again, alongside the west wall, and checked time and depth. The timer was based on the deep dive of a hundred and ten feet, but he had been at eighty to seventy feet longer than he had been at the deepest depth. He had a few extra minutes. He was comfortable enough from the exertion of breathing and swimming, but he knew he dared not push it. One of the first deadly things nitrogen did was to cloud a diver's judgment. He checked his reference light once more and was just barely able to see its glow out there in the middle somewhere. He realized he should have left another light on up at the exit hole, in case something happened to the reference light.

Crazy shit you're doing down here, he thought. His old diving instructor would kick his ass three ways for this: long, hard, and often. Along with a lot of Israelis, too, he thought with a mental smile. He ascended again, now up to fifty feet, and reversed course, going back counterclockwise around the vast cavern, looking for anything at all. He'd made it all the way around the southern and eastern sides when his timer alarm pulsed. He reset it for two more minutes and kept going; if he was going to break all the safety rules, why not one more? Was that nitrogen talking?

He had traversed what should have been the western face when the timer pulsed again, and this time he turned his face up and began the ascent, straight up the wall.

Fifteen feet up a dark shadow caught his eye. He stopped and turned around.

There.

He swam over to the shadow and saw that a

large round boulder was protruding out of the smooth rock wall like a bulging eyeball. It stuck out enough to create a shadow when his headlamp hit it from below. He swam around it, wondering why there would be this discontinuity in the otherwise smooth cistern wall. There was another shadow ten feet away. He swam over to this and discovered a narrow opening. A cave? He put his head in and saw that the cave was very shallow, a pit more than a cave. It ended about eight feet back. He pulled out and saw yet another shadow. Same thing—another small fissure that went nowhere.

He went back to the boulder and checked his console. Thirty-five feet. Air to spare. Swimming in place beneath it, he ran his hand over the slippery rock surface. Bits of rock fell away, as if it were rotten. It looked like sandstone, and the water had corroded the edges. He saw a small cloud of silt squirt out around the bottom of the boulder. Silt? Why would there be silt up here on the side of the cistern? There shouldn't be—

With a swelling wave of pressure, the boulder began to move, tipping out of the hole behind it and then coming straight down toward him. He backed furiously out of the way as the stone slid silently past him like a ship going down the building ways, grazing his chest and boots and rolling him in the water with its wake vortex. Then he was moving again, but this time, he was being sucked *into* a cave opening that had been behind the boulder. His tank and then his arms banged on the rock walls as he went in, rolling out of control, for a distance of about twelve feet before the cave narrowed to the point where the inrushing water pinned him to the walls. Finally everything settled down, and he could extract himself.

He paddled backward toward the entrance for a few feet while adjusting his diving rig and checking for problems. Everything seemed to be okay except his wildly beating heart. Then he focused on where his headlamp was pointing. The passage ahead was extremely narrow, but it was definitely a natural cave. More important, ten feet into the upwardly sloping passage he could make out what looked like a vertical stone slab. The slab was white in his headlamp light, not like the dark rock walls of the cavern at all. *Bingo,* he thought, and then remembered to look at his timer. Overtime.

He backed out and continued the ascent until his head bumped gently against the top of the drowned cavern. He looked for the reference light but could only see a faint, diffused glow well beneath him. There was no single point of light, just the glow. *Idiot* for not leaving a light in the entrance, he thought, as he fought down an impulse of panic. Then he regained control. His virtual depth was about two feet, so he had some time here, and still plenty of air. He swam around the rim of the cistern ceiling until he was pointed east again. Then he turned hard right and swam due south, trying to keep the glow directly beneath him. The first time he missed the line entirely and came up against the south wall. He turned left, went three feet or so, and then moved back out toward the center of the cavern, mentally trying to clamp down on his growing fear. The problem was that he was too far up above the damned light. If he didn't find the line this time he would have to dive again, and that could cause him some nitrogen problems later. He needed to get out of the water and start the surface interval phase. He looked at his timer, which displayed an accusing zero on its dial.

He steadied himself and his breathing, took a careful bearing on the compass, and set out again, watching the glow of the light below. From every position, it looked like it was right beneath him. He swam all the way across again and found nothing. Dammit! Had the line broken? Was the light sitting down there on the bottom? Then he had an idea. He swam back out into what he guessed was the middle of the sphere and then followed his bubble trail to the top. At the ceiling, he watched in chagrin as the bubbles turned behind his shoulder, marching in a silvery trail, bouncing across the ceiling. He followed the trail and popped up in the opening thirty seconds later, feeling like even more of an idiot. The line to the light was, of course, still there. He spat out the regulator and then hoisted himself up onto the edge using the steel pipes.

Checking his watch, he found he had been down there for twenty-five minutes, well over the calculated bottom time. On the plus side was the fact that he had not been at depth for all of that. He should be okay from the point of view of getting the dreaded bends, with "should" being the operative word. It was almost one o'clock. He would rest on the surface for two full hours just to make sure, and then he'd go back down to explore that cave. He would take a fresh tank this time, although there was still air left in the first tank— and this time, he would light up the damned entrance hole! He turned around, fished his reference light back out of the cavern, and began stripping off his gear.

22

Judith was going through the motions of working midafternoon Friday when Professor Ellerstein called. He wanted to know how she was doing and how her first week back among the living had gone.

"Not too badly," she said, suppressing an image of the previous evening. Not too badly, indeed. "It is an effort, though."

"I understand, but it is a worthy effort. I will tell you that Strauss has noticed a difference. He is very pleased with your decision."

"Well, good," she said. "The meetings are still pretty boring."

"Have you ever been to an exciting meeting, Yehudit?" he asked.

"Not here, Yossi," she said with a smile,

"How's the American doing, do you know?"

"Ah, yes, the American. Actually—"

"Yes?"

"Well, I've been seeing the American. He insisted on taking me to dinner to make amends for his indiscretion at Metsadá. I even went on a diving expedition with him, to Caesarea Maritima, which ended very badly."

"The murder there? That German tourist? You were there?"

She told him the whole story, and that she'd spent the rest of the day trying to settle the American's badly rattled nerves.

"Well, good for you, Judith. Good for you. Besides, he seemed like a nice man."

"Yes, well, he *is* a nice man," she said evasively. She'd told him about their day, but not their evening. "Although right now I'm not sure what he's up to. We were supposed to get together yesterday, but he left a message that he was still upset over what had happened. That he'd canceled his final diving tours, which I totally understand.

Then today, when I called to check on him, the hotel people say he's not there. I'm thinking the police have come back, maybe he got sick, you know."

There was an embarrassed silence at the other end.

"So," she said, bridling a little. "You think it's a brush-off, yes?"

"Um, well, I have no idea. It may just mean that he is walking around rubber-legged trying to get some fresh air. Like you say, after a night of hugging his toilet bowl."

"I suppose," she said, trying not to sound petulant, although Yossi's tone of voice sounded a lot like that damned concierge.

"Perhaps *I* should check on him," Ellerstein said. "Technically, I am his interlocutor here."

"I suppose," she said again.

"I'll do that. Then I'll call you back, at home, tonight."

"You don't have to do this, Yossi."

"I want to, Yehudit. What do the Americans say—just to close the loop? I don't know what is this loop, but I'll let you know something as soon as I know something. Shalom."

She hung up, a little relieved that Ellerstein was going to check on Mr. David Hall. It was something he could do that she could not, not without awkwardness. Then she remembered the dive shop. Maybe he had shown up today after all? She looked up the number and called the shop again. No, he had not shown up, and they had no messages. He did have four of their tanks, by the way, and they were just a tiny bit concerned about that.

"Four?" she asked.

"Yah, four."

That threw her for a minute. They had taken four single tanks to their dive at Caesarea, but she was pretty sure they had all ended up back in the lovely instructor's van. Why on earth would he have four of their tanks? That indicated either several dives or a couple of deep dives. She thanked the manager and hung up.

Something not quite right here, she thought. Unless he was going to make more dives at other sites along the coast. The manager hadn't seemed upset, just wondering where his tanks were. Perhaps that was it: David had gone diving somewhere else, just to get his nerve back after the awful thing he'd witnessed.

She would wait for Yossi's call tonight.

Ellerstein called the hotel in Tel Aviv and asked for Mr. David Hall's room. He got hotel voice mail. He called the assistant manager, explained who he was and why he was calling, and asked the man to go check the room. The manager was not exactly enthusiastic, and Ellerstein proceeded to lay a little ministry authority on him. The manager said he would call him back. Ellerstein, on his government phone, said he would hold, thank you very much. As in, do it now, please. The man was back in six minutes. "The room is made up; his things are there. Housekeeping reports no signs of illness, and they should know. The bed has not been slept in since Wednesday."

"Ah, so? Since Wednesday?"

"That's what the floor supervisor reports. Perhaps Mr. Hall has found better circumstances, yes?"

"That's always possible," Ellerstein mused. He thanked the man for his efforts and hung up. He leaned back in his chair. No signs of illness, and the maids would know. So where was the elusive Mr. David Hall? He was rich enough to have booked into another hotel somewhere while out on tour. He was supposed to be scuba diving, wasn't he? For some reason, an image of the mysterious Colonel Lazarus crossed his mind.

He had called Gulder after Skuratov's visit, but Gulder hadn't seemed very impressed. "He wants you to keep an eye on Ressner; so do we. What's the problem?"

"What's the problem? The problem is—"

"No, no, not on this phone, Yossi," Gulder had interrupted. "Look: If your scary colonel is watching the American, he's not watching other things. Then perhaps we can make him move in an unplanned direction. Keep doing what you're doing, Yossi."

He's not my scary colonel, Ellerstein thought. Still, maybe he should call Skuratov and tell him that Yehudit couldn't find Mr. Hall. See what Skuratov knew—he supposedly had the man under surveillance. Maybe the old Russian could tell *him* something, so he could then put Yehudit out of her misery. He fished out the card the colonel had given him and called the number.

"International Planning."

Right, Ellerstein thought. Spooks. He identified himself and asked for Colonel Skuratov. The colonel was not available. Could the man take a message?

"Tell him that Dr. Ressner has not heard from the American, Hall, for a couple of days. Ask him if he knows where the American is."

"Got it," the man said.

"Do you have the first idea of what I'm talking about?" Ellerstein asked.

"None whatsoever, Professor—but then I never do."

"The colonel hasn't said anything about the names Ressner or the American, David Hall? There is no special alert?"

"Look, Professor, I will deliver your message, okay?"

Ellerstein thanked him, and the line went dead. Ellerstein looked at the phone for a moment and then hung up. So much for that great idea. He snorted—all this hugger-mugger about the American. Total nonsense. Now, what *would* he tell Yehudit? Nothing, he told himself. Coward, an inner voice whispered.

23

At three o'clock, David suited up again and prepared for his second dive. The operative mean depth was going to be about thirty-five feet, since he had already inspected the bottom of the cavern. From the dive planner, the no-decompression time limit was two hundred and forty-five minutes. Over three hours. Temperature and residual nitrogen were no longer factors because he needed to be out of the cavern by four anyway, dressed and down the mountain before five-thirty, when the site closed down for Shabbat.

This time he tied off the underwater flashlight close to the slab hole before submerging. The water felt colder as he swam just under the roof of the cavern to the west side and then descended to thirty-five feet of indicated depth. It still took him fifteen minutes to find the cave opening, only to find that this was not the cave. This passage went into the rock wall about ten feet and simply ended, momentarily wedging his tank before he was able to back out. Damn, he thought. How many caves are there in here? He searched some more and finally found what looked like the cave he had seen on the first dive. The entrance was a narrow circle, which then expanded somewhat once he swam in. Following the purple beam from his headlamp, he used his hands to pull himself along the rock wall, sending up small clouds of muddy water as he inched his way forward. His tank clanked on the rock, and he looked up to see that the top of the cave was narrowing rapidly to an acute apex.

Rolling slowly in place to put his tank beneath him and then continued crawling forward, upside down, feeling the first signs of claustrophobia as he pressed forward, entering a cave inside a cave, and under thirty-five feet of water besides. He banished the distracting thoughts and kept going, inching forward now to keep his gear from being damaged. He realized he was breathing too fast and stopped for a moment to calm down. Then he realized his air bubbles were going ahead of him. *Hunh?* They should have been going behind him, out along the roof of the narrow chamber and back up to the slab hole.

He craned his neck straight back to see how close he was to the white slab. Make that the purple slab. The rock walls pressed in on all sides, and he imagined that he could feel them moving, slowly constricting like some stone python to capture him in here for all eternity. *Focus, dammit!* The slab was right ahead of him, shimmering now in the bright light of his headlamp, the colors rippling from white to purple. He reached over his shoulder like a man doing a slow-motion backstroke to touch the slab and hit—nothing.

He stopped cold. *Nothing!* He inched forward again, deeper into the cleft ahead, and again reached out to touch the slab. His hand passed right through it.

There was no slab.

It was an air-water interface. What had looked like a slab was nothing more than the refraction taking place where air and water met.

He inched forward again and felt sand along his hips, then stuck his head into the air of what looked like a round cave. He wriggled himself all the way into the cave and sat up, only then realizing that he had been swimming uphill inside the tunnel as he oriented himself once again on solid ground. The entrance back out to the main cave was now a black, rippling patch of water in the light of the headlamp. He started to take his mouthpiece out but then stopped. How old was the air in here? Was there even oxygen?

Continuing to breathe on the tank, he began to look around. The cave was not really spherical but more in the shape of an ax-head lying on its back, flat and open at the bottom, closing into a knife edge up some twenty feet above his head. There were two sheer, almost vertical walls. The bottom, on which he sat, was deep, loose sand, rising in a gentle slope like a sandy beach from the watery aperture leading back out to the main cavern. The whole cave was perhaps thirty feet in length and no more than ten feet across at the base. There was a structure of some kind, a table or bench, at the far end, under which lay a bundle of rags. Something metallic glinted dangerously near the rags as he shone the light on them.

He tried to figure out why the cave was dry. The only explanation was that the main cave had been dry at one time and then slowly filled with water over the centuries. Eventually the water would have risen past the lower entrance to the tunnel, sealed by that boulder, after which, leaking past the boulder, it would have begun to compress the air inside the sealed cave. When the water pressure outside equaled the air pressure inside, stasis would have occurred, with the air inside becoming a trapped, pressurized bubble.

He checked his elapsed time: thirty minutes. He had to move fast now, do a quick exploration of this virtual time capsule, and then get back out. He decided to stay on the scuba tank. God only knew what ancient microbes might be trapped in this place. He got up on his hands and knees, stood up, took off his fins, and then walked carefully across the sandy floor toward the structure and the rags. When he got closer, he realized that the bundle of rags contained a badly decomposed skeleton, barely recognizable as human bones, complete with a jawless skull. The bones were no longer attached to one another and were clustered around a huge dagger. He didn't touch anything but just stood there, looking down at the human remains. From how long ago, he wondered. Was this one of the Zealots? There were small clay pots scattered around the sand floor of the cave, and their blackened tops showed that they had been used as lamps. His light swept the wall, and he realized that it was covered in writing. It looked like it had been done in charcoal or perhaps lampblack. He could not begin to decipher it, but an examination of both walls revealed that they were entirely covered in some kind of Arabic or Hebraic script, to the height that a man could reach on tiptoes.

He looked up at the bench structure. It was made of wood and shaped like a large table. The legs didn't match: Some were rough-hewn; others appeared to be made of highly polished and richly carved wood. There were rough planks across the top, which was slightly higher than he could see. Ghostly remains of some kind of heavy, decorated cloth draped like spiderwebs down one side. Moving awkwardly in his scuba rig, he walked over to the right side of the cave, where the floor was slightly higher than on the left side. From here, standing on tiptoe, he could just see up onto the top of the structure, and what he saw took his breath away.

The altarlike structure was much deeper than he had thought, its top surface going back into the angle between the two sloping cave walls some four feet. There was a cracked marble slab lying on the planks, and on top of that, lying on its side, was an enormous menorah, the seven-branched candelabrum of Jewish ritual. It looked to be almost five feet from its boxy base to the top of its outflung arms, and close to four feet across. The base was heavily engraved. Two of the seven arms were damaged, bent out of the original plane, but it was still magnificent. The entire artifact appeared to be made of either bronze or even gold, he couldn't be sure. Next to the menorah were several ivory cylinders, their circular bronze or gold ends heavily engraved. The cylinders were shaped like rolling pins and were some six inches in diameter, with ornate wooden handles sticking out of each end. He was pretty sure these were scroll holders. The scrolls, if they were still there, would be sealed inside. The cylindrical sides were embossed with what looked like gold filigree. To the left of the enormous menorah was a pile of what had probably been vestments of some kind, long since rotted away, with only a few patches of color visible in his light. The only other object on the altar top was a small, very plain bronze bowl or cup, eight inches or so in diameter at the top, which was set off to one side with a small pile of what looked like old coins lying right next to it. The cup did not appear to have any markings whatsoever, contrasting dramatically with the glorious objects around it.

He lowered himself to a more comfortable position and tried to slow his heartbeat down. He'd found it. If these objects were sacred relics from the Second Temple, it would be the find of the century. Of course, he had no way of proving that, but the writing on the cave walls, once deciphered, might tell the tale. He examined the pile of bones, kneeling down to study that wicked-looking iron blade. It was almost eighteen inches long, with a workmanlike leather handle. He wanted to pick it up, feel its heft, but knew better than to touch anything. He shone the light on the walls again, covered with their strange symbols. He didn't even know where the text began and ended—but Judith Ressner, ancient language expert, sure as hell would.

He looked at his timer: forty-six minutes. He had to get out of here and back to the surface. He would leave everything right there in the bat cave, changing into his street clothes and then slipping back into the fortress for a cable-car ride. If asked, he'd make something up about trying the Serpent Path descent and then walking around under the fortress walls. The guards would be anxious to close the site down for Shabbat and just tell him to get on the damn cable car. He'd be fine—but he had to get going. Now.

He couldn't wait to call Judith and tell her of his incredible discovery. She would be furious, of course, but he was willing to bet she would come like a bat out of hell when he told her what was buried in the mountain. He tried to control his surging heartbeat. As he exited the cave mouth he anchored a chemical light-stick to a rock and then cracked it on.

Judith got home to her apartment at five o'clock. She was still depressed about not hearing any-thing from David Hall, and the silent, uncaring answering machine did nothing to lift her spirits. She shucked her coat, kicked off her shoes, and went to get a glass of wine. Yossi Ellerstein had also found out nothing, apparently. Or, more likely, was afraid to call her and tell her the truth: Mr. Hall is out on a date with Bar Refaeli.

Yet something was playing at the back of her mind. That business with the extra air tanks—something odd there. Hall was an experienced diver; he wouldn't be planning solo dives any-where, which meant he had to have set up some other diving tours. That in itself was a bit strange, given what had happened. That night together he'd been a bit of a wreck. Now he was diving again? Why hadn't he called her, dammit! Because you were no longer included in the equation, my dear, she thought. The phone rang and she jumped.

"It's me," he said when she answered.

"Indeed," she said, sitting down. "Well, Mr. Me, it is nice to hear from you. At last."

It sounded like he was on a pay phone; she could hear machinery noise in the background, and the sounds of foreign tourists. She'd heard that noise before. Wait—Metsadá? The cable-car machinery room? Oh, no!

"I'm at the hostel. At Metsadá. As you can probably tell."

She felt a flare of anger. "What on earth are you doing there?"

He was silent for a moment while a tour guide got on her bullhorn in Japanese to round up her tour group to get them to their bus.

"I've been bad again," he said. She could barely hear him. Her heart sank when she realized what he was saying.

"Bad? *Bad?!* Oh, no—for God's sake, Mr. Hall—David—tell me you haven't been digging!"

"Not exactly, but I need you to come down here. Immediately."

She pressed the telephone to her head, her thoughts whirling. What had this lunatic been doing? "Me? Why? Why *me?*"

"Because you're an archaeologist. I've made a significant discovery, but now I need a professional."

"A discovery? What kind of discovery?" She was almost afraid to ask. Masada! The authorities would kill him. *She* was ready to kill him.

"How about some major relics from the Second Temple? That strike your fancy?"

She was momentarily stunned into silence. "My God, Mr. Hall," she whispered. "Where? How? What exactly?"

"Too hard to explain this way. I have to leave now—they're closing the place down for the Sabbath. Come down here. Tonight. Please. Meet me at that geothermal building on the seashore."

"*What?* That's impossible. I would have to notify—"

"No!" he shouted and then lowered his voice. "I mean, you can't—you don't know what I've found, but if you come, you will be the discoverer of record."

"Mr. Hall—"

"Because you're the archaeologist. I'm just an amateur. I haven't touched anything. You will be the one, the archaeologist who makes the greatest discovery in modern Jewish history. Think of it."

She did think of it, and then recoiled at the enormity of what he had done. Gone excavating at Masada. After being warned off the site. The IAA would expel him from the country. Any Israeli citizen helping him, especially an Israeli archaeologist . . . well, it was just unimaginable.

"Mr. Hall, this is impossible. I *am* a professional

archaeologist, just as you say. I have responsibilities. A duty to protect ancient sites and relics. I am horrified at what you've done. I couldn't begin to—"

"A gold-plated menorah, two meters high," he whispered. "A dozen or more gold-capped theca, still sealed. A skeleton with a dagger. A cave whose walls are covered in writing."

She was speechless. Two meters? Just like on the Roman coins. *Judaea Capta.* My God, could it be?

"Meet me in three hours," he said. "By that geothermal building. South of the mountain. Drive past it, turn off your lights, and turn around and come back to it. And Judith? Bring your diving gear. It's in a fully flooded cistern. Huge— a hundred feet across, easy. Three hours."

He hung up and she just sat there, the phone pressed against her ear so hard it hurt, still in shock. Slowly she put the phone down and sat back on the couch. Almost unconsciously, she drank the entire glass of wine, while she tried to figure out what to do. Helping him was out of the question, of course. She had to call the chairman immediately. Report what this madman was saying. That he *had* been digging, illegally, on Herod's mountain. That he was claiming to have made an enormous discovery.

Second Temple artifacts!

Then she got angry again. He had lied at every

step. He had come to Israel with this crazy mission in mind all along. All the rest of it had been cover and deception. Getting them to help him gain access to the site. The bumbling amateur act. She should have known when they caught him out on the mountain at night. Communing with the spirits. Scouting was more like it.

And their evening together? More of the same. Now he wanted an archaeologist to somehow legitimize his discoveries? Right.

By now she was furious. The police, that's who he was going to get, she decided. The police, who were already familiar with this man, would treat him to a little scouting expedition to an Israeli jail. She'd call the Interior Ministry, get one of their security teams to meet him in his precious three hours and haul his impudent ass off to jail. Let him spend the night in a cellblock with some bored Palestinian teenagers.

She swore out loud, reached for the phone, and jumped when it rang again. She grabbed it up, ready to yell at him.

24

David left the hostel and went out into the parking lot. It was coming on twilight, and most of the buses had already left. The lights up in the hostel were flicking off. He walked over to his Land Rover, got in, looked around to see if anyone cared what he was doing, and then drove out of the lot. He turned right and headed south toward the bottom of the Dead Sea. A spectacular sunset was shaping up over the escarpments to the west. He drove slowly, enjoying the view but dreading what Judith might do.

Would she come? Or would she call the cops? There hadn't been a crucifixion in Palestine for a good many years, but he could imagine that they might work one up if she called the right people in. Maybe a mistake to have called her. Maybe he should drive back to Jerusalem and hold a little press conference.

The lonely road bore straight south into a landscape of glazed white evaporation ponds dotted with motionless yellow bulldozers. The gaunt shrubbery that littered the seashore up by the mountain was all gone now, the land so saturated with salt that nothing would ever grow there. He checked his rearview mirror; no lights. All the traffic from the site would be northbound, back up to Jerusalem. Then he realized that if he kept going, he was bound to run into an army patrol, and that might be awkward. He slowed and made a U-turn, lowering his own lights to parking lights. He loitered on the way back, going no more than ten miles an hour, killing time to full darkness. He planned to stay down on the seashore to wait for Judith. He'd grabbed one of the last sandwiches out of the cold case and three bottles of water before they shut the place down, so he had the makings of dinner. He was almost too excited to eat.

Would she come? What would he do if she did not?

He finally reached the geothermal complex, which had some security lights blazing on the high chain-link fence surrounding it. He turned off the coast highway and drove down the dirt track toward the salt lake, praying that the place wasn't manned, and parked between two security floodlight poles. Their amber cones of halogen light created a deep shadow right alongside the fence between them. He shut the Land Rover down, doused the parking lights, and sat back to see what would happen. Behind him, just visible in the side mirrors, the tall steel tank tower rumbled quietly in the darkness, as if something were boiling in there. From this angle he could see a large, six-inch-diameter pipe that came out of the low windowless building and ran a few feet above the ground toward the back right corner of the fenced enclosure. Just before the fence it dipped down into the ground and disappeared to the northwest. He wondered if this was a desalinization plant for the tourist site at Masada. That would account for the boiling noises. The sulfurous stench of concentrated bromine salts infiltrated the Land Rover, even though he had the windows almost fully closed against nighttime mosquitoes. Out on the highway nothing moved. The mountain and the hostelry were hidden behind the shoulder of the high mesa that projected out toward the sea like some ancient headland. He waited.

She picked up the phone again. It was Ellerstein.

"Judith, shalom. Forgive me for intruding on your Shabbat."

"That's quite all right," she said, suddenly in a quandary. She'd forgotten it was Shabbat. Should she tell him about David? Yossi probably had connections to the security people. He would know exactly what to do.

"I wasn't able to find out anything about Mr. Hall," he was saying. "His things are all still there in his hotel room, although they haven't seen him and his bed has not been slept in."

"Indeed," she said. Tell him, her conscience urged. Tell him *now*.

"Yes, well, I realize this must be a bit awkward for you. He says he will call, then he does not. The housekeeping people don't think he has been ill, either. I don't know what to say."

"Did they say his diving equipment was there?"

"What? Diving equipment? They didn't mention that. You think he has gone diving somewhere?"

"I called the dive shop where we went. They said he still had some of their tanks. I think that must be it." *Tell* him, the voice in her head was

419

saying. Shouting. "So I must suppose he is on tour somewhere, then, perhaps getting his nerve back after Caesarea," she continued, aware of the tension in her own voice. "Or he has had a better offer."

He laughed. "I can't imagine a better offer than your company, Yehudit. Still, this David Hall: He has done stupid things before, yes?"

You have no idea, she thought. Which is when she realized she wasn't going to tell him. She was going to go down there. *Relics from the Second Temple!* He had used the correct words to describe scroll holders. Hall *knew* what he had been looking at. My God! Right under their feet the whole time.

"He certainly has, Yossi," she said, "but look, this was just—how shall I say it? An interlude. We did not fall in love or anything. He was nice, we had a nice day together, a nice evening. He made no false moves, and, really, no promises other than to call. It's not the end of the world."

"Nice, nice, nice," he grumbled. "He got your hopes up and then dropped you without a word. Not so nice, I think."

"Well, what can I say?" Her voice caught in her throat and she cleared it.

"You're all right, then, Yehudit?" he asked.

"Yes, fine, Yossi. Enjoy a quiet evening. That's what I plan to do."

"Indeed. Very well. I will probably see you next

week. At the Scrolls conference. The ownership debate again. You will attend, yes?"

"Now that I am back among the earnest academics? Yes, I will attend."

"Very good. Until next week, then. Shalom."

"Shalom," she intoned, suddenly anxious to put the phone down. Her heart was beating faster. She was going to do this crazy thing? She began to think of how she would justify it, if they were caught. Nothing plausible came to mind. So call him back, she thought. Call him back and tell him. Then the siren song intruded: Second Temple artifacts. At Masada. The last stand. The Copper Scroll had described several treasure hoards taken down into the Judaean desert when Jerusalem fell. People had been looking for years. Allegro himself had searched and found nothing. Had that been disinformation? To keep anyone from looking at Masada? What more logical place than Masada for Temple artifacts? Hall's lady friend had been right all along. It would be the discovery of the millennium.

Diving gear. Bring your diving gear, he'd said. She shivered. Diving alone into an unexplored cistern inside the mountain? What an incredibly stupid, foolhardy thing for him to have done. There would necessarily be no light, no landmarks, and no rescue if anything at all went wrong, and yet he had obviously done just that—and was now asking her to do it.

She sat there in the comfort of her living room, almost paralyzed, wondering if she'd lost her mind. Then, with a start, she realized she would have to hurry. She shivered again and then got up to get her equipment.

25

Ellerstein sat at his desk, looking down at the telephone, replaying Judith's answers in his mind. The strain in her voice. The rush to put him off. Was he imagining these things? Was it just female embarrassment, or something else? Was somebody there with her, and she couldn't talk? Hall, perhaps? He swiveled around in his oak desk chair. The lights of Yafo spread before him. Beyond lay the darkened Mediterranean.

He thought hard. The American had gone with Yehudit to Masada, and had been caught by an army patrol walking around the base of the mountain at night. He had admitted to going up there at night, the stones-and-bones business. Yehudit had been embarrassed professionally by the whole incident. She should have been furious with the American, and yet they had made up and spent a day together. Two evenings as well. Then he drops her and just disappears? Hall was an attractive, wealthy man, and Yehudit was a beautiful woman, on the cusp of coming back out into the world of the living. No man in his right mind would dump her like that. Unless—what?

Now Hall was missing, in so many words, and Yehudit was being, what—evasive? No, not that, but something. Did they have an affair going, maybe? She was embarrassed to tell him? Hall was there, at her apartment?

No, he didn't think so. Something else.

The incident at Caesarea—a total mystery. The news reports said only that a German tourist had been shot and killed with some kind of spear gun at the undersea museum. No immediate suspects, but terrorism was suspected. A random killing at a burgeoning tourist attraction. Except: David Hall had witnessed it.

Masada. Hall. A senseless murder at Caesarea. Yehudit under pressure.

He swung back around and dialed Gulder's number. He got voice mail. Shit, he thought. Shabbat. He hung up and rose to stare out the window. He needed instructions, and now would be nice. He redialed Gulder's number and this time waited for the robot voice mail to take his message. "I think the American *is* up to something. It involves Masada. There's something going on, and Ressner is involved. Please call at once. There's something going on."

He hung up as suspicions were solidifying in his mind. Now he needed to wait by the phone. What in the world was the damned American up to? Was this why Skuratov was so damned sensitive about

Masada? He fixed a whisky and went into his study. The phone rang five minutes later.

"Tell me," Gulder's voice ordered without preamble.

Ellerstein reviewed the whole matter and concluded with his growing suspicions that Judith Ressner and the American were up to something, something that had to do with Masada.

Gulder was silent for a long minute. Then he sighed. "Tell it to me again," he said. "Slower."

Ellerstein went over everything he had again. This time he remembered to mention the dive shop manager's comment about the tanks. Gulder interrupted him when he mentioned the tanks.

"*Scuba* tanks?"

"Yes, of course. They had been diving together. At Caesarea Maritima. On a scuba tour. Where Hall witnessed a possible terrorist attack on a tourist. Underwater."

The line hissed for almost a half minute as Gulder absorbed that. Then he surprised Ellerstein.

"I appreciate the call, Yossi," he said finally. "Upon reflection, however, I think it's nothing. I think you may have been right with your original theory—only I think they're seeing each other, and Ressner doesn't want you to know."

"Well, that's possible, of course," Ellerstein said doubtfully, "but—"

"No, I think it is nothing," Gulder insisted.

"Well, if that's what you think . . ."

"It is. The American was caught once messing about at Metsadá. He knows if he went back there, we would deport him. Or maybe even charge him and jail him right here, no matter who he thinks he is. No." He sighed, a weary sound. "No: This is romance. This is beneath our attention, Yossi."

"You said to keep tabs on Ressner."

"So we did, Yossi, but now—well, now I think you can back off."

"Very well," Ellerstein said, somewhat baffled by Gulder's nonreaction. "You almost sound disappointed."

"In a way, I am, but not with you. It was a precaution, that's all. Now, well . . ."

"All right, then, I suppose that's it," Ellerstein said.

Gulder gave a grim laugh. "What, Yossi, you're not going to wish me to have a nice day?"

Ellerstein smiled. They both hated that trite American expression with a passion.

"Shalom," he said dutifully, hung up, and finished his Scotch, still wondering what the hell was going on. Had been going on. There was absolutely nothing going on now, it seemed.

He scratched his head. Still, he thought.

It took her just over two hours to drive down to the Dead Sea rendezvous with the American. With the start of the Sabbath, there was hardly any traffic, but always the checkpoints. She passed the tourist site at Masada, rounded the headland, and slowed to look for the turn-in to the geothermal plant. She saw the building, with its halo of amber security lights, but could not see the turn-in road. Following his instructions, she drove past the complex for a mile, doused her lights, and then made a U-turn to come back to it. This time she saw the entrance, no more than a sandy lane, and turned in. She drove nervously into the lighted zone and right past his Land Rover. He flicked on his parking lights when she was abeam of him. She stopped and backed in alongside him.

All the way down she had been arguing with herself. Her official responsibility was clear: Notify the authorities at the institute and let them take it from there. The damned American was loose again, and this time, he needed to be picked up. I can tell you right where to find him. He's been digging for treasure at Masada—that would do it. The ministry police would have been all over him. Then what, though? Would he tell them what he had found? Or would he simply say, sorry, don't know what you're talking about, and leave the country? If he didn't tell them, she would have to. There was the rub: She wasn't sure she *would* tell them. She would much rather come back on her own, or with a proper expedition, and make the great discovery herself. Which presented a further rub: Who would believe such a story, that she found something like this on her own? Did she really want to tell it and then get shoved aside by the luminaries of Israeli archaeology in their rush to the site?

At the end of the day, she told herself, it's better to rationalize. First, check it out. If the story was true, then she would tell the official world. Right. This isn't rationalization at all, she thought, as she got out of her car. This is madness, and you're going to pay for it. As he came around the back and she saw the big grin on his face, she fought back the urge to slap him.

"What have you done?" she hissed. "Tell me why I should not call the authorities."

"You can and should," he answered, his tall frame silhouetted in the glare of the security lights, "but not until you've seen it. After that, we do it any way you want."

She turned her back on him, staring angrily into the darkness. "I can't believe you went in there, alone like that. I can't believe you even came back down here, after all the trouble you caused the last time. Do you have any—"

"If I had told you my theory about an undiscovered cistern, would you have even listened?" he interrupted. He came around to stand in front of her, shielding his eyes now against the lights. "Would anyone in the Israeli archaeology establishment have given me the time of day? You know they wouldn't."

"You lied to me, to everyone, about what you were doing here," she said. "You pretended to know a cursory history of Metsadá, and yet you name the scroll holders in Greek. Everything you've done here has been a lie."

"Not everything, Judith," he said. He didn't come any closer, but his tone of voice had changed, softened. She tossed her head in exasperation.

"Look," he said, "we're wasting time. Get your stuff and come with me in my Land Rover. If we get stopped by a patrol, we are lovers who lost track of time. Leave your car right here—I checked the locks on the gate to this place. No one's been here in weeks."

"How in the world did you get up there with diving equipment?" she asked.

"The hard way. By way of the Roman ramp. There's an old military road that leads up to Silva's main camp. There's a place to hide the Land Rover up there. The entrance to the cistern is in a cave above the Serpent Path, about a hundred feet down from the east gate. I already have air tanks up there. We go in, make the dive, you see what's there, and then we back out. After that, it's your show."

"My show, indeed. They'll kill you, and then me, probably."

"No they won't. The results are going to overwhelm any archaeological crimes I've committed. Think of what it will mean to Israel to recover Temple artifacts."

She was silent for a moment. "What do you mean, my show?"

"You can claim the whole damned thing, if you want to. I don't care. I've seen what I came to see. Adrian was right. They may have committed mass suicide to defeat the Romans one last time, but they also did it to protect what's in that cave."

"You have no idea of the uproar this will cause," she said softly. "Assuming they're genuine."

"They're real, all right. You only have to see them. Now we have to move. The patrols will be coming out pretty soon."

"You have put me in a terrible position," she said finally. "I will be ruined professionally for doing this, for helping you."

"No," he said. "You are doing the responsible thing. You are going to verify that I have discovered what I say I have, and then you are going to take charge and safeguard the discovery, before the dumb American goes out and raises a horde of treasure hunters."

"How do I know you will do what you say?" she asked, her voice carrying above the noise of the machinery inside. "How do I know you aren't using me again, yes? Using me to confirm that the artifacts are authentic and then claiming the whole thing for yourself? How do I know this? Tell me,

Mr. American—and before you answer this time, the truth for a change would be very nice."

He looked away, and she wondered if she'd gone too far. Or guessed what he was really up to.

"Because," he said slowly, "I didn't have to call you. I could always have done the American thing—gone to the media. Brought a crowd of journalists down here and staged a media spectacle of the discovery. Maybe let some private treasure hunters come with me into the cistern to verify what was where and then haul it out of there into the television lights. Hell, the very existence of the cistern, the cave, and the writing on the walls would be good enough for a great show. Israel has satellite TV, right? I could have a production team from CNN down here tonight with one phone call. Is that what you want?"

"No!"

"Okay. So instead, I called you."

She stood there with her eyes averted again. She had seen the circus that could erupt with a big enough news story. She felt his hand on her forearm.

"Look, Judith, I know I've deceived you. I wanted to tell you. I *really* wanted to tell you. I didn't do this for private gain, though. I did it because I believed Adrian was right and the rest of the world was wrong. This stuff is up there. Come see it. You know you want to—and you know you'll never get another chance like this."

430

"Because I will be in jail," she muttered, but she knew he'd won. She was going to do it. A sudden and noisy release of stinking steam from the plant startled both of them. The smell made them cover their noses.

"God, what is this place?" she asked.

"I've walked around it a couple of times. I still think it's a desalinization operation. They're making freshwater out of Dead Sea brine, probably for the Masada tourist complex. They use the geothermal heat to boil off the brine and then condense the water vapor. See that big pipe—it heads toward the mountain."

She looked through the fence. The pipe he was pointing to was just barely visible in the reflected lights. The gurgling and boiling sounds from the plant confirmed his hypothesis.

"All right," she said. "Let's get this over with. We will take both vehicles, and if we're stopped, I'm going to tell the guards everything, agreed? I'm not going to play any more games."

He sighed. "Your call, Professor," he said. "Let's go."

26

An hour and a half later they were in the cave, suited up and ready to go. She had brought down a wet suit, a weight belt, and her breathing rig and mask. They had not been intercepted on their way up to the Roman camp, and her car was small enough that he didn't think it would be spotted. He'd carried her equipment up the ramp in a bag, and she'd brought some water bottles. They had changed into their diving suits by flashlight while standing back to back. He reviewed the dive plan with her at the edge of the slab hole.

"The cave depth is at about thirty-five feet," he said. "So we have plenty of bottom time. The water is not too cold, but there's air in the cave. I chose to stay on the tank rather than breathe two-thousand-year-old air."

"Yes, I understand," she said, stuffing her hair into her diving hood. "This water stinks; I would have expected freshwater."

"Me, too, but it's not. It is very, very salty. The BCD vest was useless. You'll need to stuff it with weights."

She reached out a fingertip and then tasted the water. "This is like Dead Sea water," she said. "How can that be, way up here?"

"I have no damned idea, unless it's some geologic phenomenon that's forcing Dead Sea water up into this cavern. The bottom is around a hundred ten feet, say thirty-three meters. I've already been down to the bottom; nothing there but clouds of silt and what looks like brickwork, but I didn't have much bottom time at that depth, either."

"So, we find the cave, go in, take a look,

confirm the artifacts, and then come back out, yes?"

"Right, although you might want to translate some of the writing. I think it's Aramaic."

She cocked her head at him. "You can recognize Aramaic?"

"Recognize it, yes. I think, anyway. Adrian said she could actually read it."

She just shook her head. Amateurs indeed.

"If we get separated, climb to the roof of the cavern and look for this light, which I'm hanging down into the slab hole. Surface here and I'll come back for you. There's a glow-stick at the cave mouth. Problem signal is three taps on your air tank with your knife. You have to go inverted to make it through the final neck of the cave into the air chamber. You okay with that?"

She took a deep breath. "I suppose we will find that out."

"Okay. If you get jammed in the cave entrance, rotate until you can move forward. If I could make it, you can make it, no sweat."

He reviewed the route to the cave entrance, noting that there was a second cave near the one they wanted, checked her diving rig, and asked her to check his. When they were both ready, they switched on their headlamps and masks, slipped into the water, and submerged. She signaled that she was breathing okay, and then he led her to the cave entrance, going across the cavern ceiling on a compass bearing until he thought he had the right spot and then swimming down to thirty-five feet.

Once again he found the wrong cave, but now the green glow-stick was just visible. He signaled for her to follow him, and her light kept up with him as he crabbed across the face of the west wall until he found the cave. He started in, but this time rolled inverted while there was still plenty of room. On his back now, he could see her headlamp behind him, and he gave her the sign to roll over onto her back. She was struggling with something, but then she came on. The extreme salinity of the water would probably plaster her to the roof of the cave, but that was okay because she could then hand-over-hand along the cave until they hit the air-water interface.

He pressed forward, going slower when the cave necked down. Then suddenly his face was out of the water and he was in. He dragged himself across the sand and then turned to help her come through the final, narrow opening. She instinctively reached for her mask, but he shook his hand in front of her face: Leave it on, remember? She nodded, sat up, and took a look around.

David stood up, keeping his mask in place, and took her by the hand. They walked up to the high end of the cave where he showed her the ragged skeleton and the oversized dagger. She bent down and studied the remains for a minute, touching the dagger with a finger of her gloved hand. Then he showed her where to stand to see up on the altarlike structure. She kept one hand on his shoulder while she took a look, and he felt her hand tighten on him when she saw the artifacts.

She stood there for a few minutes, just looking, shining her headlamp this way and that, before stepping back down. He put his mask close to hers and gave the thumbs-up sign. She nodded her head vigorously, her eyes ablaze with excitement. Then he took her to the right-hand cave wall and used the extra, handheld light he'd brought along to illuminate the wall. She studied the characters, tracing them out without touching them. Then she took the light from him and went searching along the wall. He figured she was trying to find the beginning of the text. He made a more detailed examination of the cave, looking to see if he'd missed anything the first time, but there was only sand and more of the small oil lamps.

He wondered how the man had gotten into the cave. He'd seen no stairs or handholds outside on the cistern wall, so the entrance had to be something that came down from the fortress, which should be just above their heads. He sat down on the sand, leaned back, and looked up. The cave walls came together like a medieval cathedral, some twenty-five feet or so above his head, but there was no visible entrance structure. He checked his watch. They should have a good fifty minutes to an hour of air remaining, more if they came off the tanks and used the air here in the cave.

Judith was playing the lights over the entire right-hand wall while she studied the script. As he got up to go over to where she was standing, he felt a distant thump. He turned reflexively to the air-water interface and noticed that the water moved slightly, as if disturbed by something. Judith was looking at him; she'd heard or felt it, too. They stood there for a moment, waiting to see if anything else happened. Definite thump, as if something very heavy had been dropped—oh, *shit!* The slab?

He waved Judith over, took a deep breath, and then took out his mouthpiece. "That sounded like the slab," he said in a rush. "I think we better go see." Then he put his mouthpiece back in. Her eyes were wide at the thought of that heavy stone slab being back in place. There was no way they could lift that. He saw the fear in her expression and moved quickly to the interface point.

When they cleared the cave's entrance, he looked up for the reference light. There was no light. He tracked his bubbles and then scanned the whole ceiling area of the cistern.

There was no light.

She touched his shoulder and pointed down. Far

below them, there was a glimmer. Son of a bitch, he thought. Son of a *bitch!*

He consulted his compass, oriented his body, and swam directly out into the cistern, rising as he did so. He felt her following along close behind. When he rose to the ceiling, he executed an expanding square search and immediately collided with something. He drew back and saw that it was a scuba air tank. He saw a second tank, bobbing with quiet clinks against the rock of the ceiling. Then he realized there were other objects, some of his supply bags, a positively buoyant flashlight, his and her street clothes. With a feeling of rising dread, he went back up to the ceiling, mask right up against the rock now, and searched along the surface until he found that rectangular seam.

The slab was back in place. They were trapped.

Yosef Ellerstein sat at his desk working on a draft of the paper he was going to present next week. It was late, and his thoughts were not really on the paper. He was still trying to work out what was going on with Yehudit Ressner and this American.

Two things were bothering him: The first was Gulder's nonreaction to his call. He'd purportedly been assigned to watch Ressner because Skuratov was watching her, and Skuratov was a possible suspect in a plot to divert nuclear weapons material. Now the American was "missing,"

Ressner was being evasive, and Gulder didn't care? The second problem was the way Skuratov's office, the so-called International Planning, had reacted to his message. Ho-hum, Professor. Thank you for your interest in national security. First, the grim old Russian had been all excited about the mysterious American, the nuclear power engineer. So much so that the American's little unauthorized excursion on the mountain warranted putting him under surveillance when he came back to Tel Aviv after his visit to Masada. Yet now? Human voice mail at Skuratov's office. First they care, now they don't.

Ellerstein got up and fixed himself a small cognac, even though he knew he'd had enough booze for one night. He wanted to light up his pipe but had rationed himself to three pipes a day now and the ration book was empty. He grumbled to himself and put the unlit pipe in his mouth anyway. He sucked noisily on it while he thought about the situation. Then something occurred to him.

What was the common denominator to all this? Herod's fortress down on the Dead Sea. He sat back down at his desk to think about that. Could it be? He picked up the phone and called the Skuratov contact number. This time no one answered. He looked at his watch. It was nearly 10:00 P.M. He let the phone ring, but there was still no answer, not even voice mail. He hung up, surprised. He did not know where Skuratov's operations center was located, Dimona, probably, with a local telephone link near or in Tel Aviv. Wouldn't it always be fully manned? A Shin Bet control room? Now no one was answering. Then he called Yehudit Ressner at home. Again, no answer, and when her voice mail came on, he hung up. He sucked harder on the pipe, the desire for just one more cognac rising again. Something was very wrong here.

Suppose, he mused, just suppose Skuratov already knows that the American has done a runner. He's taken his watchers off Judith, so he calls her, and *she's* not there. For that paranoid old Russian, the two of them together conjures up Masada again, and there's something about Masada that that old man has been reacting to like an exposed nerve. He looked out his study window into a cool, clear night. The lights of his neighborhood were subdued by the density of the buildings and the many trees. The rains would come soon.

He poured himself a small splash of cognac, thinking that soon he would be a true alcoholic. Skuratov was supposedly a high-ranking Shin Bet officer, whose responsibility was the security of the Israeli atomic weapons program laboratories. For some unknown reason, he's sensitive about Masada, which is, admittedly, only forty kilometers or so from the Dimona atomic energy center. He is also thought to be involved with what Gulder called the new Kanna'im. And where had all the old Zealots ended their days? Masada. Great God: Was there a connection? It all kept coming back to Masada.

He heaved a sigh of resignation as he put down the cognac, untouched. He got up and went to find his old army coat and his car keys. Something was telling him to go see for himself. Now. Tonight. Go down to Masada.

It's crazy. It's Shabbat. Still something kept telling him:

Go. Now—and take a gun.

27

David wasted no time once he realized that the slab was down. He signaled for Judith to follow him back to the cave. At the entrance, he pantomimed that she was to wait right there while he made an emergency dive to the bottom of the cistern. She protested, but he insisted. He gestured for her to remain at the cave entrance so he could find it again quickly, homing in on her headlamp. She finally understood and parked herself in the entrance. He swam back away from her, oriented himself with the compass again, and headed down to the bottom of the cistern.

He did the dive calculations as he went down, his ears cracking. A hundred-plus feet. He didn't intend to stay down there, but if someone had come into the bat cave and thrown everything there into the cistern, there might be some of those steel staging poles. He swam straight down, or as straight as he could with no visual cues, feeling the pressure squeeze his body. Going deep in a third dive in one day violated the nitrogen safety rules, but he had to know. Besides, he would be "surfacing" into air pressurized at thirty-five feet of water, which would act like a decompression stop. Sort of, anyway. He hoped it wouldn't be a permanent one.

As he neared the bottom his headlamp illuminated a light cloud of silt. The bottom had been stirred up, probably by the avalanche of stuff thrown down from the bat cave. He slowed, hovering vertical now, his arms extended, until he felt his fingers pressing into soft mud. Moving slowly so as not to stir up any more silt, he felt around for anything on the bottom. Nothing. Then he had an idea. He switched off his headlamp. Sure enough, the reference light was glowing about fifty feet away. He swam over there, grabbed it, fastened it onto his arm, and encountered some cans of food, but no pipes. He expanded his search area and finally felt rather than saw a single staging pipe. Then a second one. He tried to lift them both but realized he would need help getting two of them to the cave entrance. He put the pipe back down near the second one and strapped the reference light onto one of the poles, pointing up. Then he swam back up toward the western wall of the cistern, shutting off his headlamp again as he passed through fifty feet, watching for Judith's light. It appeared to his right, barely visible. He had gone way off course coming back up. He stopped and looked down. The reference light was just visible in the murky water, but it was visible.

He got to Judith and signaled that she needed to come down with him. He showed her the depth and pointed to her ears. She gave him the thumbs-up okay sign. He reached over and took off her headlamp and jammed it into a crevice near the entrance to the cave. Then he turned to swim back down, making sure she was following. Two minutes later they were on top of the pipes and the reference light. He explained with gestures that he wanted to take the two pipes back to the cave. She nodded. He tied the reference light's rubber cord to one of the pipes in case they dropped one or both going up, then got the end of one pole in each hand. Judith lifted the other ends. Then they began to ascend, facing each other with the twelve-foot-long pipes between them like a stretcher.

At one point, near sixty feet, she stopped and shook her head, as if she were having problems clearing her ears. He stopped and watched her face grimacing in the mask. Then she nodded, and they started up again. Ten feet higher she stopped again and then suddenly grabbed her right ear, releasing her grip on one pipe. He tried to hold on to the pipe, but it slipped right out of his glove and disappeared down into the gloom, the reference light going with it. Not a total disaster, he thought. I can find it again with that light.

Judith was shaking her head and pointing down. She wanted to go back down to adjust the pressure on her ear. He nodded, holding on tight to the remaining pipe, and they maneuvered back down to sixty feet again. He watched her carefully as she went through more facial contortions behind her mask to clear her ear passage. Finally she signaled okay and they started up again. By the time he realized she was going up a whole lot faster than he was, the pipe was extended out to the full length of his arm and he couldn't hold it. He almost yelled, but it was too late. He lost his grip on the pipe, which put its entire weight on her arm, and she dropped it immediately. They stopped ascending and watched it disappear into the depth below.

He swore mentally at their bad luck and then closed with her. He tried to read panic in her eyes behind the faceplate of her mask, but there was only embarrassment. He indicated they had to go back. To get one pipe this time, he signaled. She understood. Not that they had any choice, he thought. Only one pipe had a light on it. The other one was lost forever in all that silt. Plus, they couldn't safely keep going back down to that depth.

He held her hand for a moment and turned off his headlamp. He looked up and could see a faint glow off to their left. Her headlamp was still there. Good. He looked down. There was a glow, but it was so diffused now in the silt as to be almost useless. He pointed down, and they began their descent. He left his light off. At a hundred feet they encountered the bottom. The glow was more distinct now, but it was way off to the southeastern side of the cistern. They swam that way, undoubtedly churning up silt clouds behind them, but David was focused on finding that light. It looked to be fifty feet away. Forty feet. They slowed to keep the silt disturbance minimized.

Thirty feet.

Twenty feet.

The light was visible now as a small purple glimmer. It's probably buried in the silt, he thought; we're lucky we could see it at all. They slowed even more, and then they were ten feet away. He looked for the pipe but couldn't see it. It must be truly buried in all the silt, which was now boiling away from them along the bottom.

Away? Was there a current down here? He couldn't imagine how that could be, but there was. Then he saw that they were almost up against the southeast wall of the cistern. He checked depth: one hundred twelve feet. They couldn't stay here.

But there, right in front of them, at a height of about six feet off the bottom, was a four-inch-diameter pipe protruding a foot out of the rock wall. A modern steel pipe, with a concrete-collared flange. What the hell was this, he wondered. He switched his head light on to examine it, but then something grabbed his forearm with a grip so strong he almost lost his mask whipping his head around.

It was Judith. She was pointing to something to the right of the pipe, something black, with glints of metal and what looked like glass. Oh, shit, he thought. That's a wet suit . . . and a mask . . . and the white object behind the mask was a skull. The wet suit was striped with wide yellow and dark red bands. There were white bone fragments where the feet and hands had been.

Then Judith made a screaming noise in her mask, releasing a huge cloud of bubbles, and shot up out of sight like a rocket.

His immediate instinct was to follow her, but he remembered the staging pipe. He couldn't come down here again. Taking a last look at the skeleton in the wet suit, he doused the light again and homed in on the partially buried reference light. He felt around for the pipe and grabbed it, but it was stuck under something. The silt was obscuring everything, turning his lamplight brown in the water.

He felt along the pipe until he encountered what

felt like a huge timber. He swept away the silt cloud, trying to clear the water, trying to see what it was. Then he saw the glint of metal. Bright metal, like stainless steel. The silt returned, obscuring everything. He knew his time at this depth was going to kill him if he didn't get upstairs in a hurry. He felt along the object. It was cylindrical, maybe two feet in diameter. He couldn't tell how long it was. There was another one, and another one. At least three. Now he was stretched out, holding onto the staging pipe, and couldn't move to his right anymore. He felt the stirrings of euphoria.

Gotta go, gotta go!

He went back to the pipe, wrestled with it, got it loose, and started up, hoping like hell Judith hadn't gone all the way up to the ceiling at that speed. Hoping she'd remembered to blow air out of her lungs.

It was a struggle going up with the heavy pipe, but then he remembered his BCD. He adjusted the inflation slightly, and it was much easier going. He cursed himself for not thinking of that a whole lot earlier. His mind wasn't working at top form just now. Nitrogen does that, a nasty little voice told him.

As he rose slowly past fifty feet he began to work his way to the west, dousing his headlamp so he could home in on the light that he hoped was still in that crevice by the cave entrance. He wondered where Judith was, and even more, what the hell that pipe was about, not to mention a dead scuba diver and stainless steel cylinders sitting on wooden beams down on the bottom. So much for their being the first humans in this cistern during the past two thousand years. This changed everything.

Holding the pipe across his chest now, he rose to the correct depth for the cave entrance while looking around for the light. When he finally spotted it, he adjusted his BCD to achieve neutral buoyancy and then kicked over toward the west wall. He was relieved to see Judith swim out of the darkness from below him. That was a good sign: she had not gone blasting all the way to the top of the cistern. When she saw David, she swam over to the entrance and retrieved her own head-lamp. Together, they wrestled the staging pipe into the narrow cave and through the air-water interface, where they pulled it and themselves up onto the shallow sand. Then they flopped down on the sand themselves, resting on their air tanks and breathing noisily.

His headlamp illuminated her pale and frightened face. There was something major going on here that he didn't understand. He looked around the cave and made a decision. He popped his mouth-piece out, lifted off his mask, and carefully sampled the cave air. It was musty and smelled faintly sulfurous, but there definitely was oxygen.

When he felt that it was probably safe to breathe it, he gestured for her to do the same. She followed suit and then flopped back on her side, tucked her knees up to her chest, and began to sob, her headlamp shining down into the fine sand.

He slipped out of his scuba rig and shut off his air tank before going to her and securing her air. He kept his headlamp on but reached over and turned hers off to conserve the battery. She was shaking silently. He wanted to pick her up and hold her, but it would be awkward—she was still in her diving rig. She was following his instructions but keeping her eyes closed tight. He helped her out of her tank rig and then sat down beside her.

"What?" he asked softly, putting his arm around her shoulders. "Look, you panicked down there. That happens. Don't—"

"No," she sobbed. "No. I did *not* panic. Not in the way you mean."

The hell you didn't, he thought, but didn't say it. "What, then?" he asked, unsure of what was going on.

She rubbed her eyes and then massaged the sides of her face where the mask had been. Her normally composed expression was shattered. She was more than a little white-eyed, and her skin was uncharacteristically pale against the oval frame of her hood.

"That suit down there?" she said. "I recognized

that suit. Oh, David, my God! I think that, that . . . *thing* down there was my husband. That was Dov!"

Yosef Ellerstein was stopped by an army police truck on the Dead Sea highway just below Qumran. Israeli citizens were not forbidden to be in their cars at night in this area, but since there was technically nowhere for him to be going, the patrol leader naturally stopped the car and asked where Ellerstein was bound. He identified himself and then explained that there was a problem at Masada.

"Metsadá?" the young lieutenant asked. "It's closed. What kind of a problem?"

"Do you know who Colonel Skuratov is?" Ellerstein asked the young officer.

"No. He is army?"

"Not exactly. He is Shin Bet. I think. He has something to do with security at the Dimona laboratories."

"Dimona?" the officer echoed. He looked around, his face registering total confusion. "What does Dimona have to do with you, Professor? Or Metsadá, please?"

Ellerstein threw up his hands. He could see the faces of the other patrol troops looking at his car through the canvas windshields on the back of the truck. "I'm not sure," he admitted. "I have done some occasional, um, research work for

Colonel Skuratov. Listen: I believe that there is an American tourist up on the mountain, doing some unauthorized exploration. I believe Colonel Skuratov might be up there, too."

He saw the disbelief in the lieutenant's eyes. "I know," Ellerstein continued. "It's complicated. Look, let's go down there, you and me. I think we need to get up on the mountain."

"The site is closed and the cable car is shut down, Professor. That place, it's four hundred meters straight up. How do you propose to get up on that mountain?" The way he said this made it clear that he didn't think Ellerstein was up to it.

"The same way the Romans did," Ellerstein replied.

The lieutenant blinked. The ramp. "Okay," he said, "but first, I think I need to contact my head-quarters."

"Yes, you do that, Lieutenant," Ellerstein nodded. "Emphasize that name, Skuratov. They won't know me from spit, but they should recognize that name. In the meantime, I think we need to get down there. Something bad is going on. I'm sure of it."

The lieutenant gave him a faintly patronizing look, shook his head doubtfully, and asked him to pull off the road and wait. Then he went back to the truck, climbed into the cab, and got on his radio. Ellerstein maneuvered his car to the side, shut the engine down, and waited.

He was sure of it, he'd said. Something bad was going on down there. He still could not make the connection between Dimona and Masada. Or maybe it was a connection between Skuratov and Masada. What in the world could it be? He looked in his mirror but could not see what was going on inside the truck because of the head-lamps. He drummed his fingers on the steering wheel. Then there was movement behind him, a banging of truck doors. The lieutenant came back to his car.

"Battalion says to go down there and to take you with us, Professor. My orders are to sweep the site and to report."

"Did they recognize the name Skuratov?"

"You know, that's weird. At first, the duty officer gave me a 'wait, out.' Then he said to turn you around and have you return to Jerusalem. But then he said hold on, and this time he comes back and says to get down there. There will be a special security force coming over. An entire company." The lieutenant looked at him to see if he understood the significance of that. Ellerstein, like just about every other adult Israeli male, had been in the army.

"A full company?" he exclaimed. "That's a hundred men?"

"Yes. Probably special forces. He wouldn't say anything more on the unsecure radio net. Just to move out, right now. So, Professor: We go, yes?"

"Absolutely—is that military road back up to the Roman camp still there?"

"Yes. You will please follow us, Professor. Oh, I told them that you thought this Colonel Skuratov may already be up there. Apparently that's why the Dimona security reaction force is coming over. Does that make any sense to you?"

The army company was the Dimona reaction force? Oh-oh, he thought. "It just might, Lieutenant," Ellerstein said. He should be calling Gulder, but he had no phone. "It just might. We should hurry now, okay?"

"That was *Dov?*" David asked, staring at her. "Are you sure? I mean—"

"It's the suit," she said. She swallowed a couple of times to clear her throat. "There was a theory several years back about wet suits for the open ocean. If they bore the striped markings of venomous sea snakes, larger predators would stay away. Dov believed it and had a suit made with those colored stripes. It was unique. Other divers used to kid him about it. I would have to . . . to—"

"Yes, right, I understand, but I think that's out of the question right now. You shouldn't go back down to that depth again, and I damn sure can't go back down that deep for a while. Besides, we need to figure out how we're going to get out of this cave."

Her face went crooked again. "Someone closed the entrance up above, yes?"

He looked around at the dimly lit walls of the cave. "Sure looks that way. You saw all our stuff in the cistern, and I had that slab wedged way back from the hole."

"So someone must have known we were down here?"

"Yeah, and that's what's got me scared. I think someone wants us to *stay* down here."

"Just like Dov," she whispered, her eyes filling again. He pulled her over to him again, and she wept for a few minutes. He felt a wave of sympathy and had to resist the urge to kiss the top of her head. Then she took a deep breath and pulled away, wiping her eyes.

He rolled away, stood up, and began to scan the walls and the ceiling with his headlamp. Two skeletons in the mountain, he thought. One ancient, one not so ancient. A modern pipe pumping water into the cistern. A familiar-looking pipe, at that. Then he remembered the geothermal plant. The pipe coming out of that building had pointed back at the mountain. Same size. Same pipe? Was that why the young scientist had been diving into the big cistern? Or did it have something to do with those cylinders?

He was wasting time and, more importantly, air. There were two air tanks bobbing against the ceiling out there in the main cistern, but they were only partially full. Add to that what was left in their tanks here. They had three lights, all with used batteries. There was a waterproof flashlight floating up there with the tanks, but no food and no potable water, unless they went back down and looked for their water bottles. Going back down to the bottom was out of the question, and the silt on the bottom would make it impossible, anyway. He had one staging pipe and absolutely no idea of what to do next. He went back over to Judith, sat down, patted her arm, and then turned off his headlamp. She gripped his hand in the sudden darkness.

"Need to conserve the batteries," he said. "While we think this out. The big question is, how did that guy by the altar over there get *into* this cave? I didn't see any ledge or indications he came in the way we came, and there was a big boulder blocking the cave entrance when I first found it."

She thought about it, still clutching his hand. The darkness was absolute.

"If the cistern was empty at the time of the siege, there may have been ladders up to this cave."

"The bottom is a hundred and some feet down from the slab entrance. By my depth gauge, the entrance to this cave is at about forty feet. That's a damn tall ladder. Plus, the entrance to the cave was sealed when I found it. No, I think there's another way in. Up above us somewhere. And—" He stopped.

"And what?"

"Well, if there is an entrance, it must be sealed, too. Otherwise, *this* cave would be filled with water. Look."

He switched on his headlamp and pointed it down at his depth gauge. It read thirty-three feet. He switched the light off. "Once I dislodged that boulder out of the entrance, the water in the cistern pressurized the air in this side cave to an equilibrium state. There's a problem, though: If we do find a way out from *this* cave, when we open it, the water from the main cistern will fill this cave until the two levels are equal."

"Why?"

"Because the pressures would have to equalize. We're sitting in a bubble of compressed air. If we release this pressure, there'll be a small tidal wave in here."

"My God, all this would be lost. The writing is done in lampblack. The water out there would dissolve it all, especially what's in those scroll holders."

"Yeah, it might," he said, "but what are our options? I don't want to die here."

She was quiet. He was aware that every breath they took was consuming precious oxygen and beginning to fill the cave with carbon dioxide. They had to do something.

"Is there no other way to lift the slab at the top of the main cistern?" she asked.

"Not from below. Even from up top, it was very, very heavy. I had to use staging pipes to lever it. That's why I wanted those pipes—if there's another opening, above the cave here, two of us might be able to lever it open."

She didn't answer. He became aware of her breathing in the silence, along with his own. He had never experienced such absolute darkness before. For a vertiginous moment he felt as if they were floating out in deep space.

"If that is—was—Dov down there," he asked, "what do you think he was doing here? Did he ever express an interest in Metsadá?"

"Not that I recall. He'd visited, of course. Everyone comes at least once. But—"

"But?"

"The weekend before he was supposedly killed in the accident, he had gone off for a diving day with two of his college friends. They were active with LaBaG."

"That's the group you mentioned earlier. What is LaBaG all about?"

"LaBaG stands for Lochamim b'Sakanah Garinit—Fighters Against Nuclear Danger. They are anti nuclear everything—weapons, energy, everything. These are the people with whom he got into trouble with that protest I told you about. Oh, God, David, what is going on in this place? If that's Dov down there—"

He nodded in the darkness. Dov had gotten

456

across the breakers with the people who ran Israel's nuclear program. If that was his body down there in the main cave, it meant two things: Someone had killed him and then dumped him here, or caught him here, killed him, and left him here. The same way someone had replaced the slab on them? Which brought him to the second thing, and this thought really chilled him. Did this cistern have something to do with Israel's nuclear program?

"I hate to do it, but I'm going to climb that altar structure," he said. "See what I can see. Can you read the writing on the wall?"

"Yes, I can. It's Aramaic."

"Then maybe you ought to read it, because if I succeed, it may not be there for very long."

"Two thousand years it has been here," she said. "We can't endanger this."

"Judith, we don't have much air left. I can go get those other two Scuba tanks, assuming I can still find them, but they're partials. After that, we start breathing CO_2, and that's the end of us."

28

Ellerstein could barely see. The dust cloud being laid down by the army truck was overwhelming his own headlights. He kept glancing up at the mountain to his left, but there was only its silent black mass, against which the dust looked like a billowing curtain. He swore as his sedan banged and bumped over rocks and ruts that had probably felt the tramp of Roman sandals. Nothing changed out here.

When they pulled out onto the plateau on the west side of the fortress, he slowed to see why the truck was stopping. Once the dust blew aside, he saw the reason: There were two vehicles parked next to some old army Conex boxes. Four troopers piled out of the back of the truck and went toward the vehicles, their weapons at the ready. It looked to Ellerstein as if the vehicles were empty. Their windows were fogged over with night dew, and there was no movement showing through their windows in the glare of the truck's high beams.

Two vehicles, he thought. The Land Rover he guessed was the American's, but the other he recognized—it was Yehudit Ressner's Subaru. He swore again. Whatever was going on up here, they were now both involved. His beautiful minder had gone over to the wrong side of this equation. The officer was walking back toward his car. Ellerstein rolled down the window.

"Professor?" he asked. "Know anything about these vehicles?"

"I recognize the one," Ellerstein said. "It confirms my suspicions. There's something going on. Up there."

As they both looked up the ghostly slope of the

Roman ramp, the radio operator called to the officer to tell him that the Dimona security force was five minutes out.

"I used to work at Dimona, years ago," Ellerstein said. "So why in the world would the Dimona security people be interested in something happening up here?"

"Beats the shit out of me," the young officer responded with an elaborate shrug, "but once they get here, they can take over. I don't like this place. Gives me the creeps."

"This is where the Romans' Tenth Legion camped," Ellerstein said. "I suspect there's a ghost or three down in that wadi on either side of the siege ramp. Do you know how they built that thing?"

The lieutenant did not. Ellerstein told him. "Don't tell my troops that," the lieutenant said, looking over the top of Ellerstein's car. "These Metsadá patrols are spooky enough. Ah, here come the Dimona specials." There was relief in his voice.

Ellerstein looked over his shoulder and saw a convoy of at least a dozen trucks grinding up the military track, their headlamps reduced to yellow slit beams. As he watched, trucks peeled off the line at the back and stopped to disgorge troops around the base of the mountain. Just like Roman times, he thought. Circumvallation. Except, of course, for the trucks. Who knows how far Rome would have gone if they'd had trucks. Or tanks. Lord.

He watched as the remainder of the procession came up the slope and spread out into the Roman encampment. He saw one of those American Humvees leading the column. It stopped next to Ellerstein's car, and three officers climbed out. They were dressed in desert fatigues, and two were carrying submachine guns. They wore different hats from those of the desert patrol. The oldest-looking officer received the lieutenant's salute and announced that he was now in charge here. Then he came over to speak to Ellerstein, but they had to wait until the rest of the trucks spread out over the encampment grounds. Once all the engine noises subsided, he asked Ellerstein for some identification, glanced at it perfunctorily, and handed it back.

"Now, Professor," he asked, "would you mind if I join you?"

Shapiro, in his forties, was well built and looked as if he took things seriously. Ellerstein waved him in. They rolled up the windows to shut out the noise and the dust. The colonel immediately produced a cigarette and lit up. He rolled down his own window a few inches. "I'm Lieutenant Colonel David Shapiro. I'm in charge of the military security detachment at the Dimona laboratories. My information is that you think Colonel Skuratov is up on the mountain and that there's a problem, yes?"

Ellerstein nodded, wondered for a second how much he should tell this sharp-eyed colonel, and then decided to give him the full background. When he was finished, Shapiro nodded thoughtfully as he exhaled a plume of bluish smoke out the window.

"Those two civilian vehicles over there—one's the American's, and the other belongs to this Dr. Ressner?"

"I know Ressner's car; I'm assuming that the other is a rental and the American leased it. Shouldn't be hard to find out."

"No, it should not," Shapiro said. He fished a particle of tobacco from between his teeth for a moment while he considered the story Ellerstein had told him.

"Begging your pardon, Colonel," Ellerstein said, "but why does the mention of Colonel Skuratov bring out the Dimona military security force?"

The colonel just looked at him, his expression noncommittal. "You say that you know Skuratov?"

"Not exactly; he came to see me about the American's expedition down here with Yehudit Ressner. I know he's connected with Dimona." That's all I'm going to say, he thought. He dared not mention his own connection with Shabak, or the Zealot conspiracy. "I used to work there, years ago, and I remember him."

"*You* worked at Dimona?"

"Yes, but, as I said, it was many years ago. I'm a theoretical mathematician. I believe, however, that things at Dimona have probably passed the theoretical stage."

The colonel laughed out loud, two sharp barks. "You've got that right, Professor," he said. "Please wait here. As to your question, the answer is I'm damned if I know. A report was forwarded to our ops center that there was a problem up here at Metsadá and that it involved Skuratov. That report went to the laboratory director, who ordered us out to secure the site and to see what, if anything, was going on. So that, Professor, is what we're going to do."

Shapiro stubbed his cigarette out in the car's ashtray, got out, and walked around the back toward his command vehicle. Ellerstein rolled his window down and called to him. Ellerstein said, "I need to make a phone call. Does anyone have a cell phone?"

"Probably, but there are no towers out here, Professor. It will have to wait." He walked away and began shouting orders to his officers to deploy the force.

Ellerstein watched as the elite troops fanned out along the rim of the Roman camp. Some trotted down into the wadi on either side of the siege ramp, while others formed up and marched back down the military track toward the Dead Sea side of the fortress. One of the trucks was apparently a mobile communications station, and men began setting it up as a temporary field headquarters.

By now the original desert patrol group was sitting next to their truck on some rocks, smoking cigarettes and watching with the detached curiosity of soldiers who were happily on the sidelines. Colonel Shapiro took ten men and headed up the siege ramp. They set an impressive pace. The men carried submachine guns at port arms. Shapiro had a holstered pistol and a small tactical radio.

Ellerstein got out of his car and fished around for his pipe. The night was startlingly clear and cool, and he reached back in to retrieve a jacket. The gray battlements at the top of the mountain were etched in stark relief against the night sky. Behind him the black silhouettes of the Judaean hills stood guard. He could almost imagine that he could see pale, bearded faces flitting between the arrow slits up there, the ghosts of the Kanna'im keeping an eye on all the commotion in the Roman camp once again. He shivered despite himself. Colonel Shapiro and his team reached the western gate, stepped through the battlements, and disappeared. Ellerstein waited for half an hour and then decided to make his own move. The troops around the comms truck were all settled in, and the rest of the force was deployed out along the old Roman circumvallation perimeter of the site. Puffing gently on his pipe, he walked casually over to the base of the siege ramp, looked back once more, and then started up. No one seemed to notice.

With Judith's help, David climbed back down from the altar and switched off his headlamp. Judith kept hers on.

"Well?" she asked.

"I can't see anything up there that looks like an entrance. Doesn't mean there isn't one there, but if I can't see it, I can't work it."

She sighed. They walked back over to the ledge on the side of the cave. "So now what?" she asked. Her voice sounded dull, and David realized she was still in shock over finding Dov's remains.

"Well, for starters, I'll get my rig back on and go retrieve those air tanks and the extra light."

"That sounds like we're just postponing the inevitable," she said.

"That's how survival works, Judith. You keep at it, and something might break our way."

"Sure."

He patted her hand. "Give me your headlamp— I'll need it to mark the entrance here. You can use the spare, although you should just shut it off until I get back. I want to look around the entrance to this cave to see if we've missed something. Then I'll retrieve the bottles and get them into the cave."

"And then?"

"And then we keep on trying things until something works. Give me a hand with this rig, please?"

She helped him into his tank harness. He checked his weights, tested the regulator, and pulled on his mask. She was clutching his forearm. "Don't leave me here," she whispered.

"Never," he said. Then he got down on his hands and knees, flattened out, and crawled into the water like a crocodile. He bumped and banged his way through the flooded narrow passage until he came out into the main cistern. He was just able to turn around in the cave entrance. He checked his gear one more time and then took a compass bearing to get himself to where he remembered the main slab was. That's where the bottles had been; where they were now, of course, was anyone's guess, except they should still be bumping along the ceiling of the cistern. He was aware that he might have to search for them, expending more precious air in the process.

He positioned Judith's headlamp at the cave entrance and turned it on. It was not as strong as it had been. Then he launched from the lip of the entrance and headed up toward the ceiling, searching for the slab hole and the air tanks. After five minutes he had found neither and felt the first strings of panic. Then he remembered the air bubble trick. He exhaled and watched, but the bubbles now just drifted along the ceiling. Of course, he thought, the damned slab is down. He checked his compass and headed due east. If he had to, he would crisscross the ceiling from east to west until he found either the tanks or the slab hole.

He finally fetched up against the eastern wall. Nothing. Just the smooth grayish rock of the ceiling and upper walls staring back at him. He reversed course and swam back, offsetting as best he could, heading west now. He ran up against the western wall without finding anything. He reversed again. In his mind he was executing a search pattern along the ceiling, trying to offset his track by three or four feet each time, but he knew full well that, without a visual reference, he might be plowing through the same water over and over again. Have to keep trying, he thought grimly. Not going to just sit in that cave and suffocate.

The third time he hit the eastern wall something caught his eye, but it wasn't an air tank. It was another pipe, similar to the one down at the bottom. There was a mesh screen over this one, but otherwise no indication of what it was for. He paused, treading water, while he tried to figure it out. It felt like his air supply was beginning to resist his breathing, a sure sign that he was running out of air. He didn't want to look at his gauges. Pipe at the bottom with a current coming in. He felt the screen, and his gloved hand adhered to it. Current going out. A recirculating system of some kind? Water pumped in from that plant and then taken back out up here at the top of the cistern? He put both hands up against the mesh screen; after a few seconds the suction effect was more pronounced. It gave him an idea.

He turned around and swam back over to the western wall. When he hit the rock on that side, he turned off his light and looked down. His reference light was visible as a dim glow almost directly beneath him. Finally did something right, he thought, as he dived down to the side cave entrance. A minute later he broke through the air-water interface in the cave. Judith was standing next to the wall with her headlight still on, studying the symbols. He took off his mask and told her he had good news and bad news. The bad news was that he hadn't found the tanks. The good news was about the second pipe.

"I think I know how to get us out of here," he said, "but it's going to be complicated."

"I've been reading the walls," she said, as if she hadn't heard him. "Whoever wrote this was the Last Man—the one selected to make sure everyone else had committed suicide. He is telling the story of that night. It is . . . terrible, terrible beyond words."

"Wow," he said, momentarily forgetting their situation. "What was his name?"

"Judah," she said. "Judah Sicarius. Sicarius

means Daggerman. I'm about halfway through it. It's definitely first-century Aramaic."

"I can't believe you can just read that stuff. It all looks like hieroglyphics to me."

"I can read it, all right, but it is not pleasant reading. How are we going to get out of this place, David Hall?"

"Physics," he said. "I hope, anyway. There's a second pipe—at the top of the main cave. It's an outlet pipe. I think this cistern is a recirculation system. My plan is to block the outlet and hope like hell that the inlet pipe remains pressurized. There has to be a pretty big pump down at that plant to get water all the way up to the main cistern."

"And this will work how?"

"Water does not compress," he said. "So if that pump keeps pumping, the pressure in the cistern will rise until at some point the force on the bottom of that slab will be more than it weighs, and then it will pop up out of the hole—but just for an instant. I plan to be there, and, hopefully, I'll be able to jam that steel pipe over there into the crack. If I can do that, we can breathe, and if we can breathe, we can maybe think of something to get us out of here. Just one problem."

She walked back over to join him on the sand. "Just one? Wouldn't that same pressure push the water all the way into this cave?"

He smiled. "Knew you were smart, but yes, it

will. Only we're going to use that slab up there on the altar to block the entrance. That means you're going to have to stay in here when I do this."

"I do *not* want to stay in here," she began.

"We have no choice—I'm going to need your air tank, and you are probably going to have to stand on that slab to keep the water out of this cave. Stand on it and pile on any weight we can find to keep it in place. Like that big menorah up there, and those rocks."

"But—"

"I know, it's probably going to leak by—but it's all we have, Judith. That slab is around ten square feet. That's fourteen hundred and forty square inches. If I can get the pressure in the main cistern to rise just five pounds per square inch, that will exert almost four tons of force, and that slab doesn't weigh four tons."

She was silent, obviously frightened to death by the prospect of being trapped in this cave, with water rising and no breathing rig.

He gripped her shoulders. "Look: This ought to work. As long as the pump down there at the plant doesn't have some kind of back-pressure shutoff switch, the surge in the cistern water pressure ought to dislodge that slab. If I can get a pipe into the crack and wedge it open then maybe we'll have air."

"Ought to. Maybe. Okay, and then what? What do we do—shout for help?"

"Damn right. Or try to wedge the slab completely out. Or do something else—who knows? Anyway, if we can breathe, we can keep trying to get out of this mess. It's called survival, Judith."

She turned away, her face in shadow. "Maybe you should just go do this thing, David Hall. I think maybe you want to survive more than I do."

He'd forgotten about Dov, and the fact that she had been reading the testimonial of the last Jew on the mountain, describing the killing of women and children. Masada might be a mountain of death, he thought, but he was determined not to join the nine hundred and sixty souls who had died in this place. Correction, he thought: nine hundred and sixty-one.

"Help me find a round stone, Judith. Something about six inches in diameter. Then we need to move that altar slab."

29

Ellerstein stood in the western palace gate and tried to get control of his breathing. After the first one hundred feet up the steep ramp, he had knocked the ashes out of his pipe. After the second hundred feet, he had taken a silent oath never to smoke again. He looked at his watch. Well past midnight. There was no sign of the colonel and his team. They were probably searching the ruins for signs of other humans up here. He turned right and walked into the casemate walls along the southwestern rim of the fortress. A big yellow moon was rising over Jordan, casting a sepulchral light through the shattered walls.

When he got to the southernmost tip of the mountain, at the opposite end from the terraced villas, he looked down on the hostelry and tourist center, nearly eight hundred feet below. Much of it was in shadow, but he did see something that got his attention: There were two vehicles down there, Land Rovers from the look of them. They were not parked in the tourist parking lot, but rather behind the hostelry. Neither of the army detachments, coming up the coast road, would have been able to see them. They did not appear to be regular army vehicles; there were no Star of David markings, but there were whip antennas on both of them.

He shivered in the suddenly cold air. Skuratov? If so, where was the Russian right now?

It took them a long time to rig everything, and by the end of it, the air in the cave was getting difficult to breathe. David sat down in the sand near the entrance and went over the plan again with Judith. He was still in his diving rig but using her air tank this time. He had pushed the long steel staging pipe partway into the entrance tunnel. Beside them stood the half of the cracked marble slab they had taken down from the altar. It was leaning against the cave wall, ready to be dropped in place.

"As soon as I go back out into the cistern, you drop this slab across the water here. Then pack the edges with every loose rock you can find. If you have to, stand on it if the water starts to come in."

She had taken off her wet suit and was wearing just a bathing suit. He had the top of her wet suit wrapped up into a tight roll and tied to his side. That and a rock were going to block the outlet pipe. She nodded in the gloom; her headlamp was getting dim. "You know this thing is going to leak," she said, looking down at the irregularly shaped air-water interface.

"Yes, it will, but I really don't need too much pressure to lift that slab out there. Even two, three pounds per square inch ought to move it. Once it lifts, the pressure will release here."

"Where will the water go then?"

"If I can wedge this pipe into the crack, it will flow out of the cave up above. Which is good—someone will have to see that once it's daylight."

"Not on the Sabbath, they won't," she said with a sigh. Her face was perspiring. The CO_2 must be getting high in here, he thought. Time to get going.

"There's some air left in my tank. Hit it from time to time. This shouldn't take long. I'm going to swim out, leave the pipe in the tunnel here, go

472

plug the outlet, then come back for the pipe and head up to the slab. When it moves, I'll jam the pipe in as far as I can. Then I'll come back for you."

Confused, she shook her head. "We have only one tank," she pointed out. "I can't go up there."

"We'll wait here for an hour or so, let the water pump out into the cave up above and then out onto the side of the mountain. Then I'll go release the plug. That should create a small air gap around the slab. We can buddy-breathe our way back up there."

She sighed again, obviously unsure about all of this. He thought that he might be missing something, but his thinking was clouded by the bad air.

"Hang in there, Judith," he said, squeezing her hand. "This has a good shot at working. Even if we have to wait twenty-four hours, someone will see that water trail and come look."

"Not the people who dropped the slab in the first place," she said.

"Always the optimist, hunh? Okay. Time to go."

He fixed his mask and mouthpiece, turned on the tank, and slithered down into the purple water. She watched the trail of bubbles as he went and then switched off her light. The third light was still outside, at the tunnel entrance, so he'd have a reference to get back to her. She reached over in the darkness and found the remaining tank. David had said it would probably have fifteen, maybe twenty minutes of air left if she was careful.

She shook her head in the darkness. This was hopeless, in more ways than one. She didn't believe the altar slab would keep the water out, and she'd have no way of communicating that problem to David. This cave would flood, and the treasures in it would eventually be consumed by the caustic salts in the water.

Those had to be Dov's remains down there at the bottom of the main cistern, that distinctive suit and those white bone fragments. She was sure of it. There wasn't another suit like that in all Israel. An image of Dov's bones floated in front of her mind. She was doomed, and as she sat there, thinking about it, she didn't much care.

The water pipes meant that someone, and it had to be the government, was using this big cistern for some purpose besides water storage. That strange Russian had been interested in what this American was doing down here. Interested and even concerned. Skuratov had ties to Dimona, which was only forty kilometers away—and if it was Skuratov who had trapped them in here, then it was probably Skuratov who had trapped Dov in here. She found herself wanting to get that outsized dagger from under the altar for one last meeting with Colonel Skuratov.

She sat there, aware that there was something she was supposed to be doing, but her brain wasn't working very well. The air was becoming astringent, and each breath was fractionally less successful than the last. Then she remembered: the altar slab. She had to drop the altar slab over this tunnel and then weight it down. She turned on her light and took a deep breath and then another. She almost didn't have the energy to get up, but she must: David was out there, trying like hell to get them both out.

She got up, approached the heavy marble slab, positioned it as best she could, and then tipped it over onto the air-water interface. It landed with a flat splash, its edges embedding in the wet sand. Then she began to gather rocks from the cave and put them in the cracks between the slab and the entrance tunnel walls. She packed them in with sand and then more rocks, working in slow motion as she tried to get her breath. She remembered about the tank and went over to it, picked up the breathing mouthpiece, and took some air. It revived her immediately, and she started working faster now, stuffing smaller rocks and more sand all around the slab, while watching for signs of water intrusion. He had said that at first there would be no leaks, but when the pressure rose, *if* it rose, she reminded herself, the water would show up at the edges.

Finally, she ran out of rocks. She eyed the huge menorah up on the altar structure, but they had decided it was much too heavy and at the same time too delicate to move. Same with the scroll cylinders. She was aching to open them but knew better. The Qumran scrolls had been the consistency of a piece of newspaper that keeps its shape in the fireplace after being used to start the fire. The merest breath could turn such a thing to dust. She looked around the cave one more time for anything else she could put on the slab. Her body was wet with perspiration, and she could smell the fear on her skin. She looked at her watch: two-fifteen in the morning. Her depth gauge was still strapped to her wrist. It read thirty-two feet. She stepped onto the bed of rocks that covered the slab and sat down. She pulled the tank over and then switched off her headlamp. Now she could only wait. She put one hand out to the edge of the altar slab and burrowed it down into the sand. If it started getting wet, she would know she was in trouble. She laughed out loud—as if she were not in trouble right now?

David waited underneath the cistern slab, slowly treading water, the long staging pipe balanced at the midpoint under his left arm. With his right hand he held on to the iron ring on the underside of the slab. He kept his headlamp on, to watch two things: the slab itself and his depth gauge. If his theory was correct, a pressure increase in the cistern ought to register on his depth gauge. Behind him, floating next to his head, was a real prize: one of the two extra air tanks, which he had discovered bobbing along the ceiling near the outlet pipe. He had secured it to his harness with a small nylon strap and would take it back to the cave after he jammed the pipe.

He looked at the depth gauge. No change. It had read just above zero feet when he put his arm up against the big slab. He thought about Judith, waiting down in that increasingly airless cave. He felt bad enough about getting her involved in this mess, and the discovery of her husband's remains at the bottom of the cistern had been a dreadful shock. Hell, who could blame her—the government had obviously lied through its teeth about what happened to Dr. Dov Ressner, physicist of Dimona. What really bothered him was trying to figure out why someone had trapped *them* in this cistern. Was it because whoever it was realized they might discover Dov's remains? Or was it because of those two pipes coming into a two-thousand-year-old Masada cistern?

He thought he felt his ears squeeze just a tiny bit. He looked at the depth gauge. No change.

Wait—there was a change: not quite two feet. Definite movement. Good—the cistern system was being pressurized. It might take longer than he had planned on, because it was a really big cistern and a relatively small pipe. The big question was whether or not the pump over in that building would sense unusual back pressure and shut down. If it did, they were finished.

He blinked his eyes behind the mask and stared at the gauge. Now there was no doubt: The depth gauge had moved. He watched the big stone slab above his head, breathing as slowly as he could, conserving energy and air. He ran through the math again: Say the slab weighed five hundred pounds. If it was fourteen hundred square inches in area, at even just two pounds additional pressure, the water would be exerting twenty-eight hundred pounds of force on a five-hundred-pound slab. It ought to move. As long as some unknown opening in the Zealots' cave didn't fail and relieve the pressure. He refused to think about the treasure cave, the point most likely to do just that. He positioned the end of the staging pipe right up against the crack. Then he waited, and prayed.

30

Judith was drifting in a CO_2-induced haze when she thought she felt something. She tried to focus. What was it? Something, that's all. Don't worry. Relax. Then her brain sparked: Was that a pressure in her ears? She straightened up and switched on her headlamp. It was definitely more yellow now than white. She looked at the depth gauge on her wrist. Had it moved? Not much, if at all. Then what? What had she felt?

478

Her bare left hand, submerged in the sand, was tingling. She tried to concentrate, but it was very difficult. What was different? The sand was different. It was *wet* sand. She jerked her hand out and shone the light down. Definitely wet. The sand was wet. All around the slab, the sand was wet. Really wet.

She stood up too quickly and nearly tipped over. She blinked her eyes and steadied herself. Then she remembered and stepped back onto the marble slab. Had to keep it wedged in position, long enough for the pressure out there in the main cistern to dislodge the upper slab.

She focused the light. No longer just wet sand. There was visible water now, oozing up around the edges of the slab. She cast the light around the cave, but there was nothing else to pile on the slab. Every loose rock, her scuba tank, her weight belt. She wished they could have moved the huge menorah, but that was impossible. It would take four men to move that thing. She was pretty sure it was nearly solid metal, possibly even gold. An amazing treasure, the find of all finds, and it was going to be drowned here in this cave.

She sobbed once in desperation, watching the water press past the edges of the slab, wetting the marble now. David's plan was working—the cistern was pressurizing—but could she hold this thing? She hadn't followed the math he used to compute the lifting force, but this piece of marble was about one-quarter the size of the big slab up there. Then she felt it: The slab actually moved, making a squelching sound all around its edges. A small wave of water shot out from three sides before the thing settled back. There was nothing more she could do to hold it, so she knelt down, trying to concentrate her weight. The marble trembled again, a small movement, but a lot more water squirted by the edges this time. She could not hold it. She began to weep as what felt like a soft, giant hand began to move the piece of marble.

David felt rather than saw the slab move above his head. One minute he had been pressing the pipe against the crack; the next moment it had jumped up at an angle and was now wedged in the crack. He shone his light at the point where they joined and saw that he had jammed up one corner of the slab. Swirling particles in the water were streaming up into the crack. He grabbed the iron ring, repositioned his arm, and tried to shove the pipe farther into the crack, but it didn't move.

He relaxed for a moment, gathered all his strength, pulled hard on the ring as a fulcrum, and then put a steady push up on the pipe. After a minute, when he almost could no longer hold it, the slab shifted again, and this time the pipe slid several inches into the crack. He could feel the water rushing by his mask now, as the cistern relieved the pressure up into the bat cave above.

He relaxed his grip on the pipe and took a deep breath from the tank. A difficult deep breath, he realized. *Dammit!* The tank was quitting on him. He let go of the steel pipe and hung by one hand from the ring. He looked up at the pipe. He had managed to shove perhaps two feet of it through the crack. Then he realized that if the slab moved again, the pipe could slip out and plunge to the bottom of the cistern.

He got out his knife and slipped it, blade up, between his diving boot and the pant leg of his wet suit. Then he cut directly up, all the way to his thigh. The pant leg opened up but did not come off. He made a second cut, creating a strip of the rubbery material the length of his leg. He cut that off and then tied the pipe off to the iron ring as best he could. It wasn't terrific, but better than nothing. He took another deep breath and then felt a pressure dip in his ears. Not too big, but definitely something.

The Zealots' cave. That damned piece of marble had let go.

He consulted his compass, pointed west, switched off his headlamp, and then swam down hard toward the opposite wall, the extra air tank banging his hip. He saw the reference light when he was passing through twenty-five feet. He turned twenty degrees to the right and pushed down to the light and the cave entrance. He rolled over onto his back, switched on his light, and started in, but the extra tank snagged on something. He whipped out his knife and cut the tank loose from the harness, grabbed it with his other hand, and struggled backward into the tight tunnel. When he came to the end he hit his head on something: the slab. It wasn't wedged anymore, though: It was loose in the interface, and he could feel water passing around it. He pulled the extra tank up and banged on the slab to get her attention, but nothing happened. Jesus *Christ,* had the cave flooded?

Then the slab did move, and he saw her hands scrabbling along the edge, trying to dislodge it. He put his back into it then, and between them they got the thing onto its edge and he was through and standing up in chest-deep water. The marble dropped back into the hole with a flat slap.

David looked at Judith, whose white face told the story. "I couldn't hold it," she sobbed. "The water came in everywhere."

He glanced around the cave, which was now almost one-third full of water. It had risen past the bottom lines of writing on one wall. "Look," he said, pointing his headlamp. "It's going back down. I got the pipe into the big slab. The fill system should be pumping water into that cave and outside."

She collapsed onto her knees in the water and

put her face in her hands. He noticed how stuffy the air was in the cave and pushed the spare tank over.

"Here," he said, switching over the regulator connection and pushing his mouthpiece into her face. "Breathe."

She grabbed at the mouthpiece and took several deep breaths before he cautioned her to slow down. Then he took a couple of breaths himself. He watched her face. She was calming down, but the whites of her eyes were still showing.

"We'll let the water go out onto the mountainside for as long as we can stand it in here," he said. "Then I'll go unplug the outlet pipe, and hopefully we'll get an airspace up there by the slab. After that, it's a matter of time before someone sees all that water."

"Hopefully," she murmured. "Always with the hopefully."

She was trying to crack wise, but her voice gave her away. He needed to distract her. "Yeah, well, look," he said. "We're still alive, and this cave is still intact. We have some air now. Someone's going to see all that water."

"So now we what, just wait?"

"Yes. We just wait." He shone his light over the writing on the wall. "You can actually read all this?"

She straightened and looked up at the script, her headlamp throwing a bobbing yellow circle on the wall. "I've read almost half of it," she said. "It's still terrible."

"Where does it begin?" he asked, taking another hit on the spare tank.

"There," she said, getting up and wading over toward the altar structure. The water was definitely receding, he thought. The parts of the writing that had been wetted were beginning to run down the wall.

"Here. It begins like this: *I am Judah Sicarius, son of Joseph. I shall be the Last Man.*"

Ellerstein finally found the colonel and his team up on the northernmost tip of the fortress. They had apparently just climbed back up from the terraces. The colonel was not surprised to see him.

"My people reported you had come up here, Professor," he explained. His face looked even younger in the bright moonlight. Beyond them, over a thousand feet below, the Dead Sea glinted silver all the way across to the dark Jordanian hills. A night bird cried out in the darkness down on the Serpent Path. To their left stood the labyrinth of the palace storerooms, and beyond that, the cable-car tower contrasted dramatically with the two-thousand-year-old ruins. Seeing Ellerstein, the soldiers with the colonel took a break, lighting up cigarettes and enjoying the expansive view.

"So, Colonel: anything?"

"Not a damned thing, Professor. No Americans,

no Russians, no Arabs or white-eyed Palestinian Islamicide bombers, as best I can tell. How about you—did you see anything?" The colonel was trying to hide his sarcasm, but he wasn't succeeding very well.

"Nothing up here, no," Ellerstein said, fumbling with his pipe, "but there are two Land Rovers parked out in the dark behind the hostelry. Those yours, Colonel?"

The colonel looked at him for a moment and then snapped an order to the radio operator. The man dropped his cigarette and made an urgent transmission. He listened for a reply and then shook his head at the colonel.

"Goddammit," the colonel said. He turned to the sergeant. "Get somebody on that, right away. Find out whose they are." The radio operator got busy, and the colonel found his own cigarettes. "The hostelry is supposed to be covered by the regular coast road patrol," he said. "They didn't mention anything about any vehicles back there, but we've searched this whole place. There's no one up here except us."

"Did you search the cisterns?" Ellerstein asked, remembering Skuratov's concern.

"The *cisterns?* You mean along the southern rim?"

"No, the main cisterns," Ellerstein said. "The big ones you get to by walking back along the water channels from the middle terrace."

The colonel was about to answer when one of

his men called him urgently. He was standing up on the outer casemate wall and pointing down at something on the eastern slope.

"What, dammit?" the colonel snapped, his lighter poised halfway to his cigarette.

"Water, sir. There's water coming out of the mountain. Right down there. Lots of it."

Shapiro looked at Ellerstein, and then they both headed for the eastern gate, along with the troops. One of the soldiers actually trotted down the Serpent Path to where a black stream was gushing out of the ground. Ellerstein and the colonel followed him. The water was coming from a small cave entrance. He followed Shapiro and the soldiers into the cave, climbing past the remains of a stinking pile of bat-soiled sand that was being washed out of the cave entrance as they crawled over it.

Each of the soldiers had a flashlight, and they were pointing them everywhere in the cave. The floor was flooded to a depth of a couple of feet. The water seemed to be coming from a spring at the back of the cave in a rhythmic upwelling. Ellerstein tried to identify the smell in the cave, and finally did.

"That's warm water," he exclaimed. He put a finger into the water and confirmed it by tasting a drop.

"No way," Shapiro said, but then he, too, tasted a drop, as did a couple of the soldiers. "Okay, it's warm," Shapiro said. "So how the hell is a spring in the mountain generating warm water a thousand feet up?"

Ellerstein shook his head and asked one of the soldiers for his flashlight. He sloshed over to where the water was rising. Shining the light down into the swirling water, he could just make out the edge of a large slab through a cloud of turbid sand. What looked like the end of a staging pipe was jammed between the edge of the slab and the rim of the hole. When he saw the iron ring, he called Shapiro.

"Man-made," he said. "There's a lifting ring. And look at that pipe. Fresh scratches. Someone is under there, I think."

"In what?" Shapiro asked. "Under there, inside what? A cistern?"

"I don't know," Ellerstein said, "but this is new. The presence of a cistern here, I mean. We need to ·open that hole."

Shapiro straightened up, hesitated, and ordered the sergeant to get the slab out of the hole. The sergeant examined the iron ring and then had three men pull the end of the staging pipe through the crack. They all felt the slab thump back down into its hole once the pipe pulled clear, stopping the flow of water. Then they put the pipe through the iron ring. Three men got on each end, and they lifted the slab aside, revealing the rectangular hole. Water welled up again.

They shone their lights down into the hole, just in time to see a scuba air tank rising like a ghost right toward them before it popped up into their faces. Other bits of material were visible circling in the water below the opening. The sergeant hauled the tank up into the cave and read out the name of the dive shop in Yafo. When Ellerstein heard that, he signaled Shapiro and backed out of the cave.

"What?" the colonel asked.

"I think I know who's down there, in that cistern," Ellerstein said. "Have you found out who those vehicles belong to down behind the hostelry?"

"My people are checking on that," Shapiro said, visibly angry now. "Now please, tell me what the hell you're doing here."

"Colonel Shapiro, I suggest you station some people by that hole in there," Ellerstein said, "and then go find Colonel Skuratov and *his* people. I'll bet they're up in the fortress by now, what with all this commotion."

"Skuratov? What do you know about him? Goddammit, Professor—"

"Please, Colonel Shapiro. Go find Skuratov. Take him to the terraces, away from this side, away from as many watching eyes as possible. I'll wait here for whoever's in the cistern to surface. Then we'll sort it all out."

"*We?!* Who is 'we'?"

Ellerstein looked down at his shoes but said nothing.

"Look—I need to report all this," Shapiro said, pointing at the slab opening and the debris that had come out of the hole.

"Yes, of course," Ellerstein said, "but not just yet, okay? Let's see who comes out of that water, and what they were doing down there."

"But my instructions—to report immediately—"

"They will ask a thousand questions, yes? Why not wait until you have some answers, hunh? Meanwhile, Colonel, I really need a phone circuit, or even a radio, to Jerusalem. I need to call Israel Gulder in the prime minister's office."

Shapiro started to object again, but then the bit about the PM's office penetrated.

"Who the hell are you, Professor?" he asked.

"Nobody famous, Colonel—but you will be if I don't get that circuit up. Now go find Skuratov. He's up there. And, Colonel? Keep some soldiers with you."

31

Judith had almost finished reading Judah's last testament when she stopped, her finger poised above the lampblack symbols.

"What?" David asked. The water had receded entirely from the cave, but the air was getting worse. They would have to get out of here soon.

She sat back down on the floor of the cave and frowned up at the writing. "There's something he's talking about besides the last night. He makes reference to some event, some disturbance that happened forty years before the siege. In Jerusalem. It concerns his brother."

"What kind of disturbance?"

She shook her head. "It's difficult, without time to really study it. There are many possible interpretations of the words. Like the word 'brother'—it can mean his actual brother or brother in arms, like that." She studied the writing some more. "It's as if—oh, my God."

"What? What?"

She pressed the back of her hand against her lips and glanced over at the pile of rags and bones. "My God," she whispered again, "I think I know who this is. Listen."

David was baffled, but she was obviously overwhelmed by what she thought she'd discovered.

"Listen to what he writes at the very end, down here at the bottom. Damn the saltwater—this stuff is disappearing in front of my eyes. He says: *I regret, oh Lord, that we lost this war. It was madness to start it, that we all knew, those of us who had been in the hills for those many years. And now, desecration and abomination beyond words, or speaking.* Something like that. Then it goes on: *So be it. This could not have happened if it was not your will. I was just one of your instruments, as I now remain.* Then there's more, about his brother. It's, well, an apology. To or about his brother, I think."

"For what?"

"First he says he's not apologizing for betraying him to the Romans. As the long-lost, disgraced, and exiled brother, he, Judah, had been the only one his brother could trust to do such a thing, because the priests and even the Romans would absolutely believe it." She stopped again, working through the translation. "He is apologizing for *scorning* his brother, who had preached the other course, the way of love and reconciliation, just the opposite of the path the Jews had ultimately chosen, the way of war."

She stopped again, her lips moving silently, while David watched. She was totally focused. Then she put both hands up to her cheeks while she read aloud. "He puts no faith in all the talk of prophecies, the Messiah stories. He says there were Messiahs every year, before and after his brother. All of them lunatics. But there had been something innately good and—I can't make this out—innocent? about his brother. He, Judah, should never have scorned him, as a child or afterward. That was his only sin, he says. All of the things told about him later were lies, but for that, for scorning the beloved son, he repents from the bottom of his heart."

491

David felt the hairs rising on the back of his head. "Messiah? Beloved son?"

"*Att-haw baree kha-beeba.* Revered son, or beloved son. I'm transliterating here, David. It will take a crowd of Aramaic experts to get it precisely right."

"Even so," he whispered. She nodded slowly, gazing at the words.

They both stared in wonder at the writing on the wall. Then she looked at him, her face a pale oval beneath the yellow headlamp. "Say the name, David," she whispered. "Say it out loud."

"Whose? Judah's?"

"No, the whole name: Judah Sicarius. Say it out loud, three times."

David said it, and the third time he understood: Judah Sicarius.

Judas *Iscariot.*

"Holy *shit,*" he whispered. "This was Judas?" Then he looked at the plain bronze bowl. "Oh, my God, Judith—that bowl. Could that be what I think it is?"

She shook her head slowly. "I don't know. He says that if the Romans find the cave, they'll leave the bowl, and thereby miss the real treasure here."

"He must have been an old man—this was forty years after all that."

"He says he had three score years—that's roughly sixty years old. He would have been twentysomething at the time of the crucifixion. That makes sense—they were all young men."

"His *brother.* Does he name him?"

"No, and it could be brother in the sense of 'every man is my brother.' "

He looked at the bronze bowl again. It's just a bowl, he thought. Or was it? "I'm almost afraid to touch it," he said.

Then they both felt a thump of pressure in the air, as if something had squeezed the entire cistern outside.

"Something's happened," David said, almost glad for the distraction. "We'd better get out of here. Go see if we have an airspace up there."

"What if we don't?"

"All the water has withdrawn from in here. It had to go somewhere. There were grooves in the side of that big slab, which is probably how this place filled up over the centuries. If the water's down, there has to be air. C'mon."

Five minutes later they rose toward the top of the cave, buddy-breathing on the single remaining tank. When they bumped against the ceiling of the cavern, David released an air bubble from his mouth, hoping almost against hope that it would move away from them.

It did. Perversely, it went behind them. They followed it, saw lights, and a moment later popped out into the space where the slab had been. Four large soldiers and Professor Ellerstein were standing there, looking down at them.

"Shalom," he intoned solemnly, reaching for his pipe.

The soldiers brought them up into the fortress through the Serpent Path gate. They stopped while a sergeant held a brief consultation on his radio. While he did, Ellerstein took them aside. "Mr. Hall," he said, his expression anything but friendly. "Communing with the spirits again?"

"You have no idea," David said, wondering what was going to happen next. Both he and Judith were itching vigorously. He was still shaken by that wine bowl. Ellerstein was about to reply when Judith grabbed his arm, pulled him farther out of earshot of the soldiers, and spoke to him in rapid-fire Hebrew for a few minutes. David couldn't follow a word, of course, but he saw the expression on Ellerstein's face. She's telling him what's down there, he thought.

When she was finished, Ellerstein walked slowly back over to where David and the soldiers were waiting. Judith folded her arms around her chest and stood staring out over the Dead Sea.

"I don't know what to say now, Mr. Hall," Ellerstein said. "It seems you have made some amazing discoveries here. Despite all the deception."

"Did she tell you about finding her husband's body?"

"Yes, she did. She believes he was murdered, probably by the same person who closed that slab on you two."

"And the pipes? She tell you about the pipes?"

"No. What about pipes, Mr. Hall?"

David hesitated. Ellerstein was asking a question to which he sounded like he might already know the answer. He described the pipes and the cylinders. Ellerstein gave him an odd look when he mentioned them. "Whoever's been using this cistern did not know about that cave," David concluded, "but they sure as hell knew all about the cistern."

Judith came back over to where they were standing. It was light now, with sunrise imminent. A cool breeze had begun to flow up over the ramparts.

"Skuratov," she said. "He's here, isn't he?"

Ellerstein nodded.

"Take me to him," she commanded.

"Judith, are you very sure—"

"I am very sure, Yossi. He locked us in the cave, didn't he? He or his people. Now, if you please."

Ellerstein hesitated and then spoke to the sergeant, who made another radio call. Then they were escorted up to the north end of the fortress, where they were met by Lieutenant Colonel Shapiro and more soldiers. Shapiro and Ellerstein talked for a moment in Hebrew, and then the colonel took them down to the middle terrace, where they found Skuratov sitting by himself. In the soft light of dawn, his face was haggard, but his eyes were alert and angry when he saw Judith and David. He was perched on a marble bench fragment just inside the waist-high balustrade, his back to the stupendous view overlooking the sheer palisade that dropped down into the darkness.

Colonel Shapiro walked out onto the terrace, followed by Judith, David, and Professor Ellerstein. Above them, Shapiro's team waited, bored now, their submachine guns draped casually as they lit up cigarettes. In the distance, David saw lights down on the coast road, approaching the mountain, coming fast. Too fast, he thought; that has to be a helicopter. Then he heard the whining engine noise. Skuratov glared first at David, then Ellerstein. The helicopter came whopping by, actually below them, the rotor disk silvery in the morning light, and then it hooked a lazy right turn, climbing up the south side of the mountain, turning again to line up on the top of the fortress and then landing in a cloud of dust and noise in front of the storeroom ruins.

32

Ellerstein waited for all the noise up top to subside before approaching Skuratov. He was pretty sure he knew who was in the helicopter.

Skuratov just glared at him. "So, Ellerstein," he said in Hebrew. "What have you done here?"

"The question is, Colonel, what have *you* done here," Ellerstein replied. "These people tell me that Judith's husband, Dov Ressner, lies at the bottom of that cistern."

"Where you should have left him," Skuratov spat, "*and* them."

Ellerstein was taken aback. He asked Colonel Shapiro to move his men back from the terrace above; ordinary conscripts should not hear this. He also asked the colonel to keep an eye out for any more of Skuratov's people. Just then Gulder and two of the prime minister's bodyguards appeared, coming down the terrace steps. Shapiro made a gesture, and the soldiers backed out of sight. The bodyguards started down, but Gulder waved them back up the steps.

Ellerstein pulled his glasses down to look directly at Skuratov. "So this information is not news? You did this thing?"

"I did not put him there," Skuratov said. "He put himself there. I just made sure he stayed there."

"All right, Yossi, I'll take it from here," Gulder said as he walked up. Ellerstein was surprised at the aide's tone of voice. This was a different Israel Gulder. He could see that the American, unable to understand Hebrew, was totally baffled. Judith, on the other hand, looked as if she were going to explode.

"It was you?" she hissed. "*You* who closed the slab on my husband? It was you who closed it on us, too, wasn't it?"

"What are they saying?" David asked Ellerstein in English. The professor just shook his head. "That's Colonel Malyuta Lukyanovitch Skuratov, of the Israeli security service known as Shin Bet," he said softly to David in English. "Very important at Dimona. I believe he murdered Yehudit's husband."

Judith advanced on Skuratov, pushing past Colonel Shapiro to get right in the old man's face. "I *know* he murdered my husband," she said, in English now. "Just like he tried to murder us. Why? Evil bastard, look at me! *Why?*"

"Because you had no business being down there, in that cistern," Skuratov thundered in heavily accented English. "Neither of you: It is *forbidden!* Do you understand me? *Forbidden!*" He glared at David. "You goddamned Americans think you can go anywhere, all over the world, and do anything you please? Well, not here, you can't. Absolutely not. It is *forbidden!*"

"Did you know about the cave?" David asked him. "With the Temple relics?"

Skuratov hesitated but then waved his hand dismissively. "What cave? What relics? Is this some more of your emotional dreams about Metsadá, American fool? There is no cave."

"Yes there is, you bastard," Judith yelled. "Now explain yourself: Why have you done these terrible things? What are *you* hiding down there?"

"Your security, and Israel's. Your husband took an oath, and then he broke that oath when he consorted with antinuclear traitors. We knew what he was up to, of course. When he came here, to find the D_2O, he went too far. We took the appropriate measures. That is all."

"D_2O?" David asked softly. "Did you say D_2O?"

Skuratov squinted his eyes for an instant and then sighed. "Ah. I forgot. Our American here is an engineer." He rubbed the sides of his face. "Yes, I said D_2O. So now you know."

"Know *what?*" Gulder said. Ellerstein said something to him in Hebrew. Gulder's face tightened, and then he looked at David.

Judith wasn't interested in D_2O. "I don't care!" she shouted, clearly on the verge of hysteria. "You murdered my husband!"

Skuratov snorted his contempt, but Colonel Shapiro moved closer to Judith.

"In Hebrew, please," Gulder said, glancing again

at David. "Yossi, what is this D_2O business?"

"Deuterium oxide, Mr. Gulder," Ellerstein said. "Also known as heavy water. The American mentioned pipes. I'm going to guess that the cistern is part of a heavy water distiller, supplied from an evaporation plant nearby. Right, Colonel?"

Skuratov nodded once but then stared away into space. The breeze wafting up from the cliffs below carried a faint whiff of warm brine.

"They were making heavy water?" Gulder asked. "Here, in this place? In this desert?"

Ellerstein told Gulder about the cylinders. "That is why you killed Dov Ressner, isn't it? There was no radiation accident, and it wasn't because he was talking to antinuclear dissidents. He'd figured *this* place out, hadn't he? He saw the geothermal plant down there and realized there had to be a storage point, a very big storage point."

"What is this heavy water?" Judith asked, looking first to Gulder and then to Ellerstein. Then she looked to David and asked it again, in English.

"It's the key to making really big nuclear weapons," David said. "Or making smaller ones much more powerful. You can derive tritium from heavy water, and you can make plutonium in a heavy water reactor. That's why nonproliferation agencies track it—it's a marker. Large quantities of heavy water usually indicate a nuclear weapons program."

"But *make* deuterium oxide?" Ellerstein asked again. "How? The expense—it would be astronomical. There is no way—"

"Yes, there is," David interrupted. "Deuterium oxide occurs in nature, but in very dilute form, as little as one molecule in ten million in seawater, for instance." He pointed with his chin to the Dead Sea below them. "Like *that* seawater."

Ellerstein lifted his hands in a gesture of consternation.

"The key was that geothermal plume down there," David said. "If you had to pay for the energy to boil down millions of gallons of saltwater to get heavy water, you'd never do it—but this energy was free, wasn't it, Colonel Skuratov? All you had to do was fill the cistern with freshwater, distilled from the Dead Sea, then recycle all that water through a second distiller down in that plant, concentrating the deuterium oxide on each pass. Over and over again, for months on end, until the millions of gallons became, what, twenty gallons? At a ten percent concentration?"

"Thirty," Skuratov whispered proudly. "Thirty percent concentration."

David straightened up. "So you guys never did buy heavy water from Norway way back then, did you? That was all cover and deception. You were already making it right here in Israel."

Skuratov gave him a wintry smile. "The Norway

diversion—something for all you sanctimonious nonproliferators to chase after."

"Then you'd concentrate it at Dimona?"

Skuratov sniffed and looked away without answering.

There was a moment of silence. Gulder broke it, switching back to Hebrew. "There is something missing here," he said. "Our nuclear program is an open secret. What required extreme measures?"

"Because that is not what *you* wanted heavy water for, was it, Colonel Zealot?" asked Ellerstein, remembering from his days at Dimona the other use of heavy water.

Skuratov frowned at the use of the word "Zealot" but then seemed to relax, as if there were no longer any reason to pretend. "No, it was not," he agreed quietly.

"What other use?" Gulder asked. Ellerstein told him.

Gulder, obviously excited now, moved closer to the colonel, forcing him to crane his neck up at him. "We've searched this area, everywhere around Dimona, ever since you stuck your nose in when the American came. We've even overflown the fortress with radiation monitors. Monitoring trucks up and down the roads at night. There was nothing."

"First of all, heavy water is not radioactive," Skuratov said. "Second, you were looking for weapons or weapons materials. There weren't any."

"So what are those cylinders for?"

"When the water level in the cistern is reduced to a few feet and the maximum concentration has been achieved, we command the cylinders to open and fill with the product."

"The product."

"Yes, the product."

Gulder bent down to get in Skuratov's face. "A product is something you sell, Colonel."

"Just so, Mr. Gulder."

"To whom?"

"To whom do you think, Mr. Very Important Assistant? Who in this region desperately needs heavy water?"

Gulder straightened up, his face frozen in shock. "You sold heavy water to the *Persians?*"

"Yes, we did."

"Are you insane?"

"We are angry, not mad. Nor crazy, you stupid bureaucrat. The quicker the Persians get the bomb, the sooner Israel will have to strike them first. A preemptive strike, it is called. We are more like the Kanna'im than you people ever imagined, Mr. Gulder. They were the ones who started the rebellion in A.D. 67, remember?"

"And brought the destruction of Israel down on their heads when they did," Ellerstein pointed out.

"If that's what it takes, that's what it takes,"

Skuratov said. "If you strike Iran, you will have to strike *all* the Arabs. Then and only then will we have a final solution."

Ellerstein shook his head in wonder. "He *is* mad, Gulder. Stark, raving mad. No word of this calamity can leave this mountain."

"Oh, yes, that is *absolutely* correct, Yossi," Gulder said softly. He looked over at Judith Ressner and the American. Ellerstein suddenly knew what that look might mean. Then Judith stepped in and slapped Skuratov in the face.

"What about Dov?" she asked in a cold voice. In his excitement over discovering what had been going on here, Ellerstein had forgotten all about Dov Ressner. Judith had not.

"Your husband was a traitor," Skuratov said, rubbing his face where she'd slapped him. "He found out about the plant. We don't know how. We assumed he'd come here to expose the heavy water process. My people caught him in the big cistern. I gave the order to seal him in it, and I'm glad I did."

"You absolute swine," Judith said. "Then you came to my house, you, with your crocodile tears."

"Swine, is it?" Skuratov growled, finally standing up. "These were vital secrets. Vital to the survival of all Israel. Your peacenik husband, madam, who promised to safeguard these vital secrets, was ready to sell it out for his precious ideals. Well, let me remind you of something, Dr. Yehudit Ressner. You are standing on the fortress of Metsadá. Those Jews, two thousand years ago? They also had ideals, but they chose death to protect *their* ideals, didn't they? Your weakling husband ended up in good company here, yes?"

"You trapped him like an animal, and then you drowned him in your precious heavy water," she said. Shapiro saw that her fingers were opening and closing and that she appeared to be ready to physically attack Skuratov. He moved even closer to her, ready to restrain her.

"Yes, *I* did those things," Skuratov announced, pointing a finger at his own chest, "and I would do them again. Someone must, because there are very few patriots anymore in this country." He shot a defiant look at Gulder, which was when Judith made her move. First she screamed, a long ear-piercing shriek that froze everyone. Colonel Shapiro moved to grab her, but she was way ahead of him. As he raised his arms, she snatched his pistol out of his hip holster and then pushed him away so suddenly that he tripped backward and sat down abruptly. Judith swept the gun in Gulder's direction, then in Ellerstein's, motioning them to get back.

"Jesus, Judith, what are you doing?" David asked, reaching out a hand.

"This bastard killed my husband," she said in English. "He's been making this heavy water

505

business down here for a long time and now admits to selling some. To the goddamned Iranians."

"What?"

"Don't involve yourself in this, David," Judith said. She turned to Skuratov and put the gun right in his face.

"All right, then, *Zealot,*" she said, mimicking Ellerstein. "You have committed at least one murder to protect your insane scheme, not including what you did to us. We were looking for the Zealots' secret, the real Zealots', not yours. Now I'll give *you* a choice: You admire the Kanna'im? Here's your chance. Do what they did, or I'll do it for you."

Skuratov just stared at her. David didn't know what to do. He looked up to the terrace above them, but the men were not there. Shapiro, back on his feet, was also looking but remained in place. He'd told his troops to back out.

"You know exactly what I'm talking about," Judith said, putting the gun barrel up to Skuratov's right eye. He blinked and took an involuntary step backward.

"Yehudit," Ellerstein began softly, but she waved him silent. Gulder just watched with his arms folded.

"No, Yossi. This is justice here. He drowned my husband like a rat, all for the sake of his heavy water. Well, here we are, *Zealot.* In Herod's palace on the mountain of Metsadá. You wish to protect the secret of your own treason and murder? Do what the Kanna'im did, and your secret is safe."

She jabbed Skuratov in the eye with the gun. He yelped and took another step backward, toward the wall. His right eye puffed closed.

"Come on, Colonel Murderer. Whatever you were doing here, it is finished. You think Dov was in good company? Time to find out. Your life for Dov's. Hammurabi rules now, yes? Eye for an eye?"

Skuratov, never taking his one good eye off hers, slowly raised his right hand. He pushed the gun barrel out of his face with the back of his hand. Then, without another word, he turned and stepped up onto the parapet. Ellerstein yelled something in Hebrew, but in the same instant, Skuratov was gone. Judith lowered the gun and then tossed it back to Colonel Shapiro, who fumbled it and then dropped it. He bent to retrieve it, got up, and went to look over the parapet as Judith turned away.

Judith did not see Israel Gulder boot the colonel over the parapet, but they all heard him scream.

David resisted an urge to go to the edge and look over. He went instead to Judith and put his hands on her shoulders. She was trembling, but her face was set in a rigid mask as she willed back tears. The sun burst over the Jordanian hills across the Dead Sea, projecting bands of bright yellow light onto the ancient stones of the fortress. Up above, on the top terrace, the sergeant and Gulder's two bodyguards reappeared. Gulder noticed them and went up the steps. He said something to Ellerstein in Hebrew. They both looked at David. Ellerstein came over to him while Judith sat down with her arms wrapped around her chest.

"You have heard some sensitive things here this morning, Mr. Hall," he said. "How good is your memory?"

"Not worth a damn, Professor," David said, not missing a beat.

"Is that a promise, Mr. Hall?"

"Absolutely. My main concern is for what's in that cave—and for her."

Ellerstein glanced down at Judith. "Do you truly understand, Mr. Hall?" he asked. "Promises made in this place are binding, yes?"

"I understand," David said.

Ellerstein nodded slowly. "I will try my best for you, then," he said.

Gulder was coming back down the steps with his bodyguards. Ellerstein intercepted him, and they stepped aside to talk in Hebrew. David sat down beside Judith and put his arm around her shoulder. She sagged into him.

"What is it about this place?" he asked quietly. "Everything is about blood and dying."

"Not the wine bowl," she said.

Yes it was, David thought to himself, especially

508

if it's what I think it is. What had Ellerstein meant by trying his best?

Then there were soldiers standing around them. Israel Gulder came over, closely escorted by his bodyguards.

"Mr. Hall," he said in English, "will you kindly go with these people?"

"Where?" David asked.

Gulder did not reply but only signaled with his chin that David should get up and go with them. Judith didn't appear to understand what was happening.

"Now, Mr. Hall," Gulder said. He gestured again with his chin.

When they got up to the top, there were many more soldiers standing along the eastern parapet walls, looking down. The sergeant was busy shouting orders, and there appeared to be a recovery detail shaping up by the eastern gate. David had little time to watch; the bodyguards escorted him directly to the helicopter, whose turbines were already spooling up. They sat him in the left rear seat, helped him strap in, and put a headset on his head. Then one of them strapped in next to him while the other got in the right front seat, next to the pilot. A soldier outside closed the door and stood ready with a fire extinguisher until the engines came up to power. Then they lifted off.

As soon as they were safely airborne, the bodyguard next to him produced a set of plastic handcuffs and snapped them onto David's wrists. He did not resist: What would have been the point, at two thousand feet over the Dead Sea? Then the guard produced a black sleep mask, which he gently fit over David's eyes. David felt a hand on his chest, pushing him back into the seat. The gesture said it all: Relax. He slumped in his seat. After watching Gulder calmly send the colonel to his death, he wondered now if the ministerial aide had told them to throw him out of the helicopter somewhere out over the Mediterranean.

33

Judith saw the helicopter lift off without Gulder and asked Ellerstein where David Hall had gone. Ellerstein nodded at the rapidly disappearing helicopter.

"Yossi!" she exclaimed. "Where are they taking him?"

"Away?" he tried. She stared at him. Gulder had been talking on a small radio set and now ended the call. He walked over to them. "So, Dr. Ressner, tell me in complete detail, please: What have you found down there in that cistern?"

"Not until you tell me where you've taken Mr. Hall," she declared. Some soldiers were standing at the top of the steps, watching them. The morning heat was rising in shimmering waves, distorting the view.

"We've taken Mr. Hall to a safe place, Dr. Ressner," Gulder said. "Until we can sort out the ramifications of what you two have done here."

"What ramifications?"

"Well, because you chose to speak in English, after I twice asked you to speak in Hebrew, Mr. Hall knows things that he might otherwise not have known. Also, in certain respects, you are responsible for the death of a senior counter-intelligence officer. For starters."

"Mr. Gulder," protested Ellerstein, but the aide waved him silent.

"Listen to me, Dr. Ressner. Yossi here tells me you have found artifacts from Herod's Temple in that cave. Is that true?"

"Yes, I believe it is."

"And there is writing on the walls? The testament of the last Zealot?"

"So it says."

"Anything else?"

"What appears to be the remains of my husband at the bottom of the cistern," she said defiantly. "If that matters to you."

"Yes, yes, I understand that, but I'm talking about antiquities. What else is down there?"

She glared at him again as if he were inhuman. He shook his head impatiently and tried again. "Dr. Ressner," he said, "I am truly sorry that your husband was killed by that man, but now you've wiped that slate clean, yes? So: Now you must see things my way. The *government's* way. We must deal with the present, and the present is a gathering avalanche of international media interest even as we stand here talking. You know you will be the most famous archaeologist in the world in about six hours, don't you?"

"*Me?* What do you mean?"

"Because we are going to announce these discoveries, immediately, just as soon as the army can either get some divers down here or get the water pumped out of that cistern. Independent confirmation, then announcement."

"It wasn't my discovery. It was David Hall—"

"No, it was not, Dr. Ressner," Gulder interrupted. She looked at Ellerstein, who nodded his head at her. Listen to this man, he was telling her.

"This discovery was made by you, Dr. Yehudit Ressner," Gulder continued. "After years of solitary study and analysis. The American's visit was simply an annoyance, which was why you were upset by the requirement to shepherd him around this site. Then he trespassed at night and was invited to leave. He went scuba diving and then went back to America. The American is most definitely *not* part of this story, Dr. Ressner. You, on the other hand, *are* the story. Along with the artifacts, of course."

"But—"

"Yes, I know, we have Mr. Hall in custody. Of course. We will need to debrief him, and then we will send him home, but not until we have established the provenance of these amazing discoveries, in a proper public relations setting, as it were. Now: Tell me in detail, what is down there?"

Bewildered, but not sure what to do about it, she told him about everything they'd found. Gulder's eyes gleamed when he heard it. An officer called down to them from above that a navy dive team was on the way from Haifa.

"Well, Dr. Ressner: Do you think you could manage to go back down there? One last time? Based on what you've said about its size, it may take days to drain that cistern. We need to verify these things immediately."

"And preserve them," she said. "The cave must be atmospherically sealed before the water level drops below the entrance. We have no way—"

"Yes, yes, of course, Dr. Ressner," he said, steering her with his hand on her shoulder toward the steps. "Trust me, we will shortly have more archaeology experts here than there ever were Zealots. First, I think, we need pictures. Now: Yossi, take her up to wait for the dive team's helicopter. These are military divers, Dr. Ressner. They will take good care of you down there. Trust me, Dr. Ressner."

As she went with Ellerstein she realized she had not told Gulder about the wine bowl.

34

David completed his one hundredth circuit of the garden cloister and finally sat down, somewhat out of breath. After three weeks, he had not yet entirely acclimated to the altitude. Every time he was brought out to exercise, one of the monks took up station in a corner of the cloister, ostensibly reading a book of prayer. He seemed to pay no particular attention to what David was doing, walking or not walking, but he didn't leave, either.

The blindfold had come off as soon as they took him out of the helicopter. He was pretty sure that they had landed somewhere up in the Golan Heights, because the truck that had picked him up couldn't have gone more than a few miles away from the landing site, and most of that had been damn near straight up through snowy mountain ravines. They had taken him to a mountain monastery, through massive wooden gates, and into a bare white stone courtyard, flanked by thick, high walls on two sides and a stone building in front of him. Two very old men in black robes were bobbing at him and smiling a welcome. His Israeli guards took off the plastic cuffs and left without a word through a man-sized metal door embedded in one of the two enormous wooden gates.

David hadn't known what to do next. The sun was intense, and the air was very thin. He already had a headache, and he wasn't sure that any of these people spoke English. Then another monk came out into the courtyard, younger, only in his sixties or so, and greeted him in broken English. He took David through the front door of the building, down a short stone corridor with no doors, and out into a garden enclosure surrounded by a columned walkway on all four sides. There was a still fountain in the center, flower beds in four quadrants, and what looked like the entrance to a small chapel on one side. The battered remains of a stone tower rose over one corner of the walls. The monk walked straight across the enclosure and took David into yet another corridor. David noted that there were no lights or any other signs of electricity in the monastery. Finally they came to a plain wooden door at the end of the cross corridor. The monk produced a set of antique keys, unlocked the door, and showed him into a bare room that was about fifteen feet square.

Inside was a single cotlike bed with two blankets, an armoire, a small wooden desk, and a chair. There were two candlesticks, a large enamel pitcher, and a glass on the desk. In one corner was a washbasin, under which there was a chamber pot. There were two tiny windows, embrasured as if for defensive purposes, with small apertures in the room's wall opening to larger apertures outside. The walls were made of polished stone, and the ceiling was domed in a four-part arch of white tiles.

"You rest now, Mr. Hall," the monk said in what sounded like a Greek accent. "Water to drink is in the pitcher. Drink much water. Help with the head."

"What is our altitude here?" David asked, looking out one of the windows, where a stunning view of snow-tipped mountains covered the visible horizon.

"Above the sea? Nearly three thousand meters, Mr. Hall. Rest. Food soon."

He had had plenty of time to rest for the next few days, because he had not been let out of the room. A package with some of his clothes had arrived the second day. A silent monk brought him two meals a day, simple fare of tea and bread and fruit in the morning and a meal of hot soup, usually vegetable, more bread, and a glass of wine just before sundown. Once a week there was meat, which he was pretty sure was stewed goat. He had tried speaking to the monk, but the man simply put a finger to his own lips and shook his head. When David had pantomimed a book, they brought him a Bible written in Latin. His headache had finally gone away after five days. He had no way to shave, so now he was growing a beard.

There had been no question of escape. The curtain walls were easily eight feet thick, and the windows no more than a foot square. The door was made of old wood that felt like it had turned to stone. The monks got up at first light and went to bed at dark. He had candles but no matches. He had studied some Latin in preparation for the expedition, out of personal interest in Roman siege warfare. Now it seemed he was going to get the chance to learn a lot more Latin. Then Gulder had paid a visit.

He heard the helicopter hammering the mountain air but never saw it. A half hour later, what sounded like the same ancient lorry had come grinding up toward the monastery. They took him to the garden cloister to meet with Gulder, who showed up with the same two stone-faced bodyguards. Gulder had brought a stack of thin newspapers rolled up in a shopping bag.

"These are for you, Mr. Hall," he had begun. "They are English-language versions of the *Jerusalem Post* and the *Herald Trib.* So you can see what has happened with the amazing discoveries at Metsadá."

"Thank you, Mr. Gulder. Although what I really want to know is how long you plan to keep me imprisoned here."

"Imprisoned is too harsh a word, Mr. Hall," Gulder said, sitting down at the other end of the bench, just out of David's reach should he be inclined to violence. "We have prisons, and they do not have gardens."

"Same net result. Solitary confinement by any other name . . ."

"Yes, well. They are treating you all right here?"

"They are treating me just fine, although I could use some exercise and something to read besides a Latin Bible."

Gulder nodded and tapped the bag of newspapers. "These will help. Yehudit Ressner is now a very famous archaeologist."

"I can just imagine."

"Probably you can't, Mr. Hall. It has been a veritable circus. The whole world is agog."

"There were scrolls in those holders?"

"Oh, yes, and the holders were sealed with a resin mixture. They are in perfect condition. Of course, the scholars are already arguing."

David laughed. That fit.

"There was more: Did you notice anything about the bottom of the cistern when you went searching for your equipment?"

"Lots of silt. Oh, yes, it looked like there were bricks lining the bottom."

"Bricks, indeed. We hoped they'd be solid gold, Mr. Hall."

"They weren't?"

"They were not, unfortunately, especially given today's price of gold. The archaeologists said they were actually worth more than gold. They were testamentary tablets, not bricks."

"Which are?"

"Each of the tablets had a name. There were nine hundred and eighty names. They think that, once the decision was made, each man was given a tablet, and then the trusted ones took the tablets to the cave. Against the day."

"Oh, my," David said. "No longer the Metsadá myth, is it. What about those cylinders?"

Gulder reached into his shirt pocket and extracted a package of cigarettes and a lighter. He offered the pack to David, who shook his head. Gulder lit up, shocking the pristine monastery air. He smiled. It was a sad little smile, and David suddenly realized they had finally come to the heart of the matter.

"Skuratov was telling the truth about the cylinders, as far as he went," Gulder began. "Our original investigation was triggered by suspicions that someone was diverting small amounts of weapons-grade material. It was actually much worse than that."

"Worse in what way?"

Gulder described how the government suspected they had diverted enough material for a single weapon. "They had plans for making *five* weapons, Mr. Hall. Five, not just one."

"You said earlier they were diverting bomb materials. Were they actually selling plutonium or HEU?"

"No, Mr. Hall," Gulder said patiently. "They got their money by selling some of the heavy water to Iran through a series of middlemen. The deuterium oxide production system at Metsadá has been there a long time. They simply restarted it. They also needed heavy water to conceal the materials they were accumulating at Dimona. They couldn't steal both heavy water *and* fissile materials. They acquired some from other sources, but that cost money, so they then went back to the Metsadá plant."

"And when it produced much more than they needed, they saw the opportunity to sell it, make money for the other components they'd need."

"Precisely, Mr. Hall."

"So they weren't just facilitating Iran's bomb—they were working on making some of their own."

"I think Colonel Skuratov was concerned that the government of Israel might have a failure of nerve when the time came," Gulder said. "I think these weapons were going to be their insurance."

David nodded. "I have to tell you, this would be very, very hard to pull off in *our* uranium fuel production facilities. In a weapons facility, ten times harder."

"I am told that our own controls would have eventually caught them, except for the fact that they could conceal their 'stash,' as it were, using the heavy water as a shield. Hiding that diversion is not that difficult if the right people are involved. Hiding the growing mass of weapons grade material is the problem."

"So it all came back to the heavy water."

"Correct, Mr. Hall. So now you know."

"What happened to the remaining conspirators?"

"Skuratov, of course, is dead, as is Colonel Shapiro."

"Meant to ask you about that," David said.

"Shapiro was Skuratov's number two at Dimona. Impossible that he did not know what was going on. He tried his best to deflect Professor Ellerstein that night. Yossi noticed, told me. He was too dangerous a loose end, so I simply took the opportunity to let him try out the full Zealot experience, too."

"How about the rest of Skuratov's cell? You going to shoot them, Mr. Gulder?"

"No, Mr. Hall. We reserve the death penalty for monsters like Adolf Eichmann. No, these people will serve life imprisonment in a special facility down in the Negev Desert. Their nights, anyway. Their days will be spent at Dimona, cleaning up the mess they made. They may become a little 'hot,' as they say, but—" He shrugged.

"So why are you telling *me* all this?"

"Because it doesn't matter that you know, Mr. Hall."

David just stared at him until he realized what Gulder was telling him. "Are you going to execute me?"

"No, Mr. Hall, we are not."

Imprisonment, then, he thought. For life. They

were going to just leave him up here, locked up in this monastery, forever. "You can't get away with this," he said, clearing his throat, knowing even as he said it that, yes, they probably could. The image of this ice-cold bureaucrat pushing Colonel Shapiro off the wall was still vivid in his mind.

Gulder snubbed out the cigarette. "You violated our hospitality at Metsadá, Mr. Hall. Everyone at the IAA heard about that. You became, how shall we say it, persona non grata, yes? You then went on scuba excursions from your hotel at Tel Aviv, where you and Dr. Ressner became involved in an underwater murder."

"Involved?" David protested. "I damned near got killed."

"That's not what you told the police, though, was it?"

David started to answer and then just swallowed. Gulder smiled again.

"Did you know Colonel Shapiro was an expert scuba diver? Ah, well, it doesn't matter now, does it. You then took some extra dive tanks from the dive shop. You did not return them. Your rented Land Rover was found mysteriously abandoned, not at Metsadá but on the coast. Your personal effects were left in the hotel room. The assumption is clear: You went diving on your own. An accident. One should never dive alone, isn't that the rule?"

"People back home aren't going to buy that, Mr. Gulder."

"What people, Mr. Hall? Your missing girlfriend? You have no girlfriend. You never did, actually."

"What the fuck is that supposed to mean?" David demanded. One of the guards began to stand up when he heard David's tone of voice, but Gulder motioned for him to sit back down.

"Adrian Draper. How did she feel about your whistle-blowing plans, Mr. Hall? Was she enthusiastic?"

"Quite the opposite," David said. "She was adamantly opposed. Said it would wreck my career in nuclear power. We had some big fights."

"That whistle that you were going to blow, that involved heavy water, correct?"

"Correct."

"Heavy water that was being diverted within your own company. Who else, besides yourself, would have noticed such a thing within your company?"

"Nobody. That was *my* job. That's one of the reasons I'd been sent to school, for special training."

"Where you met Adrian Draper."

"Yes."

"Was it a loving relationship, Mr. Hall?" Gulder asked softly. "Were you two planning for babies and a suburban future? Or more like an exciting relationship between two intellectual equals, great sex and fiery battles? Head games and then bed games?"

David, stunned, could only blink. How could this man, this *foreigner,* know the first thing about Adrian Draper and their all too brief time together? Gulder leaned in, looking David right in the eye.

"Did you ever find out where the heavy water was going, Mr. Hall?"

"No, I didn't. The company quashed the investigation immediately. Once I got some of our government people into it, like my uncle, I was kept out of the loop."

Gulder nodded, reached for another cigarette, then apparently decided against it.

"Right after this scandal broke in Washington, Adrian left, isn't that correct?"

"Yes," David said. "The Israeli Embassy said she'd been called away on travel. I don't know if she's even alive."

"Oh, but she is, Mr. Hall," Gulder said. "Alive and well, and back in her own country. She even misses you. A little."

David was stunned. "*What* are you talking about?" he asked.

"You'll figure it out, I'm sure, Mr. Hall. Follow the heavy water. It will become clear to you. Now: Judith Ressner."

David's mind was still reeling from the

implications of what Gulder had been saying about Adrian. "What about Judith? Does she know all this, too? Does Ellerstein?"

"Well. Dr. Ellerstein works for me, after a fashion, and cares very much for Dr. Ressner. So when your uncle of the NRC calls, he will call Ellerstein, I think, because Dr. Ressner, the discoverer of the most fabulous treasure in the history of biblical archaeology, is very, very busy, Mr. Hall."

David started to shake his head. Judith would never go along with this. Gulder saw it. "Dr. Ressner is a realist, Mr. Hall. She knows that, sometimes, extreme measures have to be taken by a small state such as ours. Her husband was something of a case in point, correct? Killed by a madman, but still: Skuratov was state security. Dr. Ressner is quite fond of you, I think."

Then David got it: They had told Judith that he wouldn't be executed as long as she kept *her* mouth shut about the Skuratov conspiracy. Gulder was smiling that Cheshire cat smile again. David went back to the matter of Adrian. "Are you telling me that Adrian Draper worked for *you?* For Israel?"

"I never said that, Mr. Hall."

"Then our whole relationship was what, an assignment for Adrian, an Israeli spy? She was just playing me? *You* were playing me?"

"Much like you played Judith Ressner, is it not,

Mr. Hall? Coming here under false pretenses. All that deception, first getting close to her, then striking out at the right moment? Leaving her wondering what she had done? How does that feel, Mr. Hall?"

David opened his mouth to say something, but nothing came out. Gulder got up.

"I will ask them to let you out for exercise in the mornings and afternoons," he said, motioning to his guards that they were leaving. "These papers, of course, are for you. There will be more, from time to time, as long as you cooperate with these gentle people. They are not jailers, but they do live an exposed existence up here in the Golan. They depend on the Israeli Army, don't they, Mr. Hall? You can see Syria from your windows, I am told."

David just sat there, his mind bowled over by what this strange little man had been telling him.

"I'll send up an English-Latin dictionary, Mr. Hall. This is a very old-fashioned place. Who knows, in time they may teach you how to illuminate a manuscript."

David got up again and resumed walking, counter-clockwise this time. The afternoon sun beat down out in the middle of the square, heating the stones around the fountain and wilting some of the plants and herbs. At nearly eight thousand feet, there was over a mile of atmospheric protection missing, and David took care to stay out of the sun. Gulder had been as good as his word. He had sent the dictionary and another round of newspapers. David had been able to enjoy, if only vicariously, the triumph of the discoveries in the great cistern. Adrian's theory. His discovery. Judith's triumph, which was as it should be. There were pictures of the treasures themselves, and also of Judith Ressner, who looked increasingly exhausted by all the media attention. The discoveries made world headlines, and already the scholarly debates had begun, with various religious factions taking widely different positions on interpreting the finds, especially the contents of the sealed scrolls. He sympathized with her. Hell, he missed her.

None of that was going to change things for David Hall. If Gulder had his way, he would remain here until the end of time. The end of his time, anyway. If Judith asked about him, or suspected that he had been executed, Israel Gulder could truthfully say, no, he hadn't. He's been seized by a religious vocation.

He had thought hard about escape, but there was simply no way. No tunnels to be dug, no windows to hang from, no clambering up a column here in the cloister and scampering across tiled roofs to the twenty-foot stone wall, there to drop into deep ravines on every side except the front, where the top of the wall was rounded and covered in shards of glass. The monastery itself was perched on a spire of badly eroded rock and built to withstand the siege engines of the twelfth century.

A steady wind blew up the side of the mountain during the day, rising to banshee intensity when storms came across the Mount Lebanon massif to the north and swept down their valley.

Our valley. Listen to me, he thought.

He had not seen a single human being through the windows, and he wasn't sure he'd even seen all the monks. He'd heard them, though, when their soft chants broke the predawn silence. He wondered how long it would be before he asked to join their nocturnal vigils. He had the beard for it, if not the voice.

He was, as Shakespeare once phrased it, thoroughly mewed up.

35

Judith Ressner was alone, soaking her tired feet in the hotel's bubbling hot tub, when Ellerstein came back from the bar, carrying two glasses of wine. Judith was wearing her bathing suit under a beach wrap. She had a silk kerchief tied around her head and was wearing dark sunglasses. She had intended to swim some laps to undo the stress of three media events that day but simply lacked the energy. The government had put her up in the hotel to make it more convenient to do press conferences. When she'd gone back up to her room, there'd been a message from Ellerstein saying that he wanted to buy her a drink that evening and that he had something important to talk about.

"Bless you, Yossi," she said, making room for him to sit by her side. He took off his shoes and socks, rolled up his pants, and slipped his feet into the hot water. Judith smothered a smile; in his business suit, he looked ridiculous.

"Cheers," he intoned and tasted the cold white wine. Then he made a face. "Scotch would be better."

"This is fine. One Scotch and I would keel over into this water."

"Keeping you running, Ms. World-Famous Archaeologist, hunh?"

She nodded. A hotel guest came into the spa and gawked at Ellerstein sitting there in his street clothes.

"So, you ever hear from Mr. Hall?" he asked gently.

She shook her head. "No. I think the government boys must have threatened him. I'd really like to talk to him, but—"

"But those same government boys don't want that, either, do they."

"No, they do not. I had one call from that Israel Gulder, who congratulated me on the way I was representing the nation. He also approved of the way we finessed the discovery methodology."

"Yes, I'll bet he did. Listen: Did Gulder tell you the American went home? Back to the States?"

She looked over at him. "Not in so many words," she said, "but he certainly implied it. He said the less contact, the better for all concerned, more weasel-words like that."

Ellerstein nodded thoughtfully. "You know, well, of course, you *don't* know, I have been making some inquiries. Back in the States."

"Yes? And?"

"They don't know where he is."

She put down the wineglass. *"What?"*

"They don't know where he is. A professor I know there made a call to a friend in the U.S. Immigration Service there in Washington. Immigration haven't seen his passport coming back into the States. No one was especially concerned or anything like that, but there it is."

"So that means what, exactly? That he is still *here,* in Israel?"

"It is possible."

Judith blinked and looked away. That could mean only one thing, she thought. No, actually, *two* things. Either the Israeli government still has him, or they've—She looked back at Ellerstein, who saw the alarm in her face.

"No, I shouldn't think they did that," he said. "My guess is that Gulder has him in one of those 'secure locations' the Americans put their vice president in when he talks out of turn. To keep a lid on that weapons business."

"Yossi—"

"I know, Yehudit, I know. Of course this is all speculation. He may have gone on a world cruise for all we know. Except—"

"Except what?"

"Except I checked with the security people at his hotel. They said some police people came and gathered up his stuff—luggage, clothes in his room, his computer. No explanations, just came and got it. They signed the hotel release forms. I asked to see the forms."

"And?"

"These were not police people. These were Shabak people. I recognized one of the names."

"You never did tell me what your connection with Shabak was," she said.

"It was a temporary thing, Yehudit. Back to Mr. Hall."

"Yes, indeed. If you're telling me he's being held prisoner in this country, then I'm going to do something about that."

"That's what I came to see you about, Yehudit. I need to know something: When Mr. Gulder called you, did he imply that Mr. Hall's good health depended on your keeping quiet about his part in the great discovery?"

"What?"

"Just think back for a moment. You said 'words like that.' Like what, exactly?"

She thought about it. She had finished her wine and hadn't even noticed. Ellerstein pushed his glass toward her, and she took it. "Well," she said, "I think he said that it would be in everyone's best interest, especially Mr. Hall's, if his name never arose in connection with the discoveries. I didn't think it significant."

"How do you feel about all that, Yehudit? It was his discovery, after all."

"Don't remind me, Yossi," she said with a sigh. "I feel dishonest. But I've rationalized it this way: The discovery is the important thing, not me or my part in it. As David Hall said: Everyone remembers the Dead Sea Scrolls; no one remembers the Bedouin shepherd who found them. Plus—"

"Yes?"

"Well, when he called me down to Metsadá, I was ready to kill him. For going back down there. For digging, as I suspected he had been. He said then that he was satisfied in vindicating his girlfriend's theory and that, in return for my helping him, the discovery would be mine alone. I didn't think much about that at the time; I was too excited when he told me what was in that cave."

"I can imagine. I still can't quite believe what amazing things came out of that cave. Herod's

Temple. Incredible. Most incredible. I still haven't seen them. The lines are too long, still."

Yes, she thought. Everything was still pretty incredible. Especially the inscribed bricks. That could wait, though. Did the government have David Hall somewhere? She didn't want to admit to Ellerstein that she missed him, but she very much did. Imprisoning him was wrong, but better than putting him in the ground.

'Well," Ellerstein said, drawing his feet out of the water, "I think I'm going to make a call on Israel Gulder. If they have Mr. Hall sequestered somewhere, perhaps I can arrange for you to see him. You do want to see him, yes?"

She nodded. She had much to tell him, and something to give him.

"Not only no, but absolutely no," Gulder said, visibly annoyed. "Get out of here."

"You're thinking like a jailer," Ellerstein said. "The persona suits you, but you're making a mistake."

"Really."

"Yes, really. The longer you keep Mr. Hall in one of your boxes, the longer Dr. Ressner has to wonder what's happened to him. Eventually, she will ask."

"And I will tell her that it is none of her damned business," Gulder said.

"That's if she asks *you*."

Gulder opened his mouth to say something but then snapped it shut. He had been about to say *Who else would she ask?* when the answer dawned on him.

"If she does that, goes to the media, then we will return the favor and tell the world she was *not* the great discoverer everybody's making her out to be."

A secretary came in quietly with a sheaf of papers and put them in Gulder's in-box. He groaned. She smiled at Ellerstein and left just as discreetly.

"Or you could let her go talk to him. Satisfy herself that he is not being mistreated, that he is well and unharmed. He is well and unharmed, Mr. Gulder?"

"Hmmpf," Gulder grunted.

"I will take that as a yes. So: Let them see each other. Let them speculate on what's going to happen next. Their imaginations will probably conjure up more possibilities than yours ever can. Drop a hint or two that this situation will not go on forever. Let *them* define what that might mean."

"Why should I do anything, Yossi?" Gulder asked. "I can recalibrate her with one phone call. She promises to keep quiet. We promise not to shoot him. That's all there is to it."

"No, I think you're wrong," Ellerstein said. "Right now she is like a capacitor, slowly accumulating a big charge of electricity. Ultimately, all capacitors need to fire. Do this and you will head off a larger problem. You said that time would eventually lay this whole matter to rest."

Gulder sighed in exasperation. "What I meant was that we will cloak the whole Skuratov business in a fog of paperwork and endless investigations. If she does talk, there will be no facts to back up her story. No Mr. Hall, either."

"Has no one come looking for him?"

"Only his uncle, an official with their nuclear agency, and a brother. The uncle was seriously concerned. The brother seemed to be going through the motions. We gave them the diving-alone scenario, said we'd keep looking."

"Did they contact Ressner?"

"I doubt it," Gulder said. "The uncle knew about Hall's Metsadá project and had heard of the great discovery. We told him Hall found nothing but piqued the interest of the IAA. They sent a team down and found what they found. More along that line. Hall was not involved. We are grateful, etc., but since we can't find him . . ."

"This is the uncle in Washington who was part of the diversion investigation, started by David Hall? A diversion involving Israel?"

Gulder frowned. "What's your point, Yossi?"

"That could be a rather large loose end, Mr. Gulder. Let me try another argument on you: If this uncle tries to make a connection between Hall's disappearance and the heavy water diversion case, you will need an ally, someone outside of government. That could be Judith Ressner. If we spin this correctly, give her hope that we're working on a solution to this situation, she will be motivated to support the government's claim that the Skuratov business never happened."

Gulder sat back in his chair, tapping a pen against his teeth while he thought about that. "Ressner is a beautiful woman," he said finally. "He sees her, he's going to agitate for her to do something about his—sequestration."

"She will caution him to remain patient, not to do anything precipitous. She will give him hope."

"There is no hope, Yossi—we can never let him go."

"Then let me calibrate her, as you so quaintly put it: I'll tell her to keep doing what she's doing, being the face of the Temple artifacts. There are 'people' behind the scenes working on your other problem, the fate of your Mr. Hall. You must be patient. Like that."

"To give a man hope when there is none is a dangerous game, Yossi," Gulder said. "You'd best be very careful with your lies."

"That's a yes, then?"

Gulder gave him a long look and then nodded. He gave Ellerstein a phone number to call.

36

Two weeks later the abbot joined David in the garden right after lunch and sat down next to him. David smiled and closed his book. The abbot was known as Father Kamil, and he was somewhere between seventy and a hundred years old, with the face of an Old Testament prophet and a long white beard to match. David had told the abbot all about the Second Temple finds at Masada and explained his own presence at the monastery as a way of keeping the discoveries an Israeli triumph.

"How goes the Latin lesson?" the abbot inquired, apparently uninterested in David's backstory.

"*In res omnia, patiencia*," David said.

"Not even close," the abbot said with a laugh. "I have news for you. A visitor."

"Should I be afraid?" David asked.

"Your visitor is a woman, so I would say definitely yes."

"How would you know that, Father Abbot?"

"I was not always a priest, Mr. Hall. Many of us here lived among the Gentiles, as we like to call the rest of the world, and now we're here, of our own free will."

"Recognize danger when you see it, do you?" David asked.

"Perhaps you are here because you did *not* recognize danger when you saw it, Mr. Hall?"

"Touché," David said with a grin. "Is my visitor Judith Ressner, by any chance?"

It was evening when the helicopter announced its approach with the usual clattering roar. A few minutes later one of the monks escorted Judith into the cloistered garden, bowed, and left them alone. David stood up to greet her, not quite sure of how to do it. She solved his problem by dropping her tote bag and coming into his arms. They held each other for a long time before she finally lifted her head.

"I have missed you, Mr. Hall."

"Never thought I'd see you again," David said. "How did you manage this?"

"Yossi Ellerstein managed it, not me," she said, sitting down on the stone bench and pulling her bag over. "Have you become a monk, then?"

David looked down at his monastery garb and then tugged on his beard. "How do I look?" he said.

"Suitably holy," she said with a smile. "I must be quick. The helicopter must leave before full dark. I brought you something."

"A ladder, I hope," he said. "Or a one-way ticket out of this place? A sign that I'm not stuck here forever?"

"No ladders," she said. "Yossi tells me that he and other people are working to get you released. First the government must bury the Skuratov incident. That takes time."

"I told Ellerstein that I could damned well keep that secret," he said. "I have nothing to gain and everything to lose by opening my yap."

"Still, they must be very sure. Your uncle—Jack Hall, is it?—He has contacted the government. The fact that he is a nuclear agency official complicated matters."

David sat back with a sigh. Of course it would, he thought. Heavy water diversion. Shit.

She took his hand. "Yossi says the government knows it can't keep you here forever. He says that he and I must come up with a plan that solves the government's problem for them. Hopefully *before* the prime minister's political problems bring on an election, or the Arabs bring on another war."

"My being locked up here in the Golan Heights *does* solve their problem, Judith. Ellerstein may be more concerned about what you might say one day, not me. All I can say these days is amen."

The monk reappeared at the garden gate and beckoned Judith.

"I must go, David. Here: I have a package for you. This might well be your way out."

"What is it?" he asked. He heard the helicopter's engines starting down below the walls.

"Something very special, David. Get the monks to put it in a closed room, and then you'll understand." She leaned over and gave him a quick kiss on the cheek. Then she was gone.

As the helicopter lifted off into the darkening

sky he opened the tote bag. Inside was a cardboard box, tied up with common white twine. Inside he found a green felt cloth. The cloth contained the wine bowl from the cavern.

David felt a chill go up his back. He reached in to extract the bowl but then paused. The writing on the wall had alluded to a connection between Judah's tragic brother and this wine bowl. They had both jumped to the same conclusion, but of course there was not one shred of proof. Still, he found himself very reluctant to touch it. He rewrapped the bowl in the felt cloth. Then he remembered her suggestion: Put it in a dark room. Like the chapel, perhaps?

"So, how did it go?" Ellerstein asked Judith. "Did he look healthy?"

"A little gaunt," she said, shifting her phone to the other hand so she could mute the television. "I think he's used to more food than they are giving him in that place."

"All Americans are used to more food," Ellerstein said. "What about his state of mind?"

"He wants out, of course. He knows why he's being held there, but wonders why they won't trust him to keep his mouth shut. As he says, there is no benefit to him for revealing what happened."

"Americans are funny about things like that," he said. "He gets out, goes home to the States, then thinks about his fifteen minutes of fame and maybe wants to try that again. Americans seem obsessed with fame."

Remembering what David had said, she asked him if he was worried about what *she* might say one day. Ellerstein stared at her for a moment. "Oh, my," he said. He began to fiddle with his pipe.

"What, oh, my?"

"He saw right through it, didn't he? Your coming to him, promising him a chance at release. He knows."

"Knows what, Yossi?"

"He knows he's never coming out of there, that is what."

Judith surprised him. "I don't believe that, Yossi," she said. "Governments come and go. The past becomes the past, nobody cares. Paperwork gets lost, stories become diluted. Once all that happens, then there will be no point to keeping him."

"Well," he said, "I hope you're right. It does seem unfair, especially after he led you to such prominence. You are right about governments coming and going, especially with these uprisings in the Arab world."

"Intifada, yet again?"

"No. These Arab uprisings are generational, Yehudit. The young men throwing over the old men. The problem is that nothing in their lives will change except that there will be no wise old hands to restrain them."

"I'm glad I did what I did, then," she said. "Up there on the mountain."

"What was that, Yehudit?"

"If I am right, you will soon see."

He chuckled. "Stay in touch, Yehudit. I will do the same."

She switched off the phone and put it down on her dining room table.

Stay in touch, she thought. Just you wait, Yossi.

Late that night one of the monks knocked on David's door. He had no idea of what time it was, having taken off his watch weeks ago. He kept monastery hours, for the most part, going to bed when they did and getting up for the early morning services in the chapel.

"What is it?" he asked.

The door opened, and one of the younger monks, who spoke no English, motioned for him to get up and come with him. He held the candlestick high so David could put on his robe and sandals. Then they went to the chapel, where it looked like all the monks were gathered by the front door, including Father Kamil. The doors to the chapel were partially open, and the monks were murmuring to each other excitedly. Father Kamil gestured for David to join him on the top step.

"Look inside, Mr. Hall," the abbot said, ushering David to the doorway. "Tell me, what is that thing on the altar?"

David looked inside the chapel at the wine bowl, which he had put on a back corner of the altar after the last service of the evening. The chapel was suffused with a warm glow, but the wine bowl looked just the same, plainer than even the candleholders and the simple Orthodox cross on the altar.

"A first-century wine bowl," David told him. "From the great discoveries at Metsadá."

"How did this thing get here, Mr. Hall?"

"Dr. Ressner brought it to me. The authorities weren't interested in it. Why is everyone so excited?"

"Look again, Mr. Hall. At the chapel, not the bowl."

"Okay, I'm looking. I don't see any changes." White stone floor and walls, with no orna-mentation to speak of. The Stations of the Cross represented by simple wooden crucifixes. No windows. A white stone altar with simple vestments. Two large brass candlesticks on the altar.

With no candles.

"Where is the light coming from, Mr. Hall?" the abbot whispered. "Can you tell us that, please?"

Feeling the hair rise on the back of his neck, David looked again. No candles. There was no electricity in the tiny monastery. No batteries that he knew of. If they needed light at night, they'd get a candle. Yet there was no mistaking it: There definitely was a faint, almost golden glow to the chapel's interior.

He looked again at the bowl, but it was not glowing. It was just a plain bronze bowl, not quite perfectly symmetrical, looking a little wobbly around the rim. Dull, plain metal. It looked no different than the moment at which he'd first seen it.

"Father Kamil," he said finally, "we need to talk privately."

The abbot closed the chapel doors and instructed the monks not to go in there until he returned. Then he took David across the courtyard to his cell, which was no different from the one David occupied except for a desk and a second chair at one end. He pulled up the chair and indicated for David to take the other one.

"Proceed," he said.

For the first time, David told him the whole story of how he had come to Israel, what he'd discovered, and how he had entangled Judith Ressner into his deceptions and ultimate success. He then described the words on the wall that Judith had translated, which were probably now gone, regarding the bowl and the writer of the words.

The abbot sat there the entire time, fixing his eyes on David's face with the intensity of an eagle about to launch. When David had finished, he sighed.

"God give me strength," he said quietly.

"We were both making rather large assumptions, Father Kamil," David said. "She was translating from Aramaic, and even she said there were always many different interpretations for any word in Aramaic, especially of that age."

"Yet there is light in the chapel. Like no light I have ever seen."

David had no answer for that, but he was suddenly, perhaps irrationally, glad he had not touched that bowl.

"What will you do now?" he asked the abbot.

"We shall pray," the abbot replied promptly.

"In the chapel?"

"Oh, no," the abbot said. "At the door. Until we understand the light. So: *This* is why you are confined here? The government knows about that bowl?"

"No, the government probably doesn't know about it," David said. "They were so over-whelmed by the other things, they disregarded the bowl. I think Judith just took it and then told them it would go into a museum somewhere."

"Very well, Mr. Hall. As I said, we shall pray together to seek guidance and wisdom."

"Mind if I join you, Father Kamil?"

"Not at all, my son, not at all. Tell me one more thing, please. After your lady friend told you what was written on the wall, did you touch the bowl?"

David said yes, when they first found it, but after that, he had been afraid to.

"Why?"

"You know exactly why, Father Kamil. Do *you* want to touch it?"

"Never, Mr. Hall. Let us go back to the chapel. Ah, wait. First I must send a message. Come with me."

David went with the abbot to the far side of the garden enclosure. Father Kamil unlocked a wooden door that led to a set of steps going up into the ruined corner tower. David wondered if the abbot was going to make some kind of signal, but when they got to the top of the tower, the abbot opened another door that led into a dovecote. There was an immediate chorus of cooing and purring from the tile nesting pipes wedged along the walls.

"Homing pigeons?" David asked.

"Yes, indeed, Mr. Hall. Very reliable."

"Where's the message going?" David asked, as he watched the abbot scratch out some words on a small piece of paper and then insert it into a short metal tube.

"To our Patriarch, in Jerusalem, of course," the abbot said. "He will know what to do about this wine bowl that lights a room with no flame. He will think us all mad, of course, but he will come to see for himself."

Wow, David thought as the abbot secured the

tiny cylinder to the leg of a fat pigeon with a leather jess. Now he understood why Judith had brought the bowl here.

You'll see, she'd said.

Soon, of course, the whole world would want to see.

37

They came for him three hours after sundown, ten days after the message had flown to Jerusalem. David had been asleep when the sound of a helicopter woke him up. He got up, shivered in the cold, and looked through both window embrasures. He could see nothing but the distant snow-capped mountains in the moonlight. There was much more snow up there now, he noticed. Maybe the helo had been just passing by, he thought. He had never heard one at night. Then, fifteen minutes later, he heard the truck cranking over and knew that something was up. He lit a candle, washed his face, and got some clothes on. For some reason, this time he fished out his own street clothes.

A half hour later one of the monks who often sat with him in the garden unlocked the door, knocked, and came in. He was carrying an oil lantern, and he smiled when he saw how David was dressed. He indicated that David was to come with him. They went to the front gate, where two soldiers were waiting.

Comes now the big question, he thought. They were either going to let him go or take him to a real prison. Or worse. He took hope from the fact that everyone was acting pretty nonchalant about what was going on. There was nothing in the soldiers' faces to indicate they were going to execute him. Besides, they didn't need to send a helicopter to do that.

They slipped on a set of plastic handcuffs but this time did not blindfold him. They put him on a wooden bench in the back of the canvas-covered truck and hooked his cuffs up to a metal rod. Then the truck bumped and banged its way down the same mountain track he'd come up before. What, he thought—almost two months ago? He could see the trail opening out behind him as they went down. Briefly he considered escape. No. Nothing but wild goats could survive out there in this wilderness, and even they were pretty thin.

They did blindfold him once they put him in the helicopter and strapped him in. This time he sat back without being told to and relaxed as best he could, trying not to think of all the possibilities here. It was very cold once they got up to altitude and leveled off. He remembered stories of CIA contract people throwing Vietcong prisoners out of helicopters while other prisoners watched, supposedly as an incentive for the others to talk. He shivered again, this time not entirely because of the cold. They landed after about a half-hour flight and then ground-taxied a long way before the turbine spooled down and then went silent, which was when he heard the noise of a propjet, a big propjet from the sound of it, somewhere near the helicopter. The doors opened, and the blindfold was briskly removed.

They were parked at an airport or possibly a military airfield, he wasn't sure which. It was nearly midnight, and the field was lighted but not active. He saw some hangars in the distance and a tower with its rotating beacon flashing through the night. Parked sideways right in front of them was an Israeli Hercules C-130 decked out in desert camouflage paint. The hatch was open forward, and two engines were turning on the other side. A group of men stood by the hatch, looking at the helicopter. Two of them appeared to be aircrew in flight suits, but then he recognized Ellerstein and Israel Gulder. For some reason he felt better that Ellerstein was there.

A soldier reached in, unlocked the cuffs, and then indicated that David was to step out and go to the Hercules. He helped David out of the helicopter and then nodded his head toward the men standing by the hatch ladder. David walked over, stretching his arms and rubbing his wrists. He stopped when he reached the ladder. A warm draft from the turning engines blew under the belly of the aircraft, and he could smell the stink of kerosene fuel.

Gulder was handing him something. It was a small leather folder. David looked inside and found his wallet, his passport, and what looked like an airline ticket envelope.

"Mr. Hall," Gulder said, his face a complete blank, "this is good-bye, I'm afraid. You are leaving our country. Bon voyage."

"Is this going to be an improvement over the monastery, or something a little more final?" David asked.

Gulder just smiled, said something in Hebrew to Ellerstein, and then walked away to a waiting staff car. Ellerstein tipped his head toward the hatch and followed David into the aircraft. It was cold and dark inside the cargo bay, the only light provided by a row of small red lights in the overhead. An aircrewman wearing a cranial headset came in behind them and stood at the front end of the cargo bay.

Ellerstein picked a seat and sat down, indicating David should sit next to him. He was wearing a heavy jacket and wool slacks.

"So, what's happening here?" David asked.

"You are being released, Mr. Hall. This aircraft will take you to Greece, to the American military field at Hellenikon. A consular officer will validate that ticket back to the States, and you will leave at oh nine hundred for New York."

"That's it? No conditions?"

"Just one, Mr. Hall, and it is voluntary, of course."

"Oh, yeah, right, of course. Voluntary," David said, rubbing his wrists again.

"No, it is, really. We ask that you remain quiet about your role in the discovery of the Temple artifacts. Right now the whole world believes Yehudit Ressner is the sole discoverer. As agreed between you, yes?"

"Yes. No problem at all."

He waited for the next condition, about the weapons business, but Ellerstein was getting up. "It was interesting to meet you, Mr. Hall," he said, extending his hand. "Most interesting. If you should further, um, correspond with Dr. Ressner, please be gentle, okay?"

David shook his hand but didn't know quite what to say. "I will, Professor," was all he could manage. "Thank you." Then Ellerstein was walking back up to the hatch, where the crewman helped him down the retractable ladder and then closed it up. The crewman came down and made sure David was strapped in, gave him a blanket to wrap around his legs, and went forward. Five minutes later they were airborne over the black Mediterranean.

David undid the waist belt, removed the blanket, and stood up to stretch. The four big turboprop engines had settled into a steady synchronized whine, and it wasn't too noisy in the cargo bay. He was looking out the single porthole when he became aware that there was someone behind him. He turned around to find Judith standing there, her hands in her pockets. She looked like a football player in pads because of the oversized flight jacket she was wearing. Her eyes looked tired, and the dark pouches were back. He looked into her face for a moment and then embraced her. She relaxed and leaned against him. They stood this way for a long minute, and then David let her go and stepped back. She pressed a hand against his new beard and smiled. He led her to a seat on the long bench.

"Okay," he said. "I'll bite. What's going on?"

She smiled. "You owe this to Yossi Ellerstein. He convinced Gulder to let me come see you."

"He didn't know about that wine bowl, did he?"

She smiled. "Absolutely not, but he did figure it out pretty quickly once that story got loose in Jerusalem."

He nodded. "That could have gone two ways," he said. "They'd either give up and boot me out of the country or turn me into a good Palestinian."

She shrugged. "I'm not sure how he managed it," she said. "The media is in overload these days: Western nations defaulting, Arab uprisings, the Temple artifacts. His theory was that heavy water would be too hard a story. Too technical. No one would care."

"How did the objects look when they brought them out, cleaned them up?"

"Spectacular beyond belief," she said. "Even damaged, the menorah simply glistens, and the scrolls were intact inside."

"Glows, hunh?" he asked. "Like a certain bowl?"

She giggled. "What bowl? No one knows anything about a bowl."

"But the patriarch from Jerusalem—"

"Ah, yes, the patriarch. He went to the monastery. He returned. Apparently the room failed to glow."

David sat back against the insulation on the side of the cargo bay. "Sure as hell did when I was there."

"Yossi Ellerstein questioned me about that. Had *I* ever seen this mysterious glow."

"And?"

"I told him yes, I had. The bowl does not glow: The room it's in does. Know what he said?"

"What?"

"That the glow appears only when the bowl is in the presence of someone who believes Judah Sicarius's testament."

"That would be—"

"You and I, yes," she said. "For now, it remains at the monastery chapel, and the monks remain outside. Yossi said that the government would open an inquiry on the bowl, just as soon as you and I come back to Israel."

He took her hand. "That might be a long damned time, Judith. Especially the you-and-me part. The coming back to Israel? I don't think so."

"Well then, Mr. Hall. Mission accomplished, as Mr. Gulder would say, yes?"

He shook his head in wonder. "What about you?" he asked. "What are you doing here on my freedom bird?"

Her expression changed. "Yossi thought it might be nice for me to take a break from all the media circus business," she said. "Suggested a trip to America. Perhaps give some lectures, but mostly to get away from it all for a little while."

"At this juncture? With all the media interest?"

"Well, his 'suggestion' just might have to do with what was said up there on the mountain. About the nuclear stuff? I'm the other person who knows, remember?"

"Ah," he said. "Yes." David remembered Ellerstein's comment about corresponding. He took her hands in his. "Will you come stay with me, Judith? In Washington? I mean, I've got lots of room. A housekeeper, even. I could show you Washington, hell, the whole country. If you'd like to, of course. I mean, that is, if you don't have—"

"Yes, I would like that, Mr. David Hall," she said, a shy smile on her face. "I think I would like that very much. Although it's Yehudit, not Judith."

He grinned like a teenager. Yehudit it would be.

Maybe she could teach him some Hebrew, against the day when he went back to Israel. When *they* went back.

When pigs flew.

"I hope you're right about all this," Gulder said as the army staff car left the airbase and headed back toward the lights of Haifa.

"PM thought so," Ellerstein pointed out, "and he's the one under the gun from the Americans. The settlement question. Hamas making nice with Fatah. Egypt 'resetting' their diplomatic relations with us. Get this problem five thousand miles away from here—that's a good plan, he thinks."

Gulder grunted in the darkness of the backseat.

"You've alerted the appropriate people at the U.S. Embassy?" Ellerstein asked.

"Yes," Gulder said. "One of our special friends has had a word with one of their special friends. Once Hall gets back to the States someone will come around, quite informally, of course. Invoking old associations when Hall was in the nuclear nonproliferation world. Just a few questions about some rumors of heavy water diversion at Dimona."

"As a test?"

"Yes, as a test," Gulder said. "Who knows what he will do. If he doesn't talk, the matter is settled. If he does, then the PM can say to that dreadful woman, look, you people are pushing too hard. See what almost happened? What passions you're stirring up here? Zealots again. We need some breathing room here. Back off, Madame Secretary. Get back on your fancy airplane and go fix the Arab street, eh?"

Ellerstein smiled to himself in the darkness. One of his professors back in New York had told him a golden rule: If you can't dazzle them with brains, baffle them with bullshit. The cover stories were about right. Subtle, even, if he didn't mind saying so himself. Gulder had had his doubts, but the PM had seen it right away. Besides, the American, Hall, had done Israel an amazing turn with his theories about the ancient Zealots. Ultimately, they owed the real debt to Adrian Draper. One of their own.

"Such amazing things they discovered."

"Yes, indeed," Gulder said. "That menorah. The scrolls, even the holders. Amazing, and so beautiful. Imagine what the whole thing must have looked like, so very long ago."

"And the tablets—the bricks. All those names. Josephus got it right."

"Nine hundred and eighty, not nine hundred and sixty."

Ellerstein gave him a spare-me look. "Tell me," he asked, "what did the Pharisees and Scribes decide about that bronze bowl?"

"A run-of-the-mill first-century wine bowl,"

Gulder replied. "Nothing special. The patriarch was, apparently, not amused."

The car phone rang. Gulder picked it up, listened, and began to dictate instructions. Ellerstein tuned him out, sat back in his seat, and fished for his pipe. Judith had told him again about the final lines on the wall, what she thought they might mean, and what that plain little bowl might really be. Of course, the lines had faded after being soaked during their escape, so now, once again, there was no evidence.

Something new for the Christians to argue about for a change, he thought with a smile. Wouldn't that have been something, though.

Center Point Large Print
600 Brooks Road / PO Box 1
Thorndike ME 04986-0001 USA

(207) 568-3717

**US & Canada:
1 800 929-9108
www.centerpointlargeprint.com**